In Another Light

By the same author

Poetry

MEN ON ICE
SURVIVING PASSAGES
A FLAME IN YOUR HEART (with Kathleen Jamie)
THE ORDER OF THE DAY
WESTERN SWING

Mountaineering

SUMMIT FEVER
KINGDOMS OF EXPERIENCE

Novels

ELECTRIC BRAE
THE RETURN OF JOHN MCNAB
WHEN THEY LAY BARE
THAT SUMMER

In Another Light

ANDREW GREIG

Weidenfeld & Nicolson
London

A PHOENIX HOUSE BOOK

First published in Great Britain in 2004
A Phoenix House Book

A CIP catalogue record for this book is
available from the British Library

ISBN 0 297 84878 X

Typeset by Deltatype Ltd, Birkenhead, Merseyside

Printed and bound in Great Britain by
Clays Ltd, St Ives plc

Phoenix House
Weidenfeld & Nicolson

An imprint of the Orion Publishing Group
Orion House, 5 Upper St Martin's Lane,
London WC2H 9EA

Quotes from *To My Father* by Hugh MacDiarmid © 1931 reprinted with
kind permission of Carcanet Press Limited.

Quotes from *Scotland* by William Soutar reprinted with kind permission
of the National Library of Scotland.

Quotes from *Sonnets to Orpheus* by Rainer Maria Rilke, translated by
Don Paterson © Faber and Faber Ltd.

Every effort has been made to contact holders of material quoted and reproduced in
this book, but any omissions will be restituted at the earliest opportunity.

For my mother and father, brothers and sister

that you might pass
into the pure accord, praising the more, singing
the more ...

Sonnets to Orpheus, Rilke. Trans. Don Paterson

'It's great to be back home ... actually, it's great to be anywhere!'

Keith Richards, the Astoria, London, 2003

Love and warmest thanks to Lesley for your support, patience and guidance on the voyage.

Also to Georgina Capel, agent, friend and look-out.

Also to Khoo Su Nin, Dilys Yap, Duncan McLean, Ron Butlin, Pat Durrant and Peter Dorward for their suggestions and corrections. Ta!

PART 1

Likely the smell of it came to him first.

He opened his eyes in the grey pre-dawn and for the first time smelled the sweetness and sickliness that lay ahead. Ginger, frangipani, acanthus and jacaranda and untold acres of rubber – all those abundances that he'd never known, which until a year ago meant as little to me.

He moved like a trout in one of the burns of his childhood – one pale flick and he was kneeling at the open porthole. He stared into the dimness as a darker shape emerged off the port bow: humped wooded hills, a long ridge rising to a peak, and now first light breaking into a high corrie – surely the word came to him, he had no other.

Henderson the Canadian mining engineer – and how many hours of eyestrain over the micro-fiche it took me to get that name – was still snoring, the boat's engines thumped and grumbled as they had for nearly two weeks across the Indian Ocean and the Bay of Bengal, but now everything has changed: landfall, maybe an hour ahead.

I have him now as he stares into the yellow Far East dawn while the boat rounds Muka Head. I see the long powerful nose, heavy-lobed ears, the mouth that has not yet become obstinate, and his grey-blue eyes wary, alert, excited, measuring. He's hunkered down like a schoolboy at the porthole in striped pyjama bottoms, his long back pale and still skinny: my father at an age I never knew him, the old man as a young man first sighting Penang.

1

I woke and went up on deck once the ferry was well past the Old Man. The high red headlands of Hoy receded until we were into the turbulence where the tide race emptying Scapa Flow greets the oncoming Atlantic. There was a period of unpleasantness, then I was coming one more time round the Point of Ness towards the little town sheltering under Brinkies Brae.

I smelled once again cut grass and seaweed, glimpsed the pier where she, the window where I, the cafe where they once, and if my stomach lurched it wasn't on account of the swell. The *St Ola* slowly swung round till I was looking at the tidal Holms and the cottages where we'd disgraced ourselves.

I turned away and went below to collect my car. A couple of glances came my way, but I kept my head down. Four months away and not forgotten yet.

Bright daylight as the bow doors opened. First off, my old Audi lurched, bumped up, then I was back on holy ground once more. No reception committee at the pier head, but the jungle drums would already be beating as I headed out of Stromness towards the rendezvous.

Stevie Corrigall was waiting in his pick-up by the shores of Harray loch. We shook hands, grinning and a little embarrassed in the way of people who meet again and realise how much they like and have missed each other but don't know how to say so.

'I've rounded up the gear you asked for,' Stevie said.

'Thanks,' I said. 'Appreciate it.'

'So how's the memory these days?' he asked casually as we transferred the equipment into my car.

'I can't remember having a problem with it.'

He laughed, but after a moment of hesitation. I didn't resent it. Only looking back can you see how not all right you once were. I hefted his bolt-cutters, heavy-duty and newly sharpened. Good.

He was still looking at me.

'Don't ask,' I said, then stowed them in the boot with the rest of the kit. Sometimes you go to do something wrong knowing it's right.

'Don't need to,' he said. 'You'll be doing this on your own?'

'Like as not,' I replied.

I think he guessed then the arrangements I'd made.

'Go canny, Eddie,' he said. 'Come and see us after it's done.'

For a moment I looked directly into his round brown eyes. I knew he still felt he owed me on account of what he'd done – more accurately, what he didn't do – at that desperate Hogmanay party on the Holms, but that wasn't what I'd come back to set right.

'Thanks for everything,' I said, and we shook on that. He drove off without asking more, a tactful man.

I drove slowly on the back roads, adjusting again to Orcadian light, so thin and pale yet stinging the eyes. After months cooped up in Stoke Newington, working late into the night as *The Project* began to produce results, it was good and strange to be back moving under that wide wind-polished sky, the land like an old green tarpaulin dragged out of the North Sea, glinting pools of water in its folds, the material bleached by salt and wind and light to pale yellow, brown and olive. Few trees, no hedges, just water, sky and land.

It's a place of healing all right, but not for the faint-hearted.

I was tempted in the hours remaining to visit again the places that had mattered to me, but for now it was better to keep a low profile. So I drove straight to Evie – not so much a village as a tendency of houses – through the late September afternoon, then turned down the single track road that leads to the Broch of Gurness.

I didn't go right to it, though I could see its ruined stone tower like a squat pepperpot half a mile along the shore. Instead I turned onto a farm track I'd remembered and parked in behind the half-ruined barn facing the sea – nothing so blatant as hiding, just not being very visible.

Now I settle down to wait with flask, sandwiches, and a bunch of things I don't forget. It will be hours till dusk brings cover, enough time to consume them all if I pace myself.

I pour the first coffee, set it on the dashboard, and consider.

It began as a headache. The grainy bitterness of aspirin was still in my mouth that afternoon when young Cath turned up. I let her in, wondering how I'd got to an age where my friends' children came to stay on their way to job interviews.

By the time I'd made our tea, I couldn't eat any. I'd had headaches regularly for much of my life, but this was bad. I told her I'd stay in.

'You'll be all right?' she asked at the door. I looked up from where I sat massaging both temples.

'Sure,' I said.

I barely made it to the sink in time. Then I rinsed and spat and sat on the edge of the bath with the sweat already turning clammy. Not nice, not nice at all.

I took more painkillers and went to watch TV. Then I was back at the sink. Afterwards I changed my shirt, it was wringing. To the growling timpani in my head, some lightning had been added. Bear it. *Thole it*, as the old man would have said.

I heard Cath come in, glanced at my watch, just gone 1 a.m. Long night ahead. I groaned and retched some more into the bedside bowl. By now it was green – stomach acids or lining, I wasn't sure. She tapped on my bedroom door. I was very glad to see someone. Pain is your own but it helps to have someone around who isn't in pain, to remind you such a thing is possible.

'Eddie! For God's sake, are you all right?'

I twisted my neck and looked up at her. She was subtly strobe lit in little flashes, and with the drums and lightning and hiss in my ears it was as if we were meeting in a jungle in a tropical storm. I'd a clear memory of holding her when she was a few weeks old, marvelling at blue eyes and jet-black hair.

'Just ... rotten ... headache,' I managed then rolled onto my back. There was an easing after the stomach spasm, like coolness after rain. I blinked, gasped, let it come.

She was standing over the bed looking down at me. I was myself enough to notice what a bonnie young woman my god-daughter had become, and to be embarrassed she saw me like this. Right now she looked worried.

'I think we should get a doctor,' she said.

Doctor came. Young Aussie on the night shift. Shone light in my eyes, checked for a rash, left codeine. Call the surgery in the morning if it persists. Then he was gone, she was gone, and I dug in.

I was dimly aware of her up and about making breakfast. If I can hold down this next lot of codeine. Sleep. Get to surgery.

Her hand on my shoulder.

'I've got to go for my interview,' she said. 'Do you want me to call an ambulance? Eddie?'

Ambulance? I want sleep and no pain, not fuss. Ambulance for accidents and hearts. My heart good.

'No,' I said. ''S all right.'

She kept looking down at me. I was soaking and stripped of pretences. Some brief easing was coming after the last stomach heave.

'Okay,' she said. Then she was at the door, half in half out. 'Look, are you sure? Shall I phone the ambulance?'

It was an impulse, no more. A moment of weakening, or self-preservation. Whatever, it's why I'm still here.

'Yes,' I said.

My bare foot on wet pavement as they carried me

Dr Alexander Mackay stands in the lifeboat's shadow, out of the sun that has turned violent ever since Port Said. The breeze of the *Amelia's* passage across the Indian Ocean stirs in his open-necked white shirt – he knows that in Penang he will have to wear a tie much of the time but on board it is acceptable, just, to go without, and he's making the most of it.

A particular sound had fetched him from his stuffy cabin and *Modern Obstetrical Procedures*. He'd cocked his head, listened till it came again. That whip-crack-*wheesh* that is no other sound in the world. That went along with the smell of salt and gorse and cut grass carried on a cooler, clearer air. When it came again, exactly so, he had to come up onto deck to see if it could be true.

And it is. He's seen some odd sights over the last few weeks, but this takes the biscuit. On the fore deck the young American chap from the corridor above, in checked plus-fours, two-tone brogues, open necked shirt and maroon cap, waggles a long iron over a golf ball teed on coconut matting. He sights up at the horizon, down at the ball, steadies. Easy backswing, slight snatch on the way down, good follow through. Crack! The ball soars out over blue, increasingly veers to the left, a tiny white eruption where it hits the water and is gone.

The golfer mutters to himself, selects and tees up another ball from the bucket. Alexander watches, amused and intrigued. He spent much of his adolescence on the local links, whenever he wasn't studying. Golf was the local game of the East Coast, played by fishermen, farmers, tradesmen and artisans, men like his father. The game you struggle with all your life, but never ever master, that will always humiliate. Only a Presbyterian country could invent it, and though Alexander Mackay is a convinced atheist following certain events in the past he's put behind him, he is a Presbyterian atheist and he cares about golf.

This golfer is a good one but presses too hard on the downswing, his left side not braced enough. No surprise that the ball whistles off the deck then sharply ducks into the sea. A wee flutter of white, then gone.

'Darn and blast it!'

Alexander emerges from the shadow. He can't help it. A fellow sufferer. 'Nasty hook,' he observes.

The young man looks up, grins ruefully, takes off his cap and wipes his forehead. It is grilling out on the open deck.

'Yeah,' he says. 'Can't seem to shake it. Any suggestions?'

He's much Alexander's age, around thirty, shorter and broader, dark hair brilliantined back.

'Let me see you hit another couple.'

He watches closely. First one ball then another, their flight variations on the ones before. Plenty of power, good loft, consistent pull to the left. Then he gives his diagnosis. The grip – the right hand's too far round, get the V back pointing to the shoulder. And keep your left side straight, hit past not round it.

The American listens closely, nods. He knows this, but sometimes it takes someone else to notice. He tries again. His first is a feeble slice, the next couple are absolute sizzlers, the balls fall so far out there's just a tiny fleck of white.

'Bobby Jones himself would be proud of that,' Alexander says.

The young man blushes. For all his vigour, he's oddly pale, and the doctor in Alexander Mackay wonders if he's been ill.

'Gee, thanks,' he says. 'Do you think he's going to win your Open?'

'Wouldn't be surprised.'

'Hey, are you Scotch?'

'Scotch is for drinking.' Still he smiles. Something open and unaffected about this chap. He approves of Americans, their lack of side. He holds out his hand. 'Alexander Mackay. Doctor. Bound for Penang.'

'Alan Hayman. Water engineer. Penang and the Interior.'

They shake hands then take turns hitting balls into the big blue. They discover an equal level of ability. Good but not outstanding, like himself, would be Alexander's inner verdict. No point deluding oneself. Still, after a childhood of searching for balls in gorse and rough, it's liberating to fire them off into oblivion, just for the heck of it.

The ship's bell dongs twice for the second lunch sitting and they go in together to eat, passing with thankfulness from brilliant light into shade. Alexander wipes away sweat that's running from his hairline.

'I suppose this is how it's going to be from here on,' he says.

'I guess so,' Hayman replies. A big grin splits his chunky face. 'Spiffing, ain't it!'

In shadowlands, in a blue room where spectral figures hurried with an urgency I could not feel. Looking up at blue stippled ceiling and always choking. Shades hasten with their apparatus on wheels. Something in my throat too big, can't breathe. Can't bear this much longer.

My father came and talked with me. He was sympathetic and encouraging as I seldom knew him. *I've something to show you, laddie. Meant to tell you afore.* He seemed apologetic as he went away and then it was difficult again. More scurrying figures, more blue ceiling, more can't breathe. Panic rising hot in my throat like reflux, up then swallowed down but always there.

Graeme visited. Good to see him looking well as he cracked a few jokes, put his hand quite tenderly on my arm. *Think of Glencoe on a hard February morning – you, me and Jimmy setting out.* He was gone, but he came back from time to time when it got bad, sometimes with my dad. They seemed to get on well, like old friends. I was touched at that.

There was a gap. Still the hurrying shades seemed tense and distant, couldn't get them to help. There was someone I badly wanted to see, one whose presence would help support me, but I didn't know who that would be. Tina came to my bedside instead, which was dead nice of her. She was looking much better than the last time. *You just keep breathing. Picture that sunset at Bettyhill.* She smiled and pressed something cool, smooth and rectangular into my palm and that helped. *I'll be seeing you.*

She left and though she wasn't quite the one I missed her badly as I gripped whatever she'd given me.

2

The sun's chopped to pieces out there on the Sound. With the car window down I can hear terns piping shrill and the distant roar of the tide race by Eynhallow. A seal pops up, rotates its shining head like a whiskery periscope, submerges again.

It's worth knowing it wasn't so frightful, being in what I came to think of as the blue shadowlands, that place where you lie knowing you may be going to die. It's just lonely and uneasy, a good place to have a friend come keep you company as you wait to see what happens next.

I swallow cooling coffee and taste again the coarse, ambiguous sweetness of not being dead.

Brother's eyes looking on me.

Stippled ceiling and room the same, only it's all white now. People in white bustling in hush. Someone takes big thing out of my throat. It hurts, but much better. Still hissing mask over my face. Then brother's voice, speaking slowly.

'You've been very ill. You're in hospital. You're going to be okay.'

He talks like I'm a simple.

'You understand?' he says. 'Eddie?'

Alive, eyes open, seeing.

'Yes,' I manage.

It seems to please him. He's gripping my hand and that helps. I know who he is, he's my brother, but I can't find his name. I wonder who it was that hadn't visited me in the blue shadowlands. If I could work out who. I open my other hand but it's empty.

'They said you might be brain-damaged,' he says. 'And I said "How would we tell?"'

He starts to laugh, and I feel glad to be back again so I do too.

One of the white coats, spectral no longer, comes over and shines in my eyes. Asks who the Prime Minister is.

'Easy,' I say. 'It's . . .'

I think Nye Bevan, William Pitt, Gladstone bag. Brother and doctor looking at me. Look, I've just been born and can't be expected.

I start reciting *Sad Eyed Lady of the Lowlands* to show memory all right. I'm well into the second verse when the doctor leaves hastily, says someone will be back later to do more tests. My brother sits on. What is his name? I'm very tired and close my eyes.

Back again. No headache but hissy mask clammy on my face. I look to see how things are. Lots of tubes, some in back of hand, in arm. Monitor screen like on TV, bouncing jaggy green lines. It's true, I'm alive.

I pull at the mask and it comes off my face. Look at my brother.

'Oxygen mask,' I say. 'Peter.'

'Yes,' he says. 'Same old brilliant bro.'

I nod modestly. Look at plastic bags hung up to my left. Clear bags like what goldfish in at fairs. Tubes looping to me.

'What they, Pete?'

'I think that one's saline and antibiotic. The other's your brain fluid.'

Drops oozing from the tube. Bag half full. My brain fluid. It looked slightly thick and greasy, like that near-clear fat on top of gravy.

'Jings.'

Nurse comes with clipboard. 'We need to know your next of kin, Mr Mackay. Who is your next of kin?'

Peter and I look at each other. I'd never thought on it that way. Sounds like funeral notice.

'I suppose our mother,' he says. 'She's on her way.'

As he gives the details, I think: should be love of my life at bedside and in shadowland. My closest kin. Who she? What had Dad meant to show me? And slept.

The shadow of the flag swings across his back, up his neck then ripples over his face as the *Amelia* rolls slowly across the Bay of Bengal. He feels the cool, then heat again and dazzle is restored on the silver foil of a new pack of Players.

The first fag is the best, sucked rough and sweet into the back of his throat. He flicks the spent match at the gull following a few feet off the rail, and in its wersh cry and sheering away he sees the last remnants of his old life, the austere cliffs and shores and cold fields red in ploughing, all peel away and leave him.

He knows fine he's under-qualified for the post he's taking up, just three months of obs. and gynae. in his houseman years. It would never be allowed back home, but things are different in the colonies. He's done all the reading he can do, it's experience he's needing now. He hopes no one dies while he gets it.

Human shrieks behind him as the day's first bathers enter the canvas pool rigged over the fore hatch. The quoits line is being measured and strung, badminton has already begun, a white-gloved steward removes the last of last night's glasses all glazed and scummy, while the young Siamese barboy polishes fresh glasses, breathes on one, holds it up to the sun then polishes it some more, looking for absolute transparency.

Alexander Mackay blows smoke down his nose and envies them. They have something to do. He has read all the books of interest – the rest are just romances and other tripe. He has done his old Army exercises, breakfasted and shaved, read another three-week-old newspaper picked up in Port Said. Count Westarp is demanding evacuation of the Rhineland and an easing of armament restrictions; there is anxiety about the landing procedures of the R101 airship, the transport of the future; Aberdeen FC are second top in the Scottish League. The world is going to the dogs, a film star is re-marrying, Bobby Jones has won again. All that, and it is still only ten o'clock.

Worse, Mrs Thomas and her sexless unmarried daughter have just emerged onto the deck. They have sighted him and are heading his way. He pretends he hasn't seen them and moves off down the rail, wishing he'd never danced twice with her the first week out. There's nothing wrong with the lassie, she's not stupid and is built as women are, but she has no spirit, no gumption, 'nae smeddum' his mother would say. Yet she

12

sticks like a wet label to glass, there's a deadly determination to her sleekit downcast eyes.

'Take a seat, old man.'

Startled, Alexander looks over at Phillip Marsden. The dapper dandy of the upper deck is sitting alone at a green baize table with four hands dealt before him, cool and amused in the shadow of the big flag flying from the bridge. Gleaming white deck shoes, maroon-striped waistcoat, cream Panama, his silk shirtsleeves billow and collapse like light breathing.

'Safety in numbers and all that.'

There's something other than amusement in the man's eyes, something unexpected. Alexander sits down, picks up the nearest hand and studiously arranges it by suit and value. The two men are concentrating deeply on their game as the Thomases approach. Hats are lifted, good mornings exchanged, then the hats are replaced and the women move on.

Alexander puts down his cards, watches Marsden silently fan through his hand. Despite himself, he is intrigued. There must be more to this social butterfly, this dancer and chatterer, darling of planters' wives, favourite jester of the top table among the senior officers and Malayan Civil Service administrators.

'What's the game?' he blurts.

Marsden looks up at him. A grin flickers and is gone.

'Solo bridge,' he says. 'Do you play?'

'My parents went tae whist drives once in a while. Bridge was for posh folk.'

Marsden frowns down at his hand, puts it aside then picks up the hand to his left, fans the cards.

'You don't have to be posh to win at bridge,' he observes calmly. 'You do however require a clear mind, a smart partner, and a good memory. Would you say you had any of those, Dr Mackay?'

Alexander looks hard at the face across the dazzling baize. Light brown eyes, fair hair a little long, the neatly trimmed moustache. As the boat rolls on, the flag-shadow drifts across the cards and back. Marsden seems to be making a simple enquiry, but there's more to it than that. There always will be.

Alexander picks up the nearest hand, slowly fans through then puts it face down. Then the next. The third hand. Then the fourth. He gives ten, maybe fifteen seconds to each as Marsden watches silently. He sits back and looks after the dwindling Thomases who have attached themselves to a hapless young planter, then he begins to recite.

'Hearts – two, seven, knave, Queen. Clubs – three, five, six, King.

13

Spades – eight, ten, two. Diamonds – seven, knave.'

He pauses, slides out a Players, offers the pack but Marsden waves it away, never stops watching him as Alexander continues, pointing his cigarette at the second hand.

'Hearts – four and six. Clubs – nine, ten, four and Queen. Diamonds – three, nine, Ace, King. Spades –' He hesitates, lights his cigarette as he works to recall the story he's told himself. 'Spades – Ace, seven and six.'

He notices Marsden's fractional nod, and that he doesn't check the hands to see they're called right. Does he know or is he bluffing?

As if he can read his mind, Marsden slides a slim silver case from his waistcoat pocket, points an elegant finger to the third hand.

'Hearts three, five, nine, ten; clubs two, seven, eight, Ace; diamonds eight, ten, girl's best friend; spades are three, four, Queen,' he rattles off, then lights up a black Sobranie. Smoke comes hissing between his neat white teeth as he conjures the cigarette case back into his waistcoat.

Now Alexander has to call the fourth hand. This one is easy, the story clear and inevitable to anyone who can count.

'Hearts – six, eight, King, Ace; clubs – knave; diamonds are two, four, five, six, Queen; so spades are five, nine, King.'

The two men look at each other.

'Very good,' Marsden says. 'Do you do it by constructing a story, or by image?'

'Story,' Alexander says. 'Though I sort of see it. My brother William learned me how.'

Marsden shifts his chair slightly so he is back fully in the shade. He speaks quietly but clearly over the mounting shrieks of hilarity from the swimming pool party.

'There are ten days and nights till we reach Penang,' he says. 'Bridge won't be hard for you to pick up. I play regular rubbers with the Chief Admin Officer, a chap from Bousteads and a couple of the MCS assistants. They're keen as mustard.'

'Bellingham-Smythe is no use to man nor beast, and just the voice of yon Ramsay is like chalk on a blackboard for me. I've no wish to join them, even if they'd let me.'

Marsden flicks his ash and lets the slipstream carry it over the rail.

'What I say, old man, is if you can't join them – beat them.'

Alexander stares. There are surprises yet in the world. For all Marsden's neatness, there's a certain reckless air about him.

'There's money in it as well as the pleasure of beating them,' Marsden continues. 'These fellows like to put a few quid down, sometimes quite a few. Might help with your bar bills. Interested?'

The thin young Scottish doctor's laugh turns the bathers' heads. Not

14

wanting to be thought chit-shy, already his bar bills have exceeded his first month's advance allowance.

'I'm your man,' he says.

'When we opened up your head, I found a colloid cyst, as I'd suspected. It had taken up residence in your fourth ventricle, preventing your cerebro-spinal fluid from draining. Thus hydrocephalus and raised intra-cranial pressure leading to headache, vomiting, confusion, diminished conscious-ness and coma. These idiots left you dying on a trolley for eight hours before they called me – another twenty minutes and you'd have permanent brain damage, or be dead.'

'Help ma boab,' I said, looking up at my surgeon. He was a pink-face fella in blazer jacket and striped cuffs. He seemed very full of himself, like God at the end of a busy Sixth Day. 'Well done.'

God looked pleased, his chest puffed out like a happy budgie.

'I have a choice now,' he announced to the group clustered round the bed. 'Either to operate and resect the cyst, plus or minus a little brain, or install a permanent shunt to drain the cerebro-spinal fluid into the abdomen.'

The threat of another operation, this time one I knew about, was frightening. Now I was back in the world again, I had something to lose.

My surgeon was showing round a plate of my pre-op scan.

'Can I see?'

He traced where my brain should have been, then pointed out the miserable scraps that were actually there, flattened against the inside of my skull by the pressure.

'That's the cause of all this,' he said. 'Little bugger, size of my thumbnail. It'll have been floating around in there all your life.'

I looked. Near the base among the dark bits, another paler shape. Reminded me of a magic mushroom from those days when.

'Don't worry,' he said. 'It's quite inert. Like you, Mr Mackay.'

The students laughed at God's wee joke.

'Unfortunately this cyst is located very close to the centres for memory and abstract reasoning. There's a chance of a degree of trauma. What's your trade?'

I wished they wouldn't spring questions on me without warning. Job? Work? No idea.

'Engineer?' I said. It sounded possible.

'So,' God said to the students, 'though I'm fairly confident I can resect this cyst, Mr Mackay probably needs his memory and abstract reasoning.'

'From time to time, yes,' I said, and got a chuckle from the students.

God-surgeon didn't look too pleased. His hands were small, neat and pink. They'd been in my head.

'So I've decided to leave it there for now. I'll install the shunt tomorrow.'

Then he left, God and his trainee angels, having decided to quit while he was ahead on the brain surgery front. Seemed a good idea to me.

The shadows shorten as the sun climbs. Light flickers off the surface of hearts, clubs, spades, diamonds, the red and black and white, issuing streams of pure information to his eyes. The two men rig up an awning over the table, remove hats, roll up shirtsleeves, order lime and ice from the barboy and carry on.

The old liner rolls across the trackless blue of Indian Ocean, heading for the South China Seas with its cargo of dreams and schemes, the hopeful and the desperate. They do not go in for lunch but order sandwiches. They play on even through the sacred hours of lie-off when the canvas pool slops emptily from side to side and the rubber quoits lie stickily on the varnished deck while the young Siamese barboy sleeps in the shade of his tower of empties.

Young Dr Mackay learns the rules and basic procedures. He learns fast. Then as the afternoon wears on, and the sportsmen and bathers return to the decks, he begins his apprenticeship with Phillip Marsden in more subtle matters of conventions and signals, ruffs, finesses, discards and squeezes. It becomes apparent he could be rather good at this. He briefly wonders why he's been chosen, but mostly he is busy realising the opportunity that has come his way.

'So what brought you out here, Marsden?' Alexander asks in a brief break.

Marsden looks at him over the top of his glass. Drinks, then with a napkin dabs the trace of foam from his fair moustache.

'Left the country for the country's good, old chap.'

Alexander fights a short battle between curiosity and sense of privacy, both strong with him.

'Trouble with . . . ladies?'

Marsden seems to find this funny.

'You could say that.' He drains his glass, pats his lips and deftly collects the cards, slips them into their boxes. 'Speaking of which, I have an appointment below, followed by a set of tennis – if I still have the energy. See you for a stengah before dinner?'

'I heard you work for the Malayan Civil Service,' Alexander says quickly.

Marsden raises his eyebrows, seems to give the matter serious thought, then gets to his feet.

'Do a spot of translation for the MCS and the Chinese Protectorate,' he says vaguely. 'Jolly boring but it pays the rent, what?'

Then he is gone, threading his way through the afternoon deckchairs like a slim bullfighter, greeting and pleasing and evading with equal ease.

'Say, you've been thick with Marsden all day.' Alan Hayman slides into the vacant seat and sets down two glasses of iced beer. 'Isn't he rather what you English call a cad?'

'Scots if you dinna mind,' Alexander grunts. Certainly Phillip Marsden's dalliances on the voyage out with a French consul's fiancée and a planter's wife have been common knowledge, so blatant even the men have been commenting.

'Still, I admit the man's got charm,' Hayman continues.

'He's got more than that.' He folds up his bridge notes and looks at his principal companion on the voyage. 'So did you do a strong line with the Simpson sisters?'

'They've finally tumbled that I'm just a penniless Yank with no breeding. They like me, at least young Ann does, but I tell you there's competition out there. I estimate one free woman per ten men, and some of these guys are pretty top-drawer.'

'They're nae better than you nor me, Alan.'

Hayman raises his first cold beer of the evening.

'Darn right. Here's to you, Sandy.'

'I've never been called Sandy in my life.'

His parents and family had always cried him Alec. In primary school he was Wee Eck, then he was Big Eck. Studying medicine he became Alexander and had stayed that way.

'I'm sorry, but it sure seems like your name to me.'

Alexander Mackay examines his drink, the condensation ribbing the glass, the bittersweet promise and depths of it waiting. He listens to the name resonate in his throat, informal but upright, somehow open, even light-hearted. *Sandy*. Something he'd never been known by, never called to attention, reprimanded, rejected, commanded or patronised by. New name for a new life.

'Sandy's fine. May I call you Alan?'

'It's the American way.'

'And a good one.'

They chink glasses, their eyes meet briefly, their grins match.

'Cheers, Sandy.'

'Cheers, Alan.'

The *Amelia* beats on across the Bay of Bengal. The seas are calm and they've ceased to notice the ground beneath them is shifting, yet it makes for a certain freedom and light-heartedness, a slight giddiness of the spirit. Also quick friendships, intense flirtations, rivalries and alliances. For the *Amelia* is an island on the move, and in twenty minutes, sure as the Empire's sun sets, the ship's bell will ring for first sitting.

3

Surely my father was what the Blues singers called 'a tail-dragging man'. By which they meant someone who covers their tracks as they go. When he had his final heart attack on the golf course one autumn morning, he left only immediate personal things – his clothes, pipes, shoes, clubs, and a shelf of history books, another of biography, plus a few old volumes of poetry. And an incomplete golf scorecard Peter still has pinned to the wall.

I had never even seen a photo of him from before he met my mother, and she has none. Apparently he had never been young.

So when Mum and I cleared out the family house for sale after I came out of hospital, no surprise there was little left of him. His wooden shafted putter, found at the back of the deep press in the hall. Then on the highest shelf my hand brushed something – his black trilby, the inside band dark and still supple from years of sweat and Brylcreem.

I stood in the dimness of the press, running my thumb over it, knowing his head had touched this. Though he'd been gone for seventeen years, some of his cells would still be embedded here. My own hair was still growing over the indents from when they'd opened me up a second time after the shunt had become infected.

I'd been a sick boy, but when he'd visited me in the blue shadowlands in Intensive Care, he'd been younger and less severe. Someone I might have known and liked. I'd lain awake many nights wondering what it was he'd meant to show me, but he never came back to enlighten me.

Then under a pile of old Thermos flasks, picnic sets, a twisted tennis racket and a musty travelling rug, a little porcelain head peeked out at me. Even in the dimness I recognised it – above the red and green glaze of his robes, the plump, cheerful, quietly radiant face of the sitting Chinese Buddha.

I picked it up wonderingly. I hadn't seen this in nearly thirty years. (Kind of thing my grandparents said when I was wee and could never happen to me. Thirty years. It seems if you don't die young, you get older. Fair enough, only no one can tell you how quick it will go.)

The Buddha was dusty and cool under my fingers. He'd called it a Toby Jug.

One of the long ears was broken at the lobe. Cracked too was the rim of the crimson vase that he clasped on his lap. I smiled at the idea of Dad meditating in front of this – a man for whom any moment not being busy was a moment wasted. Justify your existence. Dinna just sit there thinking about it.

Yup, the Proddie atheist in full Go mode, not a pretty sight but bloody effective. It had got him through two world wars, made the saddler's laddie finally into a consultant surgeon who delivered hundreds of babies and only ever lost two, raised a family of his own, driven him up all his country's hills before finally releasing him to drop face down in the bunker at the long ninth.

Yet this was his, I was sure of that. So like him to pass it off as a Toby Jug, knowing fine what it really was. I turned the Buddha over and something started then, for on a patch of unglazed white porcelain on the base was one word: PENANG.

The sound of it, *Penang*, stirred dust along galleries of shuttered light in colonial buildings. Water dripping off waxy leaves, orchids, loud rainforest. His throaty voice for a moment: *In the mornings after monsoon rain in Penang ...* A myth, a legend, a word of my childhood and as distant and unlikely: Penang.

There was more. Under the Buddha was a small wooden box I'd never seen before. Stamped on it was *Federation of Malay States – Best Butter*, and scrawled on a yellowed label in his writing: *Keep*.

I hunkered down on the floor, pressed, squeezed, prised at the lid. Then with a sudden *whuff* it opened.

Perhaps if there'd been more there I'd have been less fixated. Like the pressure exerted by a stiletto heel being greater than the foot of an elephant, that sort of thing.

A small cup. No, a tankard. Blackened silver.

> Dr Alexander Mackay
> Runner up Class 'A' Billiards
> The Penang Club
> 1930

He'd have been annoyed not to have won.

The man I'd known was usually too serious, too wary, for anything as idle as competing at games. Come to that, I'd never known him at a snooker table. I remembered him after he'd retired, watching *Pot Black* on TV for hours, grunting with satisfaction or snorting with disgust, flicking the yellow dottle from his pipe onto *The Scotsman* on his lap. But he'd never said he'd played. Why keep such a small thing from us?

I put the tankard on the sideboard by the cheery Buddha and went back into the butter box.

A bundle of old pictures, once black and white, now mostly yellow, held together by a rubber band that disintegrated as I tried to ease it off.

Postcards, or photos mounted as postcards. I'd a feeling that had been common. A dozen or so of foreign street scenes, temples, some colonial buildings, a group of girls in sarongs. A wildly Gothic church. I turned over each but there was nothing written, only the printed identification: SUMATRA; THE CRAG HOTEL; SINGAPORE WATERFRONT; SIAM; E&O HOTEL, GEORGE TOWN. On the back of the church one: WIEN.

On the back of SUMATRA, one word in light pencil, his handwriting: *Hot!*

I remembered him saying you had to get up before dawn, have your work finished by noon, and drink lots of hot sweet tea to make you sweat. He'd had a friend, Alan someone, who'd taught him to appreciate classical music. He'd seemed to speak of him with regret. Then he'd count up to ten in Malay – at least, he'd claimed that's what those clucking sounds were.

Back to the box. Two small red velvet cases. The big bronze medals were heavy and cold in my palm. *Alexander Mackay, dux in Natural Sciences, Brechin Academy 1916.* The other *The James Burgon English Prize, Brechin Academy 1916.*

He said his school had just one bursary, for medicine. He'd decided he wanted it, worked and worked and got it. That was why he'd become a doctor, simple as that. So he said.

(In a Scotland still fighting the Great War, nervous, exultant, the gangly boy in short breeks goes up onto the stage to collect his medals and bursary from the headie. His mother and father the master saddler, sprushed up in their best, briefly applauding. He steps down awkwardly from the stage, knowing all he has to do is join up and survive till the war ends, then he'll be away.)

I fingered the English medal. How heavy and solid they made things then. How much turned on the very few routes of escape. My dad's older brothers all got out – South Africa, Canada, Australia, that whole Scottish Diaspora. Nothing for them in that narrow, drained country.

There was only one more item in the box. It haunts me still. Of all the things he left in Penang, he chose to bring back a double one domino.

Three days later, in a borrowed 'bum freezer' short white jacket and black trousers, Sandy Mackay joins the select bridge set in the upper saloon. Marsden makes the introductions, the whisky stengahs are ordered, and there's some chat about the progress of the boat as they sit down at the card tables.

The Guthries man, Finlayson, is a Scot with short crinkly red hair and an Edinburgh private school accent. He tells Sandy encouragingly that the main trading firms, Bousteads and Guthries, are 'full of Scots, from all different sorts of backgrounds.' Sandy Mackay nods, knowing he's the one with the different sort of background.

'That's what's so marvellous about the Straits Settlements,' Finlayson enthuses. 'It's not like India – here we're all in the same boat, eh?'

A round of nods and chuckles from the men as the cards are broken out and shuffled.

'Right enough,' Sandy Mackay says quietly, 'but still some of us sleep on different decks.'

This is greeted as a brilliant sally, and will be repeated many times in the course of the evening. But of course, he's not joking. His shared cabin on the starboard side of the lower deck is cramped and stifling. He flushes, is about to say something but Phillip Marsden shuffling cards across the table catches his eye and makes a discreet downward gesture of his palm.

With that one remark, young Mackay is in. He has a role, the chippy young humorist. His accent may be a trifle coarse, but he's a doctor, an educated man, and above all he's good at sports. Everyone knows he's just learned bridge, so they'll make allowances.

Marsden wins the cut for dealer, King to Finlayson's Queen. He shrugs, admits he's a lucky blighter. He gives a final shuffle, deftly cuts the cards three times, gathers them into his palm and deals.

The night is dark and spread with unfamiliar stars. The air's soft, passing over his shirt with light patting hands. He leans over the rail, looking down at the glitter dug up by the ship's passage. Dance band music and laughter drift from the upper saloon. With only a few days to go before the company disperses – some staying in Penang, others going on to Malacca or Singapore, and the planters and tin men bound for the

Interior – only a week before fiancées meet their match, wives are reunited with husbands, single women taken into their waiting family, everyone is what Sandy Mackay thinks of as 'a bittie raised'. 'Tears before nightfall', his mother would have added, and she was usually right.

Marsden comes silently along the rail, a shadow in black and white evening dress. Hands him two five-pound notes.

'Well done for a first night,' he says. 'You overbid in the second hand.'

Sandy nods because it's true. He'd got over-excited and carried away, never a good idea.

'Sorry I ruffed your diamond in the last rubber.'

'It helped remind them you're a beginner, which is no bad thing.'

Sandy starts to protest, but Marsden holds up his hand. 'We'll go over it tomorrow. Right now I've an appointment.'

Further along the rail a tall slim white curve is waiting, looks like the Dutch First Secretary's wife. A yellow flare contracts to a red glow, then Sandy smells the smoke. A part of him he's leaving behind disapproves, the other part is admiring of the absence of apology or pretence. It seems things are different out here, and different is what he has come for, anything to be away from his dreich exhausted country.

'Looks like you're in demand, Marsden.'

'Phillip, please, old man.'

'Sandy.'

Marsden claps him on the shoulder. *Sandy*. Already he's getting used to it. Maybe one day even the constant clinging humidity will be normal.

'They're not such a bad crowd, are they?'

Sandy has to admit it. The planters tend to be fairly upper-crust, but of the enthusiastic and unstuffy sort, here for the adventure. The young administrators are nearly all public school but seem to have been picked for their keenness for sports. It's not India, the flag having followed the trade, and the traders have no side. Apparently there's no standing army in all Malaya, so none of those military types. They've come to work, have a lively time in more freedom than is possible at home, play sports, save some money. He has no quarrel with that.

'Except yon Bellingham-Smythe – and his crony Ramsay. Sleekit wee bugger. I don't think he likes you.'

Phillip Marsden chuckles quietly.

'I don't think he does. It'll be a pleasure taking them on tomorrow.'

'It's not for the money, is it? I mean, you have your remittance and everything.'

A pause. Sandy wonders if he's gone too far. One doesn't talk about a man's finances. Then Phillip laughs quietly, a muffled drawing-in of breath.

'It's not for the money.' He seems about to say more, then stops. He glances along the rail where the white dress drapes over elegantly.

'On you go,' Sandy says. 'Better not disappoint the lady.'

'Oh, she'll be disappointed all right. Goodnight.'

Another touch on the shoulder and he glides up the rail. Murmur of voices, fair heads close together, then they go below and he is alone again. That's fine, he likes that.

He stays out there for another smoke, letting the charge of the evening dissipate and the sweat cool. He thinks back over the hands, seeing what could have been done better. He hadn't played that well, but the cards had certainly run their way.

More murmurs above his head. The topmost deck, among the stacked deckchairs. A woman giggles, not sober. Man's voice sings a snatch of 'Mad About The Boy', she laughs, abruptly cut off. A minute later above the dance music he can just hear the slither and thump and small throaty groans.

No better than a floating brothel. He draws the fire as close to his lips as he dares, then flicks it over the rail, sends it sparking down into the dark.

4

'I haven't lost my marbles, you know,' Mum said as we ate our fish suppers sitting on bare floorboards among the packing cases.

'I know,' I said. 'But you sometimes have trouble finding them.'

She laughed and fed herself a big chip.

'Like my purse in the fridge the other day.'

'Or the address book in the vegetable rack.'

When I'd left the hospital I'd been the same, suddenly lost for a word, a name. Sometimes breaking off mid-sentence because I'd forgotten what I'd started to say. And losing things – socks, money, reading glasses, watch. It still happened, but I was getting better and she could only get worse.

She scrunched up her wrapping and leaned back against the wall.

'That's better,' she said, and licked her fingers. 'In a small flat there'll be fewer places to lose marbles. It's time I had a change.'

'Can I take this?' I asked, holding up the chipped Buddha.

'Oh, *that*,' she said. 'Of course, if you want it.'

I'd asked her about the Buddha, the postcards, the billiards trophy, the domino, but she'd had little to offer. She pointed out that when my father was out working in Penang, she'd have been playing with her dolls in Perth. By the time they met, it was all long past.

'The domino is from that set you and Peter played with as children. Real ivory, you know. I'm sure he said they came from Penang.'

'So why did he throw the others out? And why keep just this one?'

She shrugged. 'Your father didn't like keeping unnecessary things. When we were first married in our tiny house, he suggested we burn all our old letters, the photos and family papers, old amours – you know. He got rid of nearly everything, the letters and photos from his brothers abroad, his mum and dad. He read each, then burned them. It took most of the day . . .'

'That's terrible!' I protested.

She looked at me almost sympathetically.

'I thought so at the time,' she said. 'Now I think he was right. I don't want to end my days surrounded by junk. I want to clear the decks. So . . .'

She got up and started clearing up our papers. Then she casually said the words that started everything.

'Of course your father had to leave Penang.'

I stared at her, wondering if she was having me on. She seemed amused, by the memory or by my reaction.

'Yes,' she said. 'He had an affair, something to do with the wife of his senior partner.'

'What?'

An affair with the wife of the senior partner was immoral, passionate, and a very unwise career move. None of these fitted the man I hadn't known.

'She was meant to join him there,' my mother said.

'Where?'

'The woman. She was supposed to join him in Vienna.'

I stared at her. She seemed calm, in her right mind. She didn't haiver, my mother, she just occasionally mislaid her marbles. I felt mine scattering in all directions.

'And?'

'Oh I don't know,' she said. 'Your father never said and I didn't ask. It was all a long time before we met, and he didn't seem very keen to talk about it. He just mentioned it the once.'

Then she turned and went slowly up the stairs. I wished I'd hugged her goodnight, there'd be only so many opportunities.

That night I sat up in bed and went through the cards that had been sent over the weeks in hospital by family and friends from my years of work, music, hill walking, love, sex, and suchlike pursuits. People touchingly pleased I wasn't dead. I was pleased too. Great sense of gratitude to still be alive, I told them.

I didn't talk about the other side of that, not wanting to make it more real by wording it.

Another thing: I'd been unconscious all the time in Intensive Care, yet the blue shadowlands place with its stippled ceiling, busy spectral figures and machines, was that ward. How could I have seen it with my eyes closed?

And if Cath hadn't been visiting and hadn't suggested the ambulance a second time, I'd be dead. Pure chance someone had been there. It had been years since I'd cohabited, Lyn and I having always kept our own places. Before that, Tina and I had intended, but . . .

The other problem was the people I felt most grateful towards, other than God my surgeon and Cath, were the ones who'd helped me through that long struggle in the shadowlands – my father, Graeme and Tina. The problem was they were all dead.

And dammit, what had my father meant to show me? I didn't believe in ghosties any more than he had, yet what he'd said had rung true. There was something he'd never shown me.

I picked up the double one domino again, felt its ivory smoothness, the hard but curved edges, the little winged dragon etched into the underside. It was the same feeling, exactly, as the unseen thing Tina had given me to hold in the shadowlands. So that's what it had been. Strange.

As I squeezed it again, my fingers slipped into the little black pits. When I pressed down, something moved. My fingers slid apart.

With shaking hand I put the opened domino under the bedside light. Something in that little cavity. A pale scrap of card. No, a tiny cutting from a photo. The chemicals had yellowed, of course, but it had been in the dark all these years and it was still possible to see something there.

I tilted the domino better to the light. Faint outline of a face, long nose, mouth slightly open, smiling or expectant. Smudge of eyes looking straight at me across years. Hair, yes that's hair by her cheek – for it's a woman and not my mother. *The* woman. Had to be.

I put my nose to the little secret cavity and sniffed the yellow dust that lay in one corner, and for the first time smelled, as the molecules escaped into the present for the first time in seventy years, a faint unnameable sweetness. Spice, and an undertone of something English, something like lilies.

Yes, I bet you had something to show me, I thought. When as children we'd played with that set of dominoes, he must have known about the secret compartment. All the time he watched us playing with it, he must have known she was in there. He'd seemed utterly, dismissively unsentimental, and gave no indication he'd ever wavered in his marriage, yet that tail-dragging man couldn't bring himself to throw out this last trace of her.

I slid the ivory lid shut, felt the click. I lay thinking of that faint face back in the dark again in its tiny tomb, wondering what her mouth had just said, what her eyes had looked upon.

Then sleep, heavy and strange, like so often after the blue shadowlands.

Two nights later he's at the upper deck bar, settling his chits with cash. A couple of hours earlier Ramsay, who had become even more silent and pale than usual during the course of the game, had proposed they double the stakes for the last two rubbers. Marsden had won the cut, dealt, and Sandy picked up a hand that went through his system like a double stengah, spreading warmth and mild delirium. He'd contracted for three no trumps and won the rubber on that hand alone. The last rubber took longer but ran up hundreds of points. If it hadn't been for the cold, flat glare in Ramsay's eyes as he joked and settled up, Sandy could have felt quite apologetic.

Phillip Marsden had melted away on one of his 'appointments', and Sandy left Bellingham-Smythe and Ramsay to bicker over who exactly had made the wrong lead when. Now he takes a gin and lime, sits in a left-out deckchair under the strange violent stars and feels almost at rest.

'Sandy! Am I glad I found you.'

'You are?'

Alan Hayman slithers inelegantly into the neighbouring chair.

'Yeah, you've got to help me. Those Simpson girls – the only hope is to split them up, right? Adele watches her sister like a broody hawk, but I've sweet-talked them into some dances with us tonight. I'm keen as mustard on Ann, the younger one.'

'Younger? Man, she's scarcely out of the cradle!'

He minded Ann from a cocktail party he'd reluctantly attended early on the voyage as they went through the Med. Right bonnie, all laugh and chat, very excited to be going back home to the East after schooling in England. Swish, that was the word she kept using. *What swish fun!* The lassie probably wasn't more than twenty, she'd have been a child during the war. Her older sister was a looker and clever with it, but with a husband waiting in Malaya. Still, it would be a change from the company of men, cards and medical textbooks.

Meanwhile Alan Hayman's laughter has turned into a cough, a searing, throat-tearing affair. He staggers to the rail, leans over and spits, comes back looking drawn. As he sits fighting for breath, Sandy can hear the light rattle of his bronchi. Something about the vocal quality, that and the pallor and the slightly hunched way his friend moves. Sandy minds meeting a line of them shuffling along a shelled road at dusk in light rain, somewhere in Belgium, and then the cases from his houseman years.

'Gas?'

'Yeah.' Alan closes his eyes, drinks cautiously. 'I'd left my mask back in the Mess,' he says at last. 'I mean we'd never used the damn things. It was maybe fifty yards, but with all the guys scrambling for theirs, I mean it was a shambles, and I . . . Well I had to breathe, didn't I? You just have to breathe.'

Sandy finds his hand on Alan's arm. Under the shirt, it's thin and trembling.

'I kept losing mine and all.'

'Bloody nuisance, weren't they?'

'They were that.'

They sit in silence, the boat cradles them on. Sandy lights up a Gold Flake. He's always smoked Players, but this lighter, sweeter, subtler brand seems to fit who he'd like to be now. He lets the smoke seep from his mouth, plucked away by their forward motion through the tropical night.

'How was your war, Sandy?'

He glances at Hayman. These Americans, they don't know what isn't to be said. It's refreshing. He inhales deeply, lets his tonsils take the shock.

'You know,' he replies. 'The usual.'

'Yeah.'

'Trick is to keep breathing, Alan.'

'Or otherwise!'

A snuffling laugh, then after a hesitation Sandy joins in.

'Anything I can prescribe for your lungs?'

Alan Hayman just shrugs. Sandy flicks his stub over the rail.

'Well – you still wanting to smooch wi these Simpson sisters?'

'You betcha!'

They hurry down the stairs towards the dance saloon, bumping shoulders and laughing on the way. After all, it's a new world and theirs for the making.

Energy. Renewable energy. It wasn't something that concerned me much till my life stumbled and it became clear some things are not endlessly renewable.

The old family house was put up for sale, Mum moved into sheltered housing and I went back to my flat in Southside to pick up my life. I'd decided not to tell her about the hollow domino – though she seemed fairly indifferent to my father's life before they'd met, I felt the secret compartment crossed some line. In any case, studying the tiny photo through a magnifying glass, it was impossible to make out anything beyond the ghostly outline of a woman's face, the grey dots of eyes, fleck of a mouth.

Another month, another hospital appointment. I had the staples taken out of my head and with my hair growing back, from the outside I looked almost normal if peely-wally. Then I went in for another scan, which was at once like being slid down a birth canal and into one's grave.

Nowadays anyone can see the skull beneath the skin. But with an MRI, we see the brain inside the skull. That's me in there.

Me too, pal.

That little voice was another unexpected extra I was learning to live with. At least it didn't tell me I was Napoleon or that I should slay the wicked.

Waiting to see my surgeon, I watched sunlight move across green linoleum. I couldn't put my finger on exactly how everything looked different these days, as though someone had changed the light to make the world sharper yet less solid and convincing, like I'd been surrounded by theatre sets.

Another lesson: someone can save your life and still be an irritating sod. My surgeon was pink and tweedy and brisk as he talked me through the plates. The latest scans showed that the parts of my brain which had been flattened against the walls of my skull had mostly re-expanded. I might experience some inconvenience or odd sensations, but my brain was nearly as it should be and he didn't need to see me for six months. The shunt was plastic and should out-live me. I should remember I was totally shunt-dependent and try to avoid blows to the head. I said I usually did.

He tapped his pen on the desk. I hesitantly tried to tell him that I felt different, as if I'd been cut adrift from something. Sometimes a voice spoke to me. I thought about death too much.

The rapping hastened. 'I'm a surgeon not a psychiatrist,' he said briskly. 'Ask my secretary for the number if you want to talk to the mumbo-jumbo boys.'

I decided not to bother. Talking would just make it real. I was alive and very lucky to be so, best concentrate on that.

Time to go back to work. Trying some old problems in my textbooks, I could do them, if a bit slower than before. But when I dropped in at the college to talk with colleagues, I was still having problems with names and anything demanded of me in a hurry. As I walked out those plate-glass doors back into the world, I knew I wouldn't be going back. Time for a change though I'd sensed that even before my head had gone wrong.

So what now? Industry – I'd already done my time. Teaching was the wrong sort of demanding. Research, I thought. Pay not so good but can use brain at own speed.

Flicking through the journals one morning, I came on a piece about aquatic renewables. Of course I'd known about the Edinburgh Duck, Donald Salter's baby, way back when I was a student. Now that the true costs of nuclear had become clear after being fiddled all those years, and carbon emissions had cast a cloud over coal, water and wind power were being taken seriously. I read through the menagerie of wave converters – the Clam, the Osprey, the Limpet, the Hosepump, the Bristol Cylinder, the esoteric Shin Hybrid. Like the early days of motoring or aviation or falling in love, there was something sweetly comic as well as exciting about it.

The hook came at the end. A renewable energy project was being set up in Orkney. The Department of Offshore Aquatics, DOA – who could resist that? – had funding for a feasibility study into tidal streams power generation. Marine biologist, marine engineer, oceanographer-environmentalist all required. Some MSc teaching work. Salary a bit of a lame joke. Interested?

It gets harder to move out of your comfort zone as you get older. I had a network of true friends, and my mum and brother in driving distance. Since Lyn and I had abruptly fizzled out a year back like sparklers, leaving us waving charred wire at each other, I'd had no lasting lover, only a friend with whom I sometimes ended up in bed when drink or loneliness or extreme amiability seized us. I had nearly accepted children were something that happened to other people. I was a free man.

I rested my fingers on the slight bulge above my ear, picked up the phone and made that call.

And so a month later, in the first year of the new millennium, I stood chilled at the deck rail in a brisk October wind as the *St Ola* ferry turned sharp right after Hoy and slid with the tide race past fields lit a violent green in the low sun, then on towards a wee town of piers, sandstone and slate huddled below a hill.

The world is wonderful just for being there. That's what I'd told family and friends before setting off to drive north with my flat let and all my possessions that wouldn't fit in the back of the car sold or dumped or given away. I didn't say the world before and the world now weren't quite the same.

Down on the pier head a grinning man with a low centre of gravity was holding up a cardboard sign with a familiar name on it, and I thought: Well, that must be me.

And so it was, more or less.

Whenever Alan Hayman mentioned the Simpson sisters, Sandy thought on some lines he'd idly read in a copy of *London Magazine* left lying on a deckchair. About two women. No prize for guessing which one the poet was after and which might have had him. Damn fool.

So there they are, standing looking out a porthole by the corner of the bar while the band takes a break. They are alone for once. The two heads offered in profile, one gold, the other fair, hair hooked back behind the ear in the new style. The same long straight nose, same mouth, one smiling, the other talking rapidly. One in pale blue, the other ivy green, they turn in unison as the two men approach. Both are quite tall and slim, but he notes the golden one's child-bearing hips, her slightly fuller figure, her unfeigned smile as though life was a treat that simply had to be delicious. They are two alternate versions of the same good idea, Ann and Adele.

The two women smile, one openly, the other with a slight shadow in her eyes or her mouth that suggests this is all a bit of a joke. Sandy hangs back a little, for after all this is Alan's idea, he's just come to help make up the numbers.

Alan Hayman makes reintroductions because Sandy hasn't talked directly to either of them since Suez.

'Lovely to meet you again, Sandy,' Ann says, holds out her hand. It's soft, warm.

Adele just stares at him. As he inclines his head, a small smile flickers and is gone.

'Dr Mackay,' she says. 'So you've dragged yourself away from the bridge table. We are honoured. I trust you won again?'

'We did,' he says. 'Though I think that's more to Marsden's credit than mine.'

'Yes, Phillip is very good – and lucky, I think, which they say counts for as much.'

'The cards like him,' he admits. 'But you still have to know how to play them.'

'Oh yes indeed.'

The eyes meeting his are blue and hazed like sea-glass. The band hits an opening chord, announces a quickstep. Adele turns to Alan Hayman, puts her hand on his dinner jacket sleeve.

'I don't believe in waiting to be asked.'

She leads him onto the floor, leaving Sandy with Ann. He has no choice, and besides she's a lively girl, and now he turns to ask her up to dance, he sees she is really a very bonnie one.

Both beautiful, one a gazelle.

5

I reach across, open the glove compartment and feel around among the recording gear till my fingers close on that cool little oblong.

I sit squeezing the double one domino, let my fingers slip into the little black pits but don't press. I try not to open it often, because each time I do the scent inside fades. It was the talisman of my quest, somehow Tina's gift as much as my father's, and I want it with me at the finish.

The Go Orkney coach shoogles up the road from the Broch. I slip the domino into my jacket pocket, slouch down in the seat till the bus passes because I know the driver slightly and CCTV has nothing on the Orkney surveillance system, which operates even in the pitch darkness of a winter storm.

That winter the main door of the house I'd rented off the square scraped then clunked no matter how carefully it was opened. This was a careful opening and I was awake in the dark with my heart knocking loud as the gale outside. I could hear the sloosh and thump on the Lighthouse Board pier, then the lash of spray on my windows though they were eighty yards back.

I wondered how we'd believed our tidal generators could ever stand up to these forces, then my bedroom door clicked. I knew who it was because it couldn't be.

'You awake?' she whispered. 'Sorry.'

'Hey, Mica. Call by any time.'

Like that night's bad news on the radio, it couldn't happen, it has happened, of course it had to happen. The pale shape detached itself from the door and drifted further into the room.

'I won't stay, Eddie,' she said. 'I've been to a party and it was too much. I'm just sheltering to avoid someone.'

There was a bang and clatter in the street outside as something came adrift. The darkness in my room swayed.

'If this is a dream, it's fine by me,' I said.

Already I felt more awake than I did most of the time when I was awake. Maybe this is how the longed-for arrives, sailing in without warning, and you wake entirely calm to see it tie up at the pier head of your bed.

'Sit down,' I suggested. 'Want me to put on the light?'

'He might see it. Don't want to involve you.'

She pulled back a corner of the curtain and let a streetlight into the room. She peered down the street towards the harbour and the Lighthouse Board pier.

'Flags of convenience,' she muttered. 'That's all it is.'

I waited, wondering how far gone she was. Eventually she turned away from the window.

'You heard about the tanker broken loose in the Firth?'

'Bad news waiting to happen.'

'Know the feeling.' Her voice trembled. 'Sorry,' she said. 'Wallowing a bit. It's been difficult recently.'

With a slight list she deposited herself on the chair by my bed. She shrugged off a big jacket and let it fall onto the floor. I put out a hand, felt wet and her lean arm hard under a sweater.

'Still raining out?' I asked.

'Hail and sleet,' she said. 'Blowing a hoolie out – Force Ten maybe. Tide's up across the South Ness road. Folks are out with their sandbags but those houses drain straight into the sea, so when the sea is higher than the drains, well ... '

'So you're cut off?'

She laughed quietly. 'Same old same old,' she said. 'But it'll turn in a peedie while. Then I'll be off.'

'Just a matter of waiting then,' I said.

So we waited in silence a while. I'd not seen her subdued like this. The first time we met was at the party of our project manager, Anne-Marie, to welcome the new intake for the Orkney DOA. I'd been on the island a few weeks. It was one of those parties where I arrived with colleagues and left with friends.

'Who's that?' I'd asked Ellen.

She glanced round at the commotion by the fireplace.

'Mica Moar,' she said. 'She's part local, recently back from South. You're interested?'

I looked again, felt the stir of energy around this oddly named woman. Pale high forehead, thick wild brown hair, strong bendy body as she danced and mocked our host's wallpaper, taste in music, joint-rolling abilities. Her eyes flicked over me then away. They were restless and very bright.

'Scarcely,' I said. 'She's not my kind of trouble.'

'You like trouble?' Ellen asked.

'No, but it's happened so often it can scarcely be an accident.'

We were just talking, flipping the phrases around but in a friendly way. I liked the project's oceanographer, felt easy in the calm that came round her like water on the leeward side of an island. As she watched her six-year-old daughter dancing with computing whiz Ray, Ellen Lorenz had the look of someone who had woken to discover she was no longer the centre of the world and felt at ease with that. No sign of a man, but I didn't know her well enough to ask.

Now Mica was wrestling with one of the musicians in the big empty fireplace, laughing scornfully and calling on him to try harder. She was quite tall, lean and whippy and our guitarist was struggling. I wondered if mixed-sex wrestling was an Orcadian custom.

'Surely that's not her real name?' I asked as we watched.

'It's just what people call her,' Ellen said. 'Her island name.'

I'd liked that phrase, 'her island name'. As if we might become another when we cross a stretch of water to a new place. Then I was dragged into an anarchic eightsome reel with Ellen and Ray, and forgot Mica for a while.

'Water'll go down,' she said abruptly from the bedside chair. 'It always does. But the disgusting smell it leaves behind ... '

A gleam of her teeth like surf in the night. I smelled gin and hash and cigarette smoke. It wasn't unpleasant on her.

'You smell like an illicit still,' I said.

'Another flag of convenience,' she muttered.

'What's with these flags?'

A pale hand flittered across the wall as she gestured.

'Everyone's flying one these days,' she said. 'Single parent, gay, dysfunctional family, embattled minority, oppressed local ... To see what we can get off with. Or who.'

Her voice dropped. I put my hand on her back and touched wet wool.

'You're soaking,' I said.

'I'll go in a minute.'

Still, she pulled off her trainers and got under the duvet beside me. Her jeans were damp against my legs. I put an arm round her shoulder and her hand drifted across my chest. We lay on our backs and were silent awhile.

On a small island all meetings happen sooner or later. So at the party.

'Who are you then?' she'd challenged me in the kitchen.

Since my brain had got squished, I needed time. Instead I said what came first up.

'Not who I was.'

Quick stab of her glance, like beak of a long-legged wader.

'How would you know?'

'I wouldn't.'

It was going too fast. Mouth well ahead of brain.

'So who are you now?' she'd speired.

'Like this country since Devolution – too soon to say.'

Then she made some crack about DOA engineers, but I hadn't come for trouble so went to dance with Ellen and her wee Cara and forgot that jolt when you bump into the eyes of an intelligence, the burning, yearning, uncomfortable kind.

The moment we really met, the one that stays with me yet, came near the end of the party. It had turned mellow and whisky, and the fiddles drifted from Orcadian to Country, sure sign of imminent collapse of all musical and moral values and an end to coherent speech. As the Zurich Brothers led us through 'Drinking To Forget', she shouted 'More pain! More loss, more dead dogs!' then fell still grinning on the hearthrug at my feet.

Being nearest, I'd hunkered down to pull her up. Her hands were strong and long-fingered, no rings but emerald green nails. She grinned sardonically up at me like I was amusing.

'You're a gent, Eddie,' she said.

'You're a bit of a hooligan, I think,' I replied.

It's like when you move in to a new place and shove say the bookcase in that corner just because it's nearest, or that tall plant goes down here because somebody came to the door at that moment. And then those accidental placements become habitual, then fixed. It was like that with our first proper exchange – a couple of flip remarks became our roles from the start. Me gent, she hoolie. Then she looked at me straight and I saw she wasn't that far gone.

'Well maybe,' she said. 'But sometimes you have to be a bit of a hooligan to grab life by the short and curlies. Otherwise you end up crying all the time.'

I felt she'd just offered me something clear and certain. It doesn't happen that often and I needed all the markers I could find. But I was pulled back into the dance and the last I saw of her that night was in a swaying threesome clutching bottles liberated from the party, heading for the golf course. She was waving a bottle at the moon, still calling out 'More pain! More Country!' as I said goodnight to Ellen and went up Hellihole Road with Stevie Corrigall and his wife Jane under that old bone-white Orcadian moon.

'Look,' I said. 'I'm glad you're here, but . . . '

'I know,' she said. 'It's not a good time for me either.'

We lay longer and she warmed and stopped shaking. I was drifting between sleep and awake when our hands began to drift vaguely. The window shook as hail drilled against the glass. I wondered how much more it could take.

'This party?' I asked as the hands moved, of their own will it seemed.

'Just another night with too much booze and dope. I mean, these are folk I've known since school. Sons and daughters of the inner circle. Solid citizens, you know? And the young ones are mostly married, some with bairns but still not quite settled enough to . . .'

She trailed off. When one pair of hands stopped, the other did too, as if they were shadowing each other down a dark street.

'Anyway,' she said. 'I was having this interesting talk with . . . this guy I used to know, about people and their masks and the tanker breaking loose, and I'm thinking this is good, we're making connections, this is where I want to be. Then I get up to go to the loo and he grabs my crotch. I was so shocked, I just looked at him. I thought we'd sorted all that. And then he does it again! And I finally get to the loo and there's this woman I know – married – arranging to go off for a drive in the moonlight out to Yesnaby with the young diver next door. I mean, come on!'

Her hands were moving down my chest. I put one of mine on hers and she stopped.

'Then I get back to the party and see Magnie slipping out with a wee lassie I know is still at school, and his bairn is upstairs asleep. Oh it's disgusting! We're greedy bastards who say we were drunk or stoned or we're not who we used to be . . . '

I winced, wished I'd never said it. When the sea gets higher than the drains, all the things you thought you'd got rid of start flowing back in.

'So you came in here,' I said.

'I just want to get home and get some purity and discipline into my life!' she said. 'Get some solid work done. But the street was blocked and this man thinks he has some claim on me and I saw your door and thought of that thing you said about not being who you were, and somehow . . . '

She tailed off and we lay there. I hadn't done this since my brain imploded. Had a notion that excitement could create pressure in my head, or pull the shunt from its root. My surgeon had told me it wasn't so, but still some fear, some hesitation remained.

Now I felt a light rapid tickling on my upper arm, as if an ant were walking there. Then I understood it must be her eyelashes flicking as she blinked. I thought too I felt a slight dampness. I was certain it would be unforgivable to ask. Her hands began drifting again. I lay and let it happen.

'Why are you afraid of me?' she murmured.

'Should I be?'

'Your stomach's tense.'

'It's been a while,' I said. 'I've been keeping my head down.'

This didn't seem the time to tell her what had happened to my head. I'd mentioned it to no one except the GP since I'd arrived in Orkney, and didn't intend to.

'My ex-boyfriend,' she began. A faint gleam as she raised herself up on one elbow. 'My ex-boyfriend would say I get interested in people who seem strong and complete, and then I find out they're only pretending to be and I lose interest and then they start getting in touch with their feelings, tears and all, and then I want to be a million miles away.'

'I'm not your boyfriend and I'm not complete,' I said. 'Or scared of you,' I added.

'Good,' she said. 'Are you anyone's boyfriend?'

'No,' I said. 'Like I said, it's been a while.'

'One of my few principles. In that case ... '

She wriggled out of her jeans then sat up and pulled off her damp sweater. Her pale neck gleamed as she shook her hair free and I knew I was in trouble. Wind punched the window and the glass creaked as she hesitated then peeled off her T-shirt.

'I'm desperate to touch you,' I said. 'Only we can't.'

I saw paleness turn my way, then the flicker of her eyes.

'Of course,' she said. Then she was over me and it was too late to protest and anyway I felt rooted and passive as the long reef beyond the harbour. She rose over me like a figurehead, her face dispassionate and staring with a small set smile into the distance as she grounded herself, lurched down on me, and though it was not a sensible time I could not stop flowing.

She stirred. 'God I'm wrecked,' she said and slid away.

I heard her dressing and muttering to herself. Dawn was in now but the gale was wild as ever, birling a dustbin lid round and round the square.

'Would you like some tea?' I asked, ever the polite host.

'No thanks.' She put her hand on my chest and pushed me back down. 'The tide's on the ebb, I can get home now.'

She stood at the door and looked back at me a moment. A wee grin, then in a quick signing her index finger pointed to her eye, at me, then twirled a quick circle. 'See you around,' she said. 'Bye.'

'Ta-ra.'

The door clunked then scraped as I lay on the moist sheet with her strong back and rapt distant face still rocking over me. Lean and hard, not voluptuous at all. I needed some sweetness and calm in my new life, not Mica Moar.

I went to the window and looked down the stone-flagged alley in time

42

to see her hesitate at the corner of Victoria Street. A volley of hail like a whirling ghost swept down on her and she turned her head aside. I saw her hand come across her collar and hold the hood of her waxed jacket. She was leaning forward at such an angle that if the wind stopped she'd fall on her face, then she was gone into the blast.

So leaves all sweetness, froth and scum.

There wasn't much I could do with that little voice, so I went back to bed and lay shivering among the leakage and the shambles. My father's chipped old Penang Buddha sat beaming on my window ledge, black eyes fixed on infinity. Together we waited for it to get as light as it ever would that winter.

'Gosh, this is jolly swish!'

Ann Simpson has eyes a shade lighter than the Indian Ocean and only slightly smaller as she looks up at him. They have quick-stepped, foxtrotted, and are now waltzing, for Adele shows no sign of relinquishing Alan Hayman. They swirl round the floor, adjusting to each other and the subtle shifting underfoot. They move well together, her warm good humour lets him relax and enjoy the movement. Dancing is like sports but more fun. And why shouldn't he have fun? Though she is surely too young and fresh for him, it's a pleasure to handle something other than cards or books, a tennis racket or golf club. Something living, something that handles you back.

And she is very much alive – and half-cut – he now realises. Her hands grips his back as the deck tilts, she presses into him, very warm and young, her skin still utterly unmarked and healthily glowing – and suddenly he responds.

It's painful, not so much in the groin as higher up, somewhere between her hands. He can feel each finger sliding and pressing, flexing on his back to the music like she's playing the piano on him.

He eases away from her a little, concerned she might feel his interest. But she presses back in on the next turn, looks up and smiles lots of neat white teeth. She has faint down on her upper lip, soft and fine. He finds it hard to concentrate on what she's saying for watching her mouth shape it.

'I'm sorry,' he says, 'that ruddy clarinet . . .'

'I said, shall we go up on deck?'

She takes him onto the small upper aft deck. On the way they pass and ignore other couples leaning at the rails, or pressed into the shadows. The moon hasn't risen but once eyes adjust there's light enough from the stars and faint phosphorescence rising where the surface breaks. Pale gleam of a cheek, two hands interlocking, a white shirt front, spark from an earring. Red tips glowing, dotted all along the rail, the brief mutterings as they pass by form lines of a fervent poem of the voyage:

> *But you really are*
> *– and if we ever do –*
> *couldn't possibly, but so far*
> *Only six days, Beth, yet you . . .*

It minds him of adolescent summer nights in Brechin, along by the golf course or out the pier after a dance on the Folly. The same etiquette: we see but we do not see, we hear but we are deaf. He has to smile, even as Ann Simpson leads him by the hand towards the stern; he remembers Jeannie Armour the minister's daughter, the first lassie he ever kissed and walked out with, his mad proposal to her after he'd been called up in 1917. And maybe she would have too, till her damn father put a stop to it.

She leads him past a stack of deckchairs by the stern. He wonders if she's been here before, on other nights with other men. It seems likely enough – she's high-spirited and much has changed since the war, especially among the young ones who missed it, and anyway on the voyage out the rules seemed to have buckled and melted in the heat.

They lean on the rail and talk nonsense about unfamiliar stars, the voyage so far, their shoulders touching. He can feel the warmth of her through his jacket. Though the night isn't cold, she shivers slightly. His heart starts charging as he anticipates what can come next. Part of him notices how absurd it is that in his life so far he has acquired proficiency with a rifle, scalpel and forceps, specialised tools of death and life, yet preparing to kiss a girl still makes him nervous.

He puts his arm round her shoulder. She silently coories in to him. It really is like Brechin pier, he could be seventeen, not twenty-nine. Neither of them is speaking now. He feels her breath warm and fast in the hollow of his neck. Perhaps she's as nervous as he is.

For all the changes since the war, the next move is up to him. He turns his head, her face is in some faint light, he is about to tilt it up to his.

'So there you are!'

It's that damned sister, Alan Hayman beside her. Sandy lets his arm slip away as he turns to face them. Cigarettes are offered and smoked, more nonsense is talked. Alan keeps glancing at him; Sandy's not sure if he's annoyed or amused. A faint twinge of guilt, but then again he'd only gone with what the women had clearly decided.

Still, he feels something is owing, so he turns to the elder sister and asks her to dance.

6

I took to Stevie Corrigall from the moment he met me off the Orkney ferry, dropped the sign with my name and shook my hand warmly. The marine biologist attached to our project, he was Orcadian born and bred – short and stocky, round headed and brown eyed, with a quick sceptical humour. He'd gone south to college and work, then like many had come back when he was ready to have family and the job was there. A returnee, the glue that held together a mixed society of natives and incomers like myself.

I liked him because he was what I was not: settled, optimistic, at home with himself and his world, a father. He had his beloved Jane, his work, his two-year-old Tanya. He also had a very handy old twelve-foot clinker-built loch boat kept on the shore at Harray.

He introduced me to the subtleties of Orkney loch fishing – the shore-hugging drifts, the curious round-arm flick cast, the positioning of the bob fly on the little crests at the end of the retrieve. He knew the Stenness, Harray and Boardhouse lochs well, knew the seasons of nymphs and the airts of the wind, the skerries and shallows beloved of the Orkney wild browns.

Out on the loch with Stevie, drifting parallel to the shore watching light on water for hours on end, talking and not talking, gently rocking below the shifting sky by the great stone circles of Stenness and Brodgar, I was beginning to feel nearly whole again.

'That woman Mica, at the party,' I said casually as I flicked my line out. 'Why the name?'

Stevie glanced at me, not fooled a moment.

'Her by-name?' he said. 'She got it at school and it stuck.'

'Bright and shiny and a bit flaky?'

He grinned, nodded.

'Lots of layers in that one! I was sorry for her at school, like, turning up in Raggedy Ann cut-down dresses of her mother's. You'll know her father, Jimmy Moar. That tall thin fella wi the stick and deerstalker, always walking.'

I pictured him. Elderly man with a face of hollowed bones. Looked like a giant glowering grasshopper. I seemed to pass him almost every day on the front street. The other morning he'd suddenly nodded to me as we passed. Now I thought of it, this was after his daughter's night visit.

'She's been South for years,' Stevie said. 'She came back because he's dying – heart condition, the word is. But they don't get on, none of that family do.'

It's been difficult recently, that's what she'd said. I remembered my father's decline, how painful it had been to go home and see the colossus crumbling. The tremor in his liver-spotted hands, the looseness round the collar and cuffs of his shirt, made me want to bolt. I'd visited little during his last months, not admitting to myself that's what they were.

So that's what she was living through. I felt again Mica's eyelashes tickling on my arm.

There was a long pause while we just fished. I had one bite on my tail fly, lost it straight away. Then he had one on the bob and pulled in a tiddler then flipped it back.

'Late in the season,' he said apologetically.

I told him I'd once been in Orkney before, on holiday. I'd visited the Broch of Gurness with someone I knew then. At her insistence – something to do with a book she'd read – I'd gone down into the well there and touched the water and felt whole, just like her book had said I would. Later I'd made a promise to go back for her, but ...

I stopped then, feeling I'd gone too far. We scarcely knew each other. It wasn't common talk between men.

'And does this someone have a name?' he murmured, keeping his eye on his bob fly as it bounced the ripples.

'Tina,' I said. 'Tina Calder.' And my voice was strange to me, her name rusty on my tongue like a lock unturned for a long long time. Stevie retrieved his line twice before he spoke, flicked it out again. I saw the tiny disturbance where his tail fly went in.

'There's always one, isn't there,' he said casually. 'The one we mark ourselves by.'

I looked at him, startled by the change in his voice. I love it when people escape the net of my assumptions.

He glanced at me, then looked back to his line, teasing it in.

'Don't get me wrong,' he said quietly. 'Jane and Tanya are everything to me, and I've no regrets. But having a family doesn't solve everything in your life, though it maybe looks that way from outside.'

Then we fished silently to the end of the drift opposite the giant Stenness standing stones. They were somewhat older than Stonehenge and the pyramids. Folk had been fishing this loch for a very long time.

Temporary accommodation, boy.

It was as if that damn tube in my head was an aerial. It had become the laconic passenger of my life.

You're the passenger, pal. I'm driving.

On my last retrieve I got a bite and brought in another tiddler. It was pleasure to catch, and a pleasure to flip it back.

'Christ, boy, yon's more a peedie anchovy than a fish.'

'It still counts. Size isn't everything, right?'

'When they tell you that, it's time to worry.'

I grinned as I washed the fish-slick off my hands. These wee games, loves, jokes, losses, catches and releases, are all we have.

'Haven't been to Broch of Gurness in years,' he said casually as we hauled the boat up onto the bank. 'But I'm sure your well is off limits now. Should you want to go back down for your friend.'

I thought about it as we seized the side of the boat and couped it over, for this was the last fishing day of the year. We were closing down for winter and the dark, but the light would come again. I was cold and hungry and oddly happy.

'So we'll have to go when the custodian's gone home,' I said, 'but before it's dark.'

'Sure,' he said. 'I'll bring Tanya, and you come for your tea after. Whenever.'

'Aye, whenever.'

We carried the rods and gear and small outboard to the car and left the loch to the standing stones reared up against the last conflagration in the west.

'I like your friend Hayman,' Adele says as they turn at the far corner of the floor. She is slightly taller than Ann and he's still making the adjustment. She is thinner and sharper in every way – her nose, cheekbones, lips, wit.

'Good,' he replies. 'So do I.'

'That's very loyal of you.'

'He's my friend.'

'And she's my sister.'

She is smiling, but he gets the message. Then something in the night, or the stir still left from what hadn't happened with Ann, or the shifting deck under his feet, loosens his tongue.

'*Both beautiful, one a gazelle,*' he says suddenly.

She misses a beat there, then catches up with him. She's still looking at him, but differently.

'*The light of evening, Lissadell, Great windows open to the south,*' she says. She doesn't say it in that daft pulpit voice most use for poetry, but as if it came from the back of her brain or the top of her heart. '*The younger dreams some vague Utopia.*' Then she laughs quietly. 'I do think Mr Yeats is improving with age. So you read modern poetry, Dr Mackay?'

He shrugs, slightly irritated by her surprise and that 'doctor' holding him at a distance.

'Willie Yeats read to us when I was a medical student in Dundee. He never looked at us, just intoned to the rafters wi his black cape and eyeglass. I thought the man was a clown but he read a couple of good things about the Rebellion. So I notice any of his stuff I see lying around.'

Now she's looking at him as if he'd grown a second head and she doesn't quite know which one to look at.

'You've heard Yeats read?'

'I told you. He was there, so I went.'

'Gosh,' she says. 'Well I never.'

'You think because I'm working class from the primitive North I couldn't read poetry?'

She looks at him. Her eyes are definitely slightly hyperthyroid, scornful, and he feels himself a clumsy peasant.

'I think, Dr Mackay, you presume too much what I think.' In an abrupt change of mood she chuckles and adds, 'But what I want to know is – which one do you consider the gazelle?'

He looks at her clever mouth and hazed wary eyes.

'I think that's fairly obvious,' he says. 'Don't you?'

She looks down but says nothing. A small tug of her lip might be a smile. They dance on through the turns, the forward and back. He misses the protective feeling he'd had with Ann, that and her radiant enthusiasm. Ann is fun. She'd made him feel light-hearted for a while, as if there were no need to be old and glum. And indeed perhaps there isn't.

> *'The beautiful and the innocent*
> *Have no enemy but death'*

She has quietly poured her cool English voice into his ear. It makes him shiver, the calm surface of her voice and the ocean depth of feeling beneath it. Now she looks at him enquiringly.

'That sounds very fine,' he says. 'But it's not true.'

'No, unfortunately it's not. So you can understand, Dr Mackay, why I have to chaperone my sister.'

He shrugs, still irritated about the kiss that had been snatched from him.

'Aye, perhaps.'

'But you think she's old enough to make her own choices?'

'Don't you?'

She moves back a little from him and glances over to where Alan Hayman and Ann are seated talking at the bar. Ann has a fresh cocktail glass in one hand and is lobbing peanuts into his open mouth with the other. Both seem to find this hilarious.

'She's just twenty,' Adele says thoughtfully. 'At that age, I decided to get married.'

'So you were old enough.'

'I thought so.'

She looks down at the floor, and for a while neither of them speak. The music ends, they drop arms and move apart.

'Thank you for the dance, Dr Mackay. I'm glad you like Mr Yeats's poem. Now it's time Ann and I went below. Goodnight.'

He bows his head a little to her, feeling a bit of a stookie.

'Aye, goodnight to you, Mrs Trent.'

She smiles slightly.

'*Bid me strike a match and blow,*' she says, and leaves him.

7

I gave it a week after her night visitation. I didn't knock and wait outside because I'd learned in Stromness only strangers did that. I went quickly up the stairs, chapped on the nearest door and went in.

She straightened up from an old typewriter and pushed her corkscrew thick brown hair back with both hands.

'Saw you coming up the street,' she said. 'Wondered when you'd decide you could call.'

I nodded, slowly unbuttoned my coat. It was my dad's, picked up from behind the door first time I was home after he died. High waisted, massive collar, heavy black wool with tiny dark red threads running through it – his winter coat from the days men still wore hats to go to work. It was older than I was and on the whole wearing better. *You might as well have it now,* my mum had said.

'What you been up to?'

'The usual,' she said. 'Signing on. I had to give up my job when I came back here.'

'Which was?'

Embarrassing to realise you don't know the most basic things about someone you've slept with. That said, if you like someone well enough to sleep with them once, you'll likely like them well enough to want to do it again.

'Selling advertising space for a local giveaway paper in the Midlands. Yes, it's as bad as it sounds. Don't ask if you ever want to talk to me again.'

'So what's with the museum piece?' I gestured towards her big black typewriter.

'That's the old man's. I've decided I had to find something to do or go mad. So I've been writing the odd feature for the *Glasgow Herald*, plus a couple of travel things. It's easy doing the usual blarney about Orkney when it happens to be true.'

She paused, looked at me then out the window. 'As far as it goes,' she added quietly. 'A while back I started writing nippy stories about my friends on the side. Some fools are publishing them, they think I'm a humorist.'

'And you're not?'

She leant back and hooted with laughter.

'God, no! I'm a sour moralist trying not to be. Only people think I'm just taking the piss and I let them.'

I nodded towards the typewriter.

'Which is this? Journalism or nippy story?'

She quickly put a cover over the machine and its sheet of paper.

'Nippy story. About some fool who runs away from a party.'

I went over to the window. From up here she could look right down the long twisting street that uncoiled through the town. She could see everyone, but they'd have to know exactly where to look to see her.

'Pull up a chair, pal,' she said.

I did. I looked at her. Same tight faded jeans, baggy sweater. Same high arched eyebrows, same long crooked mouth that had descended on me. The eyes have it, they always do, and she was well by-named for her eyes were like the mineral itself, grey with fugitive gleams just under the surface. Today her fingernails were cherry red, her only adornment.

'Well, hi,' she said. 'How's it been with you?'

'I've been working lots, which I like when it goes well.'

She nodded like she knew.

'Proddie work ethic,' she said, 'you can't beat that shit.'

'I'd like to be a layabout but ... '

' ... I get bored,' she completed it and I remembered why I enjoyed her. 'Me too. So you're with Dead On Arrival – renewables, isn't it? Wave power?'

'Tidal streams,' I said. 'We're doing a feasibility study. Orkney's got terrific potential. Our project leader calls the Pentland Firth the Saudi Arabia of tidal energy.'

She laughed, swung her long legs up on her desk.

'Yup, there's some powerful currents round here all right,' she said. 'Making them work for you is another matter.'

'And I've been out fishing, which is great.'

'I've heard,' she said. 'With Stevie Corrigall. Caught two tiddlers.'

'Three,' I said. 'Not much secret round here, is there?'

'You'd better believe it. Still, we can try.'

We looked each other in the eye for a while till it got silly and we both looked away at the same time.

'I'm from a small place myself,' I said. 'In my experience there's only one way to keep a secret in a wee town.'

She raised her arched eyebrows another notch. They were irregular, one crooked and higher than the other. Maybe that's what gave her that look as though she always might be kidding.

'And that is?' she asked.

'Plant the sapling of truth in a forest of rumours,' I said.

She laughed as I'd hoped.

'Take that mad coat off and have tea with me,' she said. 'Tell me more about the research project.'

She drained her mug then swung her legs down from the desk.

'Interesting. I sometimes think,' she said slowly, then stopped. She looked up at me, measuring my suitability for something. 'I sometimes think the only really valuable things are *not* renewable, and that's what we've got to get our heads round.'

So she knew about the one big thing.

'I passed your dad in the street,' I said hesitantly. 'He nodded to me.'

'You're honoured,' she said dryly.

She looked at me steadily and I'd have said something then, I had to, but she spoke first.

'By the way, I'm not pregnant,' she said.

'Congratulations,' I said. 'That was daft of us.'

'I know that,' she said quietly, and for once wouldn't meet my eye. 'My body keeps trying to do this to me. One day there'll be an accident. I take it you don't have children hidden away?'

'None that I know of.' I thought about it. 'In fact, none.'

She leaned forward and looked at the covered typewriter as if the answer were there. Maybe for her it was.

'About the other night,' she said slowly. 'I was nearly young, I was a bit drunk, the tide was very high.'

'Oh yes, the tide was very high.'

I knew fine what was being said, and was in part relieved.

'All the usual excuses,' she added.

I stood up and reached for my coat.

'Mica, I never asked you to come into my bed at four in the morning.'

'That was silly of me and I'm sorry.'

She put her hand on my arm as I made for the door.

'Eddie, we've got the sex bit out the way. I could do with a good friend here, someone who doesn't lech after me, or know me from school as some arty weirdo. Now I don't have to perform for you and you don't have to perform for me.'

I buttoned up my coat, pulled the belt tight, feeling as always that I'd put my father on.

'I'm a loyal friend,' she continued. 'And I'm a rotten person to want. Or I'm a very bad enemy.' She glanced up at me. 'Your choice.'

'Nice speech,' I said. 'You must have delivered it a few times.'

She shook her head and seemed delighted.

'You see?' she said. 'Some smart clerk to catch me out when I'm being phoney. That's all I'm asking.' Then she added casually 'Oh, and maybe a bit of *Yon* when a body gets frisky.'

'Oh that,' I said. 'And I thought Orkney was romantic.'

I opened the door. She was already having trouble keeping her eyes off the page scrolled into her machine. I reached in my coat pocket.

'Present for you, for the memory. A climber pal gave me it ages back, from Shetland.'

I flipped the matchbox to her. It rattled as she caught it confidently and shook it at her ear. She seemed delighted.

'Not *such* a bad memory,' she said.

I paused in the doorway as she opened the box and peered into it.

'Rivets from the Braer tanker,' I said. 'The one that broke up in Shetland. Another accident that could have been worse. Cheery Scottish outlook, eh? I want to think we could do better.'

At the end of the street I looked back up at her window. I could see the pale oval of her face, the high forehead propped on one hand, looking down. A certain feeling settled over me like a quilt, and its pattern was called Nearly But Not Quite. My father's pattern, the one that had set his mouth but helped him endure. I'd hoped to do more than endure but I hadn't got there yet.

I turned up the coat's great sheltering collar and went up Hellihole Road with its high meandering walls, out of sight if she was watching, which I was pretty sure she wasn't. At the top I turned into the Braes Hotel, hoping for a game of pool or just a quiet pint with a view of nothing very much happening in the Sound of Hoy. I wondered if I was in her nippy story, and whether I'd be pleased or miffed to find I was not.

'About Ann,' he begins warily.

Alan Hayman grins into his lime and soda.

'Not to worry, Sandy. I don't blame you – she's a lovely gal, isn't she?'

'She's bonnie enough. Have you got the sister's approval?'

'I'd say the jury's still on the porch. I'm trying to wangle us an invitation to call on the family house in George Town.'

'And then?'

Alan coughs but manages to hold it down. He sips his drink, looks at Sandy.

'I'd say – let the luckier man win. Are you lucky, Sandy?'

Sandy considers it, as he has often, though of course he doesn't believe in anything so irrational as luck. There are reasons for everything, though some are pretty damn mysterious.

'I caught bad flu in February 1918 and missed a big push,' he says. 'Two thirds of the battalion died. So I must be lucky.'

Alan Hayman nods. They sit for a while in the hot breeze of the boat's passage, and remember the faces, the names, then put them away where they belong.

'Yeah,' Alan says at last. 'I must be lucky because I'm alive too. Here's to us!'

He raises his glass. Sandy laughs, clinks his glass to it.

'*Here's tae us, wha's like us? Gey few – and they're aa deid!*' Then he resumes his normal voice and adds in explanation 'Scottish toast, Alan.'

'You guys, you can't even celebrate without bringing death into it!'

'It's our climate,' Sandy concedes.

'Well, we're in a different climate now,' Alan Hayman says, 'and I feel better already.'

'Me and all.'

They sit and drink in comfortable silence, examining the horizon though they know it'll be several days yet.

'Mackay,' Alan murmurs. 'Mac means son of, doesn't it?'

'Aye.'

'And aye is yes?'

'And always.'

'So you're the son of always ... What would that be?'

'Sometimes?'

55

'Never?'

'Damned if I know.'

Still one keeps looking up ahead though there's nothing to be seen there but sea and sky and their impossible meeting. From out here in the middle of the ocean it is possible to see, just, that the horizon has a hint of curve, and it is possible to sense, just for a moment, the size of the planet.

It's big, very big, Sandy thinks, but not beyond the mind of Man.

He clatters down the stair and along to Marsden's cabin, chaps on the door. A pause, then 'Who is it?'

'Mackay. Sandy.'

'Come in!'

Marsden's cabin is very orderly. Rows of books on the shelves, *A Malay Grammar, Cantonese–English Dictionary, The Philosophy of Emerson.* Sandy sits and watches Marsden pour cards from hand to hand. They seem charged, they flow through the air as he gathers, shuffles, cuts and re-cuts and re-shuffles, all inches above the table. He's noticed and admired Marsden's deftness, as he admires all competence, but this is different.

Marsden speaks without looking up.

'We're playing against Collingwood tonight. Don't let the stakes get too high.'

Sandy can vaguely picture Collingwood. Small, wiry, silent man, usually plays among the ladies in the forward saloon.

'Good bridge player, is he?'

Marsden glances up at him.

'Says he's a researcher, but cards are his living. He's a pro.' The deck's now on the table. With lightning rapidity Marsden cuts and turns over Ace, King, King, nods, then they're vanished back into the deck. 'I wouldn't expect the cards to go with us tonight,' he adds casually.

Sandy leans back against the door as he hasn't been asked to sit down. Stacked alongside the references books are a series of different coloured hardback files. This cabin is no boudoir. It feels like a place of intense privacy and study.

'About the ... you know, the cards? Do you?'

Marsden doesn't pause in his mid-air shuffle, the one where he interweaves two blocks of cards, marrying them crisply into one with a whirr, like wings.

'You're asking me if I cheat?'

'Well ... yes.'

'And if I said I did, I suppose you'd feel you had to refuse to partner me?'

Sandy hesitates, thinking of the pleasure of beating Bellingham-Smythe and Ramsay and even the decent public school Guthries crowd.

'Yes.'

Marsden nods to himself, slips the cards into their box and looks up. His eyes are pale and candid.

'Then I have to tell you I don't.'

8

Recently, during a midnight break as we sat and stared out over the lights of London, Ray produced a photo of the DOA project team taken shortly after I'd arrived in Orkney. We're all outside the old academy, leaning into the wind like skydivers. I'd been feeling pretty good the morning it was taken, but when I looked at myself in that photo I saw a man peering out from behind his own ghost.

I lift my hand and press above my left ear as I sit in the car watching the tide flow back into the Rousay Sound. Press quite hard, until it gives slightly. I think of a woman who gave, slightly, then release and lift my next coffee from the dashboard, listening to tiny bubble sounds in my head – my shunt, my lifeline, fuse of my mortality fizzing.

November blew itself in. The dark came ever earlier and stayed later. I was now getting up in the dark and walking home from work through the narrow back lanes in the dark. It felt as if the whole island were going underground.

For the first time in my life, sound sleep was hard to come by. One day on impulse I tried taping and playing back the sound of the sea breaking out at Warebeth beach, thinking that might help, but it sounded like white noise, just meaningless crash. So I fell back on the World Service and thinking about Penang, my father and the woman in the domino, and though I lay awake many nights with the window shaking and the muffled thump of the sea outside, the front door never scraped and clunked.

Then I woke one morning and something had changed. As I downed tea, outside I could hear the square's kids were hurrying off to the school in half-light. I listened to their voices fade as I pulled the street door to behind me. I heard a harsh *skreek*! way high up, looked and saw a big herring gull drift high over Alfred Square, and finally realised what was different today.

The wind. After a week-long gale the wind had stopped. In the silent street I could hear the regular squeak of Tammy Norrie's bike long before he eased patiently round the corner in his blue boiler suit.

He nodded as he went by, I nodded back, he pedalled slowly on like a man who knew where he was going and had no reason to hurry. Later he'd cycle back for his lunch, then back to work again, then home in the late afternoon. Evening, he'd change into his better boiler suit and bike through the streets again. I watched his heavy patient back turn the corner, bonnet pulled down over his large turnip head. Saw him cycling to his grave, stolid and expressionless to the end.

I was in joyous life-affirming Scottish mode that morning and no mistake.

I could hear everything, a cat's bell tinkle, a door closing, a car coming along behind me. I stepped to the side as it slid by. Glimpse of a weather-beaten young face, big nose, long sideburns, gold earring. My hand went up. A pause then he raised his hand.

I followed the car down the narrows towards the square with the world's best small bookshop before I remembered who it was. We'd met at a session in the back of the Flying Dutchman. Bright blue eyes, a piratical-looking fisherman in patched jeans who knew all the verses to Dylan's 'Desolation Row', which was in his favour, and insisted on singing all of them, which wasn't. His island name was Kip or Kipper, which seemed appropriate.

I walked on through the emerging morning, remembered to drop my advert letter to the British–Malaysian Friendship Society in the post box. It was almost certainly a waste of money – the whole Penang affair was seventy years back. They'd surely all be dead.

The few people in the street seemed stunned by the quiet. Now the last visitors and summer migrants had left, it was down to the hard core. Already I could at least place most of the faces. The shy girl who worked in the chemist. The skipper's widow with her headscarf, hunched back, old green coat and wicker shopping basket. The skinny window cleaner who nodded like a pigeon as he went up and down his ladder up and down the town. Our receptionist's twin sister wheeling her baby to the doctor's.

And here was Mica's dad, bending his leanness into a car window. He was talking with Kipper, glanced my way as I went by. His face had collapsed in further, he was all jaw and nose and eyes. He radiated dying.

'Aye, boy,' he said.

'Aye aye,' I said. I half-paused then added, 'Quiet without the wind.'

He and the fisherman regarded me.

'That is what it is,' he said at last, then turned back to talk to Kipper.

I dotted on along the ancient uneven flagstones that had once bedded Lake Orcadie, picked up a bacon roll at the cafe and was feeling quite cheerful as I turned up Boys Lane. I wasn't thinking much about death or not having children. I was thinking how I felt in place here, giving and receiving all these little contacts as I walked through the town.

A slight figure came quickly out of a side doorway into the lane. It was Ray, our computer modelling and electronics whiz, and he looked damn furtive. He jumped when I gave him the big hello.

'Oh man!' he said. 'Didn't see you there, Eddie.'

I knew he lived up on the Back Road, saw he wore a crumpled jazzy shirt, pale suede waistcoat, no jacket or coat. This was a man in last night's clothes.

So I just smiled and he grinned back and we said no more about it as we went on up the lane together. I'd a notion he was close to Ellen, but she stayed at the north end near the swimming pool. I hoped he wasn't messing her about.

We paused at the top of the lane to get our breath and look back down over the town, the harbour. Watched the *St Ola* cast off and move away from the pier. Checked my watch, back of nine. The ferry slid past the Holms and headed into the Sound of Hoy.

'Christ, wish I was on that!' Ray said.

'Winter getting to you?' I asked.

He shook his head, looked uncharacteristically serious a moment. Ray was always bobbing and bouncing and quipping, our cheery leprechaun though his accent was a petrol-and-water mix of Orkney and London.

'Don't you ever want to be anonymous again?' he said. 'Wish I was walking down Hackney High Street with no one caring who I am, what I do or who my friends are.'

He looked longingly after the *Ola*. I glanced at him, wondering again what he'd been up to. Not my business of course, but since moving here I'd happily entered into the principal occupation of the islands – gossiping and speculating about the doings of people. It's no place for a recluse.

'There's a saying round here,' Ray said. 'Don't mean to be crude, but if you fart in Alfred Street, by the time you get to the harbour everyone knows you've shat your pants.'

'You were brought up here, were you?'

'On Eday,' he said. 'Family moved up from Portsmouth. My father had this mad idea he'd leave the Merchant Navy and run a smallholding while my mum did B&B.'

'Didn't it work out?'

'For them it did!' He laughed. 'I hated it. No pals, no shops, no cinema. Just a lot of feuding, plotting between lost incomers like ourselves, and the last few besieged locals selling up and moving to Kirkwall.'

'Doesn't Eday have great beaches?' I asked innocently.

'Oh yeah, loads of *sand*. You ever have an interesting conversation with *sand*? Had a stimulating chat with a goat? Talked to organic leeks and parsnips? Had a novel thought while milking the cow?' He shuddered theatrically. '*Teats!* Overrated, I think. Na, I got out soon as I left school.'

'So why did you come back?'

He stared south towards Scotland where the ferry was heading.

'God knows,' he said at last. 'Maybe I wanted to see if it had changed. Or if I had.' He shrugged. 'Anyway, it's a job. Talking of which, maybe we should go and do ours.'

We went in through the old school gates, crossed the empty playground towards our offices.

'So what did you come here to get away from, Eddie?' he asked.

Well, that is personal, I thought. But personal is good. Personal is what I came here for.

'Nothing,' I said. 'But there's some things I want to get back to.'

He looked at me, head cocked on one side. It was the moment we ceased to be strangers.

'That's good,' he said. Then he laughed, held the door open wide. 'Of course it won't work, you do know that? After you, guv ... '

'Afternoon, lads,' Anne-Marie said as we came in.

'Evening, boss,' Ray replied. 'Traffic's hell out there this morning.'

Duncan yawned at his desk, ran his hand yet again across his cropped hair.

'Right enough,' he observed. 'There were two cars in front of me at the Mill Stores junction.'

Ray ignored him. He glanced over at Ellen who was making the morning brew, and she keeked back at him, and between them flew something. Anne-Marie clapped her hands.

'Right! Now we're all here can we start our "Interim Progress Meeting".'

She signed the meeting with ironic quotation marks, but she did the irony ironically so that was okay. And then we got to work.

There's quite a crowd in the upper saloon as Sandy Mackay and Alan Hayman enter. It seems the word has gone out. Even the Simpson sisters are there. Also Bellingham-Smythe and Ramsay, who looks like a sleekit, hungry wolf. After a run of evenings winning against all comers, there are several who want to see young Mackay and Marsden lose, and others are just there to watch.

Sandy shakes hands with Collingwood. The man's eyes run through him, clear and objective, finding him out. Marsden claps him on the back as they sit down, passes him his stengah. He sips; it's very dilute. They've agreed alcohol and good bridge don't mix, and Marsden has arranged with the barboy that whatever they might order, what they get is mostly ginger ale.

Adele Simpson slips into the fourth chair. She's in a dusty blue evening dress with her hair up. A green and grey opal necklace on long slim neck, head held high. *One a gazelle.* No other jewellery, except of course a plain gold band. She puts down her cocktail and smiles at Sandy. She seems amused, probably at his attempt to hide his surprise.

'I'm afraid Mr Collingwood's usual partner is indisposed,' she says. 'I've had to fill in at short notice. I trust you don't mind?'

'Not at all,' he says. 'I'm sure Alan will be delighted.'

Alan and Ann are already talking at the bar. She's laughing with him, so easy and natural. Not a gazelle but a cheerful, bright, bonnie young woman. Sandy drags his attention away. He must concentrate.

The first rubber is hard-fought and low-scoring. The cards aren't up to much, and the bidding is canny. In the last hand Sandy, perhaps distracted a moment, makes Marsden out-trump him, and they lose control of the hand and with it the rubber.

Ramsay smiles with pleasure, claps Collingwood on the back. Perhaps it's that that makes Sandy agree to Collingwood's quiet suggestion they double the stakes for the next rubber.

Again the cards aren't what he's had in the past. The boat feels as if it's rolling more than usual. He becomes aware Collingwood is in his unshowy way a very fine player indeed, counting, anticipating, calculating. Adele Simpson isn't in that class but she's good enough, shrewd and more experienced than Sandy, though her memory may not be as good.

When he hesitates over a bid, she looks at him as if she were reading his soul or at least his innermost thoughts and she's not too impressed at what she sees. It makes clear thought difficult. As does seeing Alan and Ann quietly going out on deck into the preposterous, bruise-coloured sunset.

The points rack up, they lose the rubber quickly. Ramsay is openly crowing. They're offered a chance to win their money back – a quick last rubber before dinner, double the stakes?

Before Sandy can respond, Marsden finds a gracious, witty way of agreeing to another rubber but keeping the stakes the same. Which is as well, because though Sandy plays much better, drawing an appreciative smile from Marsden, a nod from Collingwood, and even a quiet 'Well played' from Adele, still the rubber finally goes against them and they lose again just as the gong goes for dinner.

The boat is starting to roll viciously, with an additional forward pitch that brings a corkscrew twist to it. Conversation slackens off, people fall silent, examining their plates warily. For some reason Sandy has never been affected by motion sickness and morosely makes the most of his roast beef and steam pudding.

'Don't worry, old chap,' Alan says. 'You'll have plenty of time to catch up when I'm away in Kuala Lumpur. She is a dish, isn't she?'

Sandy admits Ann Simpson is indeed all right.

'All right – she's a peach!'

Sandy orders another cup of coffee. He must be sharp. He can't afford to lose again. He's near skint as it is, and he's gambling with assets he doesn't actually have. Not a time to be distracted.

He lights a cigarette, watches the waves outside march by like the Cairngorms in winter, white mountains on the move while the boat slaloms on.

✎

A small boy's father's hands are the hands of God, all-powerful to create, destroy and master. Those hands were the first ever to hold me as they eased me into the world. There are none bigger.

'I wasn't that good a diagnostician – my only real talent was in these.'

We were having a pint together in his last months. He stroked his opposing fingertips together, then peered down at his hands as if slightly amazed.

'I could feel under the skin. I could *see it*.' He laughed, looked away. 'No always so good at seeing other things.'

There were a few moments like that, near the end, when he seemed about to impart something, though of course he never did. His own nature, and the culture, made confession near impossible. Perhaps that's why he had to come and see me – or else I conjured him – in the blue shadowlands.

A few brief facts – his favourite kind – about Alexander Mackay.

He married late, in his fifties, to a woman twenty years younger, so he was always old to me. He could have been my grandfather. Yet he played football, catching and golf with us after work, and I'm old enough now to know what that takes. He was tall, lean, upright, toughened as leather. He had energy, he had power. *Vir*, he would have cried it. *Smeddum*.

He was known for being irascible. He frightened housemen and nurses, subdued tough matrons, but I'm told was gentle and sympathetic with his patients. He sometimes shouted at us, even belted us across the lug. That was his generation's way, which doesn't mean I have forgiven him.

His moments of humour, spontaneity and tenderness were as sudden and unexpected as the fistful of ice cream cones he once brought back to the car on a holiday in Ardnamurchan. I see them yet, a gleaming white bouquet sprouting from his gnarled hands.

I never knew his parents, dead long before I was born, nor any of his brothers, sown across the world on the wind of the Scottish Diaspora, so he seemed absolute, alone, without family. He had colleagues at work, and cronies among farmers and fishermen, but no intimate friends except, I think, my mother.

He was in the Lovat Scouts then the Cameron Highlanders in the Great War. Once in a trunk in the attic I found his army kilt, huge and heavy as a bolster. Under it were some medals and ribbons. I mind yet his face as he looked down at them. 'You got those just for being there,' he said at last. 'No damn merit about it. It was important to wash your feet and change your socks. We walked a lot, especially at the end.' He closed the lid and said nothing more about the war, ever. The trunk disappeared soon after.

He had an aversion to ministers and anyone who owned more land than they could walk round in a couple of hours. He respected fishermen, joiners, electricians, men of practical skills who didn't speak much. He read a lot but not novels because they weren't true. He made an exception for poetry, which he carried in his head. He used to recite Longfellow, Burns, Yeats and Robert Frost on long car journeys in the Western Highlands. My head is full of the scraps his head was full of. Poems appeal to the engineer in me – such a great size to power output ratio, wondrous wee gleaming machines, the best of them inexhaustible.

(His hand heavy and warm on my back for a moment when I finally graduated, clutching my daft scroll. *Make a kirk or a mill of it, loon.* I think that meant he was pleased and it was now up to me.)

He liked clocks, barometers, baragraphs, delighted in their accuracy and ingenuity. In old age I found him wandering round the house winding his clocks, singing quietly *Oh Jeezy-beezy loves me, the Bible tells me so . . .*

Apart from golf, he relaxed by listening to classical music. He'd stare off into space, beating time with his hand on the arm of the chair with a faint, slightly goofy smile. No one could talk then. I wonder now where he went to at such times.

Or he played solo bridge. A glass of whisky and four hands on the green baize. My father had no practical skills about the house, but he could shuffle cards in mid-air, make them hiss and glide and snap into place. He could deal aces on demand. I never wondered where he'd learned these things.

Once he looked up from one of his solitary bridge sessions and announced he'd had two lives, before and after meeting my mother, the best thing that ever happened to him. This made him a gey fortunate man and he wished me as good fortune. Embarrassed, I asked how he could play four hands, and bid against himself, when he knew perfectly well what was in the other hands.

He fanned the hand, sipped from his glass as he considered.

'You pretend to yourself that you don't know what you do.'

He had a vast general knowledge. When he didn't know something he wouldn't flannel or bluff. 'I don't know that,' he said – or, towards the end of his life when his early language resurfaced more and more, 'I dinna ken that.'

When he died, as when anyone dies, a universe went out of existence. I was too absorbed in my own life to take it in fully, though I wept at the funeral. After a while I didn't think on him much until years later he came to visit me in the blue shadowlands to comfort and console and say there was something he'd meant to show me.

> A livin' man upon a deid man thinks,
> And ony sma'er thocht's impossible.

The second coffee is sharp, strong, bittersweet as I look through the windscreen out at the tide stream through the Sound of Rousay. Our wave-measuring buoys are still out there. The difference is we own them now, my friends and I, and are using them in ways none of us had imagined back then. I think the old man might have approved, for it's my true work at last.

I see him yet, far gone in music, beating time on the armchair arm with the great flat of his hand.

9

I believed in our Orkney Tidal Streams Power Generation (Preliminary Report) project, but that morning we discovered just how preliminary we were. Which was some kind of progress, like they say realising one's ignorance is the beginning of wisdom, though I've seldom found it that enlightening.

Ellen was behind on her currents survey and had scarcely begun crustacean passage. Duncan had still to get the seabed reports, and he couldn't resolve the costing for the rotors till I'd worked out which system we were looking at anyway. Ray couldn't set up his computer modelling till we gave him something more to model, and Stevie couldn't get anything at all out of the Fisheries people. So Anne-Marie wasn't able to reassure the heid yins at Scottish Enterprise who held the purse strings.

Still, we clarified what needed to be done and after the meeting we got down to doing it. That's what I like about my trade – finding workable solutions to technical problems. Most of the work is defining the problem, and from then on in it's just application and a bit of imagination.

Of course I'd been alive long enough to know Mica wasn't that sort of problem.

I got down to committing equations for power outputs in varying currents. It meant assigning a probability density function to the tidal speed, which was a big assumption but I couldn't get started without it.

'Ellen, have you got the Graemsay Sound tidal speeds?'

She looked up. A slight creasing over her eyes. Something flickered and passed.

'We decided to let Graemsay go, Eddie,' she said. 'Remember?'

'Oh,' I said. 'Yes, of course. Sorry.'

What bothered me was her slight hesitation – not at what I'd said but at how she should respond to it. Can it be called paranoia when you suspect people are being kind?

I put it out of my head and went into that bubble of concentration, that happy immune place where the work gets done, and for an unknown time there was progress made in our little heated space in the old academy, looking over Scapa Flow as it emptied and filled its vast chill heart four beats a day.

I found myself gazing at one of my father's cards I'd pinned over my desk. The back identified it simply as GEORGE TOWN, PENANG. It was a sepia street of white colonnades with shops installed behind them, street vendors, a couple of rickshaws. Dazzling light and deep shade under the arches. In the foreground, a passing European in standard issue white suit, collar and dark tie, too blurry to identify. A sign on the right said ACHEEN STREET.

Something in the lack of clear framing, the casualness of the image, made me think it was a photo rather than a commercial postcard. I looked closer to see what the shops sold. These were maybe baskets and woks, and these might have been knives or tools spilling out onto the pavement next to the pillar ...

'Ellen, have you got a magnifying glass?'

She found one in her desk drawer. I hurried back to my desk, picked the card off the wall and had a better look.

The sign the blurred man was walking by, up on the pillar: it looked like a big domino.

I had to steady my hand. Blinked, looked again. Above the painting of the domino was a pair of dice. And to their right, what might be a deck of cards.

'Can I help?' Ellen asked.

I gave her the glass and showed her where to look, thinking her eyes were younger and sharper. I'd end up like my father, convinced in his old age everyone was mumbling.

'It's a domino factory,' Ellen said. 'In the shadow under the awning, above the Chinese lettering. Says *Green Dragon Games Factory.* And this matters why?'

I opened my desk drawer and took out the double one domino.

'My father's,' I said. 'It's one of the very few things he brought back from Penang. I think it came from this shop.'

She picked it lightly from my palm. Squeezed it, sniffed it, ran her finger over the little dragon etched into the underside. Looked back at the old postcard. At me.

'Yes,' she said. 'Maybe you do need this.'

But I wasn't looking at her, nor attending to the tone of her voice. All I could focus on was that image, trembling through the glass, of a painted double six domino and the winged green dragon above it, the same dragon as the one on the back of the little ivory tile Ellen was holding.

After dinner, they reconvene for the evening session. Alan has taken Ann dancing, so that distraction's gone. He glances at Adele, who smiles back automatically but the doctor in him notes the signs – the slight pallor, the coldness of her hand when it brushes his.

He proposes they up the stakes to thruppence a point. Marsden looks unhappy but has no choice. The first game is very even, with Marsden winning the contract and making it. In the next, Collingwood boldly contracts four no trumps and with Adele's silent assistance, just makes it. Their rubber.

Sandy has just lost a significant amount of money he doesn't in fact have. Ramsay though pale as the boat pitches on, laughs with pleasure, and Bellingham-Smythe nods judiciously, as if to say – so Sandy thinks – well class will tell. Only Adele has gone quiet; her hand rests on her forehead, her eyes have lost their brightness.

'Are you able to continue?' Sandy asks.

She pulls herself upright.

'Most certainly,' she snaps. 'I've known much rougher than this on the trip home.'

They agree to another rubber. The boat's pitch-and-screw has become continuous, and the spectators have begun to thin out. This time Sandy is focused and Adele makes a couple of basic mistakes; Marsden and Collingwood play to their usual standard, but it's become clear the junior partners are the deciding factor. Rubber to Marsden and Mackay. Sandy's still financially down but not so much. Ramsay is subdued, but that's maybe the boat.

Sandy looks at Adele. A coil of her hair has escaped and clings to her neck. She's very pale now, breathing through her mouth. Still she's holding herself upright as she apologises to her partner and proposes a last rubber with the stakes rising yet again.

She's physically hanging on to the table, which is bolted to the deck. The ship is bucking into the waves, sliding sideways then jerking on. Sandy looks to his partner, nods, accepting for them both.

As the tricks go down onto the table, the cards slide and start to fan apart. The spectators too are slipping away, the other matches have all folded. In the bidding for the third hand, Adele gulps and hurriedly closes on three clubs. For once Collingwood registers emotion but though he plays the hand as best he can, there's little likelihood. Marsden gets the lead and he and Sandy win the game and the rubber with an avalanche of points.

Overall, they're slightly in profit. He turns to Adele, who looks as if she were staring death in the face.

'I really must insist on helping you below,' he says. 'I'll find something from my kit.'

A faint ghost of a smile, a moon-shadow, flickers across her white face.

'Good show, Dr Mackay.'

I looked round. The office was empty. Lunchtime. I'd been deep in the bubble. Out the window I noticed Ray and Ellen hurrying across the playground, bumping shoulders and laughing as they went. I wondered if Ray had always had that slight limp. I'd a notion it was one of many things I'd seen but failed to notice.

Beyond them the sky had turned yellow-green as if bruised. The Flotta flare stack glowed sickly through a darkness to the south, then a pale writhing swooped on the pier. I sat at the window watching the lower town turn white as the hail squall swept over the streets and slates.

Then the fusillade hit the windows, stotting off the glass then settling over *Sharon L Magnie, DLM* 1929, and my favourite the cryptic *Fuck No!* carved into the lead flashing by past generations of school kids.

When the hail had swept through, I went outside to take a look. First white stuff of the year, bringing the appearance of innocence to my adopted home. A pale yellow glare on the dark tide-race sweeping up Hoy Sound. Bright rods of light jabbing down on the snow-mantled Hoy Hills against blue-black sky, slate sea, lime-green Graemsay. Winter was like that here, a time of brief, outlandish effects.

A thud between my shoulder blades, laughter like a child but not a child. I turned and she was already scooping together another hailball.

'Mica, don't you dare.'

She grinned and walked toward me, the ball grey-white in her hand. If she chucks that, I thought, well sod her. I don't mind being had but a little respect here would be nice.

She stopped about four feet from me. Drew back her arm. I made no effort to protect myself because that would just encourage her. I just stood with my hands in my dad's coat pockets.

'So,' she said. 'You haven't pestered me. And now I'm feeling frisky.'

Her face was blotchy with the cold but under her green woolly hat the light of life flared in her eyes.

'Frisk yourself,' I said. 'I've got work.'

Her bare fingers twitched round the ball of hail.

'You're cruising for a bruising,' she said.

'You look like you need a good feed,' I said. 'I can offer you pilchards and onions with tarragon jelly and clapshot this evening. You bring the wine.'

'Gosh,' she said. 'Temptation hollers. And what,' she leered, 'can you offer for afters?'

71

'That is for afters,' I said.

It was just patter, a bit of badinage, the old ping-pong. But in truth I suddenly wanted her very much. Something about her pale restless skinniness I wanted to fill up. I wanted to be the one.

She took a step towards me. The dark discs in her eyes grew larger. The academy, Brinkies Brae, Scapa Flow itself drowned in them.

'You know my dad's not well?' she said. 'I mean, really not well.'

'I heard,' I said.

Jimmy Moar's face had made me think of a turnip lantern – how the skin gets brighter at first because everything's hollowed out behind. The skin gets so light and tight it almost looks like health.

'It's rotten,' I said. 'I do know.' I huddled into the black wool coat, pulled my father closer about me. 'I'm really sorry.'

She held my gaze and thoughtfully lifted the ball, held it like a grey orange before my face. She blinked away the hint of water the wind had whipped in her eyes, then abruptly pushed the hailball onto my mouth. It was freezing, coarse, and as I bit a chunk off and swallowed it and felt the cold go down, it was the most pressing thing that had happened to me in a long time.

She put the ball to her mouth, bit out a chunk then lobbed the remains away. She brushed her very cold lips on mine.

'You're on,' she said. 'Your place. I'll be waiting.'

Fresh hail lashed us, we turned our faces from it. It was irresistible, and when the worst had passed and I could look up again, she was gone, a hunched figure in an oversized tatty green waxed jacket hurrying down Boys Lane. One white hand with two fingers raised above her head in what might have been an encouragement to victory or fuck off, you could never tell with her.

They lurch across the passageway. He grabs her waist, holds her tight in one arm and pulls open the door onto the deck as she points weakly. He keeps a grip on her as she vomits over the rail, for the boat's now pitching so strongly this is not a safe place to be.

Perhaps it starts then, out on the deserted rail in the tumultuous dark as he holds her shaking shoulders, feels her skin so cold and smooth, tries to calm and contain and reassure, to *make better*.

He didn't do medicine simply because there was a scholarship. As a child he watched his wee sister Janice die in their darkened front room. He heard her breathing quicken, grow laboured, then a series of brutal grunts like this woman now – and then silence. She died during his watch while his mother was at the shops. He will spend the rest of his life trying to undo this.

So as Adele shudders once more at the pitching rail, she is no longer an irritating, clever, striking woman way out of his class. She is a suffering being stripped of all poise and dignity, and he must comfort and help her.

The wind is howling along the rail. Out in the darkness he sees white flecks higher than any waves have a right to be. Finally she stops heaving. He sees the pale glimmer as Adele turns her face towards him. He's close enough to smell her bitter breath and still think her beautiful.

'Hey ho,' she whispers. 'Let's hope the boat sinks soon.' He gets both arms round her and together they stagger back into the companionway. *A bonnie fechter*, he thinks in his father's voice. There is no higher compliment.

With the help of a crewman, he gets her down the steep steps and along to her cabin. Her dress is soaking and discoloured, her hair wildly flattened. He thumps painfully into a bulkhead as the boat lurches but manages to protect her. He bangs on the cabin door. Eventually Ann opens it.

'Here you are,' she whispers. Her face too is yellow-white like the low moon in summer dusk. Behind her a child lies strapped into her bunk, mouth open as she silently stares at him.

'Our kid sister, Emily.'

He has seen her running round the boat. The large dark eyes fix on him as he asks if he can help her. She shakes her head.

'I don't get sick,' Emily says.

73

'We're the lucky ones, then,' he replies. 'You look after your sisters.'

The child nods once, vehemently. Sandy releases Adele down onto her bunk, tells her and Ann to knock on his cabin door any time day or night if they want his help. He can give them anti-emetics but that won't stop them feeling like death. They'll just have to thole it.

'I'll settle up in the morning,' Adele murmurs. Then she looks right at him and she says all he has needed to hear.

'Thank you, Sandy.'

She was reading at my kitchen table, a glass of red wine in one hand and her thick hair corkscrewed down to her shoulders like unravelling dreadlocks. She put the book down and I saw it was Stephen Levine's *Who Dies?*

'So,' she said, direct as a clean-struck ice-pick, 'who does die according to this fella?'

'Everyone,' I said.

'Good,' she said. 'I thought maybe you were going to turn out to be New Agey and expect to meet your granny in Heaven reconstituted as a bumble bee. I absolutely cannot have sex with wishful thinkers.'

'No such luck,' I said, unbelting my coat. 'She was a very nice old lady but I'll not be seeing her again.'

'Hmm,' she said. She poured out a glass and held it out to me. 'Think you'd better have a glass of this first.'

Her words were sarky but her voice was gentle. I'd loved my gran and I guess it showed. I drank, felt the warmth travel down.

'Saw your dad in the street this morning,' I said.

Her quick mouth twitched. She had a little mole by her upper lip corner and a single pale hair by it. I was seeing her very clearly now and knew what that meant.

'Did he say anything?' she asked.

'Aye,' I said. 'He said, *This is what it is.*'

'In a chatty mood then,' she said.

She drained her glass and poured another while I hung up my coat. I hoped she wasn't going to be a lush, I've no patience with them. She caught me glancing at her.

'Don't worry,' she said. 'I've been working like a bastard all week and I don't drink then. I've just come here for some jousting and R&R.'

I sat down opposite and reminded myself her father was dying. She couldn't leave but couldn't bear to be near him. She was twisting and turning like a worm on the hook of his dying.

'Can we pass on the jousting?' I said. 'I really don't need it.'

She put down her glass. She stared at me across the narrow table. A twitch at the corner of her mouth. I wondered which way this was going to go.

She stood up, scraped the chair across the stone flags.

'Hoorsmelt!' she cried. 'So there is an assertive bone or two. R&R it is, then.'

She picked up her glass and the bottle, took my hand and led me through to my bedroom.

Mica in bed was focused, expert, greedy and, yes, generous in her way. Like the North, like Orkney itself, she was many things but not comfortable.

First she switched my bedroom light off. 'Sight is hackneyed,' she said. 'Feeling is real. Feel me, here. Here. Yes . . .'

But the curtains were undrawn so the street lamp shone in, and the pale curve of her shoulders into the hollow of her back repeated the curve in other lovers I'd known, each different but all the same. She was right, sight is tired. I closed my eyes, then she clasped my head.

Silence. Her fingers hesitated on my shunt. She must have felt it under my scalp.

'This thingy in your head?'

'Yes.'

'Want to talk about it?'

Long pause, hesitation, swallowing: the works. Her fingers still now, warm, human. Lord how we need to be touched.

'Look,' she said, 'you can't be any more fucked up or scared than me. And at least you've got an excuse.'

'Later,' I said. 'Time for everything.'

Then she moved on and her hands found me where I lived.

Later, much later after she'd eaten my pilchards and onions with tarragon jelly, and I'd silently acknowledged then released the shades of other women who had eaten that with me in other places at other times, she stretched and yawned.

'Sleep now,' she said, and got to her feet.

'Do you want to stay?'

'God no! No offence,' she added.

I tried to look hurt but was probably relieved. I didn't see her as a restful sleeping companion and I slept poorly enough anyhow.

She belted herself into her big old jacket, pulled up the furry hood and suddenly looked like a child in too-big clothes. Something melted and I hugged her. She seemed surprised, but hugged me back, quick and firm, then let go.

'Look,' she said with one hand on the doorknob. 'Things I should say. Thanks a lot, this is a bad time for me, and I appreciate you telling me something real. You're not as dumb as you let on.'

'You're a terrible flatterer. But?'

'But we're *not* going to be a couple. I hate being part of anything, I couldn't even stick with the Brownies. Can we just keep it like this, once in a while?'

'Yeah yeah,' I said. 'That's all I'm up for.'

She opened the door and cold swept in. On the step she hesitated.

'I think you're up for a lot more, Eddie,' she said. 'But it's not with me. Not now, anyhow.'

Her arm came up and I had the horrible notion she was going to shake hands. Instead she pulled Levine's *Who Dies?* from her pocket and waved it at me.

'Thanks for the loan of this,' she said. 'I reckon this guy's sound – everyone *does* die. And that's why this painful shambles' – she gestured both arms wide to include me, herself, what had happened between us, the sleeping little town, everything – 'is all right. In fact it's even beautiful. Because it's really not important and it doesn't last. You see?'

Then she was gone, her footsteps fading on the flagstones. I waited for my wee voice to say something but it didn't. Perhaps Mica had spoken on its behalf.

I went back inside to set about clearing up the shambles our appetites had left.

He's woken from half-sleep by thudding on his door. The cabin stinks of Henderson's vomit, and bucks and twists like a maddened horse.

An officer, a summons. There's been an accident in the forward hold, the Captain asks if you could assist. What about the ship's doctor? He's . . . not capable. Drunk again, Sandy concludes. Or maybe just too seasick. He gets dressed and follows the officer.

Three in the morning in the forward hold. Thunderous thudding and crashing in the lamplit cavern. Apparently a cargo of mahogany broke loose, the second mate led a party to secure it. Massive log rolled and crushed his leg.

Sandy gets the hurricane lamp brought closer, hunkers down to examine the man. Pale, sweating, moaning, thin rapid pulse. Ghastly angle in the middle of his thigh. A closed fracture of the femur. The trousers ate soaked with blood. He looks strong but he could die.

Sandy estimates his weight, applies a tourniquet on the arm to bring up the collapsed vein, injects as many grains of morphine as he dares. He braces himself against the bulkhead and looks at the mate as he mutters down into unconsciousness. Considers the situation. He can't move the man till he's set the bone. He's got to do it soon before shock and blood loss kill him. The alternative, the safer option, is amputation. But then the mate will never work again.

The boat tilts to forty-five degrees, throws Sandy onto the junior officer. He wonders if it's going over and his luck has run out. He doesn't want to die trapped down here, he doesn't want to die full stop, and though he must there are things he wants to do first.

The boat hangs out for an age, then crashes back. He turns to the junior officer as they untangle themselves.

'Is it true about calm in the eye of a hurricane, or is that just blethers?'

The Captain agrees to sail the *Amelia* into the eye of the hurricane, and the ship alters course. The ship's carpenter is set to making splints, the medical stores raided for everything he could possibly need. Which isn't much – bonesetting hasn't changed much since the Greeks, apart from anaesthetics and the X-ray machine that he doesn't have anyway. This is about a sound knowledge of anatomy and *feel*. Then he hunkers back down by the mate, watches him and waits. He thinks of his wee sister and then he doesn't.

Round four in the morning the boat steadies. The howling, crashing, rolling and pitching stops, just like that. It is terribly quiet. The engines are throttled right back, just enough to keep the ship in position.

Sandy nods to the ship's carpenter, has a second hurricane lamp brought in close. Splints, tape, morphine, antiseptic. He demonstrates again to the first mate how to apply counter traction in the groin. He moves away the blanket, dries his hands one more time, grips the flexed knee and begins to pull.

10

As I sit in the car letting the home movies of time past run, a voice at my open window.

'No so cold the day!'

I start like a guilty man though I've done nothing yet. Another part of me warms to hear again the Orkney vowels give 'cold' two syllables. Cow-ald.

'It's right bonnie,' I reply.

A solid woman, dog lead in one hefty hand, plump ruddy face. She looks at the sea, the shore, the hills of Rousay across the water, her Labrador lolloping, and seems to give my reply serious consideration. I remember how in Orkney weather is a topic of prolonged discussion. It has a lot of weather, and in a place as unprotected as this, it impacts on everyone.

'It is that,' she says at last. Then she adds, 'We'll pay for it.' The thought seems to give her satisfaction.

'Maybe we already have,' I say.

'Aye, last week was just terrible,' she replies, then strides off after her dog, leaving me thinking that's not what I meant at all.

I get out, stretch, lean back on the car. Out there, great stretches of water of life-altering clarity, shallow over sand as the tide ebbs. I mind them, oh I mind them fine, those days already paid for – they seem to live and breathe somewhere still, like the children we never have, who can never grow up or die.

I stumble off along the shoreline, crunching through purple banks of mussel shells.

Stevie stopped the car and looked at me as Tanya babbled happily in the back seat. Sounded like *Ready mercury, ready mercury!* If only I could be ready, or mercurial.

'Want to drive there, or walk across the Sands of Evie?'

'There's a road all the way to the broch now?' I was outraged. The walk there had been a big part of it.

'Yes,' he said. 'I told you last week. You seemed outraged then too.'

At least my emotional reaction was consistent. Like a goldfish going round the bowl, I kept being surprised by the same thing.

We agreed a pilgrimage should be done on foot, so we took the next lane down and left the car near the shore. Tanya sang 'We are the champions' (Stevie had terrible taste in music) on her father's shoulders as we walked over the low dunes then onto hard ebb sand towards the Broch of Gurness.

Darkness was welling out of the ground, and more darkness piled up in the east, and I was tight and edgy. Like many pilgrimage sites, it was built round a slaughter, the death of an innocence.

It had been before sunrise then. Tina had read about the well in some romantic book, about how it was supposed to have these heart-healing properties. She seemed keen I went down into it. We'd walked across these same sands in half-light to get there before the site attendant, and as we walked with the big unresolved thing between us, the sky over her shoulder flared into life.

'It's my decision,' she'd said suddenly, to conclude a long-silent argument. And though I felt sick I'd nodded because, yes, it was her decision.

I found the well, and felt my way down into the dimness on wet narrow steps. I called up to ask if she was coming down. 'You need it more!' she'd called back. Her choice. And down I went till I'd finally put my hand down and made contact.

And yes, it had been true. There was something there. Even through all that had followed, I'd never forgotten the jolt of affirmation when I'd touched that hidden water. Now it was time for a top-up shot, and to keep a promise.

'You okay?' Stevie said.

'Hunky-dory,' I replied, and took the stream at a run, couple of splashes and out the other side. If you do it quick enough you scarcely get wet. On the other hand you could like Steve have wellies and a daughter, and just walk calmly through.

The attendant's hut was shuttered up, the site deserted. The tide hurried on the ebb out through the channel between Mainland and Rousay. On first moving here, I'd been confused then entertained by how in Orkney 'Mainland' referred to the largest island, the one I was living on. That place to the south was Scotland, or just 'South'. Now, I was coming to appreciate 'Mainland' was an expression of cultural confidence, not of provinciality. They're right: wherever you live has to be the centre, the main event. I was working on it.

Little Tanya had fallen silent, slumped clasping her father's neck like a koala. A couple of oystercatchers scuttered and peeped on the sand. A dog barked from a distant farm, yellow lights snapped on in the gathering dusk.

That's what it's like in Orkney, as if the sky were a wide-open eye stretched over everything. It makes no judgements and does not intervene. It simply registers.

Steve and I didn't speak as we drifted through the cluster of tiny Iron Age houses that had been built in its lee. This place was full of ghosts, some of them mine. I was looking at the basics of human life. We need shelter, food and somewhere to cook it, a place to lie down, rest, and make babies. And I live in a time so strange that there are people who live twice, three times as long as these folk but still don't get round to making babies.

I looked at Steve, the child clasped round his head. He grinned ruefully, like maybe it wasn't so easy, or just at some private thought.

'If you want to see the well at all, we'd better go there now,' he said quietly.

I nodded, and we walked round their hearths, over their beds, stepped through their doorways. We ourselves would leave as little. We ducked through the entrance into the broch and I saw again the hollow walls where Tina had stood with the dawn flush in her face. She'd just said I could go down for both of us. And I'd enquired if that was a jail sentence or an invitation.

Here were the two hearths and the well. Now there was a low square railing round it, a warning sign: *Keep Out*. Typical of the times, but it wasn't going to put me off.

Then I stopped, stared down, unable to believe it.

'I'm sorry,' Stevie said. 'I hadn't known about this.'

Across the entrance to the well there was a cast-iron metal grid. Over that was a fine mesh net. I knelt down, got my fingers round it and tugged. It didn't yield an inch. There was a big brass padlock, so the cover must be hinged. I checked – no chance of easing the hatch off its hinges.

'Fuck,' I said. 'Fuck, fuck, fuck.'

'Wheesht,' Stevie said. 'The bairn.'

'Sorry.'

We stood and looked down at the hatch in the near dark. Another part of my past was for ever out of reach now.

'Ach well,' I said at last. 'It was just a notion.'

I rested my foot on the grid for a moment and made my goodbyes.

Driving down the Evie straight heading for Finstown, Steve put on Queen's Greatest – then turned it down so as not to wake Tanya.

'Goodbye to the rock 'n' roll lifestyle,' I said.

He grinned, laughed quietly.

'Gotta move on, eh?'

When I'd cautiously climbed back out of the well those years back, I'd reached for Tina, about to say, *Let's have it.* Then I'd seen her face.

'Another time, Eddie. When we're more ready.'

There was much talking still to come, but it was done in that moment when she got her word in just before mine. I think we knew even then we never would be more ready. We hurried away into the glare of a scarlet dawn, and we never came back.

Years later I sat at her bedside, still dazed at my late summons. She put out a skeletal hand and grasped my wrist. I feel its cold bangle yet.

'I should have gone down there,' she said. Though we hadn't set eyes on each other in five years, she didn't have to spell out what and where. She licked her lips, sipped some water from her feeder tube. 'But I've always been afraid of going down into ... dark places.'

'I'll go again for both of us,' I said.

Her eyes swivelled and looked at me.

'... Neat,' she said. She swallowed. She was all lips, cheekbones and eyes. 'No hurry,' she said.

Then people came in who had more of a claim on her than I. When I'd bent to kiss Tina goodbye, she spoke into my ear.

'My decision,' she whispered.

'I'm right sorry about the well,' Stevie said as we parted outside his house, his sleeping daughter slumped on his shoulder.

'Not your fault,' I said, and tried to laugh. 'I shouldn't take it to heart. Goodnight.'

'See you the morn, boy.'

Then again, what else should I take it to? I'd promised Tina I'd go back down for her, but I'd left it too late.

I thought on her all the way as I drove back under spattered stars towards the Brig of Waith. I thought on the child we never had. For months or years after a death you carry a weight till in time you learn a different and harder sorrow. You learn that you live on, and in time find yourself sleeping again, then smiling once in a while, noticing a fine day or a good face. And the knowledge that you can and do go on living when people you love do not, that is a grown-up sorrow at last.

I turned down Hellihole one more time, with one less day to live.

When he looks in once again at the sick bay three days later, William Ancross is sitting up playing cards on a board across his lap. Sandy has insisted this is his patient, he's not letting some drunken incompetent foul up good work. He checks the tightness of the splints, then moves to examine the foot. Checks colour and sensation in the toes, checks the *dorsalis pedis* and *posterior tibial* pulses. The blood supply seems undamaged, no infection, and the setting looks sound. Excellent!

He plays a couple of hands of gin rummy with Ancross, who must have one heck of a constitution, then excuses himself.

'Got a date, Doc?'

He grins, waves, is gone.

He stands looking at himself in the mirror in the cabin's early dusk. In either hand he grips a silver-backed hairbrush with AM in swirly letters on the back, the blessing-present from his mother and father when he graduated in medicine. They must have cost his father a month's sweat in his workshop.

He leans closer and works away at the lick of hair that obstinately keeps lifting off his forehead. No, it's no good. On impulse he sweeps the brushes till he has that all-American look of his friend Alan, hair straight back from forehead and temples like he's leaning into a high wind.

He looks. He is not a man given to looking in mirrors. A voice whispers it is vanity and vanity is a sin, or at least a weakness. But this could as well be looking at someone else. This isn't wee Eck Mackay frae Brechin, the saddler's laddie.

The gleaming white dinner jacket came from the purser. 'Willie Ancross is a mate of mine, Doc, and you fixed his leg a treat. Let me know if there's anything else I can get you. Anything at all.' The black bow tie he has finally learned to make a decent fist of tying is his own, but the patent leather shoes and dress trousers are Alan's. He resolves to buy himself a dinner suit in Penang with the money saved now he no longer pays bar bills, courtesy of the ship's Captain.

Yes, he's looking at a tall, slim stranger and it's not unpleasant. This must be dapper Dr Sandy Mackay, chief consultant obstetrician, demon bridge player, dancer and man about Penang. He winks at himself, his departing old self, in the mirror. 'An unco sicht,' he says, then one more sweep of the brushes and he heads out the cabin and up the companionway for the farewell cocktail party and dance before landfall in Penang tomorrow.

'You look swell, Sandy,' Alan says, claps him on the shoulder of the borrowed white tuxedo. 'Folks might think you're in the money.'

'All dinner jacket and nae knickers,' Sandy says as they raise the first whisky stengah of the evening to Bobby Jones and the next stage of his Grand Slam.

'I've marked the cards for the Simpson girls!' Alan says jubilantly. 'You and me, time and time about. Fair enough?'

At that moment Sandy turns and sees them coming. Ann and Adele, both in identical ivory satin dresses, their hair flounced in the fashion, and because they are turned out so much the same, the difference between them comes into focus. It's summed up in the necklace each has high on her throat, and he can't stop staring and thinking how perfect: Ann's pearls and Adele's tiger's eye.

'Fair enough,' he says.

As Adele glances into his eyes, murmurs, 'There you are,' and Ann cries, 'Oh, here you are!' and smiling rests her hand on his sleeve for a moment, he registers the subtle, crucial difference in their standard greeting. With Adele it's '*There* you are,' and Ann is always '*Here* you are.' By different routes, both find him.

Fifty years on, teeing off at the ninth hole in Perth, he will hear them again so clearly *There you are, Here you are*, and feel a slight stagger inside. He blinks, drives off and pushes his shot wide into a bunker, and all the way down the fairway among the daisies and gull feathers in the chilly easterly wind they will follow him calling *Here you are! Oh there you are!*

She was in bed with no one when the summons came.

'It's myself,' the familiar, dreaded voice said.

'What's with you, then?' she'd replied.

A long pause, then something between a rattle and a chuckle.

'Me – I'm busy dying.'

'Ach, you're pished again.'

Still, she'd switched the bedside light on and sat up. Beside her, no one groaned. The old man, dying or not, was onto it quick as an adder.

'Who's wi you?'

'No one,' she said, and in that moment realised it was near the truth. 'You're not having me on – the dying bit?'

'Afraid not, lass. A few weeks or months. Can you get up here for the duration?'

She studied the green fingernails of her free hand. They scarcely shook at all.

'So the floozie's left you?'

Hardly fair to call a sixty-year-old widow a floozie, but she didn't feel fair.

'Aye, once I knew, I made sure of that.'

She turned her hand over, wondering at the length of her strong lifeline and her short broken heart line. Ah, bollocksy bollocks.

'I'm not a nurse.'

'I've already got a nurse, lassie, but she doesna make me laugh.'

'Last time I stayed, Dad, you told me to go to hell. I've been doing my best not to. I've got myself a life here.'

A long pause, heavy breathing down the phone, like the sound of a big sea caught in Bay of Skaill. So far away, that island, yet she always knows it's there.

'I fed ye when your mother left.'

She pictured years of burnt bacon and eggs, tins of macaroni cheese, piles of bread and jam. Pathetic in a way. Still, the tyrannical bitter old sod had stuck around.

'Have you spoken to Paul?'

'I wouldn't ask him and he wouldn't come. You ken that.'

She did indeed. After the last fisticuffs, brother Paul had sworn as he stepped on the ferry that he'd never set foot on Orkney while the old man was alive. Unlike herself, he tended to mean exactly what he said.

She was done for and she knew it. Still she hesitated. Beside her, no one muttered and turned over. Too young, she thought. These skinny talented lads, I must stop using them.

'Would you have trouble getting away?' her father asked. 'Is that it?'

'No,' she said. 'No trouble at all. I'll be there in a week with my joke book.'

She put the phone down then lay looking at the ceiling's blank map. Beside her, no one whiffled, his bonnie face unlined and empty.

So the summons had come at last. Back to the old man for the end game. Back to the island.

She must have had too much wine the night she told me that. Confession wasn't Mica's style, though a good yarn was.

I sit among crushed mussel shells on the north shore of the Orkney Mainland, shivering a little for the warmth is ebbing from the day along with the tide, staring out over the water, letting the hours wear on till it's time.

11

On Wednesdays, Ellen and I left work early, picked up Cara from school and I drove us through to Kirkwall. After Stromness, Kirkwall was big Sin City. Shops! The Emporium! Drapers! The ironmongers! Grooves for new CDs, the music shop by the Scarth Centre for new banjo strings, finger picks and flicking through chord songbooks.

Yes, no doubt my heart always lifted a little coming over the brow of the hill down into Kirkwall. That particular afternoon Cara was singing along lustily in the back to the *Beach Boys Golden Greats*, and Ellen beside me making lists and harmonising.

I parked by the tourist office next to the cathedral. The Vikings had knocked it up in the twelfth century as a memorial to the martyred Magnus who got it in the neck (more precisely, through the top of the skull) on the island of Egilsay. There was a lot of power in that death, as much as in the tide race. It had generated this silent calm building of red and yellow sandstone, and the *Orkneyinga Saga*, and books and music that spiralled off it. Some good can be retrieved from loss, though it takes work.

When we split up, on impulse I walked over to the cathedral that glowed in the last sun, looking more than ever like a burning boat grounded on a low bank. I went in and stood a while, thinking of people I loved, living and dead.

I'm not a believer any more than I'm a Viking, but like the well at the Broch of Gurness, the cathedral had the power of the right silence. So, thoughts to the shining nothing that was Tina. To my dad. To the ones who had fallen off sea-stacks, had high-altitude heart attacks or flown slap-bang into a mountainside. Thoughts to old lovers and friends, to Lyn now with a sound man, to my mum buzzing round town missing only a few marbles and not the ones that mattered. And to Jimmy Moar who was busy dying in a big old house back of Stromness.

Here surrounded by her children and torn from her husband lies a great glory of the female sex. The praise and the loss still lived in the worn sandstone. I wandered past the memorials, the hourglasses, skulls and crossbones, *Here lies the corps* – these people were as occupied by death as myself. I'd have been normal then.

Then it was time to hurry round the shops, the lights coming on in the early winter dark, the gust of warmth when I went in, the chat and the accents of the different islands and the incomers from all over. So I picked up a Jan Garbarek CD of him saxing with some Finnish mouth musicians, indulged in new strings and the fifteen-year-old Highland Park and a bag of chocolate gingers, then hurried up Broad Street to the Tree, which was just that: a tree set in the street. Not the only tree in Orkney, that was an exaggeration, but a gnarled, truncated, propped-up-with-concrete old sycamore that was still somehow hanging in there.

So we met there in the half-dark with the street lamps still jelly-pink and falling on Cara's excited face and Ellen's calm inward-smiling one. Then we went for tea and sticky iced cakes at the Pomona Café, and sat in the moist chattering fug of that shrine of authentic fifties veneer and Pyrex coffee cups. Then it was off to the thrills of the supermarket and wine (for me) and healthy foods (for Ellen) and sweets (for Cara).

Then driving home through the dark, headlights throwing up farmhouse, cottage, boat dragged on the shore. That was the best of it, going back warm in the car with Cara hungry-grumpy then falling asleep, past the turn-off to the Stenness stones, the dark mound of Maes Howe burial cairn, by the Golden Slipper shebeen and over the Brig of Waith, counting off those stages on our journey home like stations of the Cross.

We unloaded the car at Ellen's cottage at the North End, down a muddy path between tacky breezeblock houses. Cara and I did some drawing while Ellen cooked. We ate, drank, the bairn was bathed then I read to her in bed.

Ellen came in just as I'd closed the book for the night. Cara looked up at me, not too pleased I'd stopped.

'Why are you forty-seven?' she demanded.

'Cara!' from Ellen.

Have a long relationship, then another that ends guiltily on both sides, some short ones, a death followed by adventures and consolations, experiments in friendship and sex. Travel a bit, climb some hills, learn a new instrument, change jobs a couple of times, go to various weddings and a few funerals, hold a stream of friends' newborns in your tentative arms and pronounce them human, learn some more songs, read some books, watch plenty TV – then turn round twice and you're forty-seven, and some innocent is asking how you got there, what happened to all those years and how come you're not married or at least cohabiting and have no children?

'Why are you six?' I replied.

'Because I am,' she said indignantly, like it's obvious.

'Well then,' I said.

'Show me the string trick again!'

But Ellen insisted on her day ending, and Cara grumbled then abruptly passed out, one small unmarked hand lying open across her dinosaur.

The grown-ups, who now included me though I still hadn't quite got used to that idea, went through to the sitting room to drink and talk. And somewhere in the midst of my second whisky, I hear the true answer, the one too hard to tell children: *Because I haven't died yet.*

I tuned back in to Ellen saying she hadn't decided yet what she was doing after this contract expired. It depended. What was I doing next?

'Penang,' I said. 'I want to research more what happened, maybe even go there.'

She looked at me over her glass across the table.

'You're serious?'

'Or maybe I'll just stay on here if we get the contract extended.'

She nodded and emptied the last of the bottle into our glasses and now the child was in bed lit one of her rare roll-ups. (Smoking not being an option in Intensive Care, I'd had an enforced break, and after that, it seemed ungrateful to Life, to the NHS, to go back to damaging myself, however pleasurable it had undoubtedly been. Being with Ellen allowed me to indulge in some passive smoking. At that time I seemed to enjoy a lot of things at one remove.)

'This is a good place,' she said quietly. 'One of the best. It's healing, and trust still exists here.'

'Sure,' I said. 'It's paradise if you like it minimal.'

She tapped her ash into a shell and looked across at me. She was about to be earnest. I liked that about her, the way she was always sincere. Mica distrusted sincerity, she regarded it as the ultimate deception.

'Nowhere is paradise, Eddie,' Ellen said. 'Just some places better or worse than others.'

'Blimey!' I said. 'You'll be telling me there's no permanent Eve next.' I'd meant to say Eden, but it came out differently.

'Not on these islands or anywhere else. No wonder you're on your own.'

We looked at each other for a while. I had a strong inclination to leave.

'I'm sorry,' she said at last. 'That was unfair. Your way's as good as any.'

'You think I've got no ties?' I said and was surprised by my voice. 'Nothing and no one I'm bound to, just because I've no wife or children?'

'Like I said, I'm sorry. And you're great with Cara, I want to thank you for that.'

'Ach, it's a pleasure,' I said, accepting her slide away to safer territory. 'Lets me see what I've missed out on, for better and worse.'

She looked at me, tilted her nose up to let a stream of smoke from the side of her mouth. It was so teenage-sophisticated, must have come from an earlier stage of her life.

'Want to talk about that?' she said at last.

I looked into her glowing stove. Something brutal happens the first time someone you've made love with dies. A body you've known, touched and been in, is now ash.

'Another time, then,' Ellen said at last.

'Another time,' I agreed. 'Anyhow, your Cara's a joy.'

'She can be,' she admitted. 'If she gets to know you better, you'll find she's no angel. We have this constant power struggle and it's not always very pretty.'

'But she's yours,' I said, and felt a gust of self-pity like a draught under the door from the dark outside. 'That must change everything.'

'It does.' She looked directly at me. 'I'd die ten times over for her if I had to.' She stubbed out her roll-up and laughed, sort of apologetically. 'But the mistake you – no, the mistake people make – is thinking having children must change you, or in some way redeem you. It changes everything and nothing.'

'You mean I'm not missing out on redemption by not having children?'

I liked the brackets round her mouth when she smiled.

'Well you are missing something, that's for sure. But instead you do get a good night's sleep, some money to spend on yourself, freedom of movement and a sex life.'

'I don't always sleep so good,' I said. 'And as for the rest, less than you might think.'

She laughed, but she pursued the point.

'What I'm saying is if you do end up having children – and you're not that past it, are you? – or if you take on someone else's, just don't do so thinking it's going to solve all your problems and fears about death and loss and unresolved things with parents. Because it doesn't.'

I sat there and let it sink in. I know when I've been given a true thing, a point of leverage, and I'm always owing to the one who gave me it.

'Great,' I said. 'Thanks.'

I got to my feet, needing to be gone.

'Thanks for the evening and the meal,' I said. 'Same again next week?'

'If we're spared,' she said, and we laughed, acknowledging our doom-laden heritage even as we sent it up. At the door I hesitated, not quite knowing how to end this.

'See you tomorrow,' she said, and kissed me quickly on the cheek. 'Sleep well.'

As I meandered the big black car home, something was following, hovering over me half-attended to but always there like the darkness in my rear-view mirror. Something I could never get rid of, no matter how far or how fast I drove.

In bed, I lay awhile in the lamplight, thinking it all over, re-collecting the day under the Penang Buddha's tranquil porcelain gaze. Cara's hand flopped so open on her green fluffy dinosaur, the inscription in the cathedral, the things Ellen and I had said, the things we hadn't said.

We walk towards the fire with firewood in our hands, my wee voice murmured.

Then I was gone.

It's after midnight but the band plays on, the racket of trumpet and fiddles fading as he picks his way with only a slight stagger towards the rear of the top deck. There are couples everywhere, necking and canoodling and more. This is the last night before landfall in Penang. He understands the rules will be different then. Who knows when the women will press again so closely, offer so much with their eyes, flirt so openly, mean so little by it?

It has been heady, he admits. Since the episode of the second mate's leg (a competent piece of sawbones, he reckons, but no more than that), doors have opened to him. He's eaten with the Captain and that august gentleman has told him his bar bills are void. He has never danced with so many women, and has almost stopped feeling self-conscious. One day he may even learn to like jazz, now that he understands it's something to do with sex.

The half-moon is moist yellow like the mangoes he first had in Port Said, its light is mashed wide in the *Amelia*'s wake. He stands at the rear rail, ignoring the spooning couple as they ignore him, and imagines the wake leading all the way back across the Indian Ocean, the Canal, the Med, the Straits, Britanny, Liverpool, then the train tracks like metal stitches sewn up to Edinburgh, to Brechin . . .

He turns away, passes the deckchair bay where he and Ann almost kissed. It's taken, of course, but in behind it, half-hidden by a stanchion, is another smaller area. He unfolds a deckchair, puts his feet up on the rail, uncorks the bottle of Glenfiddich that Willie Ancross had almost shyly pressed on him when he went below to check again on the dressing and splints. No infection, swelling coming down already, and under the puffy dermatitis the settings felt good. Ancross won't just survive, he'll almost certainly work again if he rebuilds the wasted muscles carefully.

Good man, good work, good whisky. The peaty reek of it in the tropical night, cooled by the boat's passage. The long burn of it going down, the toffee aftertaste. All that's needed now is a ciggie. He fumbles through the pockets of the white tux for matches then remembers putting them down at the bar. Ach well, can't have everything.

A light rattle behind him. 'Is this what you need, Doc?' Yellow flare of a match, hands cupping it expertly against the breeze. He drags in, the little flame bends, tip flares red. Without a word she sits down on his lap, lies back till her head lolls back on his shoulder.

He knew it, and it's perfect as she twists her head, reaches up and pulls his mouth down to meet hers. It's perfect and can never ever be repeated. Not to anyone.

12

'Hyperoceanic', Ellen called the Orkney climate. Lovely word full of wind and sea, meaning cool summer, mild winter on account of being surrounded by the moderating ocean. Despite being on a latitude with St Petersburg, nearer to the Arctic Circle than to London, and the days rapidly becoming extremely short, it was if anything less biting than an Edinburgh winter.

On a bright mild Sunday, I took a badly needed long walk out beyond Warebeth, where hoodie craws sat on fenceposts by the sea like black-cloaked sinister ministers. I moved through vast simplicities of sky and land murmuring *hyperoceanic*, but that morning the healing didn't work. The sea was just the sea, the curious seal was just a large aquatic mammal, I was still looking at the world as though it were a party I'd already left.

When I got back home, it was still too early for the papers to have come off the plane. I mooched round the house tidying up, then finally made myself sit in the clean front room without toys or distractions.

This is not my midlife crisis. That ended with my brain getting squished. I can't read any more stories of men and women resisting maturity. That is no longer the problem.

I look at the light bounce off the cover of the *Mojo* magazine on the table. Not thinking, just looking. I'm not working and I'm not going out. I'm just sitting like my father's Buddha and letting it come to me.

Fuck me, there's a wee dark blotch on the back of my hand. I'm getting liver spots! I know the only way to stop getting older is to die, but still. The longer I live, the more dead friends, lovers and family pile up. I need so much more than I'm ever likely to get.

This yearning is like petrol. If I lit a cigarette now – and God knows I want one – I'd go up in flames like a protesting monk.

I could work. These figures aren't going to massage themselves. Or call on Ellen or Ray, or phone Stevie. But I won't move, won't go on to the next thing, whatever it is.

I sit in a sunlit front room in the Northern Isles and feel the world and me come to a standstill.

My heart keeps pumping though I don't ask it to. My liver spot humps tinily up and down. I'm alive now. Soon I won't be.

Make what you will of it, a kirk or a mill.

I hurried round to Mica's while I still could.

I rang the bell, thumped the door and went on up the stair, hollering as I climbed. She wasn't in her workroom. She'd got herself an old Mac and printer. Next to it was a purple file with *NIPPY STORIES & OTHER LIES* scrawled across it. Not my business.

The little kitchen was student days revisited. Baby Belling cooker, not quite empty mugs, wrappers and foil trays, spilled sugar and pizza boxes. Smell of old food and fags. Rizla packets, pack of cigarettes (empty) with the top torn off. Damp towel over chair, muddy trainers.

I chapped on the bedroom door, wondering who I'd find her with. Empty of course, the duvet slumped onto the floor by a single mattress. Thick red bedsocks and an old *Simpsons* T-shirt. She was in her late thirties and this was it. I thought it desperately sad.

I went back to her workroom, sat down at the table to write her a note. That purple file was vibrating at me. I suspected I wouldn't come out very well in anything she wrote. I was a man she called on and did over once in a while.

I glanced out onto the street and saw her coming along, talking animatedly with Kipper Johnson. She looked up and saw me at her window, then she turned her head abruptly, took his arm and said something. They stood in the narrow flagged street having some sort of argument. A car came by and they had to separate to let it between them, but still their mouths kept moving and arms waving.

I sat at her table and waited.

'What are you doing here?'
    'Looking for the Old Man of Hoy, what do you think?'
    'I told you not to call on me without phoning.'
    'No you didn't.'
We glared at each other till something had to give.
    'Your brain can't be that shit.'
    'Don't you fucking dare use that against me.'
    'Don't fucking swear at me, pal.'
We glared some more. I scrunched up the note I'd started to write. *Dear Mica – called but missed you. And miss your—*
    'I'm not doing this any more,' I said. 'I'm not going to wait till you're sex-starved or bored. You lay down these rules and conditions – don't

phone, don't come by unless I ask, don't ask me about anything personal.'

She hugged herself.

'You know what to do then.'

'Aye, I do.'

She was standing between me and the door and showed no sign of moving. I walked round her, our shoulders brushed. I had to get out.

'I thought you didn't mind,' she said quietly.

I paused at the door.

'Of course I mind! What kind of idiot do you think I am?'

Her mouth twitched.

'A passive one,' she said.

I walked fast round the Ness to kick the shake from my knees. Passed Logins Well where the Franklin expedition ships made their last call before heading off for the North West Passage on their doomed and futile quest to find a way through. I'd called an end to me and Mica, though we'd scarcely begun.

Back home, the phone answer machine was blinking. I looked at it, too weary to take on anything more. Then curiosity won, it usually did.

'Mr Mackay? My attention has been drawn to your notice in the Friendship Society newsletter. You enquire about your father Dr Alexander Mackay in Penang.'

The woman's voice was scratchy, thin, imperious. One used to having people attend. And old, I could hear her pause for breath before continuing.

'I think perhaps my aunt and uncle made his acquaintance there.'

I rose to that phone message like a trout did once to my fly on Harray loch, clean from the water to snatch it at the end of a retrieve.

He leans on the rail in his loose white cotton suit, watching the boys swarm up the cables that bind the *Amelia* to the George Town dock. The sun is just up over the mountain but already sweat is trickling from the roots of his hair. The light's opaque, thick, yellow, and there's no clear horizon. He feels he's being basted in his own juices.

He takes off his straw hat, fans himself. This damn tie, load of nonsense but has to be worn if you want respect, everyone says. And respect he wants, though he'd rather it didn't come like this.

'Better keep that hat on, Doctor. Get yourself a sola topi, all the old hands use them. And a sweat pad for your back.'

He glances at Bellingham-Smythe, from the brick-red complexion up to the clay-lined beehive he's wearing.

'Dinna think so,' he grunts, deliberately broadening his accent. 'Looks bloody daft.'

Bellingham-Symthe, First Secretary to the Governor, back for his third tour of duty, raises an eyebrow.

'It's for your own good, Mackay. The Oriental sun has rays in it that can turn a man's brains, you'll see.'

Sandy stares at him. No need to be polite any more.

'Aye, I can see that.'

'Another thing, Dr Mackay. I wouldn't spend too much time with Marsden. Bit of a rum cove.'

'He's been straight with me. I like him.'

Bellingham-Smythe shrugs. 'I tried to tell you,' he says, and marches off.

One small Tamil boy makes it to the top of the rope, jumps on deck, ducks under the purser's grab and runs aft. The purser shakes his head, puts his palm to the forehead of the next boarding child. This second boy stops, still wrapped round the rope, looks at the purser then at Sandy. His eyes are almond shaped, chocolate brown, alive and intelligent.

The purser and the boy have a rapid exchange, in Malay, Sandy thinks. The big hand stays firmly on the boy's forehead, preventing him from coming any further.

'What's he want?'

'To take your kit ashore. I told him he's too small.'

'If he eats, he'll grow bigger. I'll have him.'

His sweat is running from under his cuffs and he is scarcely thinking about last night's shenanigans as he engages the Malay laddie, points out his black tin-lined trunk. For it was the last night, that was understood, one night only.

It was perfect because it couldn't be.

The George Town quayside scene is so dense and different it's hard to see at all. Sandy blinks, shakes his head and tries to break it down into units that make sense.

Hordes of barefoot laddies in shorts, jostling, carrying, selling. Streams of thin adult coolies and stevedores carrying luggage down the gangplank and disappearing into the crowd, only the bright loads on their heads still showing so it seems the suitcases and hatboxes float on a current. Rickshaw men line up to the left, Chinese businessmen already climbing in and slowly moving off. Some motor vehicles, cars and lorries piled high with trunks, boxes, mining equipment. Bales of dark rubber on the next quay, copra laid out like brown cricket pitches. People come to buy, sell, unload, meet people, or simply to watch. Moving through the crowd are a few European men, always in white suits and dark ties. The ladies sit off to the side in rickshaws, some with parasols in their white-gloved hands. He looks, then looks away.

A mêlée. A miasma. A scrum. A rammie. The air is thick as broth with spices and flowers, copra, rubber and sweat. Air so thick it fills in the space between things. Vivid green and red sarongs, saris, men in grey pyjama suits, bullock carts and ragged shorts – it's bewildering, utterly foreign. It's certainly not Brechin.

He waves to the Malay boy standing on his trunk, waiting in the queue for the derrick. The boy grins back, does a little dance.

On the voyage out he'd read that, as a free port and safe haven, Penang has long been one of the most multiracial places on Earth. He's never seen anything like it.

Henderson stands beside him at the rail. An old hand and in no hurry to leave the ship, he helps Sandy begin to distinguish the different races. The Sikhs are easy to spot, dark and turbaned, very upright, the backbone of the police force. Then some very dark Tamil stevedores, not to be confused with the Keralan Indians – Henderson points – there and there. Mohammedans and Hindus, Chinese Buddhists and Christians – they mostly keep separate but they get along. It's to everyone's benefit. That's how it's done here.

The Chinese, Henderson continues, now they're the financial backbone of the Federated States. These softer-faced ones – see him, and him there – they're *Hokkien*, from Southern China. Got here early, live for trade in spices and opium, which you British still administer though you don't like to shout about it. Often very wealthy. Then there's the other lot, the *Hakka*. Heavy-boned, him and him, and that woman over there. Trouble is they don't speak each other's language and hate each other like poison.

'I'll tell you this,' Henderson says, 'there's trouble going on still. Just under the surface, like a boil. Their secret societies are at each other's throats, and we sometimes get caught up in it.'

'Sounds like bad Kipling,' Sandy comments. 'Secret societies – blethers!'

Henderson waves to a couple of European men in the crowd below, who wave back, indicate a waiting car.

'No one likes to talk about it. Bad for business, you know, and that's what makes this place run – or at least it did till rubber and tin went phut. If you're interested in the political undercurrents, ask Marsden.'

'*Marsden?*'

Sandy can't think of anyone less likely. Henderson glances at him.

'I suppose he told you he was a part-time translator?' Sandy nods. 'Ever ask him what he does the rest of the time?'

Sandy stares at Henderson, realises the man isn't joking. He blinks, feels the deck shift slightly.

He turns to look back down at the crowd below as Henderson points out a man sitting in a carriage in the shade of the palms, a Chinese in a wide-brimmed hat, a silver-headed cane across his knee. One of the Baba millionaires, Henderson tells him, Lee Te Fok. His people intermarried with the Malays years back. Send their children to English schools, believe in the Empire and all that. Make great food if you like it spicy. Go to his parties if you ever get invited. Wonderful jazz bands, ripping girls. Even the Sarkies Brothers go to those – you know, the Raffles and E&O people.

Sandy nods, only just keeping up with this. So much to take in, so much to learn. He breathes deeply, still wondering about Marsden. The man had come to his cabin last night, smiled and settled up, handed him his calling card then went off to console another diplomat's wife.

Henderson is still talking and pointing. Among the crowd below he indicates people from Java, Sumatra – slightly heavier faces, bulkier, maybe a shade darker. Oh and some Siamese, prettiest girls you'll ever see round here – but don't mess around with them unless you want to be sent home. If you get really desperate and don't mind paying, go to the Dutch hotel in Singapore.

Sandy nods. After all, things are done differently here. And he takes a modern, medical view of sex and its necessity. But he feels again those lips on his in the dark, the soft shock spreading to all parts of his body. Her tongue still flickers inside him, stirring up something far more unfamiliar and troubling.

He takes off his hat, obscures his face while pretending to fan himself as Henderson talks on. It won't happen again, he understands that. So now there's work. The few pre- and post-natal figures he's managed to extract from the authorities are still appalling. He's set himself a target: halve the miscarriage and infant mortality rate in two years. Mothers' deaths, well they simply shouldn't happen in this day and age. Any time free, he'll work to bring his golf handicap down to single figures. And as for periods of holiday and leave, there's all the Far East to see.

He puts his hat back on, tweaks the brim down against the sun.

While Henderson talks, Sandy watches his trunk being wrapped in netting ready for the derrick. Nearly everything he owns in the world is in that tin-lined trunk. Five white cotton suits, run up in Aden where they were much cheaper than London. His own medical equipment that he borrowed to purchase. A few books, mostly school prizes (Walter Scott, Stevenson, Burns) plus his textbooks. Clothes, a spare tie, the leather shaving case his parents had given him an hour before he caught the train at Arbroath station. An unopened bottle of Johnnie Walker, a Dundee cake, several jars of Keillor's marmalade, the remains of last night's Glenfiddich and by God that woman had a thirst for it. That's enough. All he needs is himself.

Now his trunk lifts off the deck, the boy still clinging to the netting. The derrick swivels, the trunk swings over the rail, the boy clinging on smiling as if he's riding a horse as the Tamil down on the pier starts letting out rope.

But something is going wrong. The net tears, the trunk lurches and the boy topples sideways. He grabs the side netting and clings on, dangling high above the dock. His thin legs kick the air, someone screams. The boy starts hauling himself up hand over hand, frantically grabbing the netting.

A lashing gives way completely, the net and trunk slide again and then the lad is hanging directly beneath the trunk. The mesh bulges then breaks round his grip. A quick-witted coolie is lowering the load as fast as possible but still the boy falls some thirty feet, hits the side of the pier then falls over and disappears into the oily water. With a final rip the rotten netting parts and the trunk drops, crashes onto the planking but stays balanced on the lip.

The crowd rushes to the edge. Sandy stares transfixed while other boys jump out and down into the water. He's just had a boy killed. Obviously the laddie wasn't old enough. Just because he'd minded him of Puddie Watson at the school, same impudent cross-toothed grin.

A black head breaks the surface. Then a brown arm. A collective sigh from the crowd along the quayside as the lad is gripped and dragged to the ladders. His head lolls back as he's pulled and pushed up the rungs but his legs keep working though it looks like his collarbone is broken.

He makes it to the top, stands swaying a moment then drops to his knees. Before the crowd closes round him, the boy turns his head and looks back at my father on the deck rails. His mouth opens and belches grey water. His hand comes up to make that rubbing of thumb and forefinger that serves the world over for *money* and then he collapses on the trunk, his head falling into a sun of yellow-sleeved arms.

PART 2

Against the current of humanity, the Tamil boys, the Sikh policeman, the stevedores and the British customs officials all streaming up the gangplank, he is forcing his way down. His hat has flown off and brown hair flops down across his eyebrows as he flattens himself against the side of the walkway to let by two Malays with crates of beer on their heads. On tiptoe, trying to see over the heads to where the fallen boy has disappeared in a scrum, he is all agitation and anxiety.

That bloody trunk! He should have waited for a bigger lad. When will he learn how unwise soft impulse is? He pushes on down, already running through the possibilities – concussion, internal bleeding, broken bones, shock. His medical kit is in the trunk, the key's in his pocket. He must make this right.

Behind him up on the rail of the Amelia are the rest of the cast. Alan Hayman is watching anxiously, pale beneath his tan. He is flanked by the Simpson sisters, faces dim and unreadable under cream wide-brimmed hats. Bellingham-Smythe is moving away from them, his sola topi like a white beehive, back erect and his arm raised gesturing to the Residency's rickshaw waiting at its stand. Unnoticed on the deck below, Phillip Marsden saunters towards the stern where he has a final appointment.

Dr Alexander (Sandy) Mackay has finally thrust his way to the bottom of the gangplank. In that moment when he first sets foot on the island of Penang, white-suited and intent on healing, he thinks his new life is just about to begin. In truth it already has.

13

Her address was in Trinity. Wide quiet streets, big houses from turn of last century, some subdivided but many still the family homes of Edinburgh old money. The houses with their porticoes, turrets, bay windows, glasshouses and walled gardens looked prosperous, dull, a little faded and left behind by contemporary life. I'd a notion that's what people lived in Trinity for.

I walked along in cool windy sunlight, taking my time. This might be nothing. Just an old lady seeking attention and company, with very little but a few scraps of half-remembered conversations from seventy years ago. But still I had the feeling that I was on the old man's track at last.

I turned into the wide street that ran down the hill to Newhaven Harbour. The Forth estuary was a polished gunmetal grey with little platinum shavings chiselled off it by the wind. For a minute I was walking along the Ness shore – it seemed Orkney had become one of those few places whose existence continued when I wasn't there.

It was a big square stone house, almost a mansion, with a high wall surrounding a large garden. The house wasn't pretty and the curtains and paintwork looked faded. Ivy was getting out of control round the side walls. There was a turret room with two curved windows looking out towards the river. I coveted it instantly.

There was a flicker of movement at one of the windows, then nothing.

I took some deep breaths, adjusted the file under my arm, told myself I was a grown-up not a ten-year-old come to get my ball back, mounted the steps and pressed the yellowed bell-button.

She wasn't that scary and she wasn't that old. Still she stared at me as though I were an object of interest or amusement.

'Mrs Cunninghame?' I said.

That made her laugh.

'I'll tell her you've arrived,' she said. 'Do come in.'

I stood in the hall, looked around. Loads of dark panelling, zingy smell of pine from the polish and yet still something fusty behind it. Portraits followed a wide wooden staircase up to a landing where the light seemed to get discouraged and fail.

'I'm her companion,' she said. 'Please wait here while I announce you.'

She went up the stair. I waited in the clock-ticking silence. Even in the fifties this would have been old-fashioned. Hat stand with coats and assorted dark hats, an armchair of green cracked leather by a low table with *Country Life* and *National Geographic* magazines. I glanced at them, they were years out of date.

At the far end of a dim passageway off the hall, a door closed quietly. In the ticking silence I heard footsteps click away on wooden floor. An umbrella lay over the hall table by a large ugly bowl. I looked closer. Something familiar about those porcelain dragons, that gaudy green and red demon. There'd been a vase like this in my childhood.

I took the bowl in both hands and turned it over. There on the unglazed base: *Singapore.*

'Mrs Cunninghame will see you now.'

I put the bowl down carefully, as if examining ugly curios in people's houses were my occupation, then hurried up the stair. I thought I caught a flicker of an amused smile as I went past the companion into the room.

'Good morning, young man.'

I took some steps towards the high-backed chair framed in front of the big windows. With sunlight sweeping in and bouncing off the polished wooden floor into my eyes, it was impossible to see her properly.

'Something amuses you?'

Her voice had once been authoritative. Now there were enough scratches and breaks to make it querulous.

'It's been some years since I've been called that,' I said.

She swivelled her head and looked at me. She seemed to be making no effort to get up or shake hands, so I just stood and looked down at her. She was long and thin, dressed entirely in black. Out of the dazzle of light now, I saw the mesh of cross-hatching round her mouth bend and stretch.

'You're – what? Mid-forties. From where I'm sitting, that's young enough.'

Her eyes were strong dark blue and fixed on me. Though her face was heavily lined, there was energy in it, and in the thick grey hair she had knotted at the back of her head. Because of my mother, I was used to judging the age of old ladies, and this one was a decade too young to be *the woman*. There goes that scenario.

'And old enough that you don't look so old to me.'

This time she almost chuckled. At least, that's how I took the throaty nasal exhalation.

'Do sit down,' she said, and reached for a chunky silver box sitting on the little table beside her. It too had muscular dragons writhing out from its surface. We'd once had one like it at home.

'Is that from Penang?' I blurted.

'Siam. You can tell by the conical hats.'

She flipped open the lid, took out a cigarette. She picked up a similar chunky lighter and lit up, inhaled deeply then let it out with a long sigh. Early eighties, I decided, same as my mother. The skin was a smoker's skin, probably further coarsened and dried by tropical sun.

'You do take coffee?' she said, then nodded to the companion who left the room. It was very quiet then, just a light rapid ticking from a carriage clock on the marble mantelpiece, and a slow muffled tock from a very tall green enamelled grandfather clock. She followed my eyes and almost smiled.

'My grandfather had that shipped back from China in 1900,' she said. 'When I was a girl it was so tall I called it a great-grandfather.'

As she drew on her cigarette, her eyes unfocused. I'd seen that look on my father in his last months when he'd finally stopped pretending he didn't know what he knew.

She tapped her ash then swivelled her head and stared directly at me. I'd the feeling she didn't approve of my existence. Perhaps I should have worn a tie.

'So, Mr Mackay,' she said. 'Tell me about your father.'

The long day comes back to him in flashes, like the palm-lined esplanade lit by the tropical storm that rolled in from Sumatra that afternoon, drenching him and Alan Hayman as they ran from the food stalls to the E&O hotel . . .

They are laughing and shouting to each other; the rain drives down so hard it stotts back off the ground and hangs in a knee-high haze. They run past bullock carts, abandoned rickshaws, stalls where the awnings belly under the weight of water. They sprint up the steps of the E&O, past an impassive Sikh doorman, then slide to a halt with water still gushing from their shoes at the table where the Simpson sisters and family are taking afternoon tea.

There seem so many of them, and so dry. Sandy shakes Dr Trent's hand, thanks him again for his help at the quay that morning, arranges to call in at his office above the dispensary to discuss proposals for improving pre- and post-natal care. Here are the Simpson parents, comfortably large and Edwardian, some aunts over from Singapore for the season, the kid sister and her cousin, who scarcely look up from their lemonade and ricecake.

Somehow the rain has brought hilarity. Even inside, the crash of it is quite deafening, and everyone has to talk louder, smile and laugh more. The aunts want to hear about Dr Mackay's bonesetting in the hurricane, the parents quiz Alan about his work, family and prospects. Ann is flushed as she hands Alan and Sandy their cups; Adele glances then occupies herself extracting a cigarette from her husband's case, lights up, reclines on the green cane chair and sends a series of smoke rings quivering up into the fan.

'How is the poor boy who fell?' Ann asks.

Sandy lists the injuries: dislocated shoulder, two fractured ribs, concussion. The dislocated shoulder? Trent had held his arms around the boy's chest, ready to apply counter-traction. Sandy gripped the flexed elbow. The boy whimpered, as well he might. Sandy took a deep breath, looked the boy in the eye and thought he'd received a nod, some kind of assent, or maybe it was just a shake of fear before he swiftly pulled the arm out, rotated, and the clunk as the joint reduced was audible just before the scream. He'd mend, with care. They'll check on him at the general hospital tomorrow.

Dr Trent nods, blows on his tea. He's not a demonstrative man. Sandy has noted the slight stiffness of the left elbow joint, and the white indentation around the left temple. More than that, it's in the careful way he moves, sits forward, lifts the china cup to his lips and sips through his stubby moustache, as though only close attention can ward off another catastrophe.

No need to ask, he knows the signs. Injuries apart, there's something left just over the eyes. A bit of a dry stick, the Chief Medical Officer with his clipped Edinburgh accent, but a competent and committed doctor. Sandy can only respect that.

As he eats a shortbread finger come all the way from Dundee – that buttery sweetness, those sugary crumbs! – he feels Adele's eyes on him.

'It doesn't sound as though that boy will carry much for a while,' she says casually.

'No he won't. In fact, I doubt if he'll be a wee stevedore again.' Sandy has tried to keep his voice as casual as hers. He swallows the rest of his shortbread, feels absurd with his whites hanging soggy on him. 'I'll try to find light work for him at the maternity hospital when he's fit.'

He doesn't mention the money he left, the last of his advance, with the ward sister in the general hospital. It's no damn business of anyone's. There'd been a hunger and a cockiness in that laddie's eyes that made them complicit. Brave wee bugger too. Li Tek, he'd mind the name.

'That's wonderful,' Ann says.

'I expect he'd rather be fit and well,' Sandy says, and though Adele's eyes stay down, there's a small tug at the corner of her lips.

'I hope you'll both come round on Sunday for pahits and curry tiffin,' Mrs Simpson announces. 'No need for black tie, we're very informal.'

'You betcha!' says Alan.

'Aye, thank you very much,' Sandy says, wondering about the pahits. Ann smiles on them equally. Adele watches over her teacup as she sips.

'Let's hope no one decides to have a Sunday baby, Dr Mackay!' one of the aunts says brightly. 'That would be a nuisance.'

'A baby would be a treasure any day of the week,' Mrs Simpson says firmly, then there's a pause where no one says anything and the aunts look into their cups as though they'd found something regrettable there.

Dr Trent stares at the rain sluicing down, holding his cup carefully to avoid catastrophe. Adele purses her lips and lets drift another smoky zero. Sandy watches a flush dawn in Ann's long white neck. For a minute the only sound is the two little girls muttering over a game of cards, the paddle of the fan above and the smash of rain on the terrace outside.

'So who will you be dropping cards on?' Mr Simpson asks.

His daughters roll their eyes, their father protests the old courtesies should be observed, and the conversation moves on.

Though he doesn't know it yet, that is the beginning of what will become his Sunday routine. Round of golf with Alan if he's not away in KL, a quick douse of chill water from the Shanghai jar, clean white shirt then meet to catch the little crimson bus out to the big old house in Ayer Itam.

Up the driveway between the spread fans of the traveller palms, past the bright canna beds, through fat bushes of blue plumbago where children giggled among the angsana trees and strawberry beds. Even as he still blinked at the wild coarse colours under the burning noon, Mrs Simpson would press the first of the pahits, those lethal cocktails, into their hands, and make introductions. After the pahits, the huge curry eaten sweating and woozy with cold beer and wine on the verandah with the blue chicks drawn for shade. Then always the Gula Malacca desert, slipping cool and sweet down the throat.

Then the talk would slow and falter, and some went inside for lie-off under the slow fans, while the younger set play bowls and croquet, smoke, or wander off in ones or twos behind the jacaranda, or meet half-sober as though by accident in the peeling gazebo where sharp-eyed children lie and keep watch through drifts of crimson bougainvillea.

꽃

14

I left there an hour or so later, still clutching my file, walked in a daze down to the Star Tavern by the waterside and ordered coffee and a double brandy. The place was near-empty as I chose a table by the window.

Looking back at it, she'd run the interview – for that's what it had felt like, as if I was being interviewed for a position. She asked about myself, my family, and my father, who she insisted was known as Sandy, which made me smile because he'd never been called that in his life. She said nothing while I answered, just stared at me or at the tip of her cigarette. It was very disconcerting and made me babble on.

She leaned forward when I spoke about their solid marriage and my mother's long and apparently happy widowhood. She nodded at that, said her husband had been dead for twenty years and that things had calmed down somewhat since then. She didn't elaborate.

She had a manner, the assurance of authority, the certain knowledge that she would not be interrupted, so I wasn't surprised when she mentioned she'd run a girls' school in Singapore. I liked the evident pleasure she took in her cigarettes and her strong coffee. Spirited, I thought. Eccentric, maybe. Mica could be like this in her eighties.

Then I came to the part about finding the Penang Buddha. She narrowed her eyes against her cigarette smoke and asked me to describe it accurately.

'A Good Fortune Buddha,' she announced. 'Very common among the Straits Chinese. I never cared for them myself. Continue.'

I went on to tell her about the postcards and produced them from my file. She looked at them briefly, then handed them back. She didn't seem that interested. I could feel myself losing her.

'There was also a domino,' I said. 'It turned out to be hollow.'

She nodded briefly.

'Not uncommon,' she said. 'They were novelty items. Women would keep scent in them, or lavender. Men used them for snuff – or, it was said, opium.'

'There was a photograph inside this one. Of a woman.'

I opened my file and took out the best blow-up print I'd been able to make. The image was ghostly, groupings of dots for her eyes, the open mouth, the curve of a jaw, the rest just a haze, a mist.

She put on her glasses and studied it.

'Not much left of this one,' was her only comment.

She removed her glasses and handed it back. I saw how insignificant it was. Just an unrecognisable trace of a long-dead human being. I felt foolish and apologetic.

I hurried on and told her my mother had recently mentioned my father had had an affair in Penang, something to do with the wife of his senior partner, and had to leave.

Mrs Cunninghame stared at me over her cigarette. She gave a little snort of smoke when I told her the next I knew was that my father had returned to Scotland alone some time in the thirties and bought a run-down practice in Perth.

'Men,' she muttered. 'Fairly typical. And what do you think happened to this unfortunate woman?'

'I've no idea,' I said. 'Except it must have been difficult for her. I mean in those days, with it being public knowledge and all.'

'I don't doubt it,' she said drily. 'Was there a child?'

I stared at her. It hadn't occurred to me that maybe somewhere in this world ... No, it was absurdly melodramatic.

'Not that my mother knew about. Anyway, I absolutely cannot imagine my father letting a child of his go.'

She made a face, but didn't pursue it. I had to explain just how little my mother knew about my father's early life. Or cared, for that matter. How he wasn't given to talking about it, and had burned any remaining letters and papers when they married after the war. A tail-dragging man.

She raised the remains of her eyebrows above those remarkable dark blue eyes.

'Indeed,' she said. 'What a graphic expression. I don't care much for the past myself.'

She gestured round the sitting room as if it proved her point. I didn't see how, for most of the furnishings in it were antique, apart from the little radio at her elbow – one of those little hi-tech black ones that gives you the world in a palm-top.

But now in the Star Tavern, as I drank coffee, made notes and thought back, I was struck by the absence of photographs in that sitting room, in the whole house for that matter. Old people usually accumulate lots of them in assorted frames – weddings, christenings, children, children's weddings, grandchildren – but not Mrs Cunninghame.

There had been one large black and white framed photo above the mantelpiece. A tallish slightly stout man with moustache in army uniform, dress kit presumably. Arm linked to a woman who stared out at the camera from the same eyes that had been making me nervous since I'd walked in. Palm trees and big urns on steps in the background.

'We were married out at the back of the E&O Hotel,' she'd commented, and seemed amused at the very idea. 'One of the last beach weddings. A month later, Malaya became independent.'

The companion had stirred and coughed. I had the impression she was anxious to protect Mrs Cunninghame's time and energy, so it was time to get to the point.

'So what was he like, my father?' I asked eagerly. 'Can you remember anything about him?'

She pulled a face then wafted smoke from her eyes.

'It was seventy years ago,' she said defensively. 'I was only ten or so, and I was more interested in playing with my cousin Emily than the obscure doings of grown-ups.'

She drank more coffee and considered. I wondered if she was the last person living who had known him then. Once the last person who knew us has died, then we are truly gone.

'I think he was tall and skinny with a big nose,' she said. 'He had a dreadful straw hat he'd bought in Aden, not the thing at all. When he talked with my aunt and uncle I found it hard to understand what he was saying. He had a strong Scotch accent. He didn't seem very at ease. Gauche, I suppose . . . '

She tailed off. To avoid staring at her, I looked out the tall windows down onto the garden. There was a lawn, flowerbeds, a kind of gazebo. It must have been warm out, because someone was reading in it. I could see green trousers and an old floppy hat, the flicker as a magazine page turned.

'He was playing bowls,' she said suddenly. I turned from the window. 'At one of the Sunday parties. I think they were all quite drunk.' She smiled, though her amusement seemed qualified. 'You must remember, Mr Mackay, that in Malaya people were often inebriated. The cocktails alone would stun a gorilla, and then of course they went on to drink with tiffin, and then more drinks till it was time for bed. I think there were cocktails every evening, and of course at weekends it went on from lunchtime.'

She snorted again, smoke streaming from her nostrils. Then she turned and looked at me intently.

'I often think that drink was responsible for a lot of what went on,' she said. 'People do very unwise things. Back then, a life was ruined so easily. *Ruined*. I dare say the word seems ludicrous to you.'

'I'm not laughing,' I protested. 'It's just the picture of all these people reeling about the place ...'

'As a child, I did think they became dreadfully silly,' she admitted. 'Because I wasn't drinking and I was bored, I saw a lot of what went on ...'

She seemed to go off into a dream. I glanced at the companion, who turned her wrist to show me her watch. I nodded.

'I remember!' Mrs Cunninghame announced. 'It was at one of the Sunday gatherings. I think your father and a friend took on a couple of men at bowls. I have a sense it became quite heated. Some bad feeling ... It may have been about my cousin, she was very pretty.'

'His friend,' I interrupted. 'Was he called Alan?'

She seemed to recoil slightly. Her companion stirred then was still.

'Perhaps he was,' she said. 'Where did you get that name from?'

I shrugged. 'It's just a name my father mentioned a few times. I think he said this Alan had taught him to enjoy classical music. My father didn't have close male friends, but I sensed he might have been one.'

'Indeed,' she murmured. She seemed to slump a little in her winged chair. I sensed she was tiring.

'Your older cousin,' I said eagerly, 'was she married?'

'Oh no. That was why there were all these young men around at those parties – so few single women. They would cluster round Cousin Ann like, like ... '

'Bees round flowers?'

'Wasps round jam.'

She was been silent for a time then. I let her look back down seventy years and waited.

'Phillip,' she said abruptly. 'Phillip Marsden. I think he was associated with your father. We called him "the magician" because he did card tricks, made things appear and disappear. My cousin and I liked him, he'd play with us.'

'Was he a doctor?'

'No, no,' she said impatiently. 'You have doctors on the brain. He was some kind of civil servant, like most of my uncle's friends. A neat, clever man, and a wonderful dancer. Anyway, he was a friend of my aunts and quite often came to their Sunday parties.'

I didn't see where it would get me, but I added the name to my notes.

'So you've no memory of any doctor or doctor's wife with my father at these parties?'

'Don't you think, young man, that your interest in all this is a trifle prurient?' It had occurred to me. Fortunately, my mother seemed quite indifferent to it. 'Whatever your father did to this unfortunate woman is best left forgotten. In any case, they're all dust now. I think you should, as my great-niece likes to say, get a life.'

'Look here,' I said, 'my father did whatever *with* not *to* whoever she was. It may have been the thirties but she was a grown woman. She must have wanted to. I won't have him cast as the wicked seducer here.'

We glared at each other. I'm not used to turning on my elders.

'But why must you know?' she insisted. 'It's all very unsavoury.'

'Because they're dead! Because I've nothing else left and I want something!'

That must have been lying in wait for a long time. I sweated as I sat back in my chair.

'Well well, young man,' she said at last. 'You do feel strongly. I had the impression your father was somewhat bolshie too.'

I was oddly pleased, though it wasn't a quality I admired.

'In fact,' she added, 'I've a notion Marsden joked that he'd persuaded your father to be put up for membership of the Penang Club because he reckoned they could do with a troublemaker. Phillip had an odd sense of humour.'

I had wondered about that Penang Club, because it didn't sound my father's style at all. I told her about the billiards trophy, *Runner up Class A*.

'The men played a deal of billiards,' she said. 'Of course, women weren't allowed in the Penang Club. They had their own club, known as the Hen Roost. My aunt took me there once, it was very boring ... '

She drifted off again. The companion stirred. I'd a feeling my time was running out.

'One thing more,' I said. I tried to keep my voice casual. This was the key question, the one that might give me everything. 'Would you remember the name of the head of the medical practice in George Town?'

'There would have been several practices,' she said shortly. 'I was only in Penang for a few weeks at a time – my family mostly lived in Singapore – then when I was old enough I was sent to school in England. I had no call to go to the doctor. I have absolutely no idea.'

Another dead end, another long silence. I looked out the window again, but the reader in the gazebo had gone. The garden looked like an empty stage set.

'I don't suppose any of these people are still alive? Marsden or Alan or any of your cousins?'

'You suppose rightly.' She exhaled and almost chuckled. 'They're long gone. We're not a long lived family, except for me, and I won't trouble the scorer much longer.'

There was nothing I could say to that. I picked up my file and got to ► my feet.

'My mother may have got it wrong. She's quite vague about what he actually told her. Maybe I should just let it go.'

She nodded as though that would be a good idea.

'I do have a life,' I added. 'Or at least I used to. Things have been a bit . . . difficult recently.'

'Oh yes?'

'I . . . thought I was going to die, but I didn't. Now I can't forget I will.'

I'd no idea what had prompted that confession when I didn't talk about it to anyone else. She was looking closely at me.

'Lebuh Chulia,' she said suddenly. 'Chulia Street. There was a dispensary there, and a practice that went with it. I once went with a prescription for my Aunt Dorothy. You might find that in the administrative records.'

I noted it down, more to humour her than anything else. There was a hint of a shake when she stretched to stub out her last cigarette. I bent and shook her hand, being careful not to squeeze too hard. It was bony and light but warm.

'I am sorry I couldn't help you more, Mr Mackay,' she said. 'Perhaps I just wanted to have someone with whom to talk about Penang and my family.'

'It was a pleasure,' I said, and meant it. 'You've made it seem real.'

She nodded. I could see she was tiring, and I was ready to go. She coughed then looked up at me.

'One more thing,' she said. 'I believe your father had something to do with babies in Penang.'

'No, that was later,' I said. 'He specialised in obstetrics just before the Second War.'

She nodded and shrugged in one gesture and the extraordinary gathering of wrinkles made her throat look like a lizard's.

'There may be a photograph somewhere,' she said vaguely. 'Should we come across it, I shall telephone you.'

Her left hand trembled slightly. Because of my mother, my heart turned over. I wrote down my Orkney details, and also, at her suggestion, where I'd be staying in London in case she came up with something in the next few days.

'Mr Mackay,' she said. I stopped at the door and looked back. She looked less imposing now, just an old lady trying to sit upright in a winged chair. 'If you do make any progress in this investigation, perhaps you could let me know.'

'Of course,' I said.

And that was it. Shown down that panelled stair, past the Victorian and Edwardian portraits, I had glimpses of important beards, plumed hats, sometimes backgrounds of the Far East. Still that absence of photographs – how like my father, I thought.

'Goodbye, Mr Mackay,' the companion said. It sounded very final. I'd a feeling she didn't approve of me. Nor had Mrs Cunninghame, though she may have softened a little towards the end. The door closed firmly behind me, the stained glass panel gleamed opaquely.

In the Star Tavern I noted it down: *Lebuh Chulia dispensary – practice?* It wasn't much, but it was the only solid thing Mrs Cunninghame had given me. That and the odd suggestion my father had been 'something to do with babies'.

I finished my brandy, seeing images of my father, young, awkward and bolshie, being persuaded to join the Penang Club by his pal Phillip Marsden, and the two of them drinking too much and getting into an argument over bowls. It was a human moment, a glimpse that made me yearn for more.

Alan. I underlined it twice. It was the only moment in the interview she lost control of it. It was worth being reminded that for the few living, these names still had a meaning and an emotion. He had meant something to her, I was sure of it.

Prurient, me? Get a life? Go on.

I drained the brandy, picked up my file and went out into the gathering dusk to find a taxi. Time to get back to the living, see my own family for a rare evening gathering before continuing South to whatever I'd find there.

Finally by the yellow light of the hurricane lamp, he parts the mosquito net and crawls onto his new bed, so soft and wide after weeks in a bunk. It's not moving. There's no rumble of engines. No snoring cabin-mate, no distant laughter nor squawk of jazz, the high tinkle of glasses.

The company has scattered, their floating island turned out to be temporary. Some, like Henderson the mining engineer, have taken the small steamers to the mainland, heading to Malacca, Kuala Lumpur, the Interior and what's left of the rubber and tin industries. The *Amelia* has already sailed on to Singapore – he heard the long hooting on the offshore wind as the rickshaw carried him back here from the E&O hotel through the clinging dark, and tried to dismiss the sensation in his upper abdomen as the result of unfamiliar food snatched at a stall.

The day has been longer than any he can remember since one in March 1918, and that he doesn't care to remember. But today! The first whiff of land then the promise of it coming clear through the yellow dawn ...

Lying looking up the grey cone of the mosquito net swaying to the breeze through the shutters, he smells it all again and his heart turns over. One day he will be used to this, one day he'll cease to register it as anything special. But not yet.

The day's been long but sleep's impossible. He pulls off his pyjama jacket, props himself up on the pillow and looks round the little bedroom of his bachelor quarters. Slipping his hand under the net, he picks up Marsden's parting gift, handed to him casually on the quay before that enigma rolled off in his rickshaw. Soft red leather, already slippy in his hands, gold bookmark: *Collected Poems of Walt Whitman*.

He opens it at random, reads.

I think I could turn and live with animals, they are so placid and self-contained
They do not sweat and whine about their condition,
They do not lie awake in the dark and weep for their sins,
They do not make me sick discussing their duty to God.

This doesn't read like any poetry he's come across. It's not Burns or Scott, Longfellow or Yeats. It doesn't even rhyme, but it looks lively stuff. At the very least it makes a change from Addison's *Tropical Diseases* and *The Foundations of Obstetrical Procedure.*

He flips to another page.

And nothing, not God, is greater to one than one's self is,
And whoever walks a furlong without sympathy walks to his own
funeral . . .

Already he's taking a shine to the nerve of this chap.

As he reads on, he's adjusting to the sounds of this new night. Coarse palm leaves scrape the roof tiles. High piping squeaks outside in the courtyard, probably the fruit bats he saw everywhere in the heat of the afternoon, hung like black gowned upside-down ministers in the flowering trees, among the jacaranda and frangipani. He looks up from his book at a sudden scuttle in the ceiling, a squeal then deep silence. *Mongoose,* the houseboy had said – and how daft to call an elderly Tamil, father of five, a boy – *He eat snakes and things. Very good pet.*

Snakes he doesn't like. He's already vowed not to get sick. He'll take the quinine, be vigilant with the mosquitoes, use common sense. Too many people still die too early out here. He's survived the damn war, he won't be one of them. Too many things to do, too much still to see, people to meet, all these islands lying under blue skies and giant clouds. And . . .

Lips I have met, and wish to meet again, and will. He puts down the book and blinks, sees her again, her mouth in the near-dark behind the lifeboats, the smell and taste and feel of her like a fruit falling open between his incredulous hands.

It had been going on all over the ship last night, final assignations and last chances. The slow stroke of her hand over his face before she finally slipped away, like a blind person memorising him, had made it clear it wouldn't happen again. When she'd nodded to him politely this morning, sitting by her sister at breakfast, he had blushed like a laddie as he passed on, but he wasn't surprised or offended.

He slides down the pillows, closes the book, studies the low white ceiling then blows out the lamp. Some people count sheep, he escorts himself through the intricacies of the Vertime hysterectomy, an operation so complex and precise very few surgeons dare perform it but one day he will. Thirty-four distinct stages, each with its own challenges. It is bloody and decidedly unerotic and seldom fails to quell these stirrings.

Termites scrape in the beams. The mongoose patters. Palm leaves clatter, driving moonlight shadows across the shutters. He lies sweating, near naked, almost safe, within the small-meshed drifting net, remembering her lips, her indecipherable tongue.

When the train in from the airport went underground I flinched then closed my eyes, tried to picture my way out of there. In Orkney I'd lost my protective layers, those filters you need to cope with city information overload. Think the cliffs at Yesnaby, big sea breaking. Or yellow light across empty fields above the Ness where lapwings strut like waiters in evening dress . . .

The train filled up, I hunched in small. Being carried along in the Tube was like being taken into the brain scanner in hospital. The whole city was taking a reading of my brain and finding it wanting.

Outside was not so bad. Those very high buildings were quite uplifting, and so many people of so many shapes and colours. My own species in full array. I'd eat adrenaline and information for breakfast.

I got off the bus and checked the *A–Z*. The raw buzz and clash of the centre had dissipated into dull, prosperous faded streets. I was going to see the last survivor of my father's year of medical graduates. I remembered him vaguely from the odd childhood visit, could see a high brown freckled forehead, hear a soft deep Borders voice. Even then, I knew I liked him and that he was sad under his funny. Uncle Bob aka Dr Robert Taylor.

He and my dad had been students, then housemen together during the twenties, then picked up again after my dad came back from the East. He'd been married once, divorced when that was still unusual, never had children. He was the last person alive my mother could think of who might know something about what had happened in Penang. She still got a card from him every Christmas, and after some nagging from me she'd finally come up with an address.

I turned another corner, into a small quiet street of detached thirties bungalows. My heart was uncomfortably fast and heavy. This could save an awful lot of research. I'd written to say I was coming, but had no reply and the phone number was ex-directory. I really felt quite ill and wondered if I was going to faint. Maybe the low cabin pressure on the flight down hadn't agreed with the tube in my head.

Number 39 was the last house in the street. The only one without a car in front of it. Here goes.

I walked up the gravel. The house looked neglected and tired. No lights and little colour in the paint or curtains. I adjusted my Penang notes file and rang the bell, heard a faint clanging. Come on, come on! Please don't be senile, Uncle Bob. He'd have to be about ninety. All I need is her name.

I went round the back in case he was in the garden. The grass was long, the weeds and plants indistinguishable. A rusty hand trowel lay by the back door, and a single glove. I tried the back door.

'Here, what you doing, mate?'

Young man in blue suit, holding a file like mine, mobile in his other hand. He stared at me suspiciously and of course I felt like a suspicious character. In London you didn't go round the back of empty houses and try doors.

'I've come to see Dr Robert Taylor,' I said. 'He's a friend of my father.'

He glanced at his file.

'Taylor,' he said. 'You'll be lucky, mate. He's been dead a month. Fancy buying a house?'

Once we were waiting at a railway station, just the two of us. Maybe I was seven. He'd read his paper, smoked his pipe, I'd finished my *Victor*.

'Something to show you,' he said. Produced a length of string. 'My father showed me this a long time ago.' He began to loop, twist, tie, with those deft surgeon's hands. Finally, he held it up, a loose complex cat's cradle of a tangle. He handed me one end and held the other. Looked me in the eye, like a challenge or a lesson or a joke was coming.

'Now pull,' he said.

I did, and watched the knot unravel, slip away loop after loop till there was nothing left between us but a straight length of string.

'You see, laddie, some things are less complicated than they seem,' he concluded. Then he chuckled to himself. 'The rest of them aren't.'

Odd tricks, mannerisms, turns of phrase, these are the things that remain of us. I learned it from him that afternoon while we waited for our train, and forty years later used it to bribe Cara to go to sleep.

I sit on the Orkney shore among the mussel shells and dried weed, watching the white sands of Evie rise up through the retreating water, feeling still the wonder, loss and release as that knot pulled out to nothing.

15

I left Keith and Janet's house that November morning without much hope, heading for the National Newspaper Library in Colindale. I was clinging to the idea that by some serendipity I'd come upon a lead in a Penang newspaper there – my father's name in a ship arrival notice, a photograph of the George Town Doctors' Christmas Ball, with the heads of practices and their wives' names all helpfully listed – that kind of wishful thinking.

Someone stepped back out of a parked car right into me.

When you're startled back into this world, for a moment it's oddly clear. She was tall, dark, Hispanic, steadying a VCR in her arms as my file and *Energy Engineering* flipped from my hand and fell on the pavement.

'Sorry, mister!' she said.

'No problem,' I said. 'You all right?'

She nodded, half-giggling, embarrassed maybe.

'Maria never looks where she's going!'

The woman who'd stepped from the driver's side picked up my file and journal. She glanced then handed them back. She was the flip side of her pal – quite short, fair, head bobbing like a blonde tennis ball as she spoke. A little dash line at either side of her smile, young but not entirely unmarked.

'I was out to lunch myself,' I admitted.

Maria giggled, hefted up the VCR and began to walk away.

'Catch you later, Roo!'

'Bye!'

I hesitated a moment, holding my journal and file as the driver looked up at me. I stared back. Something alive and zesty about her made it seem as if the sun had come out even though it already had. Or maybe I'd been in Orkney too long.

'I couldn't help noticing your journal,' she said diffidently. 'Maybe you can help me.'

'You need renewable energy? Or a cantilever bridge explained?'

She looked up. Her eyes went straight into me, conker-brown and wide-set, no one else's eyes, a whole life behind them. Once in a while, even in the city, a distance melts.

'Right now I need my car started.'

It wasn't a big thing, which is as well because I'm an engineer not a mechanic. Her ignition was dead, so I did the usual. Tested the battery, checked the wiring, the points, then wished I'd taken a course on car maintenance.

But I remembered one of my early junk cars. So I put her little Golf into gear, then got her to help me give the rear a couple of sharp pushes. She looked across the boot at me, laughed and her breath plumed in the cold morning. Some kind of radiance was coming from her. I knew it was called projection, but that didn't make it any less bright, or alarming.

I got in the car, tried again – it started straight off. Just once in a while something comes out right.

'That's stonking brilliant!' she exclaimed.

Her voice was northern, Geordie maybe. Husky and deep like a smoker. I looked up from the driver's seat. As she stood on the pavement smiling down at me, the light crowned her hair and my little voice prompted *the Golden Girl.*

I hurriedly explained about the starting motor sticking, told her to keep the engine running and either park the car on a hill in future or get it looked at as soon as possible. She nodded vigorously. As her blonde fringe swayed, I noticed small pointy ears.

I got out of her car. It was time to get over to Colindale while I still could.

'My mum told me to get it serviced regularly,'

I nodded, made way for a couple of schoolkids who hurried past with mobile phones at their ears, each talking earnestly but not to each other.

'Always listen to your mum.'

'I can't any more – she died two years ago this month.'

There were fine pale hairs shining on her upper lip. Something that wasn't desire juddered between us. I felt it, smack on my chest, a current that doesn't appear in my textbooks but no less real for all that.

'It's rotten, isn't it?' I said, and for once left it there.

She looked down, nodded twice. When she raised her head it happened again that current.

'Yes,' she said. 'When you can't see someone again . . .'

'When my father died I was too busy to really take it in.'

'How long ago did he?' She sounded urgent, as if it really mattered to her.

'Seventeen years,' I said. 'But now I think of him all the time.'

Her mouth opened in a little intake of breath.

'Ah,' she said. 'That long.' She looked back down the street, then at me. Then we were both embarrassed and looked away.

'Thanks so much,' she said. 'Next time you can explain about the cantilever bridge.'

A quick smile, those white teeth, and she was gone into her car. Her hand flicked up as she pulled away, and left me free to get on out to Colindale for a hot date with the *Penang Gazette*.

Just one of those small city encounters that you try to shrug off. But it was too late, I'd been done over, mugged by yearning sharp as any blade. I wonder no one remarked on it as I sat on the Tube, all that silvery darkness bleeding out of me.

A Sumatran storm had crashed through before dawn, leaving the air a little fresher than usual. Saturday afternoon at the Lone Pine swimming club beach. He takes a cold beer from the barboy, signs the chit and wanders away from the old wooden hotel, down the path that winds through the clumps of jacaranda bushes like clotted blood.

He crunches onto coarse sand, sits heavily on the nearest deckchair, drinks and stares at the warm, turgid sea. He drinks, slumps, half-watches the bathers larking about. It's been a long night.

So much blood. The smell of it, pungent and animal, is in his nostrils still. He drinks again, hears Ann Simpson's laughter among the others in the sea, closes his eyes.

Li Tek had grabbed his arm, shaken him from deep sleep. *Woman bleeds! Come now!* As they hurried through the silent back alleys, past the old men and boys bundled sleeping under their rickshaws and carts, past the Chinese temple and businesses where the Good Fortune joss sticks still glowed in bundles of three, Sandy had time to note how well the boy was moving now.

Up the stairs at a run. Second floor. Hospital dark – generator packed in again – and silent except for lamplight and panicky voices coming from Ward 4. Mrs Ashanti. He should have listened, should always listen to that wee voice that says something's not right even when your training and the evidence of your eyes says it is.

So much blood. The sheets were dark with it. Part of him noticed more gather along a fold, drip and plop on the wooden floor. He checked: the woman's in shock: moribund, but still alive. Post-partum haemorrhaging, worst he'd ever seen. The woman will die. *It's God's will,* he heard his father say, his only comment on wee Janice's death. God's will. His mother had kept staring at the empty bed, then she'd stripped the sheets to wash them and never spoke of it again.

The night porter, Li Tek, the young Welsh nurse, and the Indian Night Sister crouched by the bed trying desperately to control the bleeding, they were all waiting for him to do something. He looked down at Mrs Ashanti, looked into her terrified, pleading eyes. He shouldn't be here. Not ready for this. He should never be in charge of a maternity hospital.

But he is. And some patients die. It's God's will.

Arse it is. Night Sister is competent, and if by a miracle – there are no miracles of course – the transfusion unit's functioning this woman doesn't have to die. Blood's misleading, a little seems a lot, he learned that in 1918. Control the bleeding, get the transfusion going. Stay sterile. Follow procedure.

The moments are stretched, or his thoughts very fast. He instructs Night Sister: fist into the vagina, other hand on the abdomen to squeeze the uterus and buy him a few more minutes. Tells Nurse Gibbs what he needs from her and prays she can do it as he hurries down the corridor to scrub up . . .

'Not swimming, Doc?'

He opens his eyes on Adele Trent in a light blue knee-length dress, book in one hand, cocktail in the other, smiling down at him under a cream wide-brimmed hat.

'Can't swim,' he grunts. 'I'd drown for sure.'

She laughs quietly.

'Me too,' she says. 'Ann swims like a dolphin.'

'So I see.'

Together they look at the bathers. Ann, Alan Hayman, the athletic blond young Englishman Freddie Ellyot who seems to be everywhere, a bunch of young redundant rubber planters waiting for the boat home, a few of the MCS wives, all leaping, shouting and laughing as they play some form of water polo.

'If you're not careful, Alan will get in before you. Or don't you care?'

He lifts his bottle of India Pale Ale, lets the long neck obscure Alan Hayman. Ann jumps backwards into the swell, comes up shouting with the ball in her arms.

'She's a very bonnie woman,' he says. 'But I don't think she's that interested in me.'

'Oh come on! When you were at the house last Sunday, her eyes made love to you.'

He seems to consider this. He squints up into the light at Adele.

'That's a symptom of myopia and three Singapore Slings.'

She laughs and sits down beside him. Sandy automatically looks around for Marsden – the two of them are seen so often together, he wonders how Dr Trent can accept it. There he is, immaculate in whites, talking with someone under the trees. Trent will be working in town, he usually is.

'Maybe you're really a romantic,' she says suddenly.

He pulls a face as if he'd chewed on tinfoil.

'How do you make that out?'

'Only a true romantic would prefer a love that's impossible over a possible one that's . . . all right.'

'You should know,' he blurts, and then it's out and can't be taken back. Under her broad-brimmed hat, her eyes seem to swell. They are the kind of clear mid-blue the sea never is here. They are the blue of home.

'Touché,' she says quietly, then looks away. 'Alan says you had a bit of a flap last night. What happened?'

Though it's still on his mind – he'll check on Mrs Ashanti on his way back this evening – he's reluctant to talk. It's too close, too technical, too gory.

'I'd have thought you hear enough medicine at home.'

'No, John never talks about his work.' She pauses, hesitates. 'I don't think he believes in it any more.'

'But he works all the time,' Sandy protests.

She nods. 'I think that's why he does,' she says.

A long pause. He watches spear-shaped palm shadows stir over her face.

'He's a good Medical Health Officer. Very conscientious. He'll make a difference, especially for people who can't pay.'

'I'm sure he gets good results,' she says slowly. 'He knows medicine works. He just doesn't see the point in it. I don't think he sees the point in anything since the war. He can't say that, of course, so he works. Once I thought I—'

She looks away, her knuckles whiten round the cocktail glass.

Even under the trees and with the breeze off the water, it's too hot. The kid sister and cousin sprint by, flipping a yellow quoit between them, their feet flicking up white along the shallows. Further out, Ann waves. *I sing the body electric* ... Adele waves back then looks at him, long unfathomable look.

'These pinang trees,' she says at last, indicating the dark ones swaying above them, 'produce those betel nuts some locals chew. They're a mild drug. That's always amused me, the whole island being called after a narcotic. Not surprising people here lose their grip a little.' She pauses, sips. 'So tell me about last night.'

He begins to talk.

Night Sister and Nurse Gibbs had been very good. Miss Sharma slowed the bleeding, kept her head; Gibbs organised everything – theatre, anaesthetic drip, sterilisation – while he did the needful. Which turned into a full hysterectomy.

He pauses, glances at Adele.

'Go on,' she said dryly. 'I'm not going to faint.'

It was ... messy. But it worked. Or seems to have. The woman was still unconscious but stable when he left at 6 a.m. into the pouring warm rain. The little Welsh nurse from the nunnery had pulled herself together to act as his assistant, dripping the chloroform down onto the mask. Miss Sharma was much too good for Junior Night Sister – he'd get her in charge of the day wards, if he could push it past the governors. He's been here long enough to know if she'd been European or Malay instead of Indian, she'd have been promoted years ago.

'Mrs Ashanti – she'd already had her baby?'

'The day before, a boy. She's got another, so her hysterectomy's not the end of the world.'

'No, I suppose not. Two is quite enough, isn't it?' Adele tips back the rest of her gin sling, steeples her hands around the glass. 'You must have found it quite exciting.'

She'd found him out. For all the anxiety, the uncertainty, the hasty drama played out under the yellow-white hiss of the Tilly lamps, once he'd committed he'd felt calm and exultant. It had been the same with Willie Ancross – setting that femur down in the hull by hurricane lamp, then seeing the man back on his feet last week. Nothing else felt like it, or at least, nothing that was very likely.

'We were lucky,' he said.

'Surely luck doesn't come into it,' she said sharply. 'Or Fate. Or God. You don't believe in those things any more than I do.'

Her mind was so quick, like a blade laid over his. He spread his left hand, stretched the fingers out, remembering. What did he believe in?

'I believe in these,' he said. 'Sometimes it's like I can feel what's happening under the skin. It's the one thing I'm good at, so I must do it as well as I can.'

Her right hand leaves her glass and for a moment trails along the back of his from knuckles to wrist as if trying to read the secret. The fingertips are still cool, he'll remember them for days; he'll feel it in the nights under the mosquito net, the cool smooth pad of her touch.

Her hand jumps away. A crunch on the sand, a shadow across Sandy's lap.

'Congratulations, Mackay,' Marsden says. He's looking down, smiling his private smile under the neat fair moustache. 'Sounds like a good night's work,' he adds.

'This is an awfully small island,' Sandy says.

'Oh, Phillip hears everything,' Adele says.

Sandy's looking at her, that clean-struck profile, the quick curling mouth, as she looks up at Marsden, and he sees something travel between them. A pact, a warning, an agreement, he doesn't know. But something has passed and it's to do with him.

Adele gets to her feet, picks up her Sinclair Lewis.

'Too hot to read out here,' she says. 'I'm going into the hotel for a while.'

Then she's away, her home sky blue dress moving among the clumps of blood. The cream hat bobs, inclines, is gone.

Marsden sits down in the empty deckchair, crosses his legs, inspects his perfect fingernails.

'I need to ask a favour, old chap,' he says.

16

So I went on to Colindale later than planned that morning and a bit distracted. It's shocking when the depth of your own need reveals itself.

It hadn't been like that with Mica. The Mica I had parted from seemed all wit and wound. But that young, blonde other woman, bouncing from foot to foot in her green cords and trainers, her neat head bobbing and her wide open eyes that seemed constantly slightly amazed by what she saw, she appeared like life and hope itself.

I sat in the Tube, seeing again her parting wave, imagining a world where I was quick-witted and bold enough to ask for her phone number, one of those parallel universes beloved of SF writers and daydreamers.

But no, not in this world. I left the station and went to dig up a lost one in the National Newspaper Library.

Dim cubicles with little reading lights, and the dismal glow of the microfiche screens. I passed people who looked positively green as they stared into the flickering lights, as if some fungus of the past had grown over them. Part of me wanted to run screaming *No! No! Sleepers awake!*

The rest of me selected a spool – *Penang Gazette* 1929–30 – and lowered myself face first into the waters of the past.

What was I hoping for? My father's name listed among the arrivals and departures, or new public appointments, or in the handicap listings for golf and tennis tournaments. The Penang Club billiards tournament results. I was imagining a paragraph mentioning the Chulia Street dispensary and the head of the practice there. For once I had that name, then I had hers, and then anything was possible.

Straining my eyes into the grey grainy pages on the screen, I was fascinated and depressed equally. Depressed because after an hour or so I realised the odds against this working were about the same as Scottish Enterprise awarding our tidal energy project priority status, or Mica becoming a straightforward human being, or meeting young Roo again.

For the *Penang Gazette* turned out to be a daily. Even scanning quickly, it took thirty minutes to read one issue. So three hours for a week. Four days to cover a month. And I didn't even know what year I should be looking at for my father's arrival, the 1930 trophy being the only fixed date I had. I was asking for a gorgeous fluke.

Then again, as time passed and any knowledge of the present world outside faded, this new one became more real and pressing. I followed Oswald Mosley's resignation from the Labour Cabinet, blinked at the arrival of Amy Johnson in Australia aged 22, noted Bradman's 452 for New South Wales against Queensland. Passenger lists of new arrivals included teachers, civil servants returning from furlough, a Lady Medical Officer, a film star, a racing driver – but not my father.

There are luncheons and swimming parties and Madam Farina's Dress Displays at the E&O Hotel, adverts for Dr Morse's Indian Root Liver Pills, and monsoon breaks in the Sumatran Highlands with dancing, tennis and billiards on offer. The Moonlight Band play foxtrots on the Esplanade. Apparently, women are jumping out of aeroplanes, wearing skirts perilously high above the knee, suing for breach of promise and speaking in Parliament. At a New Year's Ball, Mr Sarkies (manager) has his daughter step from a clock on the dance floor in sequins and ostrich feathers as Miss 1930. The King and Queen of Siam sail in their royal yacht for Singapore and Java. Now Bradman is rampaging through English cricket with a current average of 150. The Black Bottom remains a scandal and a craze.

All exotic, safe nostalgia. But there are other strands. Ghandi announces the Congress Party will seek complete independence. Unemployment in Britain exceeds one and a half million. The new Labour Government proposes a new Super Tax (how my father would have smiled at that, and guffawed at the outraged editorial comparing this with the French and Russian revolutions). The war in China rages on. Germany demands evacuation of the Rhineland. The Great Experiment of Prohibition in the USA is giving rise to gangsters and shootings in the streets.

Closer to home, a Malay runs amok with a machete, kills nine, then is shot down while eating maize in a hut on Penang Hill. Eight Chinese are arrested in Singapore for assisting the South Seas Communist Party. The Kuo Min Tang becomes a proscribed organisation in Malaya. A Dutchman is found drowned 'in mysterious circumstances' in Penang Harbour. A thousand people die in a riot between the Connighi coolies and Burmese labourers. There is a shortage of berths on the boats home because the rubber and tin industries have collapsed.

Not a simple, comfortable world then. China is in turmoil, Russia is starving, the Empire is breaking up, the Western World is in the Depression. There are wars and rumours of wars, unemployment and rearmament.

And still, then as now, it is newsworthy that child star Jackie Coogan has had his appendix out, and the 'By The Way' column reports that at the Nanking Hotel Easter Dance, Miss A. Simpson was wearing a stunning frock in the new bottle green.

I stopped there, stared, checked my notes. It had to be Mrs Cunninghame's elder cousin. Didn't get me anywhere, but it gave more reality to her few memories. These people really existed, this really happened. They danced, they wore new clothes, they cut out recipes and tried to improve their tennis forehand.

I read through an article on 'The New Woman', railing against the rise of 'kissing, flirting and affairs', the breakdown of the family, the spiralling of divorce among 'a motley crowd of actors, film artists, jockeys, billiard players and sporting peers'. The good bishop concludes: 'Unhappily, the lower classes, of whom two million are unemployed, are faithful patrons of the popular Press. So circulations increase and communists are made.'

Two days later, a counter-article. It points out women now have the vote, are entering into the universities and thus the professions, and the law had best reflect this new reality 'for Jill has no intention of going back into her box'. I grinned at that crack from a Mrs A. Trent; she had a sharp turn of phrase.

The following week moves on to the Birth Control Debate. Canon Chase opines: 'Large families are necessary and maternity is a sort of holiday.' He also notes if better classes reproduce less, they are in danger of being overrun. Then Dr James Cooper responds: 'Every woman should be the mistress of her own body, and it should be her own business to declare otherwise.'

The editorial adjudicates: 'Women want everything and don't know what they want. So men must make up their minds for them!'

Ho ho. I sighed and moved on.

The cinema is showing *Rio Rita*, the new Ziegfeld. Mr Ellyot the popular sportsman gives an illustrated lecture on his motorcycle travels through Burma (well attended by the ladies). Mrs Trent's Book Circle discuss *A Man Could Stand Up* by Ford Madox Ford. Also Mr Rubelik, 'World's Greatest Master of the Violin' plays Highlights from the Classics at Penang Town Hall.

And doctors, so many doctors. Dr Jamieson going on leave, Dr (Miss) Hermitson arrives. Dr M. Philpott retires as Chief Medical Officer. Dr Fairweather and Dr Gupta lecture on malaria prevention, while Dr Martineau applauds the falling infant mortality rates . . .

I noted things down at random. It was highly unlikely I'd find anything here, but I was becoming interested in this world for itself, it took my mind off so many things.

At the end of my second day at Colindale, I scrolled on to one last edition, and on page two found an odd little story that caught at my heart. 'Mr F.G. Ellyot is critically ill after a motorcycle accident. In his late 20s, he arrived a year ago to take up employment in the Public Works Department, but has already made many friends in Penang. A fine batsman, hockey forward, golfer, and useful rugby player, Mr Ellyot is in grave condition in the General Hospital.'

I was about to switch off when another name caught my eye. 'His friend, Mr P. Marsden, who is attending him, warned the rural roads on the island can be dangerous, and should be ventured on at night only with care.'

Odd way of putting it. Am I missing something here?

Time to go home.

'Oh, this is just so swish, Sandy! Don't you love it here?'

Sandy looks at Ann, her face golden with the low sun as they all head home in Marsden's Austin Seven from the Lone Pine. The palm trees flicker with the sea behind them. Inland, the kapongs and padi fields are a deep unlikely green. The windows are all down and moist hot air flows over his skin.

'It's not so bad,' he admits.

'Oh, you Scots! Can't you just enjoy what's here to be enjoyed?' She slaps his arm, then strokes it. Her eyes are blue like her sister's, but unhazed, doubt-free. It seems churlish to resist her high spirits or her beauty.

A flock of parrots stream low across the road. Marsden brakes, swerves, and they're gone into the trees. Ann has a basket of mangoes on her lap, and the whole car is sweet with them. *I sing the body electric . . .*

'Enjoyment?' Sandy says. 'We didn't do that in school. Where can I possibly find tuition in that?'

'I have some of the most backward pupils you can imagine,' Ann says. 'Yet the funny thing is, nearly every day they seem to learn something.'

This must be flirtation, he thinks. Silly inconsequential conversation. Yet it makes him feel lighter, whizzing along like this, talking nonsense with a very lively lassie pressing against him as she peels a mango with her little silver fruit knife.

'You must be a good teacher,' he says.

She hoods her eyes at him as if she's very short-sighted or he is hard to make out.

'I think so,' she replies. 'At least my lessons are fun. Here.'

He picks the orange mango slice from the blade, pops it in his mouth. Sees the sun going down so quickly into the greasy indigo sea. Sucks and slithers down the sweetness of it all.

Poor Alan is stuck up front with Marsden, Adele leaning out the window on the far side of Ann, eyes shut as the slipstream tugs her hair. The sisters have the same ears, he notes, neat and alert as squirrels'. She may or may not be listening.

'Delicious,' he says. 'I enjoyed that.'

Her smile is mango-soft. Her lips are mango-sweet, he remembers that.

'Here, have another,' she says. 'Not so hard, is it?'

Up front, Alan twitches.

It's already dark as they enter George Town by Gurney Drive. Along Millionaires Row the gleaming mansions, mostly Chinese-owned, are all electric-lit, but still the red and yellow lanterns are hung in the porticoes at the driveway end. One of them, Sandy now knows, is the home of the father of one of his patients, famous for his parties.

He sees Marsden's face, watching him in the rear-view mirror. The merest hint of a nod as they drive past the entrance to that house.

What's Marsden up to, making a proposal like that?

'You have a patient, Mrs Chew Yoo,' he'd said at the Lone Pine, offering a cigarette.

Sandy had nodded, accepted, lit up, the flame invisible the day was so bright. He could picture her fine. Narrow, rachitic pelvis, miracle the uterus hadn't ruptured already, otherwise healthy. She was in a room of her own on the top floor, the luxury wards. First baby stillborn at the Chinese hospital, second brain damaged in delivery. Now it's the turn of Western medicine. He's been rather looking forward to it.

Apparently, her father is important. Not just wealthy, but important, Marsden had insisted as they sat fully clothed in deckchairs under the trees. Politically important. A man of considerable ... influence. Not necessarily a benevolent influence either, if Sandy got his drift.

Sandy wasn't very sure he did, but nodded and waited. It was a new and quite enjoyable experience, watching Marsden ill at ease.

Chew Yoo's father is more than a businessman, he'd explained. Secret societies aren't as dramatic as they sound – think of the Masons, the Rotary and a bit of Board of Commerce thrown in – but this secret society is engaged in a small war with one of the others. The old Hakka and Hokkien rivalry. Mostly the Babas, the Straits-born Chinese, stay aloof from it all. Most important – and this is the bit that concerns the Commissioner and the jolly old HMG back home – this man has con-tacts with certain groups that are active in the northern interior, groups that are funded from another country where elements wish the Federated States no good at all. He thinks he can use them to further his clan's interests in the up-country, but Intelligence thinks they're using him.

Sandy drained the last of his beer, which seemed to have lost its snap.

'So what do you want from me?'

Nothing much, Marsden had insisted. Just it would be helpful to know who visits Mrs Chew Yoo. Sends flowers, notes of congratulation, that sort of thing. Births and funerals, old man, that's when the loyalties surface.

'You want me to spy for you?'

Marsden winced. He lit another a cigarette, appeared to examine the shrieking bathers.

'Nothing so dramatic, old chap. Just keep a note of the names. I'm off tomorrow to do ... some work in Singapore, so pass any info on to Freddie Ellyot.'

'I thought Ellyot was with the Public Works Department?'

Marsden smiled down into his hand.

'You could call it public works.'

Sandy had put Ellyot down as another public school sportsman, amiable, well mannered, nothing more. Star of the cricket club (fast left-arm bowler, dashing bat), swimming club, a near-scratch golfer whose long iron play Sandy can only admire and hope to learn from. All done in the most disarming, self-effacing way. Terrific teeth. Straight into the Penang Club, all the sporting clubs, popular with men and women. Invited everywhere, especially by European women with marriageable daughters, not that there were many of those. One of Ann Simpson's suitors, but then who isn't?

Freddie Ellyot, well well.

'I don't know what your politics are, Sandy,' Marsden said. 'None of my business. But you've seen what happens in a war.'

Sandy nodded, looked down at the dazzling sand.

'I rather think there's going to be another one, whatever we do. We're just trying to stop it spreading into this damn nice country. I have to know what's going on, any scrap of info at all.'

Sandy looked at him, this supposed remittance man, part-time translator, man about town, his occasional bridge partner (though they still play together once in a while, the cards don't seem to run so well for them as on the voyage out), perhaps Adele's lover.

'Trust me,' Marsden said. 'Please.'

Sandy had looked into those candid eyes. Saw a bead of sweat on the bristles of his fair moustache. Remembered Marsden's mischief, his pleasure in fleecing the MCS toffs and the appalling Ramsay. *It's not about the money.* For whatever reason, Marsden also felt himself outside that crowd.

'I don't understand Chinese names,' Sandy protested. 'And I can't read a word of it, like on notes or gifts.'

'That's all right,' Marsden said. 'I can find you an assistant who does. Just have her on the rounds with you. You need a translator and general assistant anyway, don't you? She can do Malay too, of course, and some Hindi. The hospital will fund it.'

Sandy thought about it. It was true, he really could do with a translator and note-taker. There'd already been too many mistakes and misunderstandings with patients.

'Did you have anyone in mind?' he asked.

Marsden had examined the tip of his cigarette, flicked the ash off it as he got to his feet.

'Adele Trent,' he said. 'Thanks, old man.'

They've dropped off Alan at the chummery he shares with another engineer and a Guthries man. Ann has squeezed Sandy's arm then suddenly kissed his cheek as she got off to meet her parents at the E&O. Adele looked across the breadth of the back seat and smiled vaguely at him in the dimness.

She's the Chief Medical Officer's wife and that's an end to it.

He's dropped off at the end of the alley behind the hospital. Adele gets out and moves into the front seat beside Marsden. He waves them goodnight, sees the car head on towards Light Street.

As he hurries across the hospital courtyard, he is already running through the rest of the evening. First check on Mrs Ashanti to reassure them both, pick up nasi gureng from a stall, then home for a beer cool from the Shanghai jar and a think about what the heck's he's getting into.

He strides up the steps two at a time but still just fails to beat Mr Singh to opening the main door. He prefers to open his own doors, but sometimes others get there first. He grins, raises his hand in salutation as he passes into a world where he's needed.

※

17

It was one of those rare winter mornings you get in Orkney, still and clean-bright like salt has scoured the light. Hyperoceanic. I was at my desk early and feeling virtuous. My second day back from South, the town below still looked low and tiny, and there was a vast amount of open space over Scapa Flow and the Orphir hills. The low sun on the water shone like the head of a young woman in a London street.

When I looked away, the rest of the world was bleached out and dim. I blinked, then focused on Ellen and Ray crossing the playground. They must have come from dropping off Cara at school, and they were talking and laughing. She'd cut and tinted her hair while I'd been away. Now springy as a seventies filament lamp, it shone bright copper in the sharp light.

They looked up at my window. Ray cut a caper, she just waved, looking quite different in tailored slacks instead of her usual long ethnic skirts and dresses.

They came in full of the joys.

'I've a new toy for you all!' Ray announced, producing a silver palm-top computer from his coat pocket. 'We can hook this up to the wave measuring buoys,' he said. 'Then we can sit here and watch the waves as the info downloads.'

'Is this really necessary?' Anne-Marie asked.

'Not really,' Ray admitted. 'I thought it might be soothing, boss. Help us chill and focus our thoughts, instead of those clicky balls that sad execs have.'

So he hooked it up to the receiver from the buoys off Birsay and Warebeth and we all grouped round his desk. He placed it in front of his four big talking *South Park* dolls that had been last month's toy, and switched on.

We were spellbound, watching the two sets of wave troughs rise and fall as they marched in jagged irregular peaks and troughs across the screen. It was daft because the real waves were always there, anyone could go along the shore and watch them any time, but they seemed much more interesting and extraordinary like this. I recalled my unsuccessful attempt at ambient recordings of the sea. This was closer to what I'd had in mind.

'It's like a brain-wave scanner,' Ellen said eventually. 'We're watching the sea thinking.'

'Ah bollocks,' Stevie retorted, practical Orcadian to the core. 'It's just waves waving.'

'Reminds me of the movement of the Dow Jones Index,' Anne-Marie said.

I thought it was like irregular heart-rhythms, the ones I'd seen on a hospital screen after my dad's first heart attack, but I didn't say and we all watched on in silence.

'Oh look, there's a big one!'

Duncan leant forward. 'Two point five metres peak to trough,' he announced. 'The record so far is four point nine.'

'Got an idea,' I said. 'What if we wrote a program converting these wave movements to sound frequency, and set it in human range? I mean, what would it sound like if we could *listen* to this?'

Duncan frowned. 'You mean listen to the sound of the sea?'

'No,' I said. 'The sound of the *shape* of the sea.'

'Ambient,' Ellen murmured. 'It could be the ultimate ambient music. Nice one, Eddie.'

She looked at me properly for what I realised was the first time that morning. I grinned back, quite pleased with myself.

'I take it when you say "if we wrote" you mean me?' Ray said.

Anne-Marie tapped her teeth with her pen, a habit that had been bugging us all for weeks. 'In your own time,' she said, then went back to her desk to work on her Christmas shopping list.

'I'll check it out, Eddie,' Ray said. 'See what I can do.'

Then he and Duncan went back to their cubicles, leaving me and Ellen watching the pair of green lines rise and fall across the screen. The Warebeth one – it must be the early part of the tide-race – was vigorous and choppy, while the signal from Birsay was near regular, melodic. I turned the knob and brought the two signals into convergence so they ran across each other to make new patterns.

I suppose it was chaos, but it was oddly soothing. As I stood beside her, the little aerial voice offered, *This could be.*

'Still coming down to the session at the Flying Dutchman tonight?' she asked.

'What session?'

'We talked about it yesterday, Eddie.'

'Oh,' I said. '*That* session.'

I had no memory of her mentioning it.

'Like the new look,' I said. 'You seem much . . . lighter.'

She shrugged but didn't seem displeased.

'I don't know,' I said. 'It'll likely be mostly fiddles. I like songs and people saying something emotional, so long as it's not twenty-five verses about the Lancashire cotton weavers' strike in 1897, or someone's true love coming back after ten years and trying to seduce their fiancée who quite incredibly fails to recognise them.'

'Know what you mean,' she said. 'But true loves aren't always that easy to recognise. Takes a while sometimes.'

I nodded, thinking of her and Ray, their obvious pleasure in each other's company.

'There'll be Blues players there,' she offered. 'And Duncan's bringing his harmonicas.'

Duncan was not a chatty man. He was from Aberdeen. Only diving and playing harp lit him up, but he was passionate and more than competent at both.

'I'll be there,' I said. 'Ray coming too?'

'He said he might be along later,' she said vaguely. Then we both turned to look at the screen for more wave action. It went on as before, always different, always the same, so fervently saying nothing we could understand.

It's his favourite time of day in Malaya, the hour before and after dawn. Li Tek – now installed as his full-time cookboy, doorkeeper, messenger and guide through the backstreets of George Town – wakes him back of five. Leaves a mug of steaming sweetened chai and a ricecake by the bed. *Fine day, Doctor! Busy day!* he whispers, along with a wink if he's in a good mood, then opens the shutters one by one.

The dawn doesn't come up like thunder. That's complete balls. Instead as he sips his tea, the near-silence is abruptly shredded by shrieks, gibbers and wails as first light hits the dark padang trees across the courtyard. Birds don't sing in this country, they shout their heads off in tones harsh and glaring as their plumage.

Once in a while he might think of the liquid burble of the dowdy thrushes in the bush outside his parents' window, the pale haze of bluebells under the trees upriver from Perth – but on the whole he drinks his tea, enjoying the cacophony outside. He's glad to be out of his shattered country, its endless dreichness of skies and mind, the patrolling ministers and the girls either prissy or downcast. Scotland's a place where everyone explains what is not possible, that it'll all end in tears, we're here to make the best of a bad job then die and get a good rest till we're woken up to be informed we're damned.

Lot of bloody nonsense. These days he'd rather swear on Mr Whitman. Something un-Scottish and bracing in those praises of life, work, leisure, the body, desire ...

He eats the sticky ricecake slowly. Then it's time to crouch on the tiles by the Shanghai jar, ladle great washes of cool water with the wooden gayong scoop over his sticky skin, feel his mind shock awake.

Coarse towel, clean shirt, cotton suit. Black shoes, wool tie, straw hat. Cool and dry for the only time in the day, walking with Li Tek to the hospital, the boy beside him greeting the vendors, the hawkers, the first rickshaw boys out and about.

Sandy has never stopped feeling uneasy about being rickshawed. Something about watching another man – usually just a laddie, or an emaciated elderly Chinese – strain and sweat between the shafts. He can never forget he comes from a long line of domestic servants on his mother's side and farm workers on his father's. The first time he got into a rickshaw, with Alan down at the Butterworth Quay, he'd felt hilarious elation. Him, the saddler's laddie frae Brechin, up in a rickshaw! And then came unease as the boy sweated and staggered on an uphill, stood heaving at the top like a skinny horse.

So he walks to work, enjoying watching the streets wake up, the incense lit, carts loaded, charcoal fires blown back into life, babies held up to the first daylight. He likes beginnings, before it all goes arse up and agley. That's why this job is right for him. Or would be, if only he was left alone to do it.

Past the nightwatchman at the gate, *Good morning, Doctor, sir!* up the steps into the hospital. His hospital. A miraculous place where a number of people go in and a larger number come out.

Up the broad staircase two at a time. Along the silent corridors of pillars and balustrades, the shutters still barred so it's dim and cool. Lances of light through the cracks warp round his feet. Behind him Miss Gibbs starts opening the shutters; he can hear them squeak, sees the light spreading ahead as he turns the corner and climbs up to the next floor.

This is the best time, while the day is still cool and not quite begun, before his mind is cluttered and the sweat itches under his arms. This is the time he will come back to in old age when he finally allows his mind to return here. In the hour before tea, before his wife wakes him from the armchair, when he lets himself drift back to Penang it is not to the esplanade nor the temples, not the cricket ground nor the Penang Club nor the E&O hotel, nor the cock-eyed wooden bungalow that had been his home. Instead, he is walking again along the silent upper corridors of his hospital through bars of light, still cool, still fresh, as yet unmarked.

Now he walks along the topmost gallery. Shutters open behind him like sluice gates, yellow light floods the corridor. This is the floor where the first-class patients come, for the higher ceilings, the fans, the individual rooms, the better nurses and food they can order from outside. The better-off Chinese and Malays could easily afford it, but many of them still prefer to have their children at home or in their own hospital – though since his successes with Mrs Oon Hung Chong and Mrs Choon Seng (a satisfactory breech, an emergency Caesarean, both patients would likely have died without his intervention), that has begun to change.

Next floor down are the cheaper second-class wards for British government servants, teachers and the like. On the ground floor the crowded, stuffy wards for those who can't pay at all. They have to bring their own bucket, twine, scissors, catgut, and the nursing is done by irregulars. The painful inequality of this is something he and Trent agree needs to be addressed. Problem is the Colonial Office won't come up with the money so it's a matter of trying to divert funds from wealthy donors or elsewhere. For this he needs allies, people like Trent, Marsden (who for some reason is on the Board), Daniel Ng the young Administrator.

Sandy's rounds are further complicated by the languages – he hasn't found a nursing assistant who can speak Malay, Chinese, Hindi and English. Until now.

He hesitates outside the door at the end of the corridor. This is the one Marsden asked him about at the Swimming Club. Enthroned in there amid banks of flowers, fruits, cards and Good Fortune dragons is Mrs Chew Yoo. Though she's young and tiny, like many Chinese she is infinitely superior, while being scrupulously polite.

Uneasy, he turns away from her door. Miss Gibbs works her way along, opening one shutter after another onto the day. Convent girl, calm and self-contained. So few possible women here, so many men after them. No wonder everyone goes a little mad or throws themselves into sports. When a man goes down to Singapore or KL for a few days, one doesn't ask. He hasn't been yet, but it'll be hard to resist when his first holiday comes. Or maybe Java. Or Sumatra. So many islands, so much still out there . . .

Mrs Chew Yoo. The baby had felt large and awkwardly positioned when he'd palpated yesterday. See how she is today, then if necessary induce tomorrow so everyone's on hand.

'It's a fine morning, Dr Mackay.'

'It is that,' he says, stands aside as she pulls the shutters back. They stand together looking out onto the courtyard, the red tiled roofs, the murky green haze of Kedang hill, the blue-grey Strait and the mainland a low haze through the pinang and travellers palms. Smell of woodsmoke from morning fires blends with frangipani, acanthus, and carbolic from Miss Gibbs's uniform.

'Quiet night,' she says. 'Even the mice slept. Two new admissions this morning – the reports are in Matron's.'

'Aye, fine,' he says.

It's an informality between consultant and nurse that would never be allowed back home. He likes that, still resenting the slights, the near-contempt of his houseman years. Several senior consultants he'd still like to boot up the arse. Another good reason for leaving. Save some money for a few years, go back home, buy into a practice. Is that the plan? Now he's got this far, got through the war, university, survived the flu then a nasty sub-periphrenaic abscess the fools failed to diagnose, is there a plan at all?

Nurse Gibbs's flat heels click off down the stair, mingle with others coming up. He keeps looking out the window, enjoying the last minute of the day being simple and cool. Sometimes he has a feeling people are making plans for him, that all his meetings and choices are not his own, that though he got his discharge papers more than a decade ago, he's still enlisted.

'*There* you are, Dr Mackay. Lovely morning.'

She sounds cool, amused, but Adele doesn't smell of carbolic. He nods, keeps looking out the window. She stands beside him, leaning on the balustrade. Because the window embrasure is narrow, her bare shoulder brushes his arm. He can feel the warmth through his suit. She smells, oh God she smells, she smells like her sister only less sweet and more ...

'It's a wonderful country, you know,' she says quietly, as if talking to herself as much as to him. 'Especially Penang. So many different peoples here, from so many places, and it more or less works. It's not India. It's not Somerset Maugham either.'

'That's a mercy,' he says.

'My great-uncle came out to Upper Perak in 1853. He's buried in the Muslim cemetery in Malacca – converted, you see. Said that was the only way to truly understand the Malays. My grandfather thought that was going too far and moved to KL which was just a muddy village then. He loved the country in the same way. Malaria got him in the end. He was the last person to be buried in the old cemetery here, just along from Sir Francis Light ... '

As he turns his head to look at her, she tails off. She's all in yellow, even the shoes, like some tall trumpeting flower. Clutching a notebook in one hand, an orange in the other, eyes the colour of the sky back home. Either he can't look at her at all, or he sees her perfectly. This has never happened before. Right now he can see she's raised, eyes almost too bright as her lips part and chatter.

'What's Marsden up to?' he asks.

She's silent a moment, looking into his face. 'Best not ask,' she says.

'What's your part in it?'

'I was born here, I speak Malay,' she replies. 'I picked up some Chinese when I was a girl, then began studying properly at Oxford. But I left early to get married, and since then ... ' She tails off. 'Phillip's been coaching me, especially in the reading side. He's a gifted man.'

'I'm sure he is,' Sandy says.

He takes out his Gold Flake, offers her one. She shakes her head. He leans out the window and lights up. First of the day, the sweetest.

'Married women aren't really expected to work,' she says. 'I get so bored of tennis and reading and going to talks, and everyone drinking too much.' She laughs, not amused. 'Me included. Finally John ... It was felt I should go home to pick up Ann, keep her out of trouble on the boat over with Emily. I think we all hoped a break would help things, but ... '

She breaks off, looks away to the south so he can't see her eyes.

'*A talent that is death to hide, lodged in me useless,*' he murmurs. 'It must be frustrating.'

'Yes!' she cries. 'It bloody is. It's all right for Ann, she's not married, she can work.' She tries to smile. 'I suppose I was meant to be passing time until ... well, you know.'

Then she shrugs. He sees her clavicle rise and fall then in an instant he loses all medical knowledge of her. Her body is a cage of light, radiating at him. He has no prior experience of this. His cigarette burns unattended as he stares.

'So,' she says brightly. 'It's jolly fine to be of some use.'

'What does ... Trent say?'

'He's not terribly keen, but he knows enough to see it needs to be done. That it might ... help.'

He looks at her for a long time as she looks back at him. Who is helping whom? he wonders. Is this why Marsden took up with me, nothing to do with cards? Why can I no longer remember the names of the bones of her hands?

'Let's see how it goes,' he says.

18

That night the Flying Dutchman, that vile but uniquely atmospheric howff of South End, was crackling. We generated enough heat to make the yellowed walls sweat with condensation, and even the villainous red-haired one-eyed landlord – reputed to be the only surviving member of the seventies heavy rock band Three Dog Night, which I thought unlikely though he was certainly near-deaf – smiled as he turned round from the till. Maybe it was Christmas coming on, but it was one of those nights when everyone is up for it, and one of the fiddlers had repetitive strain injury so there were fewer of the same old jigs and reels.

Instead there was Western Swing from the resident Smoking Stone Band, my idea of perfect music, conjoining Texan Country with Orcadian fiddles to the advantage of each – mongrel music for a mongrel people, for that is what we are. They were followed by acoustic R&B from the eclectic Zurich Brothers (who were neither brothers nor from Zurich nor even Swiss in any way) with Duncan wailing and bubbling on harmonicas like a dolphin in heat. People talked, drank, listened, sang in open session. It was musical and emotional and social, most of the things I'd hoped for when I came here.

I took up my G banjo and did my hillbilly version of 'Honey Allow Me One More Chance' and noticed Kipper Johnson the fisherman joining in. A true Dylan fan then, knew the early early stuff. Sure enough, five minutes later he sat next to me, plonked a pint down.

I thanked him, put aside the banjo and we talked awhile under the music, it being that kind of session where listening isn't compulsory. He looked more piratical than ever, face all roughened from weather though he must have been a good decade younger than me. Dark hair back in a ponytail, earring and all. He struck me as bright and frustrated. A kind of pent-up edge to him as he drank fast and talked quickly in broad Orcadian I had trouble following.

I bought him a pint in return and he stayed on sitting among the musicians.

'Can you play 'Tomorrow Is A Long Time', boy?'

I nodded. 'Right key,' I said.

'Play then.'

He was sounding slightly slurred. Past his shoulder, I saw Mica standing staring across at us, glass in hand. I nodded to her but she gave a small quick shake of her head and looked away.

'Sure,' I said. 'Why not?'

So I played and Kipper sang and Mica watched a while before she turned away again to talk to the group of people she'd arrived with. I knew none of them and was reminded that though I was starting to feel at home here, there were circles, friendships and allegiances I knew nothing of.

He sang it well, in a raw, hesitating way that let feeling come through, a longing for something never truly had. It stilled the chatter in the room as he sang the three short simple verses. When he finished the silence went on, the best applause there is. Then the other applause.

Kipper looked down, went red. His head came up, he drained his pint, picked up a whisky from the table, knocked it back in one.

'Here, that was mine!'

It was young Douglas Anderson, one of my DOA students and a lively spoons player. Kipper glared at him. There was a long pause. I carefully moved my banjo aside.

'Was it, boy?' Kipper said. 'And whaur are you fae?'

So it had come down to that again.

'Derry.'

Another pause. One of the fiddlers started playing. Kipper silenced her with a quick sweep of his big red hand. I saw Mica standing just outside our group, watching. Then his hand went inside his denim jacket and flicked a fiver onto the table.

'Well, Mr Derry,' he said contemptuously. 'Get yoursel and me another.'

Douglas looked at the note then up at Kipper. He was younger and lighter than Kipper Johnson but his eyes were very angry. Out the corner of my eye, I could see a couple of Kipper's mates drifting closer. Douglas was with a local lass and couple of hefty student pals. He leaned forward, about to speak.

I reached across, picked up the money.

'I'll get them,' I said. 'I'm going up anyhow.'

I was standing at the bar collecting up the drinks. Glanced back, saw Mica bending over Kipper, her arm trailing over his back.

'Well done, youth.'

I turned. It was Ray, with Ellen beside him.

'Well,' I said, 'I didn't think it was time for the OK Corral yet. I hate it when a good session goes sour.'

I looked back at our table. Now Mica had her arm round his arm, smiling and laughing into his face.

'They know each other well?' I asked.

Ray and Ellen looked at each other then at me.

'Of course,' she said.

'They used to go out before she went South,' Ray added. 'Quite an item – the lobster laddie and the county planner's daughter. Big thing at the time, with her older and all.'

I nodded, hung on to that past tense.

'Interesting fella,' I said. 'Shame about the drink.'

'More interesting than you'd guess,' Ray said quietly.

Again that quick collusive glance between him and Ellen. I felt piggy in the middle and irritated.

'What d'you mean?'

Ray hesitated.

'Oh, just that he doesn't hold with the redneck values but still he's part of it. And his father – well his dad used to beat him and his brother. A lot. Nasty piece of work. You've got to sympathise.'

'Yes,' I said. 'Sure.'

I'd a feeling I'd been palmed off. Still, it did make it easier to feel for Kipper.

'You can see the attraction,' Ellen said. 'I mean, those snake hips and the sailor's eyes ...'

'Catch you later,' I said, and carried the drinks over to the table.

I sat down in the empty seat beside Kipper. Mica had seen me coming over and scarpered back to her friends. The whole thing was getting very silly. I just wanted a good night out with some songs of love, death, heartache and randiness, all our human stuff.

Douglas Anderson took his whisky and had the good sense to move away. Kipper and I did another couple of numbers at his insistence. We went on too long and it didn't feel right any more. He sang 'She's Your Lover Now', an obscure and difficult Dylan bootleg, and he kept looking over at Mica as he shouted it out.

We'd lost it. I put the banjo down.

'Play "I Shall Be Released",' Kipper slurred.

As it happened I loved the song but it was time to call a halt.

'Maybe later,' I said. 'Let someone else have a shot.'

His hand clamped down on my arm, his young weathered face was close to mine.

'Fuckin' play it,' he said.

An arm wrapped round my shoulder.

'Hey, Eddie, how you doing?' Ray said. 'Kipper! How's it hanging?'

He plonked himself down beside me, still glad-handing. Kipper muttered something then instead of hitting him got up quickly and weaved over toward the bar. He looked at Mica. She hesitated then signed him the quick *See you around* I'd come to know well, and turned back to her friends. Kipper tacked past the corner of the bar and disappeared into the night.

I picked up the guitar next to me and started to play Lou Reed's 'What Goes On'. I hadn't a clue, didn't care, didn't want to care.

I parted with Ray and Ellen outside the Dutchman. There was some hesitation when I thanked him for cutting in. Then I looked at him, waited.

He shrugged.

'Kipper owes me,' he said. 'We go ... back.'

I said goodnight and left them to walk back together to her cottage in North End, and I set off one more time alone through the silent flagstone street.

The gable ends, the slates and chimney pots and crow-stepped gables, the wynds and angles and the quick glimpses down to the old piers – in the sodium lights the empty street looked more than ever like a film set. I glimpsed my father as a young man, hurrying home through the clinging sultry streets of George Town from a late assignation or a cards game turned sour. I saw his crumpled pale suit and brown hair flopping forward, the sleeping vendors and rickshaw lads curled up in their livings, a woman in a lemon yellow dress who was burning in his mind. I saw he too was hurrying from one fire towards another.

The banjo case banged my knee. I winced and he was gone and Alfred Square was empty except for a pair of sparking green eyes on a car bonnet. A hiss and it too was gone as I went to stroke.

There were no lights on at my place, and I was glad of it. The front door clunked but a little lift of the handle and it didn't scrape. I'd surely get the hang of it before my time here was done.

So Adele Trent accompanies Dr Mackay through his morning rounds, along with Dr Dhoti the registrar, two Malay housemen, and the ward nurses. Glancing at her, trying to read the meaning of her nods and silences, her frowns and laughter, reminds him how much he knows of the workings of women, and how very little. She translates between him and his patients, she takes notes. Then once the routine is established, they call in on Mrs Choo Yew quite late in the round.

They are in no hurry; the two women chat and laugh, glance at Sandy once in a while. He notices how the tiny young woman sits up more, looks less dwarfed by her gifts, after Adele has been with her. Then as Sandy examines her, discusses the case with the registrar and arranges for the delivery, Adele idly glances at the cards, the presents. She stands behind Sandy, making notes.

Then they leave, arranging to come back again during the afternoon visiting hours.

Adele hands him her notes as they walk down Macalister Lane.

'There are a couple of names there that surprise me – the Hakka don't usually associate with Straits-born Chinese.'

He puts the list in his jacket without comment. It's not quite breaking patient confidentiality, but he doesn't like it.

'You've been a help,' he admits. 'I can't do all the diagnostic work on the evidence of my senses. I need to know what they have to say.'

'Good,' she says gaily. 'It might become quite a regular thing.' She takes his arm as they cross Transfer Street through a flow of carts, cars and rickshaws. 'Lunch at the Runnymede?'

Usually he eats something at a street stall – he's become quite addicted to anything with ginger, lime and chilli, can't have too much of that glorious burning in his throat – then goes home for the afternoon lie-off. An hour or two dozing under the slow fan, reading, or writing his short weekly letter home. Or to the E&O on Thursdays to pick up any mail off the boat then flip through the *Penang Gazette*.

Her arm tightens in his.

'Go on,' she says. 'Ice-cold mangosteen! I insist on signing the chit – my first day's wages and all that.'

'In that case – yes.'

When she laughs back up at him, it happens again. Her body is no longer a body but a long yellow flame flickering beside him as they walk down the dazzling colonnades.

19

I was sitting at the kitchen table, going through the notes I'd made in Edinburgh and London, wondering if it was worth writing to Mrs Cunninghame or whether I should just drop the whole thing. The front door had just opened, very quietly. Someone who'd learned and adapted. It was nearly midnight.

'I saw the light,' Mica said, almost apologetic. 'Okay?'

I nodded. Black cords and black crochet cardigan over grey T-shirt, carrying her big jacket over her shoulder, she was smarter than usual. It also looked like she was short of sleep. She sat down and we looked each other over.

'So,' she said at last. 'Have a good trip South?'

'Not bad,' I replied. 'The break was good for me.'

She nodded vehemently. I'd forgotten the energy she brought to being alive, her edginess, the challenge of her. She wasn't soft, she was maybe even a bit flaky, but she did glint.

'You need to get off the island every couple of months or you go stir-crazy. Or start thinking it's everything, which is the same.'

I remembered that curling quick sardonic mouth on mine as she tipped her fingers in acknowledgement to my Buddha.

'Hi, Bud,' she said. 'Hang in there.' Then she focused on me. 'So did you get anywhere in your research?'

'Why would you be interested?'

'Because you're my friend. And I like a good quest.'

I looked for irony but saw none. So I made us tea and told her about my session with the imperious Mrs Cunninghame. About going to Bob Taylor's house in London and finding I was too late. About the *Penang Gazette*. That I'd found nothing revelatory, but the glimpses had sharpened my interest.

I didn't mention my brief encounter with a life-enhancing young woman with a jammed starter motor, who had lingered in my mind long after she'd driven away. After all, it wasn't important and it was none of Mica's business, for we'd never been a couple and now we weren't even whatever we had briefly been.

She drained her mug and jumped up.

'Come a walk with me, Eddie.'

'Why should I want to do that?'

Her head was down as she struggled into her ancient padded jacket. She freed her hair out from under the collar and flicked it back. It was such a woman's gesture, so universal and unconscious, it got under my defences.

'Because it's a clear night with a china-white gibbous moon and because . . .'

'Yes?'

'Because I'm a ratbag who can say sorry better outdoors.'

We walked through the silent flagstone streets past fragments of moon collected in puddles. Past the window with the sleeping caged cockatiel, watched on our way by the cats that own Stromness by night. Out by Login's Well, past the cannon that once signalled the departure of the Hudson's Bay Company ships. All the little landmarks of my territory and the place that had claimed me.

I wondered how clear an apology I'd get, and what exactly she'd apologise for. Beyond that, I didn't think I was that bothered any more. A good night's sleep and a good day's work were more important.

We went through the little gate and onto the golf course, climbed up the brae then walked out along the ninth fairway. With the moon up and our eyes adjusted, it was quite light and we cast shadows on the grass. A faint roar from the Sound of Hoy, the cry of a gull in the night.

We reached the wooden pavilion perched like an ornamental hat on the crown of the golf course. We sat on the bench and leaned forwards onto the little rail. Across the water the Hoy hills put me in mind of dark looming breasts with moonlit tips. Naturally, I kept this notion to myself.

'I often think,' Mica said thoughtfully, 'from this angle those hills look like a man's bum. Mind if I?'

She lifted her pack of cigarettes. Not like her to ask. I waited, curious. Something of the spirit of that night, the cold and the clarity, let me feel amused at us.

She lit up. The flare spoiled my night vision but gave me glimpses of her face in the glow of her inhale. The harsh-sweet reek of cigarette smoke in the night brought back the nefarious doings of late adolescence; assignations, whispered partings, hormonal encounters in wynds of the sleeping town. Apparently, I was still at it. I hadn't expected my forties to be like this.

'My dad's decided he likes you,' she said abruptly.

'I suppose that doesn't count in my favour.'

She laughed quietly. 'Maybe not. He says you're an idiot but a grown-up.'

'Very kind.'

'You're not my type, really,' she continued. 'I mean if this was right, Eddie, if it was really right, sheet anchors wouldn't hold us back. We'd be all over each other and drowning in intense scenes.'

I remembered those days of confusing love with overwhelming need and anxiety. They weren't that much fun.

'So what is your type, Mica?'

'Oh, young, skinny, electric. Creative-destructive. There was a painter once. And a musician – well, a drummer, which is maybe not the same.'

'And a lobster fisherman?'

'Kipper? He's no intellectual, our Kip, but he's got that edge. But you ...'

She glanced sideways at me. I held my stomach in. I'm that age, I've filled out. I'm a man not a youth.

'You're *solid*. If a bit disturbed,' she added. 'Disturbed is good. In this world you'd have to be thick not to be disturbed.'

I had mixed feelings about the 'solid', but it was then, sitting looking at Hoy under the starry sky round midnight, that I knew for sure I'd passed my midlife crisis. My issue now wasn't with accepting maturity. It was with mortality. That should keep me busy for the rest of my time.

I glanced at her profile, framed by the hood of her jacket. The long ski-jump nose, wide mouth so quick to laugh or turn down in disgust, her restless hidden eyes. She dragged on that cigarette as though she was trying to suck its fire into herself.

'So – Kipper?' I said.

'Old business, believe me,' she said curtly. I did. She was one who might do many things, but I felt lying wasn't among them. She had too much pride. 'Sorry he was being an arse the other night. Drink doesn't agree with him but it's part of the culture. He turns into his father, and he hates that, which makes him more angry.'

That was too close to home for me to comment. She sucked the cigarette to its root, flipped it away and turned to me.

'So ... what about it?'

'What about what?'

I didn't intend to make this easy.

'I take back that about you being passive just because you're decent enough to put up with me. And I shouldn't have made that crack about your memory.'

'What crack about my memory?'

She looked at me.

'You know, about—'

She broke off, seeing my giggle. She punched me on the shoulder, fairly gently. 'I'd still rather you phoned before coming round. It matters to me that no one important comes into my space when I'm not ready.' I was silent. 'That's a request not a demand. It's nothing personal. Can you understand that?'

'I suppose.' I was thinking *Nothing personal.* But personal is what I want. I want very personal. People talk about boundaries and personal space, but I want an end to distance and the dissolving of personal space.

'I have missed you, you know. You have no preconceptions about me. And though you pretend you're Mr Normal, you're weird enough for me.'

'I take it you mean that as a compliment.'

'I certainly do. And we're quite good at . . . Yon.'

'Our bodies seem to like each other,' I admitted. I stepped down onto the grass and she followed me.

'So – your place or mine?'

I didn't answer as we set off back across the golf course.

'I should tell you,' she said suddenly. 'I can't do soft. You might believe there's a soft vulnerable centre to me that you can find, but I'm like this all the way through.'

'Yeah yeah,' I said as we stumbled through the bunker at the seventh. 'Mica the mineral.'

I didn't believe her, of course. Hard centres come only in certain selection boxes. The half moon was indeed gibbous and hung just over the Kame of Hoy, its light smithereened in the tide race. Still, the game was afoot again, even if the crime had yet to be committed.

'Your place,' I said. 'I haven't shared a single bed for years.'

Dear Father and Mother,

The hospital is running quite well now. I have a competent matron and a new day ward sister, and Mr Ng – a sound chap even though he speaks posher English than the minister's wife! – has formed a scheme to divert funds for the lower wards. We had seven births last week, one quite challenging.

I still have to do examinations of some Muslim women through a hole in a blanket, which is daft but better than no examination at all!

Though I'm beginning to acclimatise, I still have to change my collar several times a day. The rainy season is coming soon, so I've been on the golf course when I can. The golf here is quite fair, and I play with Ellyot who is much better than me, and Alan Hayman, who is not. It is so humid that we need to take salt tablets after nine holes. There's a hill called Penang Hill with a funicular railway, and it's much fresher up there – almost like a very fine summer day at home. I hope to go—

He breaks off writing. Marsden drops his hat on the little rattan table, accepts a beer from the Shanghai jar.

'Thanks awfully for the info,' he says. 'We have to keep an eye on these shifting allegiances. Things aren't as stable here as they might look. Cheers.'

'According to the paper, things are going to cock everywhere,' Sandy says. 'So it was a waste of money, time and men, that bloody war.' He raises his bottle of pale ale. 'Cheers.'

Marsden looks at him thoughtfully, then his fingers flicker and he opens his hand.

'This is what it was all about, you know.'

Sandy stares at the thin green pod in Marsden's palm but can see no revelation there.

'Pepper,' Marsden says. 'Spices. Curry. Before tin and rubber, while we were still running around in woad, these islands were wealthy civilisations. And they'll still be here when we're gone.'

He stares down at the pod, takes a swig from his beer. He looks weary and withdrawn, Sandy thinks. Almost defeated. Perhaps things haven't gone well in Singapore.

'Spices are what brought Francis Light here. Also the Portuguese, the

156

Dutch, and way before that, traders, farmers and refugees from China, India, Persia. All this' – with a sweep of his arm, Marsden gestures to include the hospital, the town, all Malaya in darkness outside – 'because we like a little savour to our salted meat.' He twists and crushes the pod between his neat fingers. 'We like a little spice, we do. Can't resist it.'

They sit for a while in silence under the slow turning electric punkah that pushes hot moist air around the little room. Sandy has been offered a bigger place on the outskirts, cooler too, but he prefers to be near the hospital in this makeshift bungalow. In any case, he needs to save money. He wants some kind of bulwark. Money helps, he's not daft.

'There's no end to it, is there?' Marsden says suddenly. 'Just one kind of trouble, or another kind. Sometimes I wonder why I bother.'

Sandy prefers this perplexed Marsden to the suave, amused smooth ladies' man.

'Cheer up,' he says. 'There's always work.'

Marsden fusses with his finger over his eye again, as if he were trying to rub away a headache or a sticking thought.

'And what is there after work?'

Sandy turns the cool bottle in his hand. Doesn't usually drink afternoon weekdays.

'Golf,' he says. 'There's aye golf.'

Marsden looks at him. Then starts to chuckle. Then throws his head back and laughs.

'You're right, Sandy. There's always golf.'

Marsden sits up in the only easy chair, seems to have got his snap back. 'So Mrs Chew Yoo had her baby. Boy, was it?'

'Aye. The delivery was a challenge for both of us, though she did most of the work. They seemed pleased – gave me this wee tubby chap in exchange for their own.'

Marsden picks the ceramic Buddha off the table. Turns it over in his neat little hands, smoothes fingers over the crimson jar, the shining white head, tilts it over to look at the inscription.

'This tubby chap is a Good Fortune Buddha,' he says. 'Said to be very good joss – good luck. This one is no tourist gewgaw – it comes from the temple workshop. They'll have had it in for blessing so it's even more powerful.' He sets it down carefully. 'You probably think that's a load of nonsense, but it's still an honour.'

'I'll take all the protection I can get,' Sandy replies.

'That's very wise,' Marsden says.

They sit silent for a minute, looking at the little Buddha sitting in the slatted afternoon light.

'Still, you might get the shutters secured and a decent bolt for the door,' Marsden adds.

'What you did with Mrs Chew Yoo – I may have to ask you to do that again from time to time. With Mrs Trent's assistance, of course.' Marsden pauses at the door, rotating his hat between small pale hands. 'Is that all right?'

His eyes, Sandy realises, aren't steady. They just seem that way. There's a fine rapid blinking of the upper lids, as though he's taking many pictures very fast.

Sandy just nods, wondering again how he got into this, what exactly is being offered.

'Thanks, old chap.' Marsden fits his hat on, adjusts the angle as he looks out into the dark compound. 'Oh, and if you don't mind me putting you up for the Penang Club, you'll find you'll get in.'

'Me? They'd never.'

'Mrs Ashanti's husband is on the admissions committee. He seems to think you're personally responsible for his wife still being alive.'

'That place is way beyond me,' Sandy says. He remembers the two times he's been taken there as a guest. The hush of the club room, the confident laughter from the bar, the boys moving soundlessly with trays of drinks. 'It's for the bigwigs. The *senior wallahs*,' he adds sardonically.

'Things are changing,' Marsden says easily. 'And with the bottom falling out of rubber, the membership's declining. They're so desperate they're taking in the wealthy Malays, Straits Chinese, and even impoverished Scottish doctors. And don't worry on that score – the hospital, well the MCS really, would pay your membership.'

Sandy hesitates. He's tempted and repelled by the Penang Club. It floats on a sea of green lawn off Northam Road like some stately ship from an earlier age. Part of him wants aboard. The other part is intimidated and repulsed. That gallery of past presidents, staring out half-mad from mutton-chop whiskers. One or two look like real characters, the rest remind him of more mighty versions of the people who terrorised his childhood, the teachers, ministers, elders.

'Decent food, all the newspapers and rags from home,' Marsden says, still looking out into the night. 'Drink's cheap too. A chap can have company or be left on his own when he wants – might make a change from sitting here nights. Oh, and the best billiard tables in the Straits Settlements.'

Billiards. He'd played with pals as a loon still at the school, before he dropped everything to work for the bursary. Then again at university, to relax between study sessions. The evening before leaving for the train to

Liverpool, he'd had a final game with his father in the local hall. He couldn't remember who'd won, but he was glad they'd done it.

'It'll always be the same choice, Sandy,' Marsden says. He has this gift for suddenly being intimate and natural, or maybe it's just another way of working people. 'You can either stay out of it and complain, or get inside and help change it.'

As Marsden looks at him, Sandy senses he's been passed one thing with another wrapped inside it.

'All right,' Sandy says. 'Put me up for it.'

20

Her note was on my table when I got back from an evening at
Stevie's. *Come see if poss. Bored as fuck – M.* Though it was late, I
went round. Stood in the street looking up at her light then went
up those narrow tatty stairs.

She was slumped on the bedroom windowseat, wrapped into herself in
a old green dressing gown. No curtains, so behind her was darkness,
Scapa Flow, a sprinkling of lights on the Erland shore across the bay. She
looked up, smiled faintly. Not a happy bunny, then.

'This is not a fuckfest,' she said. 'Okay?'

'Fine,' I said. 'I'll have a consolation dram.'

I nodded at the Highland Park bottle by her feet. I got and filled my
glass, chapped it to hers.

'The toast?' I asked.

'Families,' she said. 'You say I don't tell you stuff – maybe I owe you
some background.'

And she began to tell me. She spoke with pauses long and wide as the
dark patches in the moon's trail on Scapa Flow outside, and I would wait
silently till she re-formed and carried on.

Her dad was from Peterhead and ran away from sea. That was his big
joke, she said. He quit his father's boat, which was never forgiven, got
work in a Gourock builder's yard. After several years of night school, on
his thirtieth birthday he began architecture at Glasgow University, more
sure than of anything on this earth – and here Mica's pause opened up a
gulf in the night – that this was where he was meant to be.

That same evening, in a bar with his new and younger student friends,
he got talking with an angry, funny woman working behind the bar, was
attracted by her wild humour, by a will as strong as his. When the pub
closed, she took him back to her bedsit in the Gallowgate. Mica said she
wondered still about their walk through the streets, randy and half-cut
with no idea how this night would set the course of their lives.

Lizzie O'Neill was an only child too, but unlike him she was dead set
on having children and so breaking the chain of loveless childhoods she
came at the end of. All right, he said, once he'd graduated and got a job,

they'd have children, many as she pleased. They got married on that understanding.

An architecture degree takes a long time, Mica said. Long enough for someone to get impatient at the waiting. Long enough for Lizzie to decide to get what she wanted. She thought she had that right.

A pause so long the moon had shifted closer to Flotta flare stack before she spoke again. James Moar nearly made it. He nearly became an architect. Got to the end of his fourth year when Lizzie told him she was pregnant. She said she wasn't prepared to wait longer. She hadn't told him because she knew he wouldn't have agreed. Sorry.

'He could have got out then,' Mica murmured. 'Damn sure I would have, being tricked like that.'

Instead, he left university because they needed money and he got a junior town planning job. He never made a building of his own other than a garden shed and a few extensions. He never forgave Mica's mother.

'Or me, for that matter,' Mica added. 'I was that deliberate mistake. And I couldn't be the family my mother wanted so much. I can't do that mother–daughter shit, never could. I'm his child, that's the joke.'

She sort of smiled and drank from her glass of Highland Park. I wanted to hold her, enfold her, but had learned enough to know that would be disastrous.

Still, he didn't up and leave. He was only half a bastard, 'Like me,' Mica added. Another baby, her brother Paul, nailed down the lid on the coffin of James Moar's hopes.

'Or maybe he didn't want it enough,' she said. 'Maybe deep down he didn't think a fisherman's son could really be an architect. Maybe the flaw was in him.'

I'd always just accepted my father was a doctor. I'd never thought of the resolution it must have taken, especially back then, a generation before Mica's dad, to make that jump from saddler's son to professional man. And the cost of that resolve? I ran the tar-and-caramel firewater over my tongue, felt it burn inside as she went on.

When Mica was eleven, after years of simmering discontent and raging arguments when her parents had both had too much to drink, which was most weekends, her mother secretly applied for a hotel manager's post in Cornwall, and got it. James Moar had gone off to work one morning when she told the children their father would be looking after them from now on.

'Some people's lives are just crap, aren't they?' Mica said. 'If I'm ever tempted to believe life's good really, I just have to think about my parents' lives.'

Her father did look after them, she admitted. He got a promoted

161

planning job and they moved to Orkney. The children were sent to the other end of Britain to see their mother during the school holidays.

'I stopped going as soon as I was old enough to assert myself,' Mica said. 'I couldn't bear her boyfriend and I felt sick whenever I saw her. You could say I don't have too high an opinion of mother love or my own sex.'

She shivered, pulled her dressing gown tighter then held out her glass. I took it, refilled for us both, handed it back without a word.

As she took it, she looked up at me. Such a long, equivocal look, more naked than she'd ever been with her clothes off. All I could do was be there and look back at her. I sat on the other end of the windowseat; we were like bookends with volumes between us as she continued.

When Mica was in her early twenties, down in Cornwall her mother rose to get a jar of mayonnaise, grunted, turned to her boyfriend who owned the hotel, then fell across the table. She lived another six months, speechless and incontinent, before a second stroke killed her.

I could have said to Mica, well her father must have loved her to have stayed. That her mother was just trying to get her life back, and it must have been hard for her too. I could have found a cheery side, or just admitted it's a hopeless world where a dead moon shines on a sea whose sound has no meaning.

'Did you go to see her?' I asked.

Mica kept looking out at the bay. She sipped from her glass a couple of times.

'Yes,' she said. 'Once.'

She drained her glass. I did the same. It was past one in the morning and it felt like we were the last people awake anywhere. A time of confidences that would never be referred to.

'So,' she said, 'that's the whole bollocks of it. Of course, it's no excuse whatsoever for any of my bad behaviour. That's not why I'm telling you.'

'Appreciate it,' I said casually, though I felt anything but.

'It wasn't all bad,' she said suddenly. She leaned towards me, close enough to smell the whisky in her breath and see the moon glitter in one eye. 'Sometimes he made us things. There was a weird purple rocking cow, and a climbing frame that was also a maze. And my mum could be really funny, sort of wildly fantastical, and take people off.'

I nodded, remembering my old man's moments of wit or tenderness. Surely, she could see how much her mother sounded like herself. Wild, unpredictable, funny, angry – and secretive. But untrustworthy?

'Bed?' she said. 'If you don't mind the single.'

We lay together, touching this and that while the bed gradually warmed up. A few minutes later she reached down and gripped me. She spoke close into my ear.

'It must be challenging,' she said. 'To have a part of your body that can't lie.'

'It can be a nuisance,' I said. 'Sorry.'

In truth, she'd given me too much whisky. Certainly too much to have sex with her right now. Or maybe it was just the lateness.

'Like to stay anyway?'

'Yes,' I said. And did, and it felt right, her whiffling into the wall when she slept, her long back warm against my chest, left breast filling my right palm just so.

With door and shutters closed against mosquitoes, the green coil burning and a glass of Bells beside him, Sandy sits down again to the letter home. He must finish it tonight for the boat tomorrow. Every week he writes one, every week he gets one. Neither is lengthy; his father sends a couple of pages of local news and weather, with perhaps a comment on a sporting result, in his careful hand, then his mother adds a couple of lines in her less formed one.

> ... *up there next week, if work permits. On a clear day, the view is very fine, and you can see a whole stretch of Wellesley Province on the mainland. It's mostly green. Everything is mostly green here. There's not much in the way of seasons either, just continuous germination, growth and decay. It's all very dense and clinging. Still, my system must have acclimatised somewhat, or maybe I am just getting used to it all.*

He pauses. Letter writing is always an effort for him but it has to be done. He sips whisky, adjusts the flame of the desk lamp that reinforces the feeble yellow bulb.

That last evening, playing billiards with his dad – nothing significant was said, they just got on with nudging the three balls round the table. He'd noticed his father was finally slowing, had difficulty bending to the shots, and his eyes weren't as good. He was nearly eighty, had married late, and Sandy was the last of five not counting Janice.

Those hands were so worn, battered, arthritic now, from a lifetime of skilled but bruising work. As his father had bent over a delicate in-off, Sandy had seen his arm tremble and sensed then it was probable he'd never see his father again.

Outside, on their way home up Weir Street, his father had stumbled slightly, gripped his arm. 'Do well, Alec,' he'd said. 'Do right.' Then was silent all the way home. That was his last and only parental guidance.

He'd actually said *Dae weel, Eck. Dae richt.*

Sandy stares into his whisky, hearing that voice. For a moment, he has an urge to pack and be on the Thursday boat home. Get a hospital post, no disgrace in changing one's mind. Except in his own eyes. All his brothers have left the country, none have come back. That is part of doing well, he understands that.

The room is quiet. The crickets creak like football rattles. Something scutters in the ceiling. The house gecko makes a quick dart and is still. The fan stirs hot air over his clammy skin.

He glances at his new Buddha. Chap looks as if nothing could bother him unco much. Or that he's minding a joke. Do well. Do right. Exactly what, exactly how?

Some of the Chinese patients have been refusing anaesthetic because they believe the soul leaves the body then and might not find its way back. I mentioned this to our bright Administrator Mr Ng, and his solution was to have a monk come along to say some prayers while we put the patient under. This seemed to reassure everyone, and the lady in question has as much soul as she had beforehand, plus a healthy wee boy!

It's quite intriguing to find ways of working with the way things are here . . .

🌾

As Mica dressed in the dawn light, I lay in her narrow bed enjoying the extra space while thinking it striking that the family history Mica had given me last night was essentially her father's story, not her mother's.

Two firsts last night. It had been the first night we'd stayed together till morning. It was also the first night we'd slept together and not had sex – a landmark for any couple, even when or perhaps especially when they're not a couple.

She brought me tea and a slightly soggy biscuit, then carried on gathering up some writing, slid the sheets away into the *Nippy Stories* file. She seemed tense, distant, preoccupied.

I asked why the early start. She said she had to get up to the big house, her dad was expecting her before the nurse called. For the first time I asked what they actually did together up there.

'Watch crap telly and say how crap it is,' she replied. 'Or else we pick a subject, any subject, then argue about it. Or we bitch about the doctor or the nurse or the health visitor. Sometimes he gets almost sentimental, and I want to scream at him *Why don't you just be the bitter twisted shit you always were?*'

She looked down at me and for all she was grinning she was shaking.

'Know what he said yesterday? *I'm glad you were born.*' She thrust the file and a book into her canvas bag. '*Now* he tells me! What the fuck am I supposed to do with that information?'

Her hands were fisted now. She was white faced, pupils tiny in angry eyes. If I'd tried to hold her, I think she would have lashed out.

'Bolloxy-bollox,' I said. 'Your dad was giving you a tanner – go and buy an ice cream with it, *Monica.*'

She stared at me. That quick, smart mouth hung open. All kinds of lights flickered across her eyes like shadows over the Flow.

Then she burst out laughing. She dropped into the chair and slumped back. Looked up at the ceiling, got the giggles again.

'So who told you?' she asked at last.

'Ray,' I said. 'If I was called Monica I'd change it too.'

She giggled again, smeared the water from her right eye.

'I was desperate to be a boy,' she said. 'When I was ten I'd hang around the street corners in jeans and a T-shirt hoping visitors would think I was a boy. I decided I was called Mike. And then if someone challenged me, I could say I'd really said Mica.'

'And did they?'

'Sometimes,' she said. 'Then the name stuck.'

She picked up her jacket and got ready to go up the hill to her father's house. She seemed back on top and I was glad.

'You know,' she said thoughtfully, 'I liked being Mike. He was a good kid. That's what I hoped people would say, *He's a good kid.*'

'And did they?'

'Not that I remember. You getting up or what?'

We went down the stairs together. Out on the street she grabbed me and clumsily kissed my cheek.

'Thanks, smart clerk,' she said, and set off for Hellihole.

'Hey, Mica!' I called.

She stopped, turned. Waited at the curve of the street, canvas bag slung over her shoulder, my favourite hooligan.

'You're a good kid,' I said.

21

The light closed down towards the deepest dark, the shortest of those days.

The wind was a constant presence. Days of people leaning and staggering, veering and tacking along the street as though everyone in the town was half-pissed. Small children were grasped by their pixie-hoods. I remember a beagle being blown sideways then forcing its way up the street pressed to the wall, its ears streaming horizontal.

Early dusk at the back of three o'clock as I fought my way back along the grey coast from the graveyard, then the wind dragging a wordless howl from the phone lines strung over South End. Going out my door in the morning and picking scraps of seaweed off windows glazed with salt. Hair thick and matted by the day's end.

People only came out when they had to. Like sap in the few wind-shrunken, salt-burned trees in the town, life went underground, out of sight, secret as Mica's visits. I'd hear my door clunk and scrape then she'd be there. Twice to make the point I phoned her and went round. Once we just talked, the other time we employed the chaise longue and I did something to my back.

Orkney winter suited me. Struggle I can set myself to. Yet near every day there would be a brief astonishing light, making the golf course green as a padi field for five minutes, or firing the huddled grey houses lurid red and old gold.

As I hurried out of the academy from my last seminar before Christmas, the sun was rolling down the headland of the Kame of Hoy into the sea. Glanced at my watch: 3.15. A giant figure loomed up against that bloated red ball – black, eaten round with fire, waving some monstrous implement at the town below. He seemed huge, mythic, bloody rays streaming round a misshapen head.

I blinked, stepped sideways, and out of the glare saw it was Mica's father. Wearing a long-peaked baseball cap and a coat that billowed round him in the gale, he looked like a towering locust.

He stopped and stared at me. I didn't know if he had some notion what was going on, it was supposed to be secret. Mica had assured me it was better that way. 'Simpler,' she'd said. 'There's currents you can't map running through here.'

Jimmy Moar leaned on his stick and looked me up and down. I felt measured in the way my dad used to make me feel. What man does not feel lesser than his father? The flesh of his face was caving in, leaving cheekbones, nose, ears, jaw, all jutting. Death's thumbprint was in his face all right. He raised his stick, his coat blew wide and I stepped back.

'Aye,' he said. 'Fine day, boy.'

He coughed then walked on past me, leant into the wind propped on his stick as he worked his way home. Had there been a flicker of a smile? A smile of derision or conspiracy, or simple amusement?

I stared after him till he listed round the corner. It was the last time I saw him on his feet.

'Do you ever think of delivering a baby of your own?' Alan asks casually as they walk in the shade of the banana palms lining the ninth.

Sandy laughs as he towels sweat from his hands.

'Aye, why not? Babies make me feel . . .' He considers, thinking of all the babies he has helped out into the light, the end and beginning of pain, that first unseeing total stare. How often has he been the first thing seen in this world? 'Hopeful,' he says, and selects a club.

'Anyone in mind?'

Sandy bends over his niblick approach shot. Tricky one. Keep the wrists loose. Hit through. The ball flips up, hits the ridge and kicks left, more than he'd expected, ends up on the far verge of the green.

'Need more practice,' he says.

Alan laughs, marks his ball.

'Hard to get much practice round here!'

Walking off the last hole, shirts clinging, hair wet. Two fat white clouds cling to each side of Penang Hill like grizzling bairns.

'Working with ladies like that,' Alan says. 'Does it, you know, put you off?'

How many times Sandy has been asked something like this, with a snigger from men or a blush from women. Though he has far more practical experience of the workings of women than any Casanova, he's like a man who has studied and committed to memory maps of a foreign country but has scarcely set foot over the border and certainly doesn't speak the language.

'Different kind of thing,' he says briefly. 'Then she's a body trying to do what it wants to, and I'm just trying to help it.'

The stretch, the gape of it, still astonishes him at times. The sure knowledge he too came out through there. Why do we spend so much energy wanting to get back in? What's the point in that? Yet when that bairn comes free, gets a wee slap and gapes for its first breath, the question disappears like one of his father's false knots.

'I'm going to ask Ann to marry me,' Alan announces. 'Tomorrow afternoon, after Sunday tiffin at the Simpsons'.'

'Best of luck.' As Alan looks at him, he adds 'She's a good 'un. Go easy on the cocktails beforehand.'

'Thanks, Sandy.' He holds out his hand. Rather surprised, Sandy shakes it. 'Gosh, I envy you your experience,' Alan blurts.

'You haven't—?'

Alan blushes, shakes his head.

'But I reckon Ann has.'

Sandy doesn't argue with that.

'I'll get the hang of it quickly enough,' Alan says. 'Hell, you might even be delivering our first in a couple of years!'

Alan claps him on the back as they go into the long cool clubhouse bar. He remembers that. He'll remember it still in old age, and he'll stare down into his whisky, tasting again the stengahs, the slings, the sours, above all the acrid cocktail of desire and shame, poured over ice sent all the way from England.

Party night at the Flying Dutchman. I pushed in round 9 p.m. Place was steaming, hot and loud with multiple fiddles, and the condensation added a sheen to walls yellowed by thirty years of tobacco smoke. Joined my colleagues and students for a drink, then took myself and banjo to the back room where the musicians reigned. They made room at their tables. Couple of handshakes, clap on the shoulder, drink raised, a grin here, smile there. Knowing people and being known, that's what I came here for.

I hadn't seen Mica for several nights, and kept an eye open for her as I vamped through the chord changes. Plenty time to look around as we played, accompaniment for fiddle not being taxing, just fast. Tell the truth, after the tune has been played three times through each of its key shifts, it does lose its sparkle. It's for playing or dancing, not listening, and no one was drunk enough yet to dance.

But here's one who was. Mica came in holding up Kipper. He was long-legged and slim-hipped right enough, and his pale blue eyes glared round the packed room. She got him propped into a corner, said something in his ear then went to the bar.

On her way she looked over. I lifted my hand a moment then went back to whacking out A Major. No lover's greeting but still Kipper frowned in my direction.

Islands are different. The water round them lays down clear boundaries. Within them, everything is intensified. Me, I could come here as a rank outsider, make it clear I was happy to be included in, to buy a round, go fishing, play music and help out with boats and ploys. That left me free to enjoy the healing of the place, the apparent (and real) friendliness, trust, that sense of connectedness I'd always yearned for. I could disregard the complications under that surface.

But for Mica it was like the German fleet scuttled at the bottom of Scapa Flow that the divers came here for – a place full of traps and sink holes, snags and dark currents.

I put down the banjo at the end of the number and made for the bar. She was coming away from it with pints and whiskies in her long-fingered hands. I swerved towards her but she shook her head, a small movement but unmistakable.

So I got my order in despite our brooding landlord's best efforts to ignore everyone. In the back room James B. stood up to sing 'My Old Friend The Blues' and the wobble in his voice went through us all. The room quietened the way it does when true feeling jumps the gap between us, so hungry are we for one moment of emotional truth.

More pain, more dead dogs indeed. I glanced towards Mica but she was frowning at her trainers and I nearly caught Kipper Johnson's eye instead. Something told me not to meet it so I carried on as if casually scanning the room, then went to the loo.

He was there when I came out, leaning heavily against the passage wall. I nodded, made to go past but his arm shot out and braced against the other wall, blocking my way. We stared at each other.

'So,' he said at last. 'Shite weather we're having.'

Lordy, another Orkney weather conversation. Still, it was better than a punch up. He was just extremely drunk.

'It is that,' I said. 'Just rubbish.'

He leant in on me.

'If you don't like it, cunt, the ferry south is waiting.'

I could try to walk away but I didn't reckon he'd let me, and anyway I'd a pint waiting. I wondered if he was going to punch or head-butt, and felt the readiness well up in me though I was way too old for this nonsense.

'Na, I like rubbish weather,' I said. 'Suits me fine.'

Which was true enough, but it didn't seem the right answer. At this point there is no right answer.

'Oh does it?' he muttered. 'Does it in-fucking-deed. Well it doesn't suit me, out in the boat like.'

I nodded, tried to keep my voice level, watching his big hands from the corner of my eyes.

'It must be hellish out there some days,' I said sympathetically.

Kipper Johnson pushed off the wall. His jacket brushed my chest. He was younger than me but the veins had popped in his face with the drink and the weather. Certainly it was rough out there. Then again, I'd known plenty fishermen in my childhood so I wasn't going to be that impressed. And no way my dad would have backed down here. We're a bad lot underneath it all.

'So,' he said.

'So,' I said.

His right hand grabbed my lapel. Big hand, strong.

'Smart arse,' he said.

I couldn't help it. I laughed.

'No smarter than the average herring, Kipper,' I said.

Which bought me a second while he thought about it. Then his pupils flared, his head went down. The head butt it was then. My fists were just coming up between us when a blow on his back knocked him off balance.

'Hey, you guys! You must stop snogging like this!'

Mica, grinning wildly. Her glance flickered my way then she turned it all on him.

'Are you coming, big boy? Back for a spot of nookie?'

She peeled him off me and onto herself, then with one swift backward almost apologetic glance she led him out the door and into the night.

I watched the door swing to, the freezing draught cut off. She was right, there were undercurrents in this place I'd just never get. I wondered who had seen her at my place, who had talked. It had never occurred to me I was worthy of comment. I liked watching people but thought myself invisible.

I went back inside for beer and another set of Orkney reels. Then when the Country turned Western I made my excuses and left. The streets were empty of everything but wind and salt and night.

Daniel Ng leans on the huge red and gold painted gates of the temple, adjusting his spotless shoe with one hand.

'Most lovely morning, Doctor!'

They shake hands. It's the first time Sandy has met Ng outside of work, for the world of a superior Straits-born Chinese and that of a European doctor might as well be at opposite ends of the solar system. Still he approves of his quiet dedication, his clarity of thought, the unfussy way he administers the hospital, and envies the man's self-possession. He has never seen him flustered or annoyed in even the most obstructive of hospital board meetings.

'So you are on the way to the Simpson tuan's house?'

He is indeed. Unusually he'd decided to walk the whole way, hoping to settle some things in his mind, and be ready for the curry tiffin that awaited him there, among other things.

'Perhaps you would like to see round our temple?'

After a while all the painted Buddhas and stupas, dragons, demons, chants and gongs, so stunning and exotic on first encounter – like Mrs Simpson's curry – start to make him feel slightly bloated. As with the house he's going to, there's just too much on offer for one man to take in. It's enough to make him yearn for the austerity of mince and tatties and the bare interior of a kirk.

So he nods, listens, remembers, but is more than ready to continue on his way when Daniel Ng finally takes him into a small shaded interior courtyard. A little fountain bubbles before a slim-waisted bronze Buddha. It has one long finger raised like an elegant antenna, like an aerial, as if to say *Listen!* A wooden bench along each side, a red earth floor open to the sky, and that is all. An elderly man in the loose blue trousers and shirt of a gardener is sweeping up leaves with a broom, and something in the calm, methodical circling of the broom, the bowed grey head, the easy sway of the shoulders, makes the world slow and still.

For a moment, he is a small boy watching again his father sweeping up his workshop at six every evening. The same patient, scrupulous attention, neither hurried nor bored, just the act of clearing up.

The fountain burbles, the Buddha lifts his finger, the old man sweeps, and for a long moment as he stands in the shade, Sandy rests.

The gardener sweeps the leaves into a wicker basket, leans to place the broom on a rack, turns to them. To Sandy's surprise, Ng bows deeply. The gardener nods gently, takes them both in with one effortless glance, then passes through an arch and is gone.

Sandy stares: at the broom, the basket, the fountain, the Buddha, the empty shaded courtyard. There's a ringing in his head as though a moment ago someone had struck a glass bell in the air.

'I'd like to talk with that gardener,' he says.

Daniel Ng looks at him. A tiny smile creeps across his lips.

'The abbot has other business, I'm afraid.'

'The statues and gold you've seen, all the gongs and sutras, they are the show not the substance,' Ng remarks as they part at the temple gates. 'Now I have my devotions to attend to – and you have yours. Good luck, Doctor.'

Though it's a long uphill walk through the heat of noon to the Simpsons' tiffin party, he is not sweating nor exhausted when he turns up the driveway. It is as if he carries the cool of that courtyard within him.

'Here you are, Sandy!' Ann calls from the verandah where she waves in a loose green dress, then the heat and babble strike anew as he hurries up the steps into the party.

22

She came in so quietly I nearly missed it, but I smelled the gust of sea and wine as she rustled.

'You still awake?'

'Not.'

She put on my bedside light and looked down at me. She seemed flushed and hectic, as if she'd come from somewhere on fire.

'God, sorry about that,' she said. 'So many secrets in this town and so hard to keep.'

'I thought Kipper was old business,' I said.

'Well he is, kind of,' she said vaguely. 'But some old business still goes through the books, you know?'

I thought about it. I had some people still very close to me and they didn't even live here. Some weren't even living. So I just nodded.

'Think I calmed him down,' she said. 'He's probably too drunk and stoned to remember. But I'd keep out of his way for a while.'

She held up my dad's Buddha in her white long-fingered hands.

'Here, are you a Buddhist or what?' she said.

'Or what,' I answered. 'I'm not a pacifist, I eat meat and reincarnation seems silly to me – but he's right about some things.'

'Such as?'

'Well . . .' Though I knew fine that desire was the source of all suffering, I was deeply in it. The tube in my head hadn't changed that at all. I still *wanted*.

'Mindfulness and Compassion,' I said. 'And Emptiness.'

'Bolloxy bollocks,' she said. 'The world's stuffed solid with boys and girls and beasties and suchlike. He has a jolly face, though.'

She put my Buddha gently back on his window ledge, turned him to face away. Threw off her big jacket then pulled her shapeless sweater over her head. I saw the knobbly curve of her spine as she bent forward to unclip her bra.

'Here,' I said. 'About Kipper. Have you two been?'

She turned and stared at me.

'Christ, Eddie! I may be a wee jim-jam but I'm not a slag. Fuck's sake.'

'Sorry,' I said. 'Had to ask.'

She glared at me, her hands still meeting behind her back. She re-fixed the clips.

'You don't know me at all, do you?'

'Whose fault is that?'

She scowled at me and I glared back at her. She shook her head and her salt-stiffened hair skittered across her shoulders. Then she laughed wildly. I felt she was spinning on black ice with someone inside desperately turning the wheel and having no effect whatsoever.

'You're right!' she said. 'I'm a ratbag of wind and you're a gent. You're right to call me on it. Now – can I come in there?'

'Yes,' I said. 'Yes, please.'

She grinned so natural and pleased I could hold no anger as she finally unclipped and let her little harebell breasts swing my way. Then she was in bed and bending round me like fuse wire, all hard and smooth, electric.

During the rounds they do together over the next weeks, along the hospital corridors, in and out of the wards, out through the streets to the Runnymede, he collects fragments of Adele Trent's life. Her childhood in Singapore, Penang and the Sumatran Highlands. Boarding school in England where her colonial ways were smoothed over. Back to Malaya, then back to Oxford. A year of Oriental Languages then leaving to marry John Trent ...

Here she falls silent, goes somewhere inside herself where he cannot follow. He cannot ask. She is not happy, that's plain enough, but perhaps that is her nature. She speaks of Trent with respect always, warmth sometimes, love never.

Listening and looking at Adele, he begins to see in her degrees of loss and resilience – simple backbone – that he hadn't associated with her accent and her class. She seems to be enduring something, which he always respects, and yearning angrily for something else, which he cannot help but understand.

Odds are she will have a baby and that will be that. Though there seems to be some problem in that department. He cannot ask.

'Do you believe in marriage?' she demands before they part one day after lunch, amid the mayhem of Chulia Street.

He shrugs. 'It exists, no doubt.'

'Oh, don't be coy.'

A scrap of Whitman comes to him. *A woman waits for me, she contains all, nothing is lacking ...*

'I should like a mate,' he admits, tests the word, finds it about right.

'I bet you would!' she laughs. 'You and several hundred other single men on this island. Only there's very few to choose from.'

'I can wait,' he says.

'Can you?'

Her enquiry expands into the heat-stunned afternoon, is not lost under the bullock cart that creaks past, nor falls asleep with the rickshaw wallahs in the shaded alley by the Hindu temple.

'Yes,' he says simply.

A grey blustery morning as I left the house and stotted along the street, Dad's coat belted high and tight round my waist. Mica had left me groggy in the early hours, left me replaying the scene with Kipper and wondering what the hell was going on here. Everything you do comes back to you in time, my porcelain Buddha was right about that, but on a small island it comes back to you a hell of a lot more quickly. Orkney was near-instant Karma.

Right now I didn't feel like making eye contact but living here there was little choice without causing offence. So I grunted and nodded my way along the flagstone street, stepping aside for the odd car slowly negotiating the narrows. The absence of pavement made for this constant intercourse of car and pedestrian, forcing people to register each other, to connect.

I went to get a bacon roll and coffee at the cafe helpfully called The Cafe. There was a new funeral notice on the wall today, the black border framing those heavy square black letters we do death in. MRS FLORENCE (EFFIE) MANSON. I didn't know her, but plenty people here would. Seemed scarcely a week passed without a similar new notice going up here, in the Post Office, the bakery, the butchers, the Mill Stores.

I waited for my bacon, badly needing something. In a city, you're not aware of the daily deaths, but in Stromness it's in your face. It amazes me we carry on. If there was a sniper up in the church tower, picking off one or two people a week, no one would dare go outdoors.

I took my bacon roll and went out onto the street. My heart lurched as I felt those sniper sights settle on me a moment, then pass on to someone else. In time it would get everyone in the town. And still we go about our business. Astonishing.

Sheltering by the ice plant on the pier end, I had breakfast and watched a million tons of water an hour pour through Hoy Sound. Out in the Flow the sea was grey, but grey like Mica's eyes seen close to, brimming with ever-shifting light and energy. I thought of her expression when, as she was leaving in the early hours, I'd tried to offer support with her father's dying. Anything I could do? She'd stared back at me with incredulity. As if no one person could genuinely care for or help another.

I sucked the bacon sweetness from my chilly fingertips and took a last look out at the Holms, those tidal islands like elongated lily pads. My eyes were drawn to them many times a day – something about the rhythms of their connection first to each other and then, as the tide fell further, back to the mainland.

When you are dead you will love this.

No doubt. I put my collar up and turned away from the Holms, up to the DOA rooms in the old academy.

Over the weeks and months our functional office had become domesticated. We'd added desk lights to the neon, plus photos of drinking sessions, friends and children tacked to the walls by the charts. Then Duncan's pool trophy, Anne-Marie's crossbow from her archery, Ellen's wetsuit and Cara's drawings. I had my mini-disc player and headphones, some fingerpicks, my dad's old postcards of Penang.

They all looked round as I came in, last again. These nights with Mica took their toll, even though like a good vampire she always left before dawn.

'So, Edward,' Ellen said, 'I hear you and Mica are getting hitched if Kipper Johnson doesn't kill you first.'

'WHAT?' I said.

'The rumour mill grinds exceeding fine,' she murmured.

'It's more full of grit than grain,' I replied. 'I scarcely even know Mica.' Which was true enough.

Then Anne-Marie breezed in, bristling with energy and competence.

'I've got these cost-modelling figures,' she announced. 'Think you'd better both take a look at them. Oh, I hear Mica Moar is pregnant and it's yours. Congratulations all round!'

'There *is* a solution to power generation in the Northern Isles,' I said. 'It's right under our noses. All we have to do is harness the volume of rumour, gossip and sheer invention generated daily in Stromness, plug it into the National Grid, then we can leave the lights on for the rest of our lives.'

One weekday afternoon Sandy Mackay walks out along Light Street, glancing up as always at the founder's statue. He has a soft spot for Francis Light, a man with a vision, fighting a long battle against bureaucracy and indifference. He approves of Light's legendary gesture of firing small change from his ship's cannons into the jungle to encourage its clearance – something splendidly mad and impatient about that.

Like the first time he saw Hayman, whacking golf balls out into the Bay of Bengal . . . But Alan's away for six weeks working for the Water Board in Malacca, and there's no point getting soaked on the golf course now the rainy season's come.

Recently he's given up going back to his own quarters for an afternoon lie-off. Somehow it's impossible just to lie on the bed, and Walt Whitman has abruptly become a tedious bore – a man can take only so much praise of everything.

But his membership of the Penang Club has come through as Marsden prophesied, and at this hour the billiard rooms are cool and the tables as deserted and splendid as he could wish. Last week when he went there for the first time to practise, get the feel of the tables, he saw the notice up about the annual billiards tournament. It had been such a pleasure to challenge them at bridge. If he works at it, maybe he can give them a run for their money on the tables.

He's still wondering about that. He doesn't have to win, but he has to do well.

Outside the convent, the old Chinese cook with the nodular goitre blows on his charcoal fire. That smell of fuel and spicy food combined will always be Penang for him. So many stalls and street vendors it seems at any one time half the population is cooking and the other half eating. He likes it hot hot, bringing relief when the sweat comes. He glances towards the convent windows, thinking of Nurse Gibbs, pretty young lassie wasted.

I have said that the soul is not more than the body . . .
And I say to mankind, be not curious about God,
For I who am curious about each am not curious about God . . .

Aye, that's the right of it. Let God be. There's so much else interesting.

182

More cheerful now, he walks past the E&O. That first afternoon, with him and Alan running in there laughing, sodden through, water pouring from their shoes, and all the Simpson family inside taking tea so cool and dry. He sees again Ann's lips moving over each other as she talks, and Adele's home-blue eyes fixed on him.

As a laddie, his brother William showed him how to take the lid of a tobacco tin, punch two holes, thread it with string. Birl it over a few times, then pull in and out as though playing a squeeze box between your hands, and the lid spins into a blur with a whizzing sound . . . That's how it is with the Simpson sisters. Between them he is being spun and birled silly, and they don't even know it.

No more. He will concentrate on billiards. The white cue ball clicking off the cannons, pots, in-offs, straight as a die and fast as lightning those tables are, amazing how many combinations three balls can come up with. Why did Ann turn Alan down or at least put him off? Why does she look at him like that, or is he imagining it?

Past the Runnymede Hotel, all dazzling white. The cool dining room where he and Adele have eaten, sparred, talked of work and family, and then her sudden darts of frankness, those restless, hungry eyes prompting words from him he'd never thought to speak. Hoarse, emotional words about the slights and disappointments and frustrations of thirty years. His angers, his fears, memories of a childhood so unlike hers. The other week he even spoke of Janice, first time in many years, and it nearly made him greit. Her hand on the back of his then. At least she'd said nothing.

At last, through broiling light yellow and thick as mango purée, the Penang Club. Great shambles of green and white colonial building, all columns, verandahs and eaves. As he trots up the steps, the giant Sikh opens the door, *Good afternoon, tuan!*

Sandy half-smiles, half-nods, raises his hand in salutation, still unsure what the right form is as he passes from dazzling light into the shade and the deep peace of the Penang Club in mid-afternoon, mid-week, 1930.

23

ust have been a Saturday afternoon when I passed Mica's window, back from a trawl round the Kirkwall shops with Ellen for Orcadian Christmas presents. I glanced up, saw her pale face staring down at me. I waved. A hesitation, then she waved me to come on up.

Her workroom was chilly and chaotic as usual, but the table was cleared. A pile of folders next to her new second-hand laptop and small black notebooks. She was withdrawn and preoccupied, scarcely looking at me.

'He's really ill,' she said, and carried on stuffing a battered suitcase. 'I've talked with his health visitor. Can't put it off any longer – gotta move in with him till . . .'

And because she was Mica who couldn't bear certain evasions, though she adored others, she added: 'Till he's dead. Doctor says the old bugger's got another month at best, and of course he won't go into hospital. Time for the dutiful daughter bit. Oh shit . . .'

She leant over the case, weeping silently as she rolled up another sweater.

'Me and Dad,' she was saying, 'it's not whatever you're thinking. Maybe he's like me, but worse. Selfish, bad-tempered, frustrated. Mum had the good sense to get out, then she went and died. I've phoned my brother but he's not coming back till . . . So, it's down to me.'

We were in my car, sitting in the dark at the road end by Warebeth beach. There was milky light in the sky, the heater was blowing, and in the back of the car was everything she would need to stay at her father's for however long. When we'd left her place she'd asked to come down here for a last breather before going on to his house.

'It's just we never, we didn't, I couldn't.'

When Mica cried she didn't screw up her eyes like most folk do. They were wide open, staring at the break of white along dark sand as the water flowed.

'I shan't ever. He wasn't. We weren't,' she added.

I held her of course, and she gave a little to me, and I wondered if this painful feeling was love or common humanity. Perhaps one was the other raised to higher powers.

When she stopped weeping, neither of us spoke for a while. Our grip on each other slowly loosened and we didn't quite know where to put our hands. We were both far more embarrassed about her tears than anything we'd ever done in bed.

'Look outside!' she said suddenly.

I did. The moonlight on the clouds reflected palely on the sea where the small waves creased. To the left, across the tide running through the Sound, were the Hoy cliffs. Dark hump of Black Craig off to the right. Out there was our new wave-measuring device, registering the frequency and amplitude and duration of it all.

'No, look!' she insisted.

I looked harder. A brief flicker as a bird flew by, a tiny point of yellow light from a boat way out.

'Fuck!' she said urgently. 'Out of the car!'

I got out almost as quickly as she did, wondering whether a psychotic Kipper Johnson was attacking us or she was going a little mad. It was icy cold out, salty, unusually bright with moonlight.

But there was no moon.

'Fuck fuck fuck,' she said quietly.

It was more a blessing than a curse. Her hand clutched mine as we looked up. The clouds were lit by broad struts of white light soaring from the horizon to merge at the crown of the sky.

The Northern Lights, my first time. Saw them several more times that winter, but never better. So we stood and looked and I felt her fingers grow cold as mine but still we looked and shivered, and the last heat lingered in the palms of our clasped hands – the only time, I think, she held my hand. Hand-holding wasn't her style.

'My soul is a toilet,' she muttered. Then she added quietly, 'My God, it's beautiful.'

I squeezed her hand. I felt like a bungee jumper, one who's been going down for ages and now turned around and rising again.

'I'd never dare put this in a story,' she murmured. 'Don't want to turn into a love wimp.'

Then we just looked and looked while the bands of light flexed and warped and the air hissed like curtains being swished. We stood open-mouthed and open-hearted, gazing with wonder on the world the way it should be, the way it might be, the way, perhaps, it is.

At last, it faded, and we got back into the car and some warmth. I took a last look up, then flicked on the headlights.

'Thanks,' I said. 'Wouldn't have missed that for the world.'

'It happens quite a lot in winter,' she said, quietly. 'Some things you can see properly only if you live away from the bright lights.'

I drove her to her father's house, up the muddy drive past crouching bushes, the raw dog roses and twisted fuschias that could live through the salt up here. Parked round the back. There was a porch light and one upper light on. I helped her in with her stuff, piled it in a freezing passage through the back door. I could faintly hear music, sounded like Swing and a voice, maybe Sinatra.

She took my arm and led me back outside.

'I won't see you much now,' she said. 'I don't know what happens from here on, and there's a lot to take care off. But if I phone and ask you to come up, the back door's never locked. My room's first on the left.'

I tried asking her to our Waifs & Strays Christmas meal. After all, if we weren't really a couple, why not? But she cut me off.

'It's not the time,' she said. 'Okay?' She stared at me intently. 'Okay?'

I was allowed to glimpse Mica's tears and deepest fears only if I never let on I'd seen them. I nodded.

'Catch you later,' I said. 'Be well.'

'Oh fucky ducky,' she said. She squeezed my arm, took a deep breath. 'Ta, Eddie.'

She went back inside and I got into the car. I hadn't eaten and was cold and exhausted. But as I started up and drove off down the drive and round onto the back road of the sleeping town, everything wasn't lost. I had seen the Northern Lights. And I'd seen Mica's face lit as she looked up, and the sheen that fringed her lashes as she'd said *My soul's a toilet.* And the pause then *My God, it's beautiful.*

Even now, I wouldn't disagree.

He gets a tumbler of soda, lime and ice from the drowsy barboy, signs the chit then goes through to the first billiard room. He hears the click as he comes through the door, but it's already too late, dammit.

'Afternoon, Mackay.'

'Good afternoon, Dr Trent.'

The man is ten years his senior, and Sandy cannot rid himself of the respectful. He looks around; all the tables are empty and Trent is alone.

'Sometimes I come here and just knock some balls around,' Trent says. 'Helps me forget about ill people for a while.'

'Aye, know what you mean,' Sandy says, but thinks why doesn't the man go home to his wife when he finally stops working? She's probably out with Marsden somewhere. Which is cause and which is effect?

Dr Trent bends over the table, makes a neat in-off shot into middle pocket. Sandy automatically replaces the cue ball. Trent nods thanks – he's not a chatty man, which Sandy approves – then executes a couple of cannons. Nice fluid cue action, Sandy notes, no apparent fine trembling now. A heavily backspun shot just fails. Trent grunts, straightens.

'Care to join me?' As Sandy hesitates, he adds, 'We're not supposed to be seen practising, but I won't tell if you won't.'

Sandy grins, nods. So there's a hint of sap in that dry old stick. He takes off his jacket, selects a cue, makes a couple of passes then begins.

The tables are fast but true. That's all Sandy asks for – that a straight hit runs straight, gets the right rebound. A fair result. He likes that about billiards. What you do is what you get.

Half an hour of near silence as they push the balls around the long table, then Sandy raises the question of a patient he saw this morning.

'No shop, please. I come here to get away from that.'

'Fine,' Sandy says.

Trent straightens from his shot, looks him in the eye for the first time. His eyes are wide-set, brown. Perhaps it's the large pupils that make him seem to be looking right through Sandy.

'No offence, old chap.'

'None taken.'

They go back to it, the delicate, nudging cannons, the screwed in-off, the long table pots, and for a long time there's nothing but clicks and the odd muffled grunt and quiet *Good shot,* and that suits them just fine.

Trent's a good player, probably better than himself, Sandy reckons. Only every so often his shot selection is bizarre. He appears to be concentrating, yet his play is . . . disengaged. Even in a friendly, Sandy can't help but want to do well. Even playing alone, it would be the same.

I don't think he believes any more, Adele had said.

As Trent lines up his next shot, Sandy stares at the wound on the right temple.

'Depressed tempero-parietal fracture,' he says quietly, then can't believe he's spoken. Trent's cue arm hesitates, then he strokes the ball home.

'Contra coup injury. Bone fragments left behind, too far in for surgery. Medium-term prognosis – uncertain.'

Trent speaks flatly, without feeling, as if it's about someone else. Sandy nods. The man could die any time or live another forty years.

'Infantry?' he asks.

Trent shakes his head. The wound on his temple gleams palely. The delicate – too delicate, near-impossible – cut-off shot misses the central pocket. Trent straightens from the table.

'Ambulance Corps. Conchie, you see.'

'Ah.' Sandy chalks his cue, thinks about it. 'Who's to say you weren't right?'

He goes for a simple cannon, muffs it. John Trent glances at him briefly, then bends to the table and tells his story. He never looks up or round, just talks in a level, flat voice, and all the while he's nudging a series of gentle cannons up and down the cushion. All Sandy can do is listen and keep score, pushing the old mahogany markers along the board.

He graduated in 1916. Dr John Trent, MD (Edin). First one ever in his family. When the call-up papers came, he refused to join. From a long line of Quakers, he could not, would not kill. It destroys part of the soul, you see. (Sandy said nothing, just blinked and edged the marker along a couple more points.)

So he came up in front of the Board. Quite a grilling but he stuck to his, ahem, guns. No, he didn't have a sister, and if she was being raped he'd knock her assailant on the head but he wouldn't kill.

'It's quite difficult, no matter how sure you are of your core principles, being looked at across a table by six people who despise you or, worse, disbelieve you. Time comes when you even begin to doubt yourself. Maybe I am just yellow. Rightly or wrongly, other people were dying in their tens of thousands, believing they were protecting me. Chaps like you, I suppose . . . '

All this in an even monologue with Trent's back to him. Sandy sips lime and soda, trying not to cough, watches the balls being cajoled into place. Thinks of Adele, the things she's half-said and, worse, the things she hasn't said. He'd rather not hear this. Easier if Trent remained a cypher.

Trent re-chalks his cue and continues. Perhaps, he says, that's why he asked to join the Ambulance Corps. Insisted on it. Being a doctor and all, they took him like a shot. Hah! Anyway, most of the time it was well behind the lines but still it was . . . Well, in one week he saw more bodies opened up than a surgeon would in a lifetime. Saw too many. Hard to think of them all as God's creation. Sometimes they just become meat, you know?

Sandy nods, though Trent isn't looking. He remembers how the meat had once had names.

At the top end of the table, Trent turns the cue ball with a neat in-off, then resumes working the balls back down the table. It's the smoothest break Sandy has seen outside a professional exhibition.

So one day – 8 June, 1918, it was – he was out in front of the lines on stretcher-bearer duty. The mud had dried, no one was firing, all quiet. There was even a bird whistling. It got louder, became a scream – and then the world ended. He saw himself fly through the air and land face up. Eyes wide open, some extrusion in the right temple. Next to him, face down, was Prest. He wasn't in one piece.

'I've no explanation for it, Mackay, but I saw myself lying there. I saw Prest though I was unconscious. Maybe we do have a soul after all, a point of view that isn't dependent . . .'

He smartly pots a couple, by way of variation, then resumes his nudging cannons. Sandy is now staring so hard at the back of his head, the flicking cue tip, the pale smoothness on Trent's temple, he has forgotten to keep scoring.

'They got most of the shell out, grafted over the missing bone, and I survived, of course. Only, you know, you don't come back all the way. You still walk and work and talk, even fall in love, but part of you . . . Part of me, the part that watched myself lying there, it never came back where it should be.'

Sandy is sweating now. The flu made him miss the offensive where three-quarters of his battalion were killed. He's a jammy bugger. He's never been wounded, never lost part of himself. And yet he knows what the man means, knows all too well.

Trent continues. He seems as unable to stop talking as he is to stop scoring. When he met Adele – she'd walked into the surgery with a verruca, very romantic – she was a bright young thing, loved dances almost as much as she loved reading. Loads of suitors, she likes men's attention, you know. And he was just a former conchie with a bit of his head missing, but for some reason he became her cause.

Here Trent stops, cue drawn back. Swivels his head, looks up at Sandy.

'She left Oxford to marry me,' he says wonderingly.

'She said.'

'Did she also say it was her suggestion? She insisted. Said she couldn't wait, that if we didn't do it now it wouldn't happen.'

Trent nearly misses an easy pot. Though he continues, he seems to have lost his impetus. They decided to move to Malaya – she wanted to be back where she'd been a girl, and he wanted to be as far away from Europe as possible. Perhaps Adele thought she could find that bit of himself that had been blown away. Perhaps he did too. They've been here together for nearly five years now, except last spring when she . . . wasn't well and had to go home for a bit. And now . . .

Trent muffs an in-off into the bottom pocket, straightens up with a sigh. Sandy makes a guess and hastily pushes the score marker along the board.

'Wonderful break,' Sandy says.

'Yes . . . ' Trent says vaguely. He looks very tired. 'Don't suppose I'll do that again in a hurry.' He sits down heavily, his hand shaking as he reaches for his drink.

'Are you all right?'

'Had a couple of late meetings this week,' Trent says. 'Sorry I went on a bit. How was your war?'

'Not half as eventful as yours,' Sandy says.

He chalks up his cue. He's so far behind there's no chance he'll catch up now.

'I'm glad Adele's working again,' Trent says. 'She's bright and she gets . . . frustrated. She knows she's wasted just reading or going out on the bash. That generation that just missed the war – well they don't seem to know what to do with themselves. First they want to go to parties, then they want to save the world – or at least some old relic. They want a cause or a good time, but we know that's all pointless, don't we?'

Sandy stops. This has become embarrassing. The man's about to get maudlin.

'She's doing a good job,' he says. 'The hospital may want her to go full time.'

Trent looks at him directly.

'I'm glad she's working with you,' he says. 'Oddly enough, she's very fond of babies.'

The pause goes on until the boy comes in, his white tutup jacket buttoned right up to the chin, asks if the tuans would like another drink. Two gin slings.

'Can we start another game?' Sandy says. 'I'll have to concede that one.'

Despite what's been said – and neither of them will ever mention it again – Dr Trent will never suggest they use Christian names. That's fine by Sandy, the line is drawn, and that's where he wants it. They're colleagues who sometimes play billiards together during the afternoon lie-off in the rainy season, and talk a little about world affairs or sporting results from home. Before they leave the Club, Sandy puts his name down for the tournament, then they go outside to try to find a covered rickshaw or taxi home through the deluge in the gathering dark.

24

As I read through my downloaded study of axial flow rotors, for the first time I began to think this could work. What had seemed a daft and unlikely fantasy, what my dad in a certain mood would have called a *whigmalerie*, could be done.

I closed the file and sat back. Something had happened out by Warebeth while the Northern Lights flared over our heads. Perhaps it was time to admit we were not just a her-and-me joined by the hyphens of our coupling for as long as that lasted. There should be more to living than problem solving, tholing, and some energetic sexual shenanigans.

If you stopped trying you would be

Would be what? Happy? In love? Dead? The aerial voice had nothing more to offer.

There'd be further problems of course, there always are. Otherwise engineering wouldn't be much of a challenge and life wouldn't hold our interest long. That's what we do with our 9-pound brain and opposable thumb and dicky heart.

'Coming to the Hogmanay party on the Holms?' Ellen asked. 'Could be the event of the season.'

She was staring into Ray's watch-the-waves palm top screen. We all spent too much time doing that, though I was still waiting for him to try out my suggestion and convert the signals into sound.

'I've heard nothing about this.'

'You should get out more,' she said. 'Spend less time mooning after that Mica. She's taken anyway.'

'That's just to keep Kipper at bay. I think we're ready to go public.'

'Christ, you're really falling for her, aren't you?'

'Maybe it should be called rising.'

'Oh no it shouldn't,' she said firmly. 'She's not for you, Eddie.'

I looked at her. She looked back at me. Some moments later we both turned to look at the screen for more wave action. It went on as before, always different, always the same.

'I'll be there,' I said. Then we closed our files for Christmas and went to pick up Cara from school and off to Kirkwall for last shopping at the nadir of the year. Headlights on in murky mid-afternoon as I drove with the Beach Boys up loud and Cara singing 'Surfing USA' in the back. Ellen was nodding and smiling in to herself, and I thought from here on in surely things could only get lighter.

'You're in the right job,' Adele says lightly, sipping on her gin and lime as she settles down beside him on the verandah.

'Yes, I suppose I am,' he says, and in the saying knows it's true.

'Well bully for you.'

She's been like this ever since he and Alan arrived, sweet then sour. Alan has gone inside to butter up Mrs Simpson and down some cocktails so he can propose again to Ann. Sandy shrugs.

'No damn merit about it.'

'Lord,' she says, 'you really are an irritating man. You know so much about women, and you know nothing.'

'I know one thing at least,' he says.

'Oh yes? What's that?'

He's about to say it, he knows he is, something unforgivable or irreversible, but right then Freddie Ellyot rumbles up the drive on his motorcycle, grinning and waving to one and all. While everyone's attention is on the new arrival, Sandy turns back to her. She is looking at him, her mouth slightly open, tip of her tongue flicking over her lips. Her pale eyes widen.

Through the gateway comes a small green Humber, and Sandy and Adele move apart. Dr Trent jumps out, claps Ellyot on the shoulder, hurries up the verandah steps.

'John! You're just in time!" Mrs Simpson calls.

Dr Trent is bright-eyed, almost feverish. The brisk moustache twitches.

'So I see,' he says. He puts his hand on Adele's shoulder then bends to kiss her cheek. Sandy studiously watches the children clustering round Freddie's bike.

'I gave Sharma the report to finish,' Trent says. 'Got to take a break sometime, eh Mackay?'

'Oh aye,' Sandy says. He's hypnotised by Trent's hand on Adele's shoulder, the way the knuckles whiten as she rises.

'I'm glad you changed your mind, John,' she replies. 'You need to relax.' Her smile is vague, unfathomable. 'Shall we go inside?'

Sandy watches them pass through the half-shutters, so familiar with each other, in step, that hand still clasping.

'I'm going to propose after lunch!' Alan announces beside him. 'The other week I lost my nerve, but not this time.'

Ann has joined the group clustered round Ellyot. She's let herself become tanned and golden, in the new American fashion. In white slacks, she rests one hand on the bulging headlamp, the other on Ellyot's broad shoulder.

Sandy raises his Singapore sling, lets it trickle cold down his throat.

'Best not wait too long,' he says. 'I might get in there first.'

Alan hesitates, then laughs.

'It's not you I'm worried about, Sandy,' he says. 'It's that damn motorcycle! How can a guy compete with that? Do you think she'll have me?'

Sandy looks at his friend, all eager and brilliantined, paler than he should be, and wonders how long he's got. Thinks of Trent inside, his hand on Adele and shrapnel in his brain. Looks again at Ann, young and golden as honey, laughing as she sets wee Emily or Vanessa on the pillion.

'Seize the day, Alan,' he says. 'I'll talk to Ellyot, then you can get Ann away and weave your Yankee magic.'

Freddie Ellyot has large, perfect teeth. His fair hair is thick, his eyes clear and direct, his jaw clean-cut as he forks more curry. He reminds Sandy of any hero in his boyhood adventure annuals.

'Where's Marsden?' Sandy asks. 'Not often he misses a Sunday here.'

Ellyot glances at him, cracks a poppadom.

'Some . . . business has just come up.' He lowers his voice. 'Anything new to report?'

'No.'

They go back to talking about sport. Sandy can do this on automatic. He digs into heavy, fruity curry, drinks cold beer, looks down the long table crowded with Simpson family, friends, another bunch of unemployed planters and tin men needing to be fed as they wait for passage home. Two single women – though if Alan is accepted, that'll be one though Miss Gibbs hardly counts – and maybe twenty single men. It's not healthy. No wonder there are carry-ons.

At the far end of the table, Dr Trent sits close to Adele, fiddling with his food. Sandy wonders about his presence and Marsden's absence. Now he thinks of it, the two men are very seldom in the same room. Is Marsden away because Trent was coming? Yet Adele seemed genuinely surprised to see her husband. Does that mean he came *because* he heard Marsden was away? And what does that mean?

He pushes his plate away. The fans clunk overhead, the voices rise, the birds outside scream fitfully. The two girls are playing 'Chopsticks' very badly on the piano in the next room. His shirt is clinging damp, his fingers smell of cigarettes and Brylcreem. Adele shouts 'Oh *no!*' and sets off more laughter down the table.

He blinks at the brilliant light as the verandah door swings open. Ann smiles briefly at him as if there's something he should understand. Behind her, he glimpses Alan wandering in the garden, hands in pockets, the giant urn of Mrs Simpson's beloved acanthus trailing like fiery rockets above his down-turned head.

I got home round eleven from our pre-Christmas Kirkwall outing with Ellen and Cara, feeling more comfortable with myself and Orkney and life in general. That morning I'd gone for another check-up and it seemed my shunt was still working and my brain fluid still drained into my abdomen. The other week Mica had run her finger lightly over the little scar.

'I've heard of men carrying their brains in their balls,' she said, 'but you're the only man I know who has his draining into his belly.'

I was still smiling at the memory when I came in the door and saw the phone answer light was blinking. I thought of leaving it till morning but I always have the notion this might be the call that changes my life.

'If you've nothing better to do, you could pad on up the brae, big boy.'

Though she was trying to make a joke out of it, Mica sounded like she was on the end of a choke chain she couldn't stop pulling against. I went.

The clouds were racing through the moon and the night wind was full of salt and seaweed as I plodded up Hellihole Road between its high drunken leaning walls. I'd been told there was a burn channelled under the road, I could sense its dark passage under my feet. It was fine and raised and lonely in a good way as I walked up onto the single track Outertown road. Nothing and no one up there, just a green flash of a cat's eyes in the moonlight.

I came at last to her dad's Gothic heap on the right, with low salt-shrivelled trees by the drive. A single light in the front window – his bedroom, I thought.

I went round the back. The door was unlocked like she'd said. Dim light under the door first left. I chapped lightly and went in.

Her bleak little bedroom was lit by two candles but there was nothing romantic going on. She was sitting up in bed with the duvet wrapped round her and her arms tightly round her knees. I could practically see that choke chain glitter.

'I can accept he's dying,' she said hoarsely, 'but I can't take *Songs For Swinging Lovers* any more.'

So I got in the bed and held her. She was stiff and trembling, I could feel the thump of her heart as we lay in that cold little room listening to Sinatra coming through the wall. I began to realise the accompanying sounds weren't singing but grunting. It sounded like resistance not despair, but it was all the worse for that.

'How long's he been like this?' I asked.

'The last couple of days,' she muttered. 'On and off. He says the music helps. Course the old sod won't go to the hospice, won't leave the island. Says he wants to die here – how's he think that makes me feel?'

She ranted on, her fierce whisper hot against my neck. How typical this was of him, doing what he wanted, never thinking how it affected anyone else. How she wanted to be a million miles away but her brother wouldn't come and there was only her and the nurse. How she hated this, hated him, hated being tied like this, how no one else could or ever would do this to her. How she was as selfish as him, a rotten apology for a human being.

I just held her – there was no point saying soothing things. Gradually she softened, her arms relaxed round me. The music went on and on and finally, that terrible grunting stopped.

'Sorry if I got you here under false pretences,' she said then abruptly fell asleep, snoring quietly into my collarbone.

I lay awake a long time, feeling the birth of something new.

She was standing by the bed in a long crumpled T-shirt, glass of water in her hand in the half-light.

I watched her crouch as she groped for cigarettes and I saw her knees, I mean really *saw* them, and in that moment I felt the vulnerability of her entire body. Felt how she breathed and her heart beat, knew the ageing and indignities that must come her way, that she must die early or late, suddenly or slowly, but she must die. I knew the inevitable physical suffering that went with her body, however whippy and desirable it was to me, and from then on I never saw her the same.

That's why I say when she came back to bed we made love.

At the crux, my hand across her mouth because the walls were thin, then her long fingers smothering my shout.

It's not the sex, of course, it's the feeling that goes with it. It feels like a kind of dying, and in a way it is, if dying is a reluctant, painful letting go of self.

After I'd dressed and was about to go, she slung her arms round my neck.

'This isn't the best time to have a love affair,' she said. 'But thanks.'

And all the way walking homewards through the dawn I thought *Is that what we're having?*

The sands of Evie are uncovered now, still wet and shining. The light, the unique light of Orkney comes of sky reflecting sea-reflecting sky, two vast mirrors set facing each other, an infinite feedback of light. You could say it is a place of reflection.

But her knees, her bloody knees, that's what I remember now.

Ellyot pushes the disputed bowl away with his foot and mutters something about 'poor sport'. There is no deadlier insult. Alan pushes him away, restores the bowl. Ellyot laughs scornfully. Sandy gets between the two of them, tells Alan he's being ugly and Ellyot he's a pompous . . . Dr Trent takes his arm.

'Look, chaps, it's only a game.'

'Yes, but let's play it square, eh?'

'Hayman, I don't need you to tell me to play fair.'

Alan and Ellyot glare at each other. People are starting to notice. Ann and Adele turn away from their conferring, Mr Simpson frowns. The two pairs, Dr Mackay and Alan Hayman, Dr Trent and Freddie Ellyot, agree to replay this final, decisive end.

The jack is rolled down the short lawn, a good imitation of an English bowling green, though somehow it can never be. Alan, who is still quite drunk, bowls badly in a sullen silence. Ellyot is superior, nonchalant. His faint smile says it's only a game as any gentleman knows, and he can't help being good at it. John Trent looks withdrawn, his bad elbow is a hindrance.

Sandy glances at the bowls. His last shot, the opposition are lying two, only hope is to blast them away. Doesn't matter whether Ann and Adele are watching or not. He sights, swings and bends . . .

His bowl runs fast and straight, almost as fast as the two girls who burst out of the bushes in their chase, kick the bowl off its course, scatter the others into Mrs Simpson's cherished strawberry beds, then run off laughing onto the lower terrace.

Here comes a man about my age, nearly young but with traces of grey in his short trimmed beard. As we talk briefly about – what else? – the weather, Orkney and its wonders, I see the nicks, lines and creases in his face, the white, puckered scar across his hand, all those bits of damage we pick up along the way. I wonder what he sees.

Meanwhile his son, a lively little tyke of the sort I'd like to have had, is poking among seaweed with a stick. He spears a dead crab, examines it with an urgency, an absolute attention I have long longed to recapture.

The wean spins the crab shell away and is ready to move on to the next wonder. 'C'mon, Grandad,' he says and my head quietly explodes. Good Christ, yes it's possible. My father could as well have been my grandfather, and I too could have been on to grandchildren and watch my genetic immortality footer along the shore.

Still could, of course. My dad lived to see Peter's bairns. He treated them with a humour and patience I don't remember him showing with us. Less stressed, I suppose.

'Better get on,' the young grandfather says apologetically. 'After all, it's not for ever.'

The two of them dwindle along the shoreline beneath a huge sky and I think: he's right of course. That knowledge haunted me when I first arrived here, and it drained the sun from the brightest day. It made my friends insubstantial, and people on the street into flickering shades. There is nothing solid in the nearly dead, of whom Jimmy Moar was only a more extreme case than the rest of us. Knowledge of our brevity was with me constantly, and though it's true for sure, it's near impossible to live with.

What sustained me through that winter? Those things Orkney so freely offered. I mean the gift of weather unscrolling across sky, water, land; the small courtesies, humours and recognitions in the street, pub and office; a world stripped of clutter and the third-hand, so my poor bashed brain no longer had to cope with many small stimuli but only with a few huge ones ...

I mean the Tree in Broad Street, or yellow dawn light flaring over Scapa Flow as I walked to work, or a curlew turning over the Ness like an airy key in an invisible lock, letting some door within open again. And though the light was short, each day I'd look out at a horizon wide enough to give a glimpse of the curve and true size of the Earth.

I mean Cara's sleepy song in the back of my car driving back from

Kirkwall; a cast fizzing out into the dusk over Harray loch; a fish supper warming my hands through last week's *Orcadian* as I came along the echoing empty flagstone street and suddenly came to myself again as a voice said clearly *When you are dead you will love this*, and I felt again the hunger, warmth, damp, the smell of hot fish and vinegar, and folded the miracle of being here at all deeper into my father's coat as I hurried homewards.

As I stretch cramped legs then crunch through the mussel beds onto the sands of Evie, I can see something has changed between now and then, and whatever else might have happened I know I have these islands to thank for it. For I can look around me at this howl of light, at the distant figures by the Broch, at the disappearing nearly-young man and his grandson, at everything that's not for ever, and a voice murmers, *But it's now.*

He wanders through the Simpsons' upper garden in the thick soft night, needing a break from the music, the chatter, the bodies. Something too feverish in the party tonight, or in him, God knows. Several of the planters are drunk, can't blame them, going home, poor sods, they cluster round the few women, married and unmarried. After the fiasco of the bowls, Alan was put on a rickshaw home by Mr Simpson. Adele and Trent have left early. They're well out of it. There's something sordid, even ugly, in all this hunger and need. Time he went home.

A thump from inside, something breaks, laughter. A new record comes on, one of Alan's boogie-woogies. *If you knew/ What I'd gone through/ You'd be crazy too* ...

He turns away from the house, wanders towards the little gazebo. Someone has lit red night-lights inside it, and even from here he can smell the mosquito coils, see the smoke rising. It's like a little abandoned stage. Empty glasses glint on the near rail.

Whisky in one hand, cigarette in the other, he goes up the three steps with just a trace of a stumble.

'*Here* you are.'

Ann detaches herself from the shadow and stands before him.

She lights up one of his Gold Flake, blows the smoke out through her nose and grins at him. She is, he realises, a bit squiffed. But then so is he, or he wouldn't say what he's about to.

'So why did you turn Alan down?'

She turns and looks at him, eyes squinting through the smoke.

'I haven't.'

'So you're thinking about accepting him?'

She sighs, as if he's a dense pupil or she's been asked too often.

'Sandy, there are a number of men I like, and I'm enjoying myself. I've seen what comes of an impulsive marriage. Regrets. Then first guilty thoughts, then guilty ...'

She trails off, looks over back at the house. He wonders just how much the sisters share.

'It won't do, will it?' The words jump from her. 'Once you're married, you can't jump ship halfway across. You'll end up drowning in the mid-ocean.'

He shrugs, not at all comfortable. The night is very warm, and the dark's solid outside the flickering lamps. He's slightly worried about malarial mosquitoes among other things.

'Alan's a good chap,' he says, trying to steer the conversation back. 'He thinks the world of you.'

'I know,' she says. Then she turns and looks right at him. 'Do you believe in marriage?'

He leans back on the rail. 'It exists,' he says dryly.

Ann bangs her glass down, takes a step closer.

'Oh, don't be smart, Sandy! You know what I'm asking.'

He carefully drains his whisky, thinks about it. About Ann, who suddenly seems more substantial than her sister. He and Adele spar and bicker between bouts of confidences. This is different, this is head-on challenge, and deserves to be met.

'I believe in a lifelong mate,' he says slowly. 'Some marriages are good, I don't doubt that.' He thought of his parents. He had no idea what their marriage was. Had they had any dreams and hopes? Had they been realised? 'And when people make a promise, they should stick to it if they've any backbone.'

'But if they're miserable, or just disappointed? What then?'

Ann's voice is urgent and throaty. The red night-lights set around them flicker conflicting shadows across her face, making it not just bonnie but for the first time a mystery. She is close now, her presence seems to fill the little lit octagon. Outside them is nothing but unknown night and jungle, so much of it.

He hesitates. He has no clear view on this. Even if he did, he suspects his actions don't bear it out. If he's not careful, he will fall into the hypocrisy he so loathes in the previous generation, the ones who made the war. Perhaps he already has.

'What then, Sandy?'

With difficulty, he looks at her, so urgent and alive.

'Then perhaps one should leave it,' he says, and for a moment it seems even the cicadas and the jungle have fallen silent.

Ann turns away, adjusts her shawl over her arms, her face down, her bobbed hair flickering red-gold. Across the garden, voices come faintly, and 'What'll I Do?' on the gramophone. The air is overpowering with frangipani and smoke from the mosquito coils. He feels a prick, slaps the back of his hand. They should go inside.

'Sometimes a person marries another person, thinking she is saving him.' Ann's voice is low, he has to come closer. 'It can look that way, but perhaps it is her that is being saved.'

Now she turns, looks straight up at him.

'She's highly strung. You understand? You mustn't believe everything she tells you. I'd do anything to protect my sister.'

'Yes, I understand that.'

'I'm not sure you do,' Ann said. 'I don't think you understand at all.' Then one step closer, and she kisses him.

They clutch and sway, turn slowly like dancers on the summerhouse stage. As her wrap slips from her shoulders, there is a small human sound from under the acanthus.

'Who's there? Who's that?'

A giggle, then one, two small shapes glimmer in the dark, running back to the house. Where a door opens and revellers stagger out, carrying a lantern, heading their way.

Sandy hears a muttered and rather impressive curse, then he is alone. He lights a cigarette, feels the carotid artery pulse in his neck, that and the other stirrings. He draws deep with a shaky hand, tries to think of England or something equally unerotic, not the softness of Ann, nor the unexpected heat of Adele.

He pictures again the tobacco tin lid, blurring between two skilful hands.

25

Party time in the far North, when people get together at the darkest of the year, looking for a spark.

Christmas in Orkney was fine, as I'd decided it would be. I told myself I was lucky to see it at all, phoned my mum staying with Peter and his family, and we opened our presents to each other during the phone call. Music CDs, and an electronic guitar tuner, and a hand-held virtual fishing set.

Everything must go.

My instruments, my books, my car, even my shoes will end up with someone else or in the skip. The agenda of my life will be shredded. As if I could forget.

I unwrapped my mother's parcel to find an old book bound in soft cracked red leather. *The Collected Poems of Walt Whitman.* On the flyleaf, I was astonished to see my father's signature. I knew he'd had a prodigious memory for poetry, but mostly of a traditional sort, learned at school by rote. Judging by its condition, this one had been read a lot, travelled a lot.

Then on the title page, another surprise. *For Sandy – well played, partner! Yours, PM.* Had to be Marsden. So old Mrs Cunninghame was right, they really had called him Sandy. I wondered what game they'd played as partners. Billiards, most likely.

The third surprise was the best. According to Mum's note, *Thought this might interest you,* she'd found it in the Whitman.

Two men in white tropical suits stand looking into the camera. My father tall and thin, straw hat in one hand, a cigarette in the other. I've never seen a photo of him this young. Left side parting in thick hair, tight-knotted tie, slim shoulders sloped like a coat hanger. His grin could be cheery – cheery, for God's sake! – or defiant. The other man is shorter, perhaps older, has one hand casually in his pocket, the other pointing at the camera. Most of his face is shaded by his Panama hat, leaving his eyes unfathomable. Below his neat moustache, his mouth is slightly open, as if he were speaking at that moment. They are a couple of feet apart, and between them I can see a window filled with jars and little boxes.

I turned it over and read in my father's hand *Lebuh Chulia, May.*

I dug out the map of George Town I'd had sent me by the Malaysian Tourist Board. Found Lebuh Chulia. Yes, it really existed, behind the port, in the centre of the old colonial town. Mrs Cunninghame had mentioned it as the street of the dispensary. This could be it.

I wondered about the man with his face in shadow. Alan? Marsden? The head of the practice? Mrs C. might be able to identify him. Time to get in touch again.

I stared at the picture, hearing the sweltering street sounds, the clack of rickshaws and clogs, babble of Malay, Chinese, Indian, English voices. Why was this photo taken? Who took it? Why was it kept? Only one thing for sure: on Lebuh Chulia my father as a young man had stood with a companion for a moment with sun splashed over his face, as real and present as me now, quick-burning as the cigarette cupped in his left hand.

The Waifs & Strays Xmas Party, held at Duncan's house, was one of Ellen's ideas: a gathering of ten of us (plus three children) who had no families or partners here, come together to celebrate their good fortune. A soundtrack was playing when I walked in the door, a warbling cacophony of swoops and howls and soars, not in any recognisable key, nor with any recognisable musical intervals or rhythm.

'Congratulations, Ray,' I said. 'A Christmas number one for sure.'

'December 20th, off Warebeth,' he said, checking the mini disc label. 'Rising tide with westerly force four. Wait till you hear the sound of the shape of the Birsay ebb on an easterly wind!'

'Is it much better?'

'Na, not really,' he admitted.

I flicked through more tracks while everyone started to get their knees under the table. They were all rubbish, unlistenable, like that Theramin Dr Who electronic instrument left on random. I'd been hoping we might have stumbled on something original with our music of the shape of the sea. Bit disappointed, yes.

Crackers already being pulled, wee Cara and a couple of her chums getting over-raised already, the vast browned bird resting on the table. Odd how cooked meat, unemployed actors and the dead are all wrongly described as 'resting'.

But we are grown-ups, we make Christmas in whatever groupings we find ourselves, and this will be a good one because we've decided it will be so, and for today we'll ignore that sniper in the church tower.

Ellen handed a long knife to me.

'You're an engineer and a carnivore – do something useful to that defenceless bird.'

I carved, as my father always did, first stropping the blade to a lethal edge. Then his hands went to work, quick, devastating and delicate in the way of talented surgeons and chefs. I can see him yet, bent over the bird, concentrating, almost communing with his patient as the neat pile of slices grew.

When we were all ready, Duncan called for disorder and held his glass up.

'This life!' he toasted. 'Love it or loathe it.'

We raised our glasses and drank to that. Ellen squeezed my shoulder as she went on by.

(The photos that were taken that afternoon, of people flushed and jubilant with daft paper hats, hugging and pulling faces across a strewn table of ravished earthly goodies, Ellen's hot cheek on mine, Cara on Ray's knee reaching for her new crayon set, and the others holding glasses and flutes, cigars and fiddles, people who are scattered now, some whose names I struggle to remember – years from now our images will turn up in drawers, attics, or between the pages of a book, to say we were alive and back then then was now.

Let's correct that toast of Duncan's – *Life: love it or leave it.*)

I came home late that night, very tired but humming quietly. The company of friends, the gathering of self-proclaimed waifs and strays, is good. I thought of Mica, up in that big dark house in Outertown, attending her father's dying, and my heart went to her.

In my bedroom, my Buddha had grown a small blue flower from his Good Fortune vase. Her note by it read *Loving all things and so hating them to avoid turning into a love wimp – Merry Xmas! – Monica.*

Despite the heat, they've eaten their way through this special dinner in the little creaking bungalow he now calls home. Once Alan had deduced that morning what was going on – the package from home, the telegram from brother William in South Africa – Li Tek was sent on a shopping spree. Oysters, langoustines, tinned ham and pineapple, tin of plum pudding, foil-wrapped French cheeses, oatcakes and shortbread. The Malayan bachelor's birthday meal. They've had two bottles of wine, toasted each other's health and that of the immortal Bobby Jones, and are now on to brandy and cigars, Rachmaninov's *Second Piano Concerto* lugubrious on the wind-up gramophone.

'So she turned me down, dammit!'

'Put you off till later, I'd say,' Sandy says. 'At least you're on the waiting list.'

Alan groans.

'Seems like every single chap in George Town calls on her. I know Freddie Ellyot's taken her out round the island on his motorbike again. Bit of a chump, isn't he?'

Sandy chooses to let that pass. The *Penang Gazette* has been full of the arrest and deportation of Chung Kai Chuan, and when he'd made some mention of it to Ellyot on the fifth tee, the man had flushed then hooked his drive into the pinang trees.

'Maybe he'll break his neck on it some day,' he suggests.

Alan brightens at this prospect and accepts another brandy.

'I'm off to the tin mines in Perak for a month,' he says. 'I'll ask her again when I get back.'

Sandy raises his glass. 'Have a good trip.'

'Happy birthday!' They touch glasses and drink. 'So what's it feel like to be thirty?'

Sandy looks round the little room, the row of books, the Good Fortune Buddha perched high on the shelf by the door, the small framed photo of Father and Mother on the ice at the curling. He's thousands of miles from home, thirty and still single.

'Very well,' he says. 'It's just another day. I don't hold with—'

There's a rap on the door. Giggling and scuffling on the step outside. Li Tek never knocks. It's almost unknown for anyone to call on him at night.

In they come, grinning with glee at his surprise: Marsden, Adele, Ann. 'Couldn't let this occasion pass, old man,' Marsden says. 'Here, congratulations.'

A bottle of Glenfiddich. As Sandy turns the long angular bottle over in his hands, he is jolted by a sense of exile, touched almost to tears. While Alan – now looking very cheery – and Marsden sort out glasses and folding chairs, Adele and Ann stand in front of him, side by side. With her little mocking smile, the one that tugs her lip and shows two white teeth for a moment, Adele formally hands him a small wooden box.

'From both of us,' she says.

Ann nods happily. In the lamplight her face is golden, flushed with life.

'You mentioned the old men used to play it in your village,' she says. 'So we thought you're probably old enough now. Happy birthday, Sandy.'

She kisses his cheek. He slides open the lid, blinks as he looks down on the packed rows of ivory dominoes, the round black spots glistening like contracted pupils.

When they've gone, he stacks away the chairs then steps outside into the courtyard with a last cigarette. It's very late for him, for Penang, and the only light is a dim red flickering from the Hindu shrine at the street end. He doesn't know much about Hinduism, only that they have a clutter of gods and that feels ... messy. One is more than enough.

I have said that the soul is not more than the body,
And I have said that the body is not more than the soul.

He exhales, looks up at the night. Feels night air like moist silk slipping over his throat and arms. Charcoal from the night fires, sandalwood incense from the shrine, whisky from home – though he is tired, his senses are wide awake. Thoughts like fireflies spark, go out, re-appear, tracking their journeys across the dark.

In sixty years they'll all be dead and gone. And tomorrow he expects to deliver more children into the world. What's he to make of this?

He looks back into the room, seeing again his friends grouped round the table under the lamp, the rattle of dominoes and the clack of laughter. Marsden quipping but ever-watchful, Alan frank and open. Above all he sees Ann and Adele, one smiling, the other with her lips pursed, as they consider over the possible combinations hidden in their long-fingered hands. How could he have first seen them as near twins? Now they appear as alternative fates.

'From Mr Lu's workshop in Acheen Street,' Adele had murmured as he'd first shuffled the dominoes round the table. At that moment, Marsden had been busy setting up chairs, while Ann and Alan were at the gramophone sorting out some less lugubrious music. 'A Malay proverb says there's another blessing hidden in each gift, for those who have the wit to find it.'

Now he draws on his Gold Flake, thinking about it.

Marsden hadn't played. Instead he'd sat near Adele, freshening drinks and changing records, putting on the jazz and crooners that Ann had brought. But at one point he'd been twiddling a domino in those deft, neat hands, making it stroll from finger to finger, when he'd coughed and said almost apologetically, 'My father used to have a hollow domino. In the old days gentlemen used to keep snuff in them – or in his case, opium . . .'

Very unusual of Marsden to mention anything of his family. Maybe that's why he'd remembered it. But someone had chuckled, Ann chapped her last domino triumphantly, and looking round the table at that moment Sandy had been swept up in a glow of thankfulness for his life, these friends, the age he'd come to when many of his contemporaries had not. For a moment it seemed to him this is what life could be, an adventure, moving forward constantly into the new. Then Adele had glanced up into his eyes as if there were something he should understand.

He's sure he hadn't imagined it. Marsden had said that, then Adele had looked up into his eyes. A double act? He knew there was speculation on the island as to just how much they shared.

He leans back on the doorframe and inhales deeply, thinking it over.

Just before leaving, Adele had packed all the dominoes away in the box. No, nearly all. From here he can see one propped up beside the Buddha.

He doesn't credit that supposed Malay proverb. *A blessing hidden in each gift, for those who have the wit to find it.* No, it sounds too laboured.

Still he stays out a minute longer, smoking and looking up at the different stars. From somewhere behind them comes Father's voice. *Dae weel, Eck. Dae richt.*

26

I picked up a copy of the photo of my father and his unknown companion in front of the Lebuh Chulia dispensary, posted it with a short note to Mrs Cunninghame, then drove up out of Stromness in the short-lived light of the last day of the year.

Late March would be the payback, everyone assured me, when light returned like a flood tide. My contract would be up then and I wasn't sure where I'd be. Anne-Marie was still politicking for resources to take our report further. There was a chance of our pushing further into proof-of-concept and running a couple of prototypes ...

I took the single track road out to Yesnaby, up the last incline that rises into the blue then stops where the land does, abruptly in a strew of fragmented sandstone and concrete left from the war. I stopped the car, pointing at the sea. Outside, the wind was very strong; it slammed the door closed and the windscreen went quickly opaque with salt spray.

Buttoning my dad's coat up to my neck, I pulled down my woolly green *Lochinver* hat, fumbled into gloves then walked out carefully to the edge. Three hundred feet below the sea was smashing turquoise into a storm of white. A few hundred yards out a small boat rode the big swell, heading back for Stromness. I wondered if that was Kipper. He was known for going out in roughest weather, and when Mica spoke of this lack of wisdom her eyes shone.

I turned away from the cliff edge and walked south battered by the gale. Yellowish dods of gunk flew through the air where the cliffs dipped into a bay. I staggered cautiously to the cliff edge again and looked down. The whole bay was covered with yellow-brown foam. It rippled and heaved in the wind like some vast breathing hide. Scuds of it were whipped off and went flying up the cliffs and away inland.

I walked on, felt a soft cold paw on my face. Put up my hand, pulled down a clod of yellow sea foam and watched it fizz and dissolve. I kept pushing into the gale as more attached itself to my jeans, and soon I was half covered in the stuff and looking vaguely abominable.

I brushed it off, kept moving. The wind and spindrift were a fine distraction, an easing in a way. I was thinking about the Waifs & Strays party, about Mica who hadn't answered my calls or been in touch since Christmas, about the lives in Penang gone for ever, of Tina's skeletal fingers closing on my wrist and my promise to her unkept. This knowledge of dying I carried in the marrow of my bones and the stem of my brain. It wasn't so much I thought too much of Death, more as if Death were thinking too much of me. Wherever I went, I felt a vast, indifferent eye turned on me.

Then up ahead I saw a steaming, a soaring of smoky-grey water up a slit in the cliffs. It rose clear into the air then bent back and shot off inland where the turf was shining. It was like the cliffs themselves were smoking, and I couldn't understand it because the sea was well back at this point in the bay.

I'd get soaked if I got closer but I had to see. So I staggered through the buffeting down the dip towards this baffling spout, staring at its rising and whipping back and the sodden shining puddles it formed inland round some baffled-looking gulls. I wanted an explanation, I always do.

At the bottom of the dip, a small burn flowed under the barbed fence, heading towards the spout. I got closer and my coat was being steadily spattered before I could see what was happening.

The burn ran over some flat stones then dropped over the edge. I leaned out and watched the water fall as water should – then it was caught, sucked away from the rock and hurled up into the sky and blown back across the land. The stream kept pouring out but none of the little waterfall actually got to the sea. It was caught in a natural energy feedback loop – the inland spray-pools fed the burn which leapt over the cliff and was blown back again into the pools and so on and on, endlessly renewed.

I stared and stared. Then when I was thoroughly wet and had what I needed, I turned and set off back to the car, to call on Mica at her father's house.

I came up Hellihole onto the Outertown road, turned into the drive and saw the ambulance by the front door. The ambulance doors were as open as a newly dug grave. As I stepped from the car Mica hurried out of the house. She came up to me, her face pale and tight.

'This is a bad time,' she hissed. 'You shouldn't—'

Behind her framed in the doorway came a short procession: stretcher man one, man on stretcher, nurse by stretcher wheeling oxygen trolley, stretcher man two, then Kipper Johnson. Everyone was concentrating on what they were doing except him. He was looking at me.

I stared at her. At him. At her.

Behind her shoulder, on the stretcher her father stirred. He partly sat up, an oxygen mask on his face, he grimaced and waved me over.

I stood by the stretcher by the ambulance doors. Jimmy Moar was half propped up on one elbow. All the stuffing had leaked out since I'd seen him last, transparent skin and burning eyes. He crooked his long boney finger, beckoned me in. I bent towards him as he fumbled down his oxygen mask.

'Just an ordinary day, boy,' he whispered hoarsely.

Then he fell back and they had the mask back on him and carried him into the ambulance. Mica leant her hand on my shoulder.

'It's the final taxi,' she said. 'To the hospital. What did you come here for?'

It didn't seem the time to talk about parties on the Holms or endless energy loops or any of the other things I was ready to say to her.

'Can I help?' I managed. 'Lift to the hospital?'

She shook her head, looked back to Kipper who was still standing glaring in the doorway.

'Kipper will take me.'

The ambulance began reversing and we ended up on opposite sides of it. Then it shot off and we were left with only space between us.

'Go to the Holms party,' she said quietly. 'Have a hoolie on me. Catch you later.'

Then she walked back to the house, to Kipper who put his hand on her shoulder as she passed inside, gave me one last stare then went in after her.

I drove down to Warebeth beach, sat in the car looking out in the general direction of Greenland with Jonathan Richman's *The Modern Lovers* playing quietly. Somewhere out there the wave measuring buoy was sending the brain waves of the sea back to the old academy without meaning, break or end whether anyone was there to see them or not.

I sat on till the music had long flown into the mystery and it was dark at the end of an ordinary day, then I drove home to change for the Hogmanay party out on the Holms.

Sandy Mackay could divide his time in Penang into before and after the day Marsden found him practising billiards in the Penang Club.

'Thought I'd take a drive to the Botanical Gardens,' he'd said straight off. 'Fancy a spin, old man? Could do with a chat.'

Sandy stayed down till he'd made the long-table pot.

'I've got my semi-final next week,' he said. 'Need to practise.'

Marsden popped the red back onto the table.

'I'm told Van Oerstrat's drinking again – you'll win. I've put money on it.'

Sandy knocked the two reds in then straightened up.

'I wouldn't mind a trip out of town,' he said. 'This place is a goldfish bowl.'

Marsden drives easily, one-handed, through the outskirts of George Town. The day is hazy and colourless, and though it's sweltering, he keeps the windows up. His voice is matter of fact as he fills in the background to the request Sandy knows must come.

It's a matter of balancing forces, it appears. Of good intelligence. The Kuo Min Tang – Sandy has heard of them?

He has indeed. Some Chinese political organisation, linked to the new government in Canton. It had been banned about the time he arrived in Penang.

Marsden nods. Suppressing the KMT was not necessarily a good idea, and it had raised a bit of a rumpus because the new Governor had done it without clearance. Banning the Malayan KMT is inflammatory, will drive out the moderates, and probably won't work anyway, which makes the administration look both oppressive and weak – the worst possible combination.

Here Marsden pauses, says something Sandy never forgets.

'You see, our power in the Far East can hang on prestige or bayonets. Given that we have no standing army here, prestige is preferable.' A quick grin, a sideways glance. 'We administer this place but we don't own it. We couldn't hold out long against any serious attack, though Singapore is safe as long as we have a navy.'

'I see Bill Tilden's won Wimbledon for the third time,' Sandy says.

'Remarkable at his age,' Marsden concedes, but isn't deflected. 'We're going to hand over anyway, sooner or later,' he continues. 'What matters is that we leave the place in good order, and free from outside dominance.'

'Straight sets too.'

'Which could be China or Japan.'

They're driving past Millionaires' Row now, the gleaming mansions where money resides. Marsden explains Governor Clementi has been reminded by the FO that he is in Malaya to do what he's told, however clever he may think himself. The problem now is to retreat without losing face. But that's a political problem. Marsden's department is, ah, neither political nor military.

'So you're spies?'

Marsden winces.

'We prefer Intelligence, old man.'

The Kuo Min Tang are still printing and distributing Chinese Humiliation Days, holding banned meetings, calling for non-co-operation, like Gandhi in India. The long-term aim isn't Malayan independence but to extend China's power in the Far East. Chinese are a large part of the population of Malaya, and are economically dominant, so their loyalty is crucial.

So, Marsden continues, on one hand we've the struggle within the Kuo Min Tang, and its attempts to undermine the governance. Then there are the secret societies, with the Hakka and the Hokkien feuding – the stabbings, the odd murder you read about in the papers, they're mostly about that. Then there's the Communists.

'That's three hands,' Sandy says.

Marsden nods, smoothes his moustache.

'Told you it was complicated,' he replies, and drives on.

Despite himself, Sandy is interested. It explains glimpses he gets in the *Gazette* of things hinted at, the scuffles, deportations, searches. Despite knowing he's being used, he finds he still likes the man. Enjoys, he must admit, the little fizz of excitement that comes with a challenging obstructed labour.

Now Marsden fills him in on Communist activity in Malaya. They're opposed to both the British administration *and* the Kuo Min Tang. At the moment they're more formidable on paper than in fact.

Sandy nods. He's read about the Tiverton Lane seizures. So that's what Marsden is up to in Singapore. Well, well.

'That was one of Onraet's successes,' Marsden says. 'But it doesn't stop there.'

Marsden pulls up his little Austin outside the gates of the Botanical Gardens, switches off. In the silence he looks at Sandy. Here it comes.

'There's a man called Abdul Raman,' he says. 'At least, that's one of his

names. It's said he's back in Penang, where his brother's wife is eight
months pregnant ... We would rather like to find him.'

27

We gathered down by the shore by torchlight, clutching carrier bags of booze and food, some with guitars and fiddles. Stevie was there with his wife Jane, Ray sucking on a cigarillo, Ellen with Cara and a crowd of our students. Duncan was absent-mindedly blowing Blues harmonica as we changed into wellies, and the notes persisted long after they'd gone out under the stars.

So many stars too, once we'd turned our backs on the yellow lights of Stromness and looked out to sea. We were quiet as we began to walk out into the dark, trusting that at the bottom of the tide the seaweed-strewn rocks held no deep pools. I could hear the sea out on either side as we slithered and stumbled on, following the faint torchlight, aiming for the steady light from the cottages on the inner Holm.

Reek of seaweed on freezing air, the faint strains of the harmonica under the glittering stars, heading out towards the island with these pilgrims, I felt my father all around me in his coat. Thought of Mica at her father's deathbed, of my mum with her humour growing sharper as her memory gaped and let in more light. I glimpsed again the golden girl met for ten minutes in a London street when some portal had opened onto a new world. Above all, bobbing in front of me while we sploshed through the pools, I saw Jimmy Moar's collapsed face staring up at me. Pulling off the mask, saying those simple extraordinary words: *It's just an ordinary day.*

'We're just in time,' Ellen said at my side.

Right enough. In her torchlight the turning tide was running over our feet like pale rats, sploshing and muttering, a thousand tiny hisses as the weed rose. She slipped, grabbed hold of my arm and together with wee Cara we hurried across the last of the dark and up onto dry sand.

We were in it now. No one could leave this party till the next low tide.

The two adjoining Holm cottages were brightly lit, hung with candles and streamers, loud with competing musics, packed with a cross-section of Stromness life. Word must have gone out. Here were the faces I'd come to know, DOA staff and students, the Heriot Watt crowd who shared the academy offices with us, the Zurich Brothers already energetically thrashing country blues, the folkies sawing away in the next room, the young smokers passing large joints around in the kitchen.

As I moved around the rooms, letting the red wine go down and the chill leave my bones, I heard the accents range from broad Orcadian (and even I was beginning to distinguish between the accents of Stromness and Kirkwall) to southern English, urban Scots, a couple of Lewis voices, Aussies, the South African couple who'd come to visit on a world-hitch and never left, the urbane New Delhi murmur of Surinder discussing New Psychology with a native graphic artist and an incomer plumber.

A mixed bag, a mixter-maxter as they say. Natives and incomers and returnees all coming together in these bright rooms. In cities you choose your company, which means you end up with people like yourself – same interests, values, income bracket, aspirations, sexuality. But on small islands you make do with whoever happens to be there, and so are put into the company of folk you wouldn't otherwise know. At a glance I could see a retired professor, two evangelical Christians, a baker, a sculptor, a cook on the tugs and two amiable barflies, all drinking home brew with a skeletal vegan.

I'd been putting this to Stevie and Ellen. She laughed and said when she told friends South she lived here mostly for the social life they thought she was joking.

'Enough shouting our heads off,' she said. 'Dance?'

But I wasn't ready yet and drifted off for refills beside Stevie. I told him about Mica's dad going into hospital. He nodded, knew already. The jungle drums never sleep.

'And Kipper Johnson was at the house,' I said casually. 'What's that about?'

He scooped peanuts into his mouth, followed by a slug of Jack Daniels, washed down with red wine.

'They have a history,' he said vaguely.

Everyone said that. What did it mean? Above the clash of fiddles on my right with thrash metal on my left, Stevie leant in and shouted in my ear.

'It's natural that Kipper would be there. He's Jimmy Moar's great-nephew.'

'That means Mica and Kipper ...'

'Aye, sure,' he said. 'They're half-cousins or something.'

'She didn't tell me that,' I muttered.

He scooped more peanuts down his maw.

'I've tried to tell you,' he shouted. 'Things aren't always as nice and simple here as you'd like. There's circles and secrets and histories. We're on an island, boy.'

I thought about it. Could explain why Kipper had been up at the house. This could be good news.

'Let me try that Jack Daniels,' I said. And then I was called through to add some faux-Bluegrass banjo to the Zurich Brothers harmonies, and lost track of Stevie for a while.

We had hollered 'Don't Sit On My Jimmy Shands' and were halfway through a heartfelt version of 'Keep Your Distance', fine Richard Thompson song bitterly acknowledging attraction to a dangerous woman, when I felt the draught. Then a bit of a commotion by the front door. You could feel the change ripple through the party.

Kipper plus his brother and boat-partner had just come in with a huge carry-out. It was as startling as if they'd come down the chimney, because everyone knew we'd been marooned for a while now. That's what made the party special, the knowledge we couldn't be interrupted and no one could leave till the tide fell again. That's what screwed the lid down and let the pressure cook.

'Must have come by boat,' Andy muttered between verses. 'Be careful.'

I got a long baleful stare from Kipper. I nodded back, he looked at me hard one more time then turned away.

The two adjoining cottages weren't that big. Nor was the Holm itself, maybe a hundred and fifty yards by eighty and nothing on it apart from the houses. We were on a very small island and it would be hours till the tide was down. I couldn't avoid him all that time. Maybe if we talked while he was still sober. This whole Neanderthal thing was corny and daft and well past its sell-by.

I found him in the kitchen, half bottle in his hand. Big hand, already red and swollen. It was a hard job, no mistake. I'd taken to him, something sardonic and yearning in him I liked. Any Dylan fan is distant kin.

He broke off talking with a very drunk schoolgirl. Looked at me hard. Pale blue eyes, distant or unfocused under tow-coloured hair.

'Aye, boy,' he said, and drank.

'You surely didn't wade over?' I said. And drank.

'Christ no! Took the blue boat, like.'

'So how's Jimmy Moar?' I asked.

The mist in his eyes blew away. They were very focused on me now, and I became aware of his brother leaning by the kitchen door.

'What do you care, pal?'

'Well, just because,' I said. 'He's a very sick man.'

He looked at me long. I stood with my arms down, open and loose. Damned if I was going to play this confrontational game – or be intimidated by someone at least fifteen years my junior.

Kipper swallowed. I saw his Adam's apple rise and fall, noticed a pale scar line across the side of his neck. These moments when the world becomes so clear, so absolute. Maybe it was that way for Jimmy Moar dying. *Just an ordinary day, boy.*

'He's no dead yet,' Kipper said. Had another slug of whisky. I drank my wine, the brother stirred, the drunk girl giggled and Kipper glared at her.

A warm hand brushed across my cheek, pressure on my thigh.

'Hey lover – you owe me a dance,' Ellen said.

And she led me away into the next room, still draped round me like clingfilm. Once we'd made our space in the crowd and begun to dance, she eased away from me. I could feel the warmth where she'd been and my body rising to it. She looked at me and laughed.

'I do hope that's not a gun in your pocket,' she said.

I looked away, saw Kipper and his brother standing in the doorway staring at us.

'Body has a mind of its own,' I said. 'Sorry.'

She'd seen them too. She put her arms round my back and swayed into me.

'Don't let it come between us,' she murmured. 'I think you need some protection – make like we're an item.'

I took her point and we slow-smooched in our tiny jostled space. It wasn't unpleasant. Her cheek on mine was softer than Mica's. Wasn't supposed to notice that but I did. No lines at the edge of her mouth, her neat lips uncreased. She was a good friend.

'Hey,' she whispered, her breath soft and alcoholic by my ear. 'Relax.'

I was getting tired of women telling me to relax. She glanced off towards Kipper and his crew.

'Eddie?'

'Yes?'

'Think we'd better snog.'

I looked at her, the little grin on lips I'd never thought to kiss, and then I did.

The young lad at the gate decapitates the coconuts with a casual swipe of his machete, hands one each to Sandy and Marsden. These are nothing like the brown hairy novelties he remembers from fairs, but huge, green and smooth. They are, as always, cold and delicious inside, the thin sweet juice trickling down to clear the dust and choke of the day.

They walk by the empty bandstand, past the zoo enclosures and greenhouses. (Wouldn't it be grand, Sandy thinks, if in this country there were coolhouses in the public gardens?) The golf course apart, this is the largest clear space on Penang, and it's a relief being able to move unobstructed. The rest of the island is mostly either the dense streets of George Town or solid jungle. Here it's quiet, mid-afternoon, mid-week. Ornamental pheasants stroll about, a group of macaque monkeys come running down the path, cuffing and swearing at each other.

He's not happy with Marsden's requests. They include approving a particular temporary doorman, and if necessary admitting his patient early, perhaps keeping her in for a few extra days. He doesn't like it at all, though Marsden argues he's not asking him to practise bad medicine, only to be over-zealous.

More than that, it means further days with Adele walking the corridors at his side, more lunches and confidences at the Runnymede, more awkward delayed partings. Ever since he opened the domino he can feel words rising hot and burning in his throat, demanding release.

He risks being a knave or a fool, perhaps both. Odds are he is mis-diagnosing both Ann's flirting and Adele's restless sparring and sudden confidences. Even the tiny photo hidden in the double one could be a little joke, a wee pliskie. There'd been no inscription, just a pinch of pollen and her unreadable eyes looking out at his. Could mean anything.

Recently he's been calling less on her help, found reasons for not coming to the elder Simpsons' Sunday parties. He can still extricate himself. Perhaps if he goes to Singapore on his leave ...

They have reached a large pond at the far end of the gardens. Marsden sits on a bench, glances at his watch then conjures a cigarette from his case, lights up. Sandy has never been this far into the gardens before. Something about the pond draws him, its steaming yellowish clarity, the little island in the middle, the stillness of it all and then the dark green of the jungle soaring behind, so thick and unkennable ...

'*I too am not a bit tamed, I too am untranslatable,*' Marsden murmurs behind him.

'*I sound my barbaric yawp over the roofs of the world,*' Sandy automatically continues the quotation, hears Marsden chuckle.

'So you like the Whitman? I noticed it at your bedside the other night.'

Sandy glances round at him, so immaculate and elusive.

'The man goes on a bit, and he does seem rather full of himself.'

'Oh yes, he is that.'

Sandy tears his eyes away from the jungle, the silent-steaming pond.

'But I like yon bit about animals. *They do not sweat and whine about their condition.* What if I don't do what you want?'

He's already decided if Marsden threatens him, that's it.

'You don't like politics, do you?'

'They get a lot of people killed.'

'Yes, they do.' A pause. 'That's why they matter.' Another, longer, pause. Marsden puts his hand on his arm. 'You must do what you think is right, Sandy.'

Do well. Do right. He stares at the wall of green across the pond. Beside him, Marsden jumps up.

'If you don't mind waiting here, old man . . . '

Then he's gone, hurrying down the path towards a couple of men who are disappearing over the brow of the slope.

It's the still and stagnant hour of the afternoon. The light is so haze-bright it leaches the colour from everything except the slab of dark green jungle. He can see now a faint gap in its curtain, what looks like the opening of a path. Trouble is, he hasn't a clue what's in there and if it's dangerous.

He's stares at the broad steaming pool then closes his eyes against the glare. It's a relief. A bit of peace and quiet. Maybe this is what Daniel Ng meant the other day, in that courtyard in his temple, this calm in the muddle . . .

Then he feels it. A force that's swept across the park breaks on his chest and passes on through. Shocked, he opens his eyes and sees a gold-green ripple dying across the pond. But he has heard no fish jump or stone thrown, and there is no wind.

Across the pool, in a pale blue dress, she is crouching with one hand trailing in the water. She looks at him with a simple enquiry.

28

I was kissing Ellen. It was that kind of party. All round us, things were getting out of control. A drunk local girl was draped over a skinny student while two local lads looked and muttered. What looked like strip poker under the table in the corner. All bedroom doors closed now, someone peeing out the window because of the queues at the loo. Joints the size of telescopes navigating from hand to hand. The kind of party that had brought Mica to my door in the first place. When Eden goes wrong . . .

Ellen pulled back.

'That was pretty half-hearted,' she said. 'You're a rotten method actor.'

'Sorry,' I said. 'I got distracted. We can try again.'

She reached up, put her finger on my lips and gave me an unfathomable look.

'You've had your chance,' she said. 'Anyway, he's gone now.'

I looked, and so he had. We moved apart a little, carried on dancing but something had gone out of it. Eventually she put her hand on my shoulder.

'Cara's playing with the other kids in the back room,' she said. 'Better check she's okay.'

'Sure,' I said. 'And thanks, Ellen.'

'My pleasure,' she said lightly, and was pushing away through the crowd.

The mood of the party had changed. The social fabric I loved to wrap round me was fraying at the edges. As I stood at the door to get some air a lad pushed by me and threw up over the flagstones. He spat a couple of times, rubbed his stomach then went back in for more. Inside I saw the woman of the couple who'd rented the house for the Christmas period. I didn't even know her except by sight, and I guessed most of the people here were strangers to her. She looked taut and anxious. There's a line between accepting hospitality and taking advantage, and most of us were on the far side of it.

I looked round. There were many hours to go but already the first spillages and breakages, the mashed crisps, beer-stained shirts, the first baleful looks and muttered curses.

A tearful girl came out of a bedroom. I saw her hugged, though it looked more like trapped, by two girlfriends. She was led away then one of the girls hurried into the bedroom and the door closed.

The musicians were shouting more than singing, Duncan and Blind Cal were blowing Blues harmonica into each other's faces; a couple stood motionless on the dance floor, only their jaws working as they sucked the souls from each other. And back on the Mainland Jimmy Moar was dying. Mica was with him and I wasn't with her. I wanted to be there but had no right to be. I wasn't related. We didn't have a history.

'Okay, boy?'

Stevie, looking concerned. Him at least I could rely on. I felt a wave of affection, remembering our pilgrimage to the Broch of Gurness, and though the well had been sealed off, just making the trip together was a bond.

'Not really,' I said. 'I'm kinda . . . disappointed.'

We looked round the room, through the archway into the scrum that was the kitchen, the various competing dins where speech became babble. Some hoarse shouting squeezed through from the other sitting room where I thought Kipper had gone.

Stevie shrugged.

'It's just an Orkney party, boy. No as bad as it looks.'

A crash and tinkle from the kitchen followed by laughter. The harmonicas were now wailing through Robert Johnson's 'Crossroads' and I thought it was this kind of party when that dark genius made an unwise pass and drank the poisoned wine.

This is not right.

'Maybe it's me,' I said.

He put his hand heavily on my shoulder. We were both fairly drunk, I could tell by the way the movements of his mouth and his words had become uncoupled.

'There's nowhere perfect on this earth, Eddie,' he shouted in my ear. 'Just some places better than others, and this is one of them.'

'I'm going outside,' I said. 'Need a break from this.'

'Further you can keep away from Kipper the better. He's getting tanked up in the kitchen.'

'Can't get very far from him here,' I said.

Outside with Stevie it felt better as we let our eyes adjust to the dark. There were many many stars. Off to the south the Flotta flare stack burned its giant candle, lots of non-renewables being non-renewed there. Away to our right the lights of Stromness strung along the shore, the yellow streetlights and the little glowing curtained rooms, the houses clinging up round Brinkies Brae, the lights suddenly stopping below the top leaving it dark.

I breathed deeply. The air was very cold. I wanted to be in Stromness, walking along James and Dundas and Alfred Street to my bed, to lie down and declare the first year of the new millennium ended and this ordinary day done. Shouts, laughter and music and light spilled from the house behind us.

We began walking, stumbling in the darkness down to the glimmer at the shore. Following the sand along to the promontory, round the corner, back towards the house lights again. We talked of Orkney, life and love and death. He told me something of the tensions and losses of his life as well as its satisfactions, and I told him back. We talked in circles as we walked a circle round that tiny tidal island and back to the two low cottages. I remember we seemed very close.

We came round the back, past an outhouse. As I followed Stevie, my head exploded. Light flashed black and white and I was falling, acrid taste of violence in my mouth.

I was lying on cold flagstone. Looked up, saw it all against the outside light. Kipper standing over me, grinning and flexing his fist, his brother on one side and Stevie on the other.

'For Christ's sake, Kipper,' he said. 'Get a grip.'

But he did nothing. Johnson looked down at me as I rolled, trying to get away.

'Happy New Year, cunt,' he said and lashed out with his boot. I was rolling and the toe caught my ribs and all the breath yelled out of me. I dimly heard Steve say, *Aw c'mon, Kipper.* I looked up and he was standing looking very worried but doing nothing. For a moment our eyes connected. Someone stamped on my thigh and it went numb and I couldn't roll away.

Then Ray was there. Little Ray took Kipper by the shoulder and said, 'That's enough, Kip.'

Kipper stopped dead. Looked at him and something passed there. Then Kipper's brother yanked Ray aside.

'Stay out of it, ya poof,' he said.

Then there was a flood of other voices. Our hostess, looking pale, Ellen and a couple of other women swamped Kipper and his brother and somehow got them out of there.

Then silence. Everyone had disappeared except me and Stevie. I got to my feet; my legs seemed to be still working though my right thigh was numb. I looked at Steve, he looked back at me.

'You all right?'

'Still breathing,' I said. 'Fuck, it hurts.'

'He shouldna have kicked you.'

'You didn't stop him.'

He opened his mouth to speak, closed it. Looked away off to the Stromness lights across the water as though the reason was there.

'I'm sorry,' he said at last. 'I have to live here, Eddie. You can move on.'

So that was the bedrock. Fair enough. When it came to it, all that had passed between me and Steve on our walk round the island was hot air and non-renewable haivering.

Steve spread his arms like he was being searched.

'I'm *connected*, man,' he said. 'Wife and bairn and family.'

'Sure,' I said. 'Forget it.'

A silence between us. From inside there was a shout, hoarse and angry. Then raised voices, quietening down. Another shout, a crash.

'Just another Orkney party?' I said.

'Some are wilder than others,' he admitted.

The crash this time sounded like a window going. Some thudding sounds like a bull in a stall.

'You'd best get out of here,' he said. 'Better for everyone.'

'What did you have in mind?' I said. 'Yogic flying or swimming?'

He hesitated. 'The blue boat,' he said. 'I'll row you back.'

꒰ꢀ

Inside the rainforest the trees are tall and thin, so close together. Everything is entwined, creepers grow up trunks, lianas hang down from branches and feed back into the ground. Orchids white, yellow, crimson, have latched into every cranny. The sky isn't visible, not a speck of blue up there, just dark solid green. The cackling, screeching, clicking, scuffling, slithering, is constant, but he can't see a single living thing in the thick dim light.

Except Adele. She has led him in here by the hand, now turns to face him. Her pupils are huge, her lips part.

'Help,' she says quietly.

Their mouths meet, add low sounds to the jungle din.

꒰ꢀ

He took a torch from his pocket and together we hurried down to the shore and the wee pier. The boat was there, swinging on the rising tide. Steve shone the torch down on it.

'Hell's teeth,' he said. 'They've taken the rowlocks.'

We looked at each other, his face pale in reflected torchlight. The faint shouts and cries drifting down from the house sounded ugly.

'Okay,' he said. 'Nothing else for it – better wade back.'

'You're bloody joking!' I stared at him. 'There must be feet of water out there.'

He glanced at his watch, thought about it.

'I've done it before,' he said. 'In summer admittedly. Trust me, it's possible and it's for the best.'

Then as we hurried down to the shore nearest the Mainland, he added, 'You can swim, can't you?'

'Not that well,' I said. 'Certainly not for long with boots on.'

'We'd best stick together then,' he said.

We were on the sand by the water's edge. It was pure black out there. Faint swishing as the water sucked and scoured by. The Orkney mainland shore, a slightly deeper dark with the lights of Garson farm beyond that, seemed a mile away. There was a dirk under my ribs every time I breathed.

'I swim like a herring,' he said. 'Life-saving badges and all. At worst we'll get very very cold and wet.'

I hesitated. I could see it in next week's *Orcadian. Tragic accident after party – two bodies missing.*

'Let's do it,' I said.

We walked into the shallows. For a couple of seconds my boots held out, then icy water swept in. I breathed in, it hurt. Breathed out, that hurt too. We resumed, stepping forward into the darkness. It went against everything I knew.

Water up our shins, then calves. Another ten yards, stumbling about over rocks. Now up to our knees. My lower legs were going numb. The going was getting harder and slower, it was wading through icy black syrup. Worse, the tidal current was sweeping across right to left, the way it did on Ellen's charts. I knew about that current, had been working out how to use it for months now.

My numb feet slipped off some underwater ridge. I fell sideways, felt the current tug me even as Steve grabbed my arm and pulled me upright.

'Better hang on to me,' he said. 'This is as deep as it gets. Trust me.'

'Oh yeah,' I said. My mouth was going numb, couldn't speak right. Still we pushed on into the water. It gripped my crotch, squeezed me freezing right where I lived. If I'd told Mica to get lost first time she showed up, melt back into the night she'd come from . . .

'Don't like this,' I mumbled. 'Better sing.'

'Amazing Grace?'

'River Deep, Mountain High?'

'By the Rivers of Babylon.'

'Boney M? You must be fucking joking. Jeez, I can't feel my knees.'

'Don't know that one! We could sing hymns.'

So we waded on deeper into the dark, terribly slowly now, bawling 'All Things Bright And Beautiful' till we ran out of verses. I couldn't feel my legs at all. The lights behind at the cottages looked miles back and the darkness in front had no end. He gripped my arm and I knew then he was worried.

'Carrickfergus!' I said. '*The water is wide, I cannot swim over* . . .'

We ploughed on into the dark, his torch flashing ahead, looking for the shore.

'Knew those life-saver badges would come in handy. Not so far now.'

'*I wish I had a handsome boatman* . . .'

'*But the sea is wide.* Hang on, Eddie. Whoops! Thanks, boy.'

'Here, you know you're not planning on having any more bairns?'

'How does that one go?'

'It goes – I don't think we're going to make it.'

'Hmm, don't think Jane would be too chuffed. She likes her oats. Hey, we're getting shallower!'

'We were never that deep. Shit . . . '

'Don't get carried away now. Okay?'

'Okay.'

'Look, I'm sorry I couldn't . . . '

'It's okay,' I said. 'Understood. Island life.'

And we hurried through the last shallows, the water unmanacling our frozen legs, fell full length in a foot of icy water. Salt in my mouth, the whole taste of the sea like eating oysters but cheaper, then we knelt gasping on the shore of the Mainland at the end of the year.

Finally she brushes down and straightens her dress, belt, hair. Marsden is calling. They have to go to him.

'But won't he ... mind?' Sandy said.

'*Mind?*' she said. She stared at him as if he were backward. 'What did you think was going on?'

He shrugs, feels some certainty ebb away. He'd imagined this moment so often, so many nights lying under the fan, and he'd always thought it would change everything, resolve everything. Make the path clear.

'I thought maybe you and he ...'

She stares at him.

'Well, you do go everywhere together,' he says. 'You put your arm through his. People talk. I could never understand why Trent put up with it.'

She laughs then, and the wild sound of it sets off scuffling overhead.

'You poor booby! Phillip isn't interested in me like that.' She pauses, picks a tendril off her shoulder. 'Not the way he shuffles his cards, if you see what I mean. John knows, that's why he doesn't mind me going around with him.'

'Oh,' he says. 'Ah.' Interesting condition, one he knows little about. He remembers it was an effective way of getting out of the Army. 'Good.'

'Good?'

'Well,' he says, 'I'd much rather that than ...'

She laughs, quietly this time, kisses his neck.

'Phillip's a true friend,' she says. 'Please don't be beastly to him.'

She takes his hand, ready to lead him out of the woods, but he holds her back.

'What do we do now?'

'I haven't the faintest idea.'

A sharp crack! above their heads. Something slithers down through the trees. Then directly above Adele he sees something that will haunt him for the rest of his life: a cloud, a swirl, a column of tiny yellow butterflies silently streaming up into the gloom.

'Whoops – there goes my immortal soul!' she laughs.

Her wondering upturned face is green in the half-light. He feels around them the rainforest rising and rotting, the growth and decay rushing through their own bodies, no difference, no distance at all.

Marsden makes no comment when they walk out of the jungle together.

Perhaps there's a hint of a smile, a sardonic tinge in his voice when he apologises for being away so long. As he drives them back to town, Adele sits up front and Sandy is alone in the back. And when he gets out at the street corner, feels the momentary damp press of her hand on his, he seems to have agreed to everything Marsden requested.

29

Standing on the Sands of Evie at the bottom of the tide, my forearms gooseflesh at the memory of that crossing. At the time I thought it was as bad, as mad, as desperate as it got.

Island life is a lesson in quickfire karma. What you do comes back to you sooner or later. On a small island, it's always sooner.

I look down-light at the way I've come, see the weight of my feet has printed an erratic trail of hollows across the tidal sand, shining as they fill.

My front door scraped, a pause then it clunked. I was awake again with heart whuddering. Mica? Kipper? Glanced at my watch – nine in the morning, first day of the year. Tide well down by now. Should have locked the door but I've got out of the habit living here.

Footsteps in the hall, into the kitchen, then out. Thump on the door.

'Come on in,' I said. Might as well face it. I sat up in bed in the grey light, wincing at the sword thrusts between my ribs.

Ray was still in last night's party clothes, spangly shirt and all, but he didn't look very glittery.

'So you made it across,' he said. 'That'll be the talk of the town for a while.'

'Better than being beaten to a pulp by the Lobster Crew,' I said. 'And a Happy New Year to you.'

'Happy New Year, Eddie.'

He held out a half bottle. Observing the formalities, I took it, wet my lips then returned it.

He sat on the end of my bed. We looked at each other. He glanced at my Buddha, so jolly and indifferent. Then we looked at each other again.

'I think . . . ' He cleared his throat. 'I think it's time for a few words of explanation.'

'That might help,' I said. 'There's some decent coffee in the kitchen cupboard. I'll join you in a minute.'

'I assumed you knew,' he said and blew the froth off his cappuccino. 'Neat little gadget this.'

'Christmas present from my brother,' I said. 'I assumed you were with Ellen.'

He laughed quietly as I put the choc shaker in front of him.

'What's convenient isn't always possible,' he said. 'We're great pals and she's a lovely woman, but it's not what turns me on.'

I nodded and watched while he shook a great shake of chocolate onto his froth.

'I've been blind,' I said.

'Ah, too much Mica in your face,' he said. We laughed a bit, and it did seem funny when it didn't hurt. 'Not so much blind as looking in the wrong direction,' he said at last. 'It could have been Ellen and you, you know.'

I thought about it. The party where we'd talked and danced, but me caught up with the swirl of energy round Mica. Our shopping expeditions, the evenings that followed them. The conversations once Cara was asleep. Her abrupt change in style after the last time, the sense I'd got that I'd done something wrong and she was trying to act as if I hadn't. Yes, it should have been.

'Past tense?' I asked.

He looked up at me across my table, eyes round and the colour of the chocolate he'd shaken.

'I'd say that window of opportunity has closed,' he said at last. 'Anyway, you're stuck on Mica and you can't do much about that, any more than I can. Being gay isn't exactly the lifestyle of choice in Orkney.'

'Not a big scene, then?'

'Not even in Kirkwall,' he said dryly. 'Though you'd be surprised the people that have made passes at me, and some more than that.'

He sounded quite pleased and bitter at the same time. I thought of the morning he'd darted out of a door onto the lane in the night before's clothes.

'Kipper being one of them? That's why he vanishes whenever you're around.'

'Very good,' he said. He licked away his foam moustache apprecia-tively. 'No, not with me personally, though I admit he's got a certain something.'

'What, then?'

'Kip went into the Merchant Navy after he left school,' he said slowly. 'To get away from his bastard dad. And like a lot of straight men, after a while at sea he wasn't averse to a bit of how's your man. Happens I know about it through a pal, and Kipper knows I know. I had a word on our way back this morning, and I don't think you'll have any more trouble from him.'

'Thanks,' I said. 'I appreciate that.'

'Nice to have the blackmail going the other way for once,' he said.

I got up and set up the wee coffee maker again, took out the jar of Ellen's flapjacks.

'Your limp?' I asked. 'Trouble?'

He nodded.

'London,' he said. 'They broke my leg and a few other bits. That's one of the things that made me apply for the job here.'

'Jesus,' I said. 'Man, I'm sorry.'

'I assumed it was common knowledge,' he said.

'Looks like the jungle drums didn't beat in my direction,' I said, and felt bereft to be outside the tribe.

'Once I realised you didn't know, we were too embarrassed or something to say. And I think Ellen was kind of annoyed, because she'd fancied you and you didn't get it.'

I thought about it, listened as the refill pot frothed its top. Turned the knob and released the pressure. I thought of her snog at the Holms party. I'd assumed it was just to protect me from Kipper, and maybe it was, by then. Which made it even more generous somehow. It had been nice, too. Nice mouth, nice lips. Good person.

'You're right,' I said. 'Our desires aren't convenient.'

'Nope,' he said. 'Sometimes they give you a good kicking.'

'Certainly had that,' I said. 'Thanks again.'

He nodded, champed on his flapjack.

'Oh, another thing,' he said. He put his coffee down and looked at me, serious now. 'Jimmy Moar died round six this morning.'

I plodded up Hellihole Road to Mica's on that grey blustery morn with my head blurry and right hip feeling it had a stake driven into it. Thinking about what Ray had shown me of the way things really were.

I thought too about Jimmy Moar going up and down this brae slower and slower until he stopped. Now he'd never be seen here again. It's such a simple shallow thing, death, only there's no bottom to it and no way across.

As I tightened my dad's coat, I saw him walking down Chulia Street, stepping in and out the colonnades, seeing and smelling and glad to be there, all young and hungry and alive. He's going for lunch with *her* – and a friend. Yes, of course she'd have a friend, a chaperone, a cover . . .

A peewit tilted black and white over my head. I looked up and its wing beats moved in me, no distance between us. I saw it, felt it, each wingtip feather spreading, and there was no *out there* for a long long moment. These things happened – the glimpses, the aerial voice – every so often since my brain got squashed, moments of existence that made all the rest a dwam, a daze, a half-dream. It was some compensation for feeling subtly posthumous the rest of the time.

The bird settled on a long flat glide down towards the flooded fields and I limped on.

Up the drive, past the stunted twisted sycamores. The house was dark except for a light in Mica's bedroom. A car I didn't recognise was parked outside. Because of it I rang the bell and waited, feeling more like a tradesman than a lover.

'Yes?'

The stranger standing there all burly and fair-haired turned out to be Mica's brother, finally back from Canada. I didn't ask if he'd made it in time, just said I was sorry about Jimmy Moar and asked if she was in.

'Not available. Sorry mate.'

So I left the card I'd brought, suspecting she'd despise all such conventions. *I'm very sorry. Be in touch whenever. Love, E.*

I turned and walked back down the gravel, past where Jimmy had raised himself on the stretcher then stared into my face to say that one simple unfathomable thing. Rain had cleared the air to the south, way beyond the cliffs of Hoy I could see the blue-grey mountains of Scotland across the water. It was another ordinary, irreplaceable day.

As a doctor, Sandy Mackay knows more about sex than most men of his generation. Unlike them, he has a clear understanding of menstruation, fertilisation, conception and delivery. He knows about hormones, their various effects on the brain, the central nervous system, heart rate, blood pressure, erectile tissue. It gives him a certain satisfaction to see himself and others, politicians, kirk ministers, film stars, shopgirls and street-sweepers alike, all in the grip of biology.

He has read Freud and agreed we are driven by a backseat driver no one wants to talk about. He has read *Married Love* and knows about the clitoris, its surprising blood supply and extensive wiring. He has a good objective understanding of sex as biology rather than object of morality. All else is delusion. It is important not to be deluded. He has been fooled before by talk of God and Empire and Duty.

His sexual experience up to this point? A degree of initiation with the minister's daughter before leaving home. In London then in France he had the messy, urgent experiences typical of young men not wanting to die a virgin. Then in the last year of his degree, he was selected by one of his few female fellow students for a thorough mutual exploration of anatomy. She was intelligent, pretty enough, and very clear she would never marry. After graduation she briskly shook hands with him, wished him good luck, then boarded her train to London.

He has known crushes. He has read of passion, mad love, romantic love, in novels, seen it in films, and has always considered it somewhat ridiculous, not for serious people. Before coming to Penang, he'd studied maps, checked the statistics, read accounts by others, glanced at some pictures – but none of his research prepared him for standing on deck above the Butterworth Quay, finally smelling and seeing and feeling Penang.

So it is now for him with love, if it is love, or desire, if this is desire. At the age of thirty this serious, wary, reticent man has arrived at a place he thought a myth.

Since the Botanical Gardens encounter, he is gone, fallen as if into poison ivy. He itches and aches in places he didn't know he had, for instance that place in his chest whose workings as a pump he understands well, but whose other aspects are a mystery. He must walk the wards beside Adele as if everything were as before, concentrate on this swollen abdomen, find that foetal heartbeat – with her only feet away, calmly taking notes.

He has called Mrs Raman in early as Marsden had requested. The new doorman, a shifty-looking Javanese, is in place. Abdul Raman's brother, the woman's husband, has visited, but not the man himself. Looking her over this morning, Sandy is a bit concerned about the delivery – this is another small woman with tiny feet. Worse, she has a fibroid the size of an apple lying low in the pelvis.

He should be thinking only of this woman's delivery, not Adele's lips light as a moth fluttering on his, the little gasp of her breath in the underwater forest light. He must concentrate on one woman as a biological mechanism he must deliver, not another one his whole being yearns to touch again.

He lifts his hand, smoothes down Mrs Raman's nightgown. It could be another breech or even a shoulder, but the baby has a good heartbeat. The fibroid is large, but shouldn't impede delivery. This at least he can do.

They part on Macalister Lane. The street is crowded with hawkers, rickshaws, bullock carts and a few motor cars, traders, coolies and businessmen. It is not a private moment. Private moments will be hard to come by. No lunch at the Runnymede today – she says she's promised to meet Ann outside her elementary school in Perak Street.

'I expect she's going to give me a good talking to.'

'What does she know?'

'Enough.' She pulls a face. 'My little sister has always been rather possessive of me. Don't believe everything she tells you.'

Sandy has heard this warning before, from Ann in the gazebo. Modern obstetrical procedures are a doddle compared to working these two out. She is about to walk off when she hesitates, and for the first time today her eyes meet his.

'When you put your hand on her belly like that – was it just for reassurance?'

'I was determining how the baby will present itself – breech, head, shoulder. And checking the size of its head.'

'You can feel that through the skin?'

She seems incredulous, as though he were claiming special powers.

'Yes, of course,' he affirms. He has no idea that his intent absorption in examination has moved her more than any flirtation could. 'It's just practice and concentration.'

'And her feet? When you held her feet – what was that for?'

He grins at her.

'Believe it or not, there's a relationship between foot size and . . . pelvic brim diameter.'

She can't help glancing down at her long slim yellow shoes.

'Then I'll hold no surprises for you,' she says.

She is still laughing at his expression as she pats him on the arm then walks off down Kedah Road, a yellow flame moving without harm through crowds of sarongs, suits and saris. He feels himself fall, fall and burn with helpless longing. It seems she has made some kind of promise, her smallest gesture blazes him.

30

The funeral notices went up in the usual places, the baker's, Post Office, Mill Stores, by the harbour. JAMES EASTON (JIMMY) MOAR. Folk stopped, read, agreed it was no surprise and went on with their shopping. It happened nearly every week, after all.

I was standing in front of the notice at the Post Office, thinking it might give us a more balanced outlook if there were also bright cheery public notices announcing the town's new babies. With that invisible sniper up in the clock tower picking off the population one at a time, a bit of good news might help.

'So he's gone, then.'

First time I'd seen Ellen since the Holms party. She looked trim and perky in a new brown leather jacket. She seemed to have completely shucked off her old earth mother look I used to tease her about. Her lashes were darker, and her fingernails were a flash of crimson on a dull day. The mouth I'd kissed was bright too.

'I was thinking about babies,' I said.

'Well count me out,' she said. 'I've done my time.'

'Ellen, I didn't mean—'

'There's a season for everything,' she said. 'And I think it's passed, don't you?'

I looked at her and saw a determined young woman heading into a new life.

'Yes,' I agreed. 'I suppose it has.'

'Any more stunts like crossing from the Holms mid-tide and you'll not have babies with anyone.' She put her neat hand on my arm. 'I was so worried that I'm still angry at you.'

'Thanks,' I said. 'I mean, sorry. I think Ray's taken care of it.'

'Yes,' she said. She bit her lip, looked up at me again. 'Look, I'm sorry about that. I kept meaning to tell you. I mean, we knew you'd be cool about it. Maybe I wanted you to ... '

She tailed off. Her eyes were bright as she looked and blinked at the funeral notice. Then she flipped her scarf back over the collar of her new jacket.

'*If wishes were fishes* ...' she said briskly.

'*Men would swim free,*' I supplied the rest, and it felt good to walk on with her down James Street like we were friends again. Which we always had been, which was all we were ever meant to be.

Sandy sits in the shade of a small cafe stall, reading the latest *Penang Gazette*. The world is on the verge of an abyss. At home, in Europe, in America, the Depression is spreading. Trade is dying, there is mass unemployment, everywhere rumours of wars and revolutions. China's civil war rages, the Far East is falling apart, markets have collapsed in tin and rubber.

It's bad, bad. He looks up from the paper, orders another coconut, lights a cigarette and turns the page. The New Woman is flighty and unstable, hemlines are rising, the civilised world is obsessed by sex, marriage is in terminal decline.

He quickly turns another page. The Australians, led by the irresistible Bradman, are humiliating England at cricket. Wimbledon is dominated by Americans. Having completed the Grand Slam, Bobby Jones has announced his retirement.

Bad times to be sure. Yet the voices around him are friendly, this clear cool coconut juice is delicious, his cigarette smoke mingles with the smells of spices, sweat and sea. He is nearly young, he is in the Far East – and here she comes in a taffeta dress of blue pale as her eyes, crossing the road toward him, so slim and urgent.

He rises to his feet, removes his hat as she approaches, and in that moment he is terribly, terribly happy.

'This weekend!' she says quickly. 'We're all going up the Hill to the Crag Hotel. Phillip says he can arrange that we . . . Please say you'll come.'

As he stares into her eyes, the world situation has gone up in smoke and left no residue but a hint of ash in the wind blowing down Light Street.

I took the morning off work to go to Jimmy Moar's funeral. Stevie and Ray came too. As we walked along to the kirk in black ties and best jackets, I felt I was being escorted by a bodyguard.

Maybe I was at that. Standing at the gateway below the church, among a small group of old men in dark coats, was Kipper Johnson in black suit, white shirt, black tie. Shaved and with the thick ponytail tied back, he looked pretty good if pale.

He went paler when he saw us. His eyes flicked to Ray, then away. If pirates could look embarrassed and discomfited, he was one. We kept on walking up the steps, the bruise above my right eye throbbing again. I wanted to hammer him. I'd never make a Buddhist.

'Easy,' Ray said quietly. 'Sometimes you have to take it and let be.'

I nodded as we went into the gloom. He'd had a much worse going over and was trying not to let it sour his life. I had to do the same and neither fight nor run away, if that could be arranged.

The church was less than half full. Jimmy Moar had been a difficult character, and according to Mica certainly not a churchgoer. I think most of the people were from the golf club. The long box was near the pulpit, the waxy white lilies must have been flown in.

The organ tootled on, a baby cried. Then a small procession, led by the minister. I recognised Mica's brother before her. She was in a turquoise two-piece suit that might have been her long-dead mother's. It was of a completely different era, like the small dark red hat perched high on that unruly hair. Pale, and she wasn't looking at anyone, nor at the coffin.

At the end of the short service, she came forward. For the first time she looked across at the coffin, the white lilies, then she focused over our heads and began to speak.

'To the living we owe discretion, to the dead we owe only the truth. Some smart clerk said that, and I think my father would have agreed.'

She paused, swallowed several times. I thought she might fall over, but when she continued her voice was firm, matter of fact, almost defiant in its clarity.

'So here's the truth.

'My father's life was a disappointment to him. Neither his work nor his wife nor his children were what he'd hoped for, and there was nothing anyone could do about that.

'James Moar was not a sweet man and life didn't please him often and he never pretended otherwise. He didn't pretend. You can call that arrogance, or honesty.

'He did the work that dissatisfied him well. He loved his wife to the best of his ability, and when that wasn't enough he brought up his children as well as he could though it was not what he wanted to do with his life. There was a lot of burnt toast and beans but that's better than no toast and beans at all.

'He did have satisfactions. Most of them were on the golf course, or in the clubhouse bar afterwards. He had a strange passion for Frank Sinatra and the Nelson Riddle Orchestra and the songs of Jake Thackray. He liked watching birds, dogs and seals being themselves. He relished watching the television and seeing his gloomy prophecies fulfilled.

'He liked knock-knock jokes.

'He endured his life and he endured his dying. He came from a generation that were good at enduring.

'It's a shame there wasn't more joy in it.

'That's all I can say.

'So goodbye, the old fella.'

We queued up to shake hands with the immediate relatives, me still clearing my eyes. In her words, I'd said goodbye to my own father all over again, for they'd not been unalike. For a moment I stood in front of Mica and wanted to hug her, fold her into me. But we were a secret if a widely known one, and she held out her hand automatically and I shook it as I had her brother's.

'Thanks for coming,' she said formally. Her mouth, her whole face was stiff like she'd had botox injections.

'I had to,' I said. 'I'm very very sorry.'

Her eyes flickered, just for a moment.

'Thanks, Eddie,' she said.

I hesitated and started to turn away, and as I did so she rapidly and minimally signed, *Catch you later* then turned to the next person and we were done.

I walked slowly down the path towards the street. Someone seized my arm and I turned to face Kipper. It's hard to look straight at someone who's given you a beating, but I made myself.

'I'm sorry, man,' he said. 'About the other night. It was, you ken, the drink.'

I kept looking him in the eye, reminding myself about his father. He'd embarrassed himself and that was bad enough.

'It'll no happen again,' he said. 'Definite. Right?'

'Sure,' I said. 'Don't think twice, it's all right.'

But I said it like it wasn't that all right, and he got the message. He held out his hand.

I looked at it, at him. Wondered how long I intended to live here. After a long hesitation, I shook it, briefly, once. And was about to turn away when he spoke again.

'She's told you, right?'

'Told me what?'

He looked at me, then away. A couple of elderly men were waiting to speak to him.

'She'd best tell you herself,' he said, then I walked home with my escort, my friends.

The funicular carriage clicks slowly up the cogs of the track with just enough momentum to stir some air through the open window. The railway up Penang Hill is still a novelty, the green painted wood and brass rails still shiny, and the carriage is packed. All the races and cultures of Penang are here, jammed close together. The Malays courteously avert their eyes; the Chinese stare indifferently; the Europeans look and talk to each other over the heads of everyone else.

Sandy looks at Adele who leans back against the rail opposite him. Her white oval face is calm, distant. Two fair tendrils have escaped the body of her hair; they bob over her left ear with each jerk of the railway's gearing and he feels quite sick with longing.

She smiles faintly at him, then turns to murmur to Marsden beside her. That dapper magician twiddles his fingers around his mouth, says something and she laughs quietly. Perhaps Sandy imagines the man's quick glance his way.

The track steepens. The carriage is now enclosed in a narrow gully, pulled upward through plummeting jungle. The air is dark green, lit by glowing sparks of flowers. They rise slowly past a pale monkey that hangs by one arm and waves the other across its face as though wiping them out of its sight. Ann exclaims at the tiny baby clinging to its shoulders, *Sweet!* she murmurs. '*So sweet!*'

Sandy glances at her beside him. Her face is quite lit up in the green gloom. Impossible not to sense her full breasts, her hips, her fecundity. He has no doubt she would deliver babies like peas from a pod, plop plop plop. She squeezes against Freddie Ellyot at the window to glimpse the monkey a moment longer, then she looks back at Sandy with an almost apologetic grin at her enthusiasm.

Just then, the carriage becomes pitch black as they enter the tunnel section. A couple of quiet gasps, a giggle, then complete silence in the crowded carriage.

A hand, soft and warm, touches his. Strokes the back of his hand, then works round into his palm. A thumb caresses the hollow there, fingers flicker along his, then grip tight. It is so dark, the touch so intimate, his erection is almost instantaneous.

The hand abruptly loosens, leaves his – and the carriage is light again. He looks at Adele opposite, but she is gazing calmly out the window.

Ann? Her head is turned towards Ellyot. Marsden looks coolly back at him; for a moment his eyelid flickers.

Sandy's heart is still thumping as he steps off the carriage at the top of Penang Hill. His palm tingles as he lights a cigarette. At the very end of his life he will feel again that touch in the dark, and still wonder whose it was.

'Right,' Ellyot says briskly. 'Anyone for a beer at the Crag?'

31

We sat opposite each other in The Cafe, at the seat by the window over the harbour. I looked at her looking at me. For once no quips or challenges. At other times that would have pleased me.

'I did warn you,' she said.

I nodded, wondering how much that excuses any of us. She looked down and found some salt grains on the table worth prodding into place with her ringless ring finger.

'I'm not proud of it,' she muttered. 'I've behaved like a dickhead without even the excuse of a dick.'

She licked her fingertip, gathered the salt on it. She looked up.

'I'm leaving,' she said. 'South, maybe abroad. The house is going up for sale.'

'I know,' I said. The jungle drums had beaten that one out. 'And what about us?'

'Eddie, there wasn't an us. I kept telling you.'

'But it had got to the point where there was going to be,' I said. 'Either that or we'd just be fucking and disgusting ourselves.'

Once, twice, she opened her mouth then changed her mind. She looked sideways out the window as the Hoy ferry scudded away.

'I know,' she said quietly. 'Maybe that's one reason why I'm off. Dad's gone and I don't know yet where that leaves me.'

Pure lust, I'd noticed, eventually collapses under the weight of its own contradictions – rather like capitalism, but much quicker. Sleep with someone a certain number of times and you start to get to know and feel for them, then the ignorance that generated the lust in the first place has gone.

I put my hand on hers. It was warm and human and mortal.

'Let it go, love,' I whispered.

She looked startled. She looked down, gripped my hand. Then she sat back, well back, and laughed.

'Men always want to get to the heart of me. They think there'll be a soft vulnerable person there. Well, maybe there isn't! That's what you want, isn't it? Me to open up to you.'

Nothing I could say to that, it was true enough. Still, I felt she was arguing with herself, so I just looked at her and waited.

'That's what I liked about Kipper,' she continued. 'He left my soul alone. Given half a chance, you'd want everything.'

'And give everything, yes,' I whispered. I was sweating now as we closed in on the core of it.

'Maybe you want too much.'

'Maybe you fear too much.'

We stared at each other. For once, she looked down first and I knew there was more.

'Something else I have to say. God, this is difficult.' She swallowed, looked out the window at the ice-plant and the pier. 'That mistake I once said my body's always trying to make? Well – it's happened.'

'Bloody hell,' I said. 'Blimey.'

I looked at her and felt dazzled, almost giggly. I looked out the window. Right now, the Holms were joined to each other but not the shore. I'd lost track of whether the tide was rising or falling, but I could see a life, a different life, an utterly different life beginning.

'I thought. I shouldn't have. So so stupid.'

Then she stopped. Her hand lay on mine, she squeezed hard. Her eyes were so large and bright blue-grey it seemed like pigeons flew through them.

'Eddie, I don't think I can have it,' she said.

'Of course we can.'

'It's not that simple.'

'Of course it's bloody simple,' I said, and for once in my life felt complete conviction. 'You have baby, I earn money, we don't sleep very much but baby grows. You write book, I create sustainable energy, Scottish parliament finds visionary leadership, child walks!'

I was getting a wee smile from her now.

'Your book gets published, tidal currents become major renewable energy source, Scotland grows up – child starts to talk sense!'

I had this feeling as long as I kept talking, something might come out right.

'It's easy as driving a car, Mica – morons do it with ten per cent of their attention. I'm at the far end of forty with a tube in my head, and you're a flake with attitude, but we can do this.'

Just a hint, a tiny curl at the edge of her mouth. Then her eyes darkened like cloud-shadow passed over the sea. She leaned closer across the table.

'I have to tell you,' she said. 'Paternity's not guaranteed.'

They say the world stops, or your heart does. It's more a matter of a world ending, the one you thought you knew, and a new one, a poorer and more weary one, starts to take its place.

'Kipper?'

She nodded, looked down.

'Could be,' she whispered. 'I haven't been entirely . . .'

I never found out what she hadn't been entirely. I was out the door and into the street of this grey new world. I walked home wishing to bash my head off the walls, break open my shunt, anything at all to obliterate what had just been dreamed and lost.

The top of Penang Hill is something very like paradise. At nearly three thousand feet, the air is completely different, almost like a hot summer day back home. It's sweet to take off jacket and tie, roll up sleeves, feel the coolness passing over his arms and neck as they stroll along the terraces, paths and promenades of the rolling wooded summit plateau.

Up ahead, Adele has her arm linked with Marsden's. Her white hat bobs among the peaks of Kedah across the Straits, one more oval cloud among many. Ann has one arm linked through Freddie Ellyot's, and she takes Sandy by the other as they pass through the shade of the pinang trees. She is almost skipping between them like a child; she tucks up her legs and the two men swing her down a short flight of steps.

They're all raised, high spirits and energy flow between them, buoyed up by the fresh air. Up here, looking out over dizzying slopes of solid green broken by the odd red tiled roof, or thin smoke rising from a kampong, then the endless sea in three directions and the Straits to the east, up here it is possible to feel anything is possible.

'There's nowhere like this in Singapore or KL,' Ann says as they alight on a lawn outside the Crag Hotel. 'Penang's a pearl!'

'One mostly cast before swine,' Adele murmurs as she lies back on the bank. 'Present company excepted, of course.'

She adjusts her hat over her eyes to keep out the sun, already getting low over the Indian Ocean. In forty minutes it will roll into the water; in an hour it will be completely dark, with none of the long gloaming of Sandy's home. And once it is dark, the impossible, the longed-for, may come.

Iced watermelon juice, then gin and tonic for the quinine. They sit outside as it gets dark and most of the crowds disappear. Paper lanterns are lit and brought out onto the terrace; they flicker orange, yellow, red, like fat fruit dispersed among the tables. Most wonderfully, there are few mosquitoes up here, so they can sit out as long as they want.

Marsden has changed into a sarong, which he claims was common practice among the tuans in the old days. Bright green and red, which looks so lively on Malays, seems less convincing against his paler skin, but he carries it off. It signals the new freedom they seem to have entered up here. It reminds Sandy of the kilted regiment the remnants of his battalion were transferred into. After an initial awkwardness – he'd never worn a kilt before, as an East Coast man why would he? – it had been practical, comfortable, even pleasurable to wear.

George Town is out of sight below, but a spatter of tiny lights glow at the Batu Ferringhi resort, and out in the darkness at sea two bobbing sets of navigation lights move towards each other, briefly coincide, pass through each other and move apart.

Fireflies begin to blink in the trees like faulty fairy lights. Ann takes his hat, shakes a twig then passes his hat back. He looks down at the sparks where his head has been, and for a moment is enchanted as a child.

'Bet you never thought you'd catch Tinkerbells!' she laughs. Adele groans, Sandy tips his hat and watches the little cascade fall then scatter on their erratic journeys through the night under stars that now seem familiar and right.

Watching the faces dip in and out of the pool of light round their table as they talk and laugh, Sandy thinks he diagnoses what's going on here. Now he knows the truth, if it is the truth, about Marsden, he can see that Phillip is cover for Adele. He always has been. And the assumption by anyone who sees them is that Sandy is Ann's suitor, competing with Ellyot and Alan. So Ann is Sandy's cover in turn, though he wonders if she would wish to be. He can still hear her in the gazebo, her whisper 'You don't understand at all,' the flutter of her butterfly kiss. The heat of her mouth.

She said she would do anything to protect her sister. Or are they locked in competition as Adele had hinted, so she wants whatever her sister has? After all, he's just a young doctor of limited means and no matinee idol, why should she want him other than because her sister does?

And Ellyot? Sandy drifts out of the talk about Coward's new play, all adultery, wit and alcohol. Freddie's hand lingers on Ann's as he lights her cigarette. He is Marsden's man, of course. Enlisted by him to distract Ann from Adele's doings tonight. Or perhaps he is genuinely keen on Ann. Who wouldn't be? What the hell is really going on here?

'But to be serious,' Ann says across the laughter she has just caused, 'these people feel longing and call it love. But it is only longing.'

'Why should they stay in miserable marriages?' Adele snaps. 'Don't people have a right to try to be happy?'

Ann looks at her sister, puts her hand on her arm. At that moment, she seems the elder.

'Yes, but what are we to do when our happiness is purchased at the cost of someone else's wretchedness?'

There is no irony in her voice. Adele examines her nails, Marsden breathes on his cigarette case then polishes it on his sarong, Ellyot stares into his glass.

Then talk turns to Mr Ghandi and his salt tax march, and whether he is madman, scoundrel or hero, and they are on safe ground again.

Who touched me? Sandy wonders as they cross the lawn to their quarters. He knows well enough the question is small beside the fate of India, but like a hand held up close enough to the face to cover the sun, for him it's pressing enough to eclipse the future of the Empire.

Who touched him?

32

O f course we couldn't leave it there. We agreed to meet and behave
like grown-ups, though it was rather late in the day for that. Her
condition: I didn't try to change her mind. My condition: she
gave me the truth.

Warebeth's not a picture-postcard beach. There's sand, stones, skerries,
seaweed, scattered about the place. It is what it is, Stromness's nearest bit
of beach, destination of dog-walkers, runners, Sunday afternoon drives,
and of course lovers.

I'd always liked it because it wasn't obviously beautiful. Also it's just
along from the graveyard, which looked a fine place to be dead if you had
to be and you certainly did – lichen-stained tombstones and the wind
from the sea, peewits, oystercatchers and curlews mewing as the odd seal
pokes up its whiskery snout.

So there was a fine backdrop of intimations of mortality as we walked
along Warebeth, picking our way among sand and rocks and weed. I
looked at the side of her averted head of salt-stiffened hair. Beyond us,
the sea creased white stress marks over the offshore reef.

She said now both her parents were gone she felt light, untethered in
the world. It made her giddy, she said, as though she might fly off or fall
over. I understood?

I took her arm so she wouldn't take off. We reached the far end of the
beach, wheeled about and started walking back.

She told me one of her nippy stories had just won a competition.

'I know,' I said. 'It was in the paper.'

Ellen had brought it into the office and we'd all read it, trying to
identify people and places. Not the most literary of readings, but
inevitable. Mica had given a version of me a good doing-over, but saved
the harshest for a version of herself.

'That's another reason why I have to leave,' she muttered.

'I thought it was funny,' I said. 'But some of it isn't right – like the Post
Office doesn't face the harbour, and you have the ferry leaving at the
wrong time.'

'I know that!' she cried, and scattered a scuttling of sandpipers. 'Think of it as a parallel universe.'

'Hmm,' I said. 'So that's what goes on inside your head. A parallel universe.'

'That's what goes on inside everyone's head.'

'Do these parallel worlds ever meet?' I enquired. 'And isn't that the kind of pessimism people girned about in the early twentieth century?'

'Maybe they do touch,' she said softly. 'Maybe once in a while. Maybe they did here, once.'

I was silent, remembering.

'The Arts Council have offered me a bursary,' she said briskly. 'So I'm in the money, and then there'll be the house. Market research won't see me for a while. I'm going to go away where no one knows me and write and try to save my life.'

Maybe a part of me was relieved. The rest was sinking like a weighted creel, going way down.

We got back to the car and sat in it a while.

'Kipper?' I asked.

We sat on with only the sound of the sea and her breathing.

'It was . . . easier at the time,' she said. 'To do it than not.' She paused. Her long pale throat convulsed. 'I didn't like myself and behaving badly made me feel worse. Which felt good because I wanted to feel bad because I was.'

'Cut the crap – you looked me in the eye and you lied.'

She flushed, opened her mouth to protest. Her pride was the size of a tennis ball when she gulped it down.

'I've been a cunt,' she said quietly.

'You haven't,' I said. 'I *like* cunts.'

She flinched as if I'd struck her.

'So have you told Kip he could be a proud father?'

'I'm not a complete idiot! It's really, really over with him now Dad's dead. I don't feel pleased I can make someone cry, you know.'

I glanced at her. Her eyes were like sand on a falling tide, shiny with water just below the surface.

'One thing Kipper and me always had in common,' she began. She glanced at me, silently asking whether to go on. I nodded. 'We're restless frustrated angry types, so we always understood that in each other. But that's not your problem, is it?'

I considered it, tapped my fingers on the wheel.

'Tell you my problem, *Monica*,' I said. 'I keep doing arithmetic in my head. I keep counting backwards.' I turned and by sheer will forced her to look at me. 'So was it when I was away in London? Or after the gig in the Dutchman when you took Kip away then came round? Or before all that?'

I kept thinking: she was so hectic that night. If she hadn't been home after leaving the pub with Kip, she wouldn't have her cap in. I thought she'd come from a fire, all flushed and raised. Dear God, not that night.

She stared at me for the longest while.

'I don't know,' she said simply.

It'd all been arranged. Marsden and the Simpson sisters are staying in the main hotel, Ellyot is booked into the annexe, and Sandy is in a former gardener's cottage at the end of the croquet lawn. The boy leads him there, hands him the lantern and a key, bows, then leaves.

Sandy looks around. It's tiny. It's perfect. His dinner suit is laid out on the bed. A rattan easy chair. Recent copies of *Punch* by the bed, the *Illustrated London News* by the blue-tiled Shanghai jar. He blushes, remembering how on his first evening in his quarters he'd awkwardly climbed into the unfamiliar receptacle, thinking it a small bath not a storage cistern.

He strips off, ladles the chill water over himself, towels down, reaches for his dinner clothes. A tiny Indian is challenging the British Empire, and a moral atheistic Scotsman is almost ready to commit adultery, if the opportunity arises. The world is changing, no doubt about it.

As he dresses, throwing wild, awkward shadows in the lamplight, he finds himself singing a song of his childhood, one brought back by brother Andrew from his war:

> *Aunty Mary had a canary,*
> *Whistled 'The Cock of the North',*
> *It whistled for oors*
> *And fleggit the Boers,*
> *That dandy young cock of the North . . .*

Marsden lightly grips his elbow at the bar. 'There's been no joy on the Raman case,' he says. 'Can you find a reason to ask her husband to come in again?'

Sandy stares at him, then turns away.

'There's nothing wrong with the woman.'

Marsden drops his hand.

'Sorry I asked,' he says. 'Not very square of me. Just I'm a bit desperate – there's a lot rides on this Abdul Raman affair. I wouldn't want you to do anything unprofessional.'

He looks quite sincere, far as Sandy can tell.

'If she hasn't gone into labour in the next three days, there might be grounds for asking the husband in,' he concedes.

'Thanks,' Marsden says. He glances back at the dining table, sees Freddie Ellyot coming to join them. 'Turn in early, old man,' he says quickly, 'I'll see what I can do.'

I drove slowly along past the scatter of farms, cottages, breezeblock houses, until the Outertown road ended in mud and we got out.

The day was still brimming blue, the shortest day clearly past, as we went through the gate and up the brae. I reached out and grabbed her arm.

'About this baby,' I said.

'*Please*,' she said. 'I should never have told you, that wasn't fair. My problem, my fault, my decision. I'll deal with it but I've got to get off Orkney first.'

She pulled her arm free and steamed on up the brae. I could have called her, said I didn't mind whose bairn it was, but by God I did. I'd known she was difficult, wilful, headstrong, but I'd never thought she would lie.

She slowed and I caught up with her near the top.

'You'll come back some day?' I asked.

'Maybe,' she said and kept her head down. 'Grow up here and this place is always with you. Even when I was South and mad at it, I never forgot.'

The slope in front of us crested and we came out on top of Black Craig by the old wartime lookout. The wind was clean and strong and the sky went on to the edge of the world. The Old Man was a stumpy prick off the Hoy cliffs and the sea, the brimming sea, went on.

She turned her wide eyes on me.

'Don't try to shape this into what it's not, Eddie,' she said. 'Don't kid yourself or me – we never were a fine or tragic romance.'

'But we could have let it become something else,' I blurted.

'And what's that?'

I hesitated, not quite knowing how or why I'd got here.

'Whatever comes after lust and friendship.'

'Which is?'

'What do you think?'

Then we were silent as we looked from that high place out over the big glinty world.

I dropped her off at the foot of the drive of her father's house. We'd said our goodbyes and I'd promised not to see her off when she left.

She paused as she got out of the car.

'There's nothing I'm expecting that anyone can bring.' She shrugged. 'Maybe next time round, eh?'

The sheer nerve of it took my breath away. By the time I'd organised a reply, she was at the front door. She turned and looked back at me, and I'd aye remember her like that: long-legged in old blue jeans, battered green waxed jacket with high collar framing her pale face and shining eyes, and her mouth quivering between tears and mischief. My hooligan, taking life by the curlies.

I raised my hand and quickly signed, *See you around*, then drove away.

Back in his little room – more of a Wendy House than a cottage, he decides – he takes off his jacket, sits in the rattan chair, picks up *Punch* and waits.

No, this won't do. His stomach burns. The night is so quiet, only the whisper of breeze in the atap thatch. If only he'd had a chance to talk with her, but either Ann or Marsden has been by her all evening. On the few occasions he's caught her eye, she's smiled vaguely then looked away. Ann on the other hand has been flirtatious and gay, as though trying to dispel any memory of her earlier seriousness.

But he hasn't forgotten it. Happiness purchased at the cost of another's misery . . .

He gets up, yawns, stretches out on the three-quarter bed, looks at the rough thatch ceiling.

He waits some more.

He hums *Aunty Mary had a canary*, then stops.

Then it comes to him in a flash of certainty. It'll be Ann.

That's what all this is about. That's what Marsden will arrange. There'll be a tap on the door, a giggle in the dark, and Ann will come to his bed.

What would he do then? He blinks and almost groans, for he knows he would not say no.

And after he has lain contemplating his moral depravity, the shameful hollowness of his attempts to do right and do well, the emptiness and vanity of all human desire, and still no one has come, he finally rolls on his side and blows the lantern out.

A double tap at the door. A creak and the thick sweet guff of the night blows in. And some other scent, lilies of the valley. He can smell it where he lies, eyes wide open and seeing nothing, for he is in utter dark.

A thump as she bumps into the table. He reaches out, his fingers close round his matches.

She giggles. He strikes the match.

'*There* you are,' she says.

※

When the alarm went off and I opened my eyes to see my Buddha's cheek glimmering in half-light instead of true dark, I knew the year had turned. I made breakfast, ate and shaved, not hurrying.

When it was time I frothed up a second mug of coffee and took it across the square, down the alley onto the short pier where I used to sit on fine autumn mornings when I'd first arrived. I sat on the bollard by the old derrick and waited.

The morning was fully lit by now, mild and utterly still, a faint mist rose from the flat, electric-blue water, where the low sun and its long, butter-yellow reflection dazzled my eyes. Today the Holms were elliptical lily pads floating separate from each other and the shore in the brimming tide.

The *St Ola* slid away from the big pier. As it gathered pace, the bow wave pushed up white and curling, like wood shavings rising from my dad's plane in his workshop when I was wee. The ferry steamed on through the narrow channel, right by my pier.

She was there at the rail, of course she was.

We stared at each other across the distance. I wanted to shout *Why did you have to tell me?* I wanted to yell *Don't do it!* But there was no way she'd hear above the engines, so I just raised my hand and saw the pale smudge as she raised hers, and we stayed like that, our palms facing across the distance, till the boat had taken her by.

I sat on a while, the old stone bollard cold on my arse, waiting for the wake to hit. By the time it did, the ferry was already rounding the golf course and heading into Hoy Sound. The water slapped and gurgled on the piers all along the waterfront, long-delayed echo of the boat's passing. Then it was gone and the bay was empty again.

The water was glass-clear. I could see to the bottom where a shoal of minnows turned and moved as one thought. I saw everything perfectly clearly as the wake smoothed away, and off the Holms the blue boat slept on its own reflection, for a while.

PART 3

He lies awake in the lantern light, watching it shift across Adele's shoulder-blades, her white skin turned pale rose. She is still lying partly across him, her breathing steadied to a steady whiffle, her face turned away.

Her skin hot on his, the dig of her rib in his side, fair whispy down on the nape of her neck – he fights to stay awake and witness her five minutes longer, for this may never recur.

When one has no Faith, one must at least be moral. He has always rather despised those weak-willed enough to fall. But he has fallen, off the ledge of his morality if nothing else. And the falling, oh my God, the falling feels like freedom, feels like flying, as in those childhood dreams.

But this is not childhood. They are falling and some time must hit bottom.

Before dawn he must wake her, send her back to the room she's sharing with her sister, who is perhaps with Ellyot. He does not know what arrangements they have made between them. All he knows is this stunned lightness, as though he has been biffed by a pillow the size of an elephant.

He laughs inwardly. Moral codes are helpless in the face of the lightning storm that lit this tiny room. Her body minded him of the fireball he once saw roll down the street in childhood, not solid but a crackling hoop of energy and light. Now she is just a body again, breathing and vulnerable. He knows a thousand ways in which a body is vulnerable. Till now, he didn't know it is also beautiful.

This happiness will cost but for now there is lamplight rosy on her shoulder, her precarious and precious breathing. The night breeze flutters in the palm thatch, then sleep.

33

I was huddled on the shingle beyond Warebeth one bitter afternoon after Mica's departure, numb with cold, which seemed to help but not that much.

A note had finally come from Mrs Cunninghame the week before. She thought it possible – underlined – that the man with my father outside the Lebuh Chulia dispensary was Phillip Marsden. She reminded me it was seventy years ago, she had been only ten, and the shadow on his face made it hard to tell, but the moustache was familiar.

Her writing was formal, cursive, and began to wobble near the end.

Interesting to have an image of Marsden but by no stretch of the imagination could he be the 'senior partner', and Mrs C. had said she didn't believe he'd been married anyway.

For lack of anything better, I lifted the binoculars and found amid the chop the bobbing red tip of our wave-measuring buoy. The 'music' Ray and I had cooked up from it and the one off Birsay hadn't been ambient, it had just been meaningless mess.

We need meaning, I thought. The world might not have any, but we need it. The problem with those signals was not randomness but lack of structure. There was no scale, just endless swoops and dips without musical intervals, rhythms or pauses.

Meaning is something we have to make. And that's okay, that's what we do if we can.

What if we selected signals at intervals? So the rising or falling pitch could hit recognisable musical notes, still reflecting the wave action but making sense to the human ear.

The sea's voice, yet our meaning.

But how to make it in tune? I thought first of the guitar tuner Peter had given me for Christmas. Then a memory flash of Keith in London in his digital den on my earlier visit, showing me how his new software not only let him generate rhythms no human hands could possibly play, but even took his dodgy voice and tweaked it it. At the click of the cursor he could flip his voice from Blues gravel to operatic baritone. Above all, it could compensate when he went flat (which, he freely admitted, he tended to).

What if we wrote a program that did that automatically? A kind of computerised tuner that sought out the nearest note on a scale. It should even be possible to pre-determine a major or minor or pentatonic scale ... Then if you bring in the second signal source, the Birsay one, or a third and a fourth, there'd be strange chords, unpredictable aquatic harmonies ...

I was no longer shivering. I wasn't thinking of Mica or Tina, dead fathers or children unborn. It felt like my brain had finally woken from a long slumber as I imagined the sea round Orkney endlessly generating a music at once natural and technological ...

To make the sound of the shape of the sea meaningful. Another fantasy, like the one I'd woven in idle moments around a golden head, or believing I could change Mica's mind, or recover my father in Penang?

I had to know what it sounded like, that was all.

I went round to Ray's that evening and put it to him. Half a bottle of Highland Park later, we had the basis of our project. We christened it Wave Action Modal Music, or WAMM.

We'd take the wave signals from the buoys. Break them up so the information comes through only every quarter second or whatever. In terms of pitch, it would convert a continuous curve into a series of steps, i.e. notes. The programme automatically corrects the pitch to a note on our selected scale. Then we use a sequencer to play with tone and tempo. The sea could sing like Eva Cassidy or wail and buzz like an electric guitar. So that it didn't become tedious, Ray suggested a variable rhythm could be triggered by, say, the wind. Not simple, but do-able.

In our minds, it was already done. We were already discussing the company we'd form, where we might go for grants, the CDs and the software packages we could market, the art installations, the contents of the WAMM website ...

I wafted home late that night through the empty Stromness streets with a whuddering heart. This project pooled the enthusiasms of my life – music, the natural world, technology – into one intriguing synthesis. It might prove a foolish and profitless quest, but it was ours and had to be done.

Renewable energy music. It was as good as falling in love, only more reliable.

Back home, the phone machine was giving me the red eye wink. Mrs Cunninghame, suggesting I might try Colonial Records at the Public Records Office in Kew. *Look in the gazettes,* she insisted. *Please inform me of any discoveries you may make.*

Her voice was bossy but weary and I was touched by her continued interest, though that particular quest was no longer foremost in my mind.

I drank a pint of tea as I lay in bed flicking through my dad's Walt Whitman till I came across a vigorous pencilled tick against one passage:

> *They do not sweat and whine about their condition,*
> *They do not lie awake in the dark and weep for their sins*

That was the old man all right. I said goodnight to the Penang Buddha who seemed to have developed a sly grin, put out the light and pressed Play in my mind's ear.

Strangest dreams. Deepest sleep. Water everywhere.

'*Here* you are!'

In the corner of the dining room, Sandy looks up from his mango juice. Ann is smiling but looks strained or perhaps just tired. Behind her, he can see Marsden and Ellyot talking outside on the terrace. No sign of Adele, last glimpsed as a paleness slipping across the lawn in the hour before dawn.

'More or less,' he says. 'Good night?' he asks.

She blinks, flushes.

'I thought so,' she says. 'You?'

'Oh, I enjoyed it.'

She sits down, puts the napkin over her knees as the boy approaches. 'Something I have to ask you,' she says. 'I—'

'Please, Dr Mackay please?' The boy seems flustered. 'There is telephone for you. The mother hospital—'

He sits alone in the taxi down the hill road. Mrs Raman's baby is malrotated, face to pubes, according to his registrar, who wasn't happy with the progress of her labour and already anticipated second-stage obstruction. So he'd phoned as arranged. The Empire might totter, people embark on adulterous affairs, but still babies have to be born right.

He glances at his watch, urges the driver to hurry. He'd left without packing or seeing Adele, just a quick word to Marsden. He'd never learn what Ann had to ask him.

Kieland forceps. Rotational mid cavity delivery. Ensure empty bladder – the patient's and his own. Make a generous episiotomy. Apply the anterior blade of the forceps first. Imagine it's the head of *your* child, gently cradled in those metal blades.

They join the surfaced main road into town. Nurse Gibbs should have scrubbed up and sterilised by now. The sun is still low, the day is fresh, he is wide awake. In his pockets, his hands are flexing.

So Mrs Raman's baby is delivered after a scary amount of pulling. A girl, all present and correct. He congratulates the husband, a very tall young Javanese, then he goes back to stitching up the new mother.

She has a number of visitors that afternoon. Among them, a slim silent man who is followed when he leaves by the new doorman, down obscure alleys till he slips into the side door of a workshop off Ah Kwee Street. The doorman hesitates then hurries to the police station. Over the next hour, an assortment of hawkers, fortune tellers and rickshaw drivers appear near the various exits to the rambling workshop.

Abdul Raman emerges at dusk, hurries down the quay and boards a small steamer to the Mainland. He is not the only one.

Then for a while, nothing very much. The baby feeds and sleeps and grows.

Next morning, struggling up to the offices through late January sleet and a hangover, WAMM looked horribly like a weekend fantasy.

I sat watching the signals on Ray's palm-top. I was at least halfway through my life. Sooner or later, you have to get to your feet and find music you can dance to, or moulder away muttering curses in the seat in the corner.

Ray sat down beside me with a carrier bag full of electronics.

'Last night was the biggest load of hot air I've enjoyed all year,' he announced. 'Now we need to find the balloon to hold it.'

The day became brighter.

'We'll need help,' he continued. 'Inga Unwin in London is the best algorithmic programmer I know. She's authentically strange, though her musical tastes stop at Siouxie and the Banshees.'

'So we can remain in awe and patronise her.'

'That's what I thought. So I phoned her this morning. She thinks it's possible and she might be interested, but she insists on meeting you to check you're not a wanker.'

I'd been thinking of another quick trip South anyhow, to try this Colonial Records Office. According to Mrs Cunninghame, it might contain summaries, reports, census results, lists of deportations for Penang. It could be a short cut. Her insistence had revived my interest, and I'd promised her I'd give it a go.

I borrowed the palm-top display and set it up on my desk below the card of the domino factory on Acheen Street and one of a street market somewhere in Sumatra. Then I got down to finishing the section on stress loading in underwater turbines, feeling for once pretty renewable myself.

Penang is a small island, roughly turtle-shaped and only fifteen miles by nine. A good deal smaller than, say, Orkney Mainland, with five times its population. Much of it is impenetrable jungle, the rest is densely populated. Europeans are a small minority, not much more than a thousand in all, highly visible to each other and everyone else in their white suits, buttoned up jackets and ties, their dresses, gloves and hats. Their principal occupations are work, sport, and talking about each other. They have their own clubs, entertainments, recreations and places of worship – as do the Chinese, the Malays, Indians, Siamese. The cultures intersect only at points of commerce, in hospitals – and on the cricket field (though the Chinese, even the Straits-born, remain mysteriously indifferent to the game).

It is no place to conduct a secret affair.

They cannot safely meet in his little wooden bungalow. Nor at the Lone Pine swimming club. There is no such thing as an anonymous hotel room in George Town. The cinema might well be showing *All Quiet On The Western Front* or *Ladies Love Brutes*, but nothing goes unnoticed when the lights come up.

The likelihood is wherever they go, the doctor officer's wife and the head baby wallah at the hospital will be known. There are no secluded meadows or hilltops where they might meet and lie. The whole bloody island is covered in gargantuan vegetation and malevolent biting insects. They cannot even go somewhere alone in a car or on a bus together without the risk of it being seen and mentioned. (In any case, Sandy doesn't have a car and Adele can't drive.)

So it is that one Saturday morning, after the birth of Mrs Raman's daughter, Sandy Mackay packs a bag, says goodbye to Li Tek, walks down to the Sweetenham quay and boards a small steamer bound for Singapore. He has ten days off, his first proper break since arriving in Penang nearly nine months ago. He admits to his colleagues he needs it, he has been a bit seedy lately.

He eats and sleeps well on the boat to Singapore. He sits up at the bar at night but doesn't drink too much. He goes out to look at the southern stars before bed, but not for too long. And if he mutters *All is vanity* from a book he doesn't believe in, it doesn't keep him awake at night, for he is resolved now.

Singapore is interesting but not so very. After Penang, it is rather flat, too British, one-dimensional. He writes postcards to his parents, brothers, and, on impulse, to his friend Taylor from student days now working in Austria. He goes to a few clubs, plays golf, visits a notorious hotel but is not tempted.

He leaves Singapore earlier than expected, takes a steamer bound for Java. But when it calls first at Sumatra, he gets off. He isn't tempted by the coast and instead sets off for the Highlands. From Bengkulu, he takes a bus to Curup.

The kampong is a collection of thatched houses, a Dutch church, an outdoor market. Goats, chickens, bright sarongs, a cage of tiny yellow songbirds. *Aunty Mary had a canary* . . . The dirt road is lined with stalls and people squat under green and blue parchment umbrellas. Though the air is much cooler up here, the sun is even fiercer. Nearly everyone is dark, the Chinese have disappeared, and whatever language the people are speaking, it is not Malay. In the distance, there's a volcanic peak with what may be cloud or snow on its summit. It's all wonderfully unfamiliar, it's the kind of adventure he dreamed about as a boy poring over the school atlas.

But he doesn't stay. He checks the slip of paper in his pocketbook, finds the village's taxi, and establishes he wants to go to Bukit Kaba, higher and further into the mountains. *Ah, outerworld!* one of the men gathered round says gravely.

He is indeed about to go off the map of everything he has known and believed in.

The taxi stops at the new hotel outside Bukit Kaba. The sun is just setting, the air is almost chilly. The mountain range across the valley covers the western sky. The manager, a young Batak, offers him *Namaste!* He is a little later than expected, the journey was tiring, yes? Memsahib Allways is out walking but she will no doubt be back before dark.

He sits in the bare lounge, drinking bitter coffee spiced with cardamom. A wood fire burns in the grate, for the evenings are chilly. He watches the light grow thin over the mountains, and he remembers the hills beyond Braemar, a day on Lochnagar with Robert Taylor before their finals when he'd talked earnest nonsense about self-discipline and hard work being the only values he recognised.

He hunches closer to the fire, sticks his nose over his coffee, tries to prepare himself.

'Ah, Mr Allways!' She stands in the doorway, white hat in her gloved hands. 'There you are.'

'Here I am,' he replies, gets to his feet and kisses her lightly, as a husband would. Her hands press into his back as he looks into her eyes and thinks he would do anything to enter the light there.

Then they go to their room. They have four days.

※

34

D riving south from Orkney in early March, the transitions set in as I crossed the shabby grazing and sorrowful sheep farms, then the wilderness of Sutherland. Orkney presents for my family and the Penang file were my only passengers. I had ten days holiday due me and I was going to use it.

I was off-island, back in the big world. Mica was out there somewhere – I'd heard nothing from her since she'd sailed. Presumably, she was no longer pregnant. She wouldn't do it lightly, but she would do it.

To the west the ragged peaks were like the ones on the read-out of our wave meters, still sending signals I wasn't there to see. I hit the Latheronwheel junction, then turned to follow the bucking road down the coast, mountains on the right and to the left the sea like beaten tin, pock-marked with light.

As I accelerated out of Dunbeath, in acknowledgement of the writer of that place I flicked 'The Bends' into the cassette player. Turned it up to a roar, sure Neil Gunn wouldn't have approved but knowing I did. As I put my foot down in the old Audi – my first grown-up motorcar after a lifetime of post-student heaps – I felt at one with the power steering and grease-smooth shift of the gearstick, the wild coast, the desolate land, sea glittering hundreds of feet below. I sang 'The Bends', sang rage at the lives, loves and children lost, and joy at being still in the game and on the move again.

What might it sound like, the shape of the sea? Not a clue, but I had to find out. Though I was formed by the twentieth century, I didn't want the second part of my life in this new century to be an afterword. Here was the big new ploy at last.

So I sang myself hoarse as ancient and modern worlds collided, all the way down the twisting coast. Then it was south to big trees, high buildings, and the sky shrank – and though the people became more plentiful, it would be harder to attend to them there.

Dear Father and Mother – I'm staying near this Batah village in the Sumatran Highlands. It is quite cool here, about the same as a spring month at home. Gives one a large appetite! It's a misty season here and there isn't much chance of walking up the hills. But there is a very fair hotel, an active volcano, and even some hot springs where I took off my clothes and bathed the other day!

I hope you are well, as I am. With love, Alexander

Her arms slide round his shoulders as he finishes writing. It is the end of their last afternoon, though they have not allowed themselves to talk of this, nor of what happens next. The sleeves of her dressing gown are cool across his neck as he turns to look at her. In white satin, she is a tall single lily.

'I'm out of johnnies,' he confesses. 'I didn't quite realise ... '

'I told you,' she says. 'It's pretty clear I can't – and anyway, this is the most unlikely time. I'm getting more irritable by the hour, you said as much.'

It's true. Between the wonders, they've got on each other's nerves. He finds her cool and distant. She says he is too pushy and impatient. While making love and for long minutes afterwards, he has her as she has him. Then it's lost again. It drives him crazy. He longs to heal her and so complete himself, but she won't let him.

He kisses her thin wrist where the artery beats.

'Seize the day!' he says. 'Why not?'

Then while she closes the shutters, sending slats of light into the dimming room, he takes a moment to add to his postcard.

P.S. This is where our sudden storms come from.

When does it happen, that point where you worry about your parents more than they worry about you? My mother's front door was open so I went in. Called her name. No answer. Odd. I'd phoned of course, she should have been expecting me. I went quickly through the flat, looking in every room but no sign.

The back door was open. I stood in the doorway and watched her sitting reading on the garden bench. A cup of coffee beside her as she bent over her book in her blue fleece jacket in the warm sunlight, one hand thrust deep in thick white hair. I stood taking it in, knowing there'd be a time when I'd need to return to this.

She looked up.

'Oh, there you are,' she said.

I put down my bag, sat beside her on the bench. Hugged her gently.

'Here you are,' I said.

Inga Unwin led me down into her basement in Stoke Newington. Its walls were matt black, black as her fingernails and the shawls hung on the walls like bats' wings. The black leather handbag on the silver settee was coffin-shaped. 'A bit strange, Ray had warned, 'but one of the good.'

She made Roibos tea – the only thing I ever saw her consume, other than vitamin pills and cocaine – then took me up three flights of stairs to her other room in the shared house. I watched her as we climbed. She was tall and so thin, thin enough to get away with those black leather trousers. Her neck was moon-white above her black T-shirt, her cropped hair a silver stack.

She led me into an attic room, put the tea things on the black table and pulled up the silver blinds. I loved that high room straight off, which was as well because we'd spend months working there. It was octagonal, with worktops built into five sides and windowseats in the others. The worktops were strewn with computers, monitors, keyboards and silver CDs. An unfeasibly black sound system dominated one wall.

'Sleep in the earth and dream in the sky,' she said. 'The cellar and the attic are the only rooms worth living in.'

Her accent was broad Suffolk. It was hard to keep a straight face.

She poured the tea, folded herself at black angles in a windowseat and stared at me for a long time from the sooty hollows round her eyes. The old tweed jacket that was my daily Orkney wear now seemed out of place.

'My, you look pretty weird,' she said at last.

'Aye, so do you.'

(Even now, back sitting in the car as the sun settles into the low haze over Eynhallow Sound, I have to smile. That was very Inga – the straight-faced testing out, the brief glorious smile at the right response.)

What she really wanted to know, she said, was why she should devote months of her valuable time – did I have any idea how much she normally charged for her skills? – to making this sea-shape music idea work.

I started on the sales pitch, but she interrupted me.

'I'm not asking *what* it is,' she said. 'Ray's already explained. I'm asking *why*.'

'Because I was nearly dead once,' I said. 'And I'm trying to live with that.'

I had her attention then. I told her about the blue shadowlands and the dead people who helped me there, the renewable energy project, insomnia and the meaningless onrush of the sea.

'We're all dead, Eddie – it just hasn't sunk in yet.'

'And do you find this a helpful point of view?'

'Very,' she said. When she smiled, her teeth were so white. 'Imagine the worst has happened and you're already dead, but you've just been popped back for a day or few.'

I thought about it, sniffed the miracle of tea, stretched my legs to get up and look out at the lights coming on across London. It would already be dark in Stromness. The end of another ordinary day in that brief break from not-being that we call life. I looked at the back of my hand, the fine criss-cross of lines, the faint veins that beat. The worst had already happened. There was nothing more to fear.

I went back to my windowseat and picked up my tea again.

'Yes,' I said. 'So let's talk about the soundtrack for this philosophy.'

Certain people give you pointers along the way, and Inga the ultra-Goth with her sardonic negativity was one of them. As I take the mini disc recorder from the glove compartment to check the batteries and the mike once again, I know what I'm going to do is for her, among others.

In the months I've known her since then, Inga gave no indication whether she had a lover, or indeed of her sexual orientation. Ray had no idea either. Then the other week, at the end of an all-nighter trying to set the parameters for note-correction – our single biggest problem, especially when I was insistent that the program had to be fast enough to run in real time, which somehow mattered – I had the nerve to enquire about her love life.

'I don't go there,' she replied flatly, and that was that.

The mini-disc recorder is fine and there's a new battery in the mike. Must remember to switch it on when it comes to it – this is a hell of a distance to come for a dud.

Though the yellow fuzz of the sun through the evening haar still rolls on the surface of the sea, I rack away the necessary electronics in my jacket pockets then let myself move on to the good bit.

'Gee, it's good to be back and see your smiling face again,' Alan says as the bus shoogles through the crowds out towards the racetrack. 'Cheer up, Doc! What's up with you and Ann anyhow?'

When they'd all met up in the E&O that morning, Ann had pointedly snubbed Sandy's greeting, taken her sister by the arm and turned away to talk to Dr Trent. Even Marsden's flow of banter couldn't cover it.

'Lord knows,' he replies. 'I'm not a keen reader of women's minds.'

His friend looks at him.

'Say, there's not been something going on between you and her while I was away? I want to know before I propose to her again. Chap doesn't want to be an idiot.'

Sandy looks back at him steadily, trying not to recall her kisses in the summerhouse. *You don't understand at all.*

'No,' he says. 'Absolutely not. I just forgot to do something she asked ... to have a quick look at one of her pupils.'

Alan's face lights up, and Sandy knows he has done the right thing.

'These Simpson ladies!' Alan says. 'They do like to have their way. That's what's so swell about them!' He takes off his hat, fans his face. With the bus stuck behind a bullock cart in the full midday sun, it's not so comfortable. 'Has Freddie Ellyot seen much of her?' he asks casually.

''Not since I've been back,' Sandy says. 'He seems to be away a lot.'

Marsden has hinted Ellyot is busy working on something to do with Raman and terrorist cells in the North. No arrests or deportations have been made yet. Marsden seems to be playing a waiting game.

'More good news! I'm going to put a bundle on Running Water in the third,' Alan announces. 'Reckon the name's a sign. If he wins, I'll propose again at the dance afterwards.'

❦

35

The words 'Public Records Office' had made me picture some fusty old mausoleum, but I'd turned the corner that morning in improbably warm and fertile Kew to see a swish temple of steel and glass, complete with ponds, fountains and resident ducks. Inside was hi-tech, hi-security. The usual searches, then a lengthy registration and a wait till I was issued an electronic ticket. A compulsory induction tour that left my head spinning. Rules that included no mobile phones or laptops, no food, drink, folders or pens. Only loose-leaf notes allowed.

I bought a coffee, went out through the glass doors, stood and drank it in the morning sunlight. It was so much milder down here, like spring already, a world of crocuses, blossom, birds that sang in budding trees instead of the harsh *kaak* of seagulls or the lonely *pirl pirl* of curlews. For a moment, the yearning for that chill clear light, that austerity, everything contained in the word *North* . . .

But that was another country, and besides the wench is fled. I went back inside, bought a couple of pencils, swiped my card and went upstairs to track down the Malayan gazettes that should hold the reports, files, confidential correspondence between the people who had tried to administer that long-lost world.

I came down for a late lunch break, my mind mazed with another time, another place. I turned away from the cafeteria till with my tray, thinking about Marsden's reports on the Kuo Min Tang and the stushie surrounding the new Governor's banning of the secret societies, the opium trade and the seizure of explosives, and she was sitting at a table with a purple file in front of her.

She glanced up and I knew her straight away because I'd met those eyes before and something had passed between us on a cold bright street.

She hesitated, then smiled. Small white teeth, full soft mouth with only the faintest lines at its margins.

'Hi, renewable energy man,' she said huskily. 'I got that starter motor fixed. Join me?'

I sat down opposite her. I didn't want or expect anything from her, just wanted to be near that radiance. She was bonnie rather than beautiful but she was so alive she was hope itself.

'Eddie,' I said. 'Eddie Mackay.'

She took my hand. Not Mica's vigorous challenging grip, but a soft warmth, her palm laid against mine for a moment.

'Roo Cullen.'

The image, the outline of the Golden Girl, probably comes from my cousin Anna. We played one summer together, I'd looked at her as she swung down from the tree house we'd built and landed beside me as if she'd dropped from the sky, all golden and exhilarated, the sun behind pouring out of her, and it was as if my heart took a photograph.

We all have them, those templates, the silhouette of the beloved – like those jokey cut-outs of King Kong or Monroe that an ordinary person sticks their head through and becomes not quite themselves. It's irrational, unsound, no basis for anything. I do know that. But once it's lodged there, it can't be helped. For me it's a certain contour, a certain build, colour of skin and hair, and life flaring in the eyes. Tina had had traces of it but Mica not at all. Mica was only herself. Now here by a miracle was Roo again, looking at me intently as I ate.

'I'm looking up military service records for my friend Maria,' she said. She tapped the purple file like it was evidence. 'Her grandfather.'

'Any luck?'

'I've got most of it. You?'

'It's been interesting, but I'm thinking of packing it in,' I confessed.

'Oh you shouldn't do that,' she exclaimed. 'Everything's here if you look long enough.'

Looking at her, I tended to agree. Roo looked as though she'd been spread all over with honey. Pale hairs stood up along her golden forearms. She was so alive and glowing, eyes undefended, open wide as if everything she saw surprised her.

I kept asking her about herself for the pleasure of watching her lips move, the little lines bunch and smooth away above the bridge of her nose, her short almost chubby fingers spooling her words. Her voice was low, throaty for someone a generation younger than me. She had a nicotine stain on the inside of her left index finger. When we went outside, she smoked a roll-up. The sweet-acrid pale smoke drifted from her to me and I breathed in happily.

She paused abruptly, midway through telling me about her biological father in Vancouver, looked at me. She tapped my file.

'So what's all this about?' she asked.

I gave it to her briefly – my tail-dragging dad, Mum's casual revelation of an affair in Penang, a scandal, his departure. How the need to know more had grown in me. How whenever I thought about it, about the truth just beyond my grasp, the people who could have told me all being dead now because I hadn't known ten years earlier, it drove me nearly mad with frustration.

'So you want to find out who she was,' she said. 'Why they split up, what happened to her afterwards, if she went back to her family, if there was a baby – all that?'

'Well, yes,' I said. 'Wouldn't you?'

She pursed her lips.

'There was nothing secret about my mum's affairs,' she said. 'She called herself a free spirit. So you want to get back at him?'

'No, I want to get him back!' I said.

I grabbed my coffee and swallowed down hard.

'I can understand that,' she said quietly. 'It's wanting something you can't have any more. My mum . . . '

Her fingertips inches from mine, and her eyes damp and shining like chestnuts straight from their shell. I see my hand covering hers. Of course I didn't, I know the boundaries.

For a moment I may be looking at Rowan Cullen, not the Golden Girl. She shakes her head rapidly like a retriever emerging from water, then she smiles again at me.

For the rest of the afternoon, I whipped quickly through the gazette files I had ordered up. These weren't microfiche or photocopies, these were originals, hand-typed with mistakes, handwritten in scrawls, creased and sometimes stained. Letters of recommendation, private notes between Penang administrators and the Foreign Office in London.

I found out why J.P. O'Farrell didn't get the promotion he was expecting – it had taken just one line *There is concern here as to his unnatural proclivities* followed by indecipherable initials. Also the inside story of how the new Governor Clementi was roasted for his banning of the secret societies without referring to the Foreign Office, the reprimands, strategies for placating the current Nationalist Chinese government and the Chinese community in Malaya without losing face. All this on files labelled Most Confidential, now released under the 60-year extension rule. It was fascinating, seeing how power, influence, string-pulling were actually done – but it scarcely got me closer to my father.

I speed-read (glancing at the clock, thinking of Roo downstairs) secret reports on the organisation and activities of the Kuo Min Tang in Malaya, with an appended handwritten note on the internal struggle within it between Nationalist and Communist elements. It concluded *Our power here can rest on bayonets or prestige; on the whole (given our lack of a standing army) prestige is preferable. Marsden.* That name again. I'd a feeling I'd have liked him. That sardonic turn of phrase in his neat cursive hand. I wondered if it had made him smile to himself before he sealed his report, dropped it in the diplomatic bag for London, then went out into the broiling haze to catch a rickshaw to his club . . .

Only half an hour before the closing bell. I pressed on. The Annual Report for the Straits Settlements 1929 and 1930 detailed the rapidly improving statistics for infant mortality and public health, but also the total collapse of rubber and tin prices. A proposed 'retrenchment' in administration costs included cutbacks on staff, expenses, even the suggestion of selling the Governor's yacht.

Not all-blithe confidence, then. In fact, the more I looked through the gazette headings, the more anxious, uncertain and unstable the times appeared – Chinese demonstrations in Penang; seizures of opium; commutation of death sentences; circumstances surrounding the death of Sgt. H.G. Weekes, Malay States Volunteer Regiment . . .

The next file contained details of several deportations over the years 1930–34, such as that of J.D. Martinez for fraud; the lengthy saga as to who would pay for the ticket home of the penniless con-man James Villers; the repatriation of F.N. Quinn. No mention however of the abrupt departure of Dr Alexander Mackay.

Nor of his arrival, for that matter. There were thin files on a number of appointments, seemingly at random – an inspector for the opium packing factory in Singapore, a new commander of the MSVR, a new school-mistress for the English School, Miss Ann Simpson – surely my old lady's cousin. Her application contained another name I'd seen before – Dr J.B. Trent as a character reference. After his name was *Assistant Medical Officer.* I noted down what I could for Mrs Cunninghame, though it was scarcely sensational. Still, there was a feeling I was getting warmer.

The last file I opened was the one I had most hopes of: *A report on current medical services in the Straits Settlements and Singapore.* There were dozens of doctors listed there, none listed as heads of practices. I noticed Trent was now listed as Chief Medical Officer – a civil servant rather than a doctor.

The one significant discovery I made was in a separate column, the one concerning the hospitals. *Dr A.W. Mackay, Chief Consultant Obstetrician, Edward VII Maternity Hospital.*

I blinked and sat back at my carrel. So Mrs C. had been right, he hadn't been in general practice at all. Which was interesting but cast doubt on my mother's recollection of what he'd said sixty years ago. He couldn't have had a senior partner. Maybe the director of the hospital? I noted down *Sea Ah Song* without much conviction then closed the files, handed them in at the desk and hurried downstairs.

She was waiting by the glass doors in an old Afghan coat. I could remember them first time round. She brandished her purple file.

'I'm finished here, Eddie. Any luck yourself?'

I managed to refrain from saying I'd already had one piece of extraordinary luck that day. Instead as we walked through the cold and now dark streets to the Underground station, I talked about the picture of Penang I was starting to build up, and the traces of people I was beginning to feel I knew – Ann Simpson, Trent, Marsden, the luckless Ellyot. And the discovery my father hadn't been in general practice at all, which rather cast doubt on my mother's recollection.

She listened, nodding and exclaiming from time to time. Her eyes kept snagging on mine. I guessed she was like that with most people. She was unguarded, someone who made contact.

'It was interesting,' I concluded as we waited at the platform, 'but it looks like there's nothing more there.'

'So what do you do now?'

I shrugged. 'Maybe go back to the newspaper library. But there's months of reading to be done there. If I haven't made a breakthrough by the end of this trip, I'll pack it in and get on with another project I have in mind.'

She looked at me then, those round velour brown eyes in the poor light. The train was coming and I was already rehearsing what I was going to ask when she gripped my arm.

'If I can get away, I'll give you a hand reading those old newspapers tomorrow. You never know, we might get lucky.'

Oh send another carriage chugging down your smoky tube ... The Northern Line dirty as ever, swaying and rattling and throwing my neighbour against me but no irritation this evening. Instead a warm glow like good whisky in the belly and I smile to my fellow citizen. After hesitation he grins back ruefully like *Well this isn't everything I dreamed of but here we are*, and for a moment there's contact and humanity as on Orkney except here when we part it's with the certain knowledge we'll never see each other again. Whereas in that place where I'm not, the big O, every meeting is given weight by the likelihood that we will.

But that's okay. And being anonymous and unknown is okay. I'm just another molecule slipping through the solution. Indeed, you could say I'm part of the solution, just as everyone in this carriage is. I smile again (but this time to myself because I don't want to alarm the neighbours) because I recognise this feeling from way back, my brain happily gibbering and the honey whisky glow in my belly, and I can only smile because I'd thought those days were way past and apparently they're not.

Yes, London is redeemed, even the old Northern Line that shunts the brain cells of the city around invisibly as the shunt I carried under my skin bore tired fluid away from my brain, even that is working as it should.

She got off the train two stops ago, touched my arm (I feel it yet), smiled down *Tomorrow if I can make it*, then shimmied out the closing doors and was gone into the crowd, the last gleam and bob of her hair as she ducked down the stairway like a winter sun setting off the Kame of Hoy.

Here's where I get off.

It's stifling at the races, which for some reason are held through the heat of the day. It's one of the big events of the year, nearly all the Penang Europeans are there, and many more have come from the Mainland. The Simpson group have gathered in their finery on a stand near the halfway mark. The hats are particularly outrageous, as if there's been an explosion in a parrot farm, while Mrs Isabella Simpson opts to labour under a shrubbery. For today, dresses are longer, ties are black. A few of the old guard, including Mr Donald Simpson, wear their cream sola topis. Even Trent has taken the day off. He nods to Sandy as he and Alan climb up onto the little stand.

'I expect you're still missing the cool of the Highlands,' he says. His tone is neutral.

'I never got much beyond the Sumatran coast,' Sandy replies. 'I spent most of my leave in Singapore.'

Impossible to see the man's eyes under his broad-brimmed straw hat.

'I meant the Scottish Highlands,' Trent says.

Marsden takes Sandy by the elbow, twirls the silver-headed cane he's brought in honour of the day.

'I need your scientific opinion on the form, old man. As a medical man, how would you say a seven-year-old would go in this heat?'

Sandy knows little about horses, but accepts the intervention gratefully. He cannot bring himself to look Trent in the eye, though he must, he must. Even less can he look at Adele, who stands below him in her bird of paradise hat, talking with her mother and the two little girls. All his life he has striven for the self-assurance, education, means, and morality that would allow him to look anyone straight in the eye, to be lesser than no one. Now for the first time in his life he is in love, and there are at least three people whose gaze he flinches from. Worst is the person he faces while shaving each morning.

Sweat and grass, tobacco smoke, coconut, putrid durian fruit, women's scent and the pure animal reek of horse as the thoroughbreds crash by – he is quite dizzy with it. The light is painfully bright yet murky and so sultry it feels as if any moment something – another cigarette, a cheer, an unwise remark – could bring thousands of tons of water condensing out of the air to drown men, women and animals alike.

He wipes his forehead with his jacket sleeve, replaces his hat. Perhaps that old buffer Bellingham-Smythe was right, something in the tropical sun's rays is bad for Westerners, undermines our health on every front. We're not made to live here.

Superstitious unscientific balderdash. It's just a matter of being careful. He signals to the water carrier. The old man hoists up his bagpipe-bellows type sack, skooshes out two horn mugfuls. Sandy hastily drains them, feels the icy water give him a sharp occipital headache.

'Worst time of year, Mackay,' Mr Simpson says in his ear. 'Our second rainy season. Family can't wait to be back in the Cameron Highlands. We up sticks there every year at this time.'

'Envy you,' Sandy says. He rather likes old Simpson. Genial buffer, not half as daft as he looks. The white eyebrows and whiskers, brick-red complexion, may come straight from some picture-book, but the man's eyes are clear and direct. He usually speaks sense. 'If it's anything like up on Penang Hill.'

'Oh, better,' Simpson laughs. 'Much better! Five thousand feet up, you know! Need a blanket on the bed and a jolly fire at night.'

A blanket and a fire. Sounds like paradise. It was. He remembers opening the shutters in their room onto the chill blue morning air, the whole day ahead, her stirring in bed, propping herself up on one elbow and pushing the hair from her eyes . . . He's just about to say something about the Sumatran Highlands, then remembers he mustn't, he was never there.

'Fact is,' Mr Simpson says confidentially, 'it's good for the ladies' health, you know. We're hoping it might do Adele some good – she's been a bit off-colour recently. We thought her trip to Sumatra might help, but it doesn't seem to have.'

'Your daughter's going with you?'

Sandy tries to keep his voice casual, but still his smoke gets caught in his throat and shrinks his vocal chords. He's very aware of Trent standing just behind Mr Simpson, next tier up.

'Just for a couple of months, at first. Shame Ann can't come, but she does insist on working. Modern women, eh? Still, she's tough as old boots, that one.'

Sandy swallows the last of his cold water.

'Oh,' he says. 'That'll be . . . '

He tails off, can't say what it'll be. The afternoon seems to have jammed solid. Dr Trent leans down.

'Adele's never been very strong,' he says quietly. 'A touch tubercular. She does like to keep it quiet – only family and close friends know.' His eyes seem to bore in on Sandy, the grizzled moustache twitches sardonically. Or perhaps he's imagining it. The man never was a ray of sunshine.

'Surely she shouldn't be in a climate like this.'

'Born to it, old chap!' Mr Simpson says. 'This is her home, she was desperate to get back out East.'

'So you'll just have to manage without her at the hospital, old man,' Trent says. 'After all, her health must come first, eh?'

'Aye, of course,' Sandy replies. He waves again to the water carrier, wondering if he's going to faint like some chinless wonder in a drawing room comedy.

He watches Trent work his way down through the stand to intercept Ann and Adele. He leans solicitously over her, puts an arm round her waist. She does look very pale, it's true. He can't believe he missed the TB. Is that connected to her infertility? He must look it up.

'Of course, I'll carry on making trips down to KL when the big chief needs advice,' Mr Simpson continues. 'I'm only semi-retired, like to keep my hand in.'

'What do you advise him on?'

Mr Simpson chuckles; his blue eyes squint at Sandy while he lights a cheroot.

'On which advisors to listen to! These are difficult times. Unstable. Uncertain. Nothing but rumours and a bad feeling down here.' He pats his comfortable stomach.

He puts his hand on Sandy's shoulder, leans closer. Now there's nothing old bufferish about his eyes at all.

'Exit with dignity, young man,' he whispers.

As Sandy stares, Simpson straightens up. His wife has returned.

'Yes,' he says more loudly. 'It'll be India first, then here, sooner or later. You'll see. All we're working for is an orderly withdrawal.'

'Oh, Donald,' his wife says affectionately, putting her arm through his. 'Don't listen to him, Dr Mackay – he's such an old Jeremiah.'

Sandy excuses himself, goes to find Alan before the next race begins – a novices handicap. Through the multi-coloured throng of sarongs, suits, tunics and dresses, he sees Trent approaching, with Adele still on his arm, Ann on the other side of him. He hurriedly joins Alan in the queue for nasi guring and fresh coconut till they've gone by.

'Sorry your Running Water didn't win. Does this mean you won't propose again?'

Alan laughs as he sucks his snack off banana leaf.

'I put it on each way. I'm a cautious guy, when it comes to it.' He flicks the loose rice from his lapels, glances up. 'And a stubborn one. Sure, I'll be doing the old bended knee again tonight. When you want something, you gotta keep plugging away, don't you reckon?'

36

'Your jacket smells of peat smoke,' she says. 'Orkney must be stonking good!'

As Rowan picks her file up from the seat in the Newspaper Library lobby, I'm trying not to grin inanely like a lovesick elderly admirer. Though she's too young for me, of course – two months short of her thirtieth, which now seems a remote period of history, certainly somewhere I'll not visit again – the real truth is, I'm too old and grim for her.

She walks ahead of me to the security. She's wearing loose olive pants with pockets everywhere and a short top that flashes her golden waist and belly as she turns. She's quite short, full hipped and almost stocky, but she moves so lightly and easily over the ground you'd think she was on rollers. Her hips swivel on oiled bearings.

'I'll give it one last time,' I say as we wait for the spools I've ordered. 'Don't give up yet,' she replies. 'One of us might get lucky.'

She smiles at me, I smile back, and there is suddenly a lot of sunshine about in the British Newspaper Library.

I switched on, spooled to where I'd left off three months before. This is absurd. I'm feeling like bloody seventeen not my late forties.

I finished with sport – some golf medal winners but no Dr Alexander Mackay – spooled on to the next issue, by-passed the front page that was just adverts and notices. Loads of interesting stuff but nothing relevant. On to the next issue.

Sad death of Frederick Ellyot, popular young sportsman. So he never pulled through from that odd motorcycle accident. Reading the eulogy, about his youthful energy, contribution to the sporting life of Penang, and his useful role in the Public Works Department, for some reason I'm touched across the years by the death of someone I never knew.

I hiss to Rowan to come have a look. She stands and leans across me, stares silently at the screen for a long time as she reads. She smells faintly of patchouli and Golden Virginia tobacco, and her belly is inches from my nose and now I smell only the warmth of her skin.

'You should make a copy of this for that old lady of yours,' she says at last. 'I hope this encourages you to keep going.'

I sit back to a safe distance. Our alcove is dim, light and sound die here. Only the light-pools from two other screens where two other obsessives labour away in silence. I want air and big sky and her nearby.

'I'll give it today and Monday,' I say. 'But if nothing more helpful turns up – that's it. I really do have a life to live.'

She looks at me, one side of her face lit in the screen. In the pale white light for a moment she looks like some of the women in the photos I've flicked through, admiring horses or attending fashion shows or going to funerals. As her eyes hold on me, I begin to know what my father might have felt, what it is to fall disastrously.

'There's plenty of time, Eddie,' she says.

I look at her, knowing that the years between her age and mine will pass quicker than she could ever imagine. I'm trying to think what I can tell her that's of any use, but I'm distracted by the tiny fair hairs on her cheek, backlit in the gleam from Ellyot's photo on the screen.

'Go to it,' I say.

Mid-afternoon, the photographer works his way along the stands, taking pictures spectators can buy from him later. He catches the Simpson group as Ann points out to Adele the swish horse she's put her money on.

Alan is looking the same way, hand on his chin, the other clasping his elbow, trying to appear judicious.

The kid sister Emily and her cousin Vanessa hide then peek out.

John Trent's hands are clasped behind his back as he bends to say something to the aunts; the wound on his temple gleams palely in the shadow of his hat.

Phillip Marsden and Mr Simpson have their heads close together, and whatever they are talking about it appears more serious than horses.

And Sandy, who has seen the photographer coming, turns away. A strand of tobacco has left his unfiltered cigarette, and he reaches to pick it from his tongue.

The photographer takes another three shots, all in the informal style that has become popular. After all, who wants to look like a set of rigid, stuffy Edwardians? But it is the first one that Mrs Simpson will select at the studio two days later, because it shows her beloved, difficult daughters and her husband at their best, and the day is one she wants to remember, for it went well despite the upsetting rumours, and part of her senses, rightly, it will never happen this way again.

✻

'Eddie – I've got something!'

I jerked forward in time, from the menu of a lunch at the Runnymede Hotel. She was bouncing from foot to foot so her blonde tennis ball head bobbed in the dimness of the cubicle.

'I took your suggestion and went back months before the billiards tournament,' she said. 'I tried my birthday and there were none of the names you mentioned. But then I tried my mum's dates, and – come see!'

I bent over her console, then felt faint. For there it was at last: a date, and the names, the names of real people who lived and breathed and sweated as they came down the gangplank at the Butterworth Quay in George Town one morning seventy years ago.

SS Amelia arrives from England . . . Then a list of senior administrators, couple of minor aristocrats, a racing car driver, a long-forgotten famous novelist. I followed her finger down the list till it stopped among various small fry. In among them was the name I'd been looking for, and a few others I wasn't entirely surprised to see.

Mr P. Marsden, Chinese Department liaison officer
Dr A. Mackay, Head Consultant for King Edward VII Maternity Hospital
Miss A. Simpson, schoolteacher at the English girls' school
Mrs Trent

Without thinking, I hugged Roo. For the first time, her thick hair tickling my cheek, her breath moist and warm on my neck.

'There's more!' she said. 'You won't believe this!'

Arranging the photocopying took us till closing time. On Monday I'd be able to pick up *Alarming incident at Butterworth Quay*. A photographer had been there to take a picture of the racing driver and his starlet companion. Instead he'd got an image of something bulky wrapped in netting and a thin boy hanging under it, one leg cocked up, one hand flailing. Many heads in the foreground, and a row of pale dots up on the ship's rail. Quite possibly my father and his friends were among them. I'd stared and stared till my eyes watered, but they'd remain for ever just out of reach.

Maybe all I'm doing is scratching an itch, I thought as I watched Roo duck her head to light a roll-up as we left the library, but I can't stop now. She inhaled sharply, smiled as she let the smoke whistle out through her teeth.

I couldn't believe she'd got so lucky. Her mother's birthday, for God's sake. Enough to make you think there was a pattern and a meaning to things, some improbable connection across times and places.

Even more remarkable, and something I'd phone Mum and Peter about that evening, was the story Roo went on to find.

Dramatic operation in hurricane off Sumatra. One of my dad's yarns in his old age, something my brother and I had never fully believed. True, all true, down to the cargo of teak and sailing into the eye of the hurricane to fix the second mate's leg.

Below the three paragraphs was a photograph.

My father is standing awkwardly beside a stretcher at the foot of the gangplank. His crumpled white suit and straw hat make him look like a fugitive ice cream salesman as he looks back at the camera. On the stretcher, a burly man is propped up on one elbow, grinning broadly. And right behind him, leaning forward as if in a hurry to be off, with a small slash of a smile under his stubby moustache, is the man I think I last saw standing in front of the Chulia Street dispensary.

There's a simple, helpful caption: *Dr Mackay, Second Mate Ancross, Dr Trent.*

It's late in the E&O ballroom bar. The last perspiring dancers have flopped into their rickshaws, the last residents have pulled themselves up the grand staircase. Even the punkahs seem weary as they slowly chop the smoky air.

A plump, balding Armenian is dancing alone, waltzing himself slowly round the sprung floor while the last remaining member of the orchestra drags Strauss from his fiddle. The man – who with his brother owns the E&O hotel, jewel of the Orient, more sumptuous even than Raffles, which his family also owns – holds his arms out, encircling a lost partner. On his head he balances a glass of brandy and soda. Every so often he takes it down, sips, carefully replaces it then dances on.

Slumped in an armchair, Sandy watches Arshak Sarkies' stately, solitary progress round his own dance floor. In the fatigue at the end of the revels, he glimpses tonight the truth of what old Simpson and Marsden have been saying; the E&O hotel, for all its size and splendour, is decaying. The penniless planters have gone home, the tin men can no longer afford it, even the Civil Service is cutting back its staff, their wives no longer flock to the fashion shows, their discussion group mornings are ill attended.

A tide is going out, he can feel it. Before leaving, old Simpson was rambling on about the great banquets of the past, with ice sculptures, iced buffets, hundreds of guests dancing and chattering in the cool air from all that ice. They used to dance till dawn, then set off in fleets of rickshaws for an early swim followed by breakfast. Now it's all over by one in the morning.

'We've seen the best of it!' he announced. 'Orderly retreat!'

'Yes, dear,' his wife said as she took him by the arm. 'I think it's time we made ours.'

And so they left, the Trent and Simpson clan, with a last parting look from Adele. The only time she met his eye all night, and he has no idea what that brief stare meant. It's been utterly impossible to get her on her own.

An hour on, he's still here, nearly everyone's gone but he's unable to get out of this green leather armchair. Alan stirs beside him, signs the chit for a last cold beer.

'Ann says she's waiting,' he mutters. 'Says she has to know her sister will be all right before she can decide about marriage. Doesn't make any sense to me.'

Sandy closes his eyes, but it doesn't help. What comes instead is an old scrap of poetry from the school.

> *Yestreen when to the tremmlin string*
> *The dance ga'ed through the lichtit hall . . .*

'What's that, old man?' Alan mutters. 'Gaelic? Think you'd best lay off the Scotch.'

Sandy opens his eyes, but still sees Adele at the races, standing by Ann, one in cream, the other in blue, pleated skirt, her blue eyes shaded by an oval hat.

'Burns,' he mutters. 'I'm no that taken wi Burns, but it's the bonniest thing he ever wrote.' He closes his eyes again, and lets it come back. He's drunk, he knows it, alone and drifting, about to become emotional.

> *Tho' this was fair and that was braw,*
> *And yon the toast of a' the toun,*
> *I sighed and said among them a*
> *'Ye are na Mary Morison.'*

Mr Sarkies is still dancing alone, spinning slowly with a slight wobble like the Earth itself. The whole effect is no longer ludicrous, it's unspeakably sad. It's time to leave but he cannot.

The violinist stops playing, bends to pack his fiddle away. Two Tamil boys lean on their brooms, cautiously watching their boss. In a year the bankrupt hotel will be sold and he'll be dead, but for now Arshak Sarkies dances on, brandy glass balanced on his head and his eyes tight shut, lightly embracing the partner only he can see.

❧

37

'It's for you,' Keith said. 'That Orkney woman you don't want to talk about. Ready to speak to her?'

Mellow with wine, I took the phone. What with today's discoveries in the library and Roo's proposal for tomorrow, nothing Mica could say could touch me much. It had been six weeks since I'd sat on the old pier and watched the *Ola* take her away. Unless – heart thudding – she'd changed her mind about the baby.

'Hey, fuckster!' she greeted me. 'How's the mad quest going?'

She'd done it.

'What can I do for you, Monica?'

I heard her intake of breath. I waited, offered nothing.

'I'm passing through London and it seems you're here too,' she said rapidly. 'Could we meet?'

I made the necessary arrangements and rang off.

Mica wasn't so wired or glittery now. Away from the salt-stiffening Orkney air, her hair wasn't so wigged out from her head. She'd even got a faint tan, though I didn't ask. The jeans, old sweater, battered jacket were the same but they didn't make the same sense as they had back there. Now she looked merely eccentric.

She'd pushed into the cafe, spotted me sitting and strode straight over. I didn't get up so she bent to hug me. I watched her getting coffee and cake – her idea of breakfast – at the counter, her energetic gestures, the way her hand, her head moved. I'd known this woman, she had known me, in another place, to a degree.

'So,' she said as she sat down, 'much to talk about!'

I looked at her, waited till her eyes lifted from her carrot cake to me. Sea eyes, blue-grey, perhaps calmer than before.

'Let's be clear about this,' I said. 'We met at a difficult time when we were both desperate. Lots happened, some of it good. But what I'm left with is this: you slept with Kipper, probably several times. Second, you lied about it. You could be a pain in the arse, but I always thought you were a truthful one. And then—'

She grasped my wrist, squeezed to the little bones.

'You had too high an opinion of me, Eddie,' she said. 'I can be as cowardly and second-rate as anyone. Now I'm trying not to be.'

Her long white fingers moved up my arm as she leaned closer across the table. I watched her long mouth frame improbable words.

'I'm very, very sorry about Kip. I'm even more sorry I told you about ... well you know ... I dumped it on you.'

'I take it you're unpregnant now?'

She blinked, just once and quickly.

'Yes,' she said. 'I'm punished by my dreams.'

Then we couldn't look at each other.

'You used me,' I said at last, though it wasn't what I was thinking.

'And you used me – for sex, for company, to keep your heebie-jeebies away.'

I couldn't deny it, though I had to smile a little at the *heebie-jeebies*. She hesitated, then took a big bite from her cake. Washed it down with coffee.

'Mm,' she said. 'Not too sweet. Fact is,' she continued, 'that's what people do in relationships. Use each other. I just hoped we could use each other well, and kindly. You see?'

And there she'd laid it bare. Use each other kindly. If life is shite, let's at least use scented bog-roll.

'It must be possible to do better than that,' I replied. 'There's a whole other level.'

She stared at me. Her lips parted, then she changed her mind. Her tongue flicked a sweet crumb into her mouth.

'Fuckly duckly,' she said. 'You old hippie.'

'Don't pretend you don't know what I'm talking about.'

She held my gaze for a moment then looked down and dabbed her long thin fingers in sweetness.

'Sure,' she said quietly. 'But it hurts so much when you lose it.'

Then she shrugged, sucked her fingertips as if that made up for it.

'So what are you,' I asked, 'a free spirit or a mouse?'

'Jeepers, you've changed.'

'Or something.' I dealt with her much better now I cared less. 'Well?'

She stared at her fingertips, now licked clean. For once, no colour on her nails, just clear varnish. She looked at me, sort of smiled. I flinched as she put her hand on my arm again.

'You're looking at a rare case of a bad girl turned good,' she said.

After a pause where something could have got said by either of us but didn't, she lifted her hand away. But she was smiling, a relaxed, natural smile that let me glimpse how much she'd calmed since her father's dying was done.

'So – any hot goss from Orkney?' she asked, and the moment passed.

Then it was easy to sit there in the morning cafe exchanging news. I told her about two of the three things that were uppermost on my mind. I told her briefly about WAMM, and she didn't mock. She looked up and for a moment our eyes met.

'Sounds worth pursuing,' she commented. 'Because you think it is. I'd like to hear it some day, long as it's not boring hypno-mush.'

I promised her this music could be as agitated as she could wish. Then I filled her in on Penang, the lucky breaks I'd had with a friend's help at the Newspaper Library, my plan to go see Mrs Cunninghame in Edinburgh on my way north. I had the sense I was finally closing in on something.

Mica listened, nodded, asked questions, even made suggestions, like the Mormon database for birth, marriage and death records if I ever got the woman's name.

I glanced at my watch then asked casually where she'd been since she'd left Orkney.

'Once I'd . . . taken care of things . . . I had to get some sunshine on my brain.'

I got a short version of her swallow's flight to North Africa – Tunisia, then Morocco, a village by the sea where she'd found a cheap room and set up with her typewriter. She'd slept a lot, walked the wind-blown beaches, wrote some, stopped drinking. Resisted the advances of many handsome young men offering hashish.

'And their undying love?'

'Oh yeah, that too. But I'm not mucking about any more. And now I'm back here.'

'Staying?'

'It . . . depends. I'm flat-sitting in Clapham for a friend and working on new stories. The latest is now only partially about this smart arse who behaves like a jerk, and how she then tries to put it right.'

'And does she?'

She grinned down into her coffee as she spooned out the sweet brown fluff.

'It's a comedy of sorts,' she said, and left it at that.

I'd the impression that after years of faffing and drifting, she'd found something that was truly hers. She nodded.

'Twenty years of pissing away my life to piss off my old man. Or maybe just scared of failing at something that actually mattered to me.' She paused, looked beyond me as the doorbell tinkled. 'Or succeeding,' she added. 'So many things I want to do now and there isn't so much time. Eddie—'

She broke off. I turned and Roo was there.

'Sorry I'm late,' she said. 'God I'm starving!'

Radiance in Stoke Newington.

I looked back from the counter as I ordered up her big breakfast and our picnic sandwiches. The two of them were deep in conversation. I heard Rowan's throaty voice then Mica's huffing laugh, the one that wasn't quite her, but Roo couldn't know that. The two heads bent closer together across the table. I hoped Mica wasn't amusing herself at Roo's expense. Her kind of gaucheness, the optimistic emotional openness, often prompted a savagery in Mica, as if someone being hopeful and excited about the world offended her.

I'd told myself that this was the only way I could have fitted Mica in. There hadn't been time to see her south of the river then keep my rendezvous with Roo. I could have not seen her at all, but that would have been cowardly. So I'd set this up, which was adolescent of me. Just wanted Mica to see me with this gorgeous young woman, let her speculate.

But now, watching Roo lean forward eagerly towards Mica, her golden head bobbing as she nodded and replied, I could see her from Mica's point of view – young, inexperienced, uneducated, no match in the verbal arm-wrestling. Roo didn't read books or newspapers, she'd left school early with the encouragement of her mother who scorned schools. If she could pass two evening class exams, she might go to college 'to learn something proper' as she said, but it was a struggle.

'Me and books don't get along,' she'd said. 'My mind goes all hazy and I start looking out the window. Stuff in books doesn't seem as real as things out there. So,' she'd laughed, 'I guess I'll always remain pig ignorant.'

Still she seemed as vital as Mica but happier. She made me happier to be around. But a small and unworthy part of me saw her as I imagined Mica did, and I was ashamed that I was embarrassed.

I took the tray of her full breakfast – if Mica lived largely on her nerves, the golden girl clearly liked her grub – and carried it carefully over to the table.

'Roo's just been telling me her cure for sore throats,' Mica told me brightly. 'She takes clippings from her big toe and puts them under this little model of the Great Pyramid she has by her bed. Isn't that so amazing?'

'It's ... different,' I muttered. Roo seemed undeterred as she tucked into her fried bread.

'Tell me, Roo,' Mica continued innocently. 'How do you deal with period pains?'

Roo glanced up at her, then at me.

'Stick a new Tampax in the pyramid,' she said, and speared a sausage. 'Works every time.'

A long, terrible pause then Mica spluttered and sprayed her coffee. Then she was hooting with laughter and Roo grinned and sunshine spread like butter over the morning cafe.

'Must be off,' Mica said, getting to her feet. 'Miles to go and promises to keep.'

'Would you like to come with us?' Roo asked. 'We're going out to chill in this amazing wasteland I've found.'

Of course I'd known this was not a date. An unworthy part of me was disappointed that Mica now knew it too. She declined politely, said she needed to get back to work. I went with her to the door.

'I like your wee pal, Eddie. Think she might be good for you?'

'It's not like that,' I replied.

Mica sniggered quietly as she zipped up her battered jacket. She flipped her hair free of the collar, and I remembered the gesture from another time and place. She gave me a quick hug, more a clasp of the shoulder.

'I really am sorry,' she said. 'Think about it. Cheerio.'

Then she stepped back, waved to Roo, and was out the door and gone, leaving me wondering what part of what had passed between us I was supposed to think about.

Sandy fits a new steel needle then carefully lowers the arm onto the outer grooves. A click, a hiss, then Mozart's *Piano and Violin Concerto* uncurls like incense from the squat little radiogram. The fiddle and piano, the simple sad gay air, mind him of dances back home.

Behind the screen, Alan is still coughing and retching. Worse is the shuddering inhalation that follows. In his houseman days, Sandy has heard people die like this, the same desperate clutch for breath before the end.

The piano pauses then moves into its second theme, the one with the bonnie little stumble where it seems to fall, then the fiddle lightly reaches down, picks up the melody and twirls it away. For years Sandy couldn't see much point in music except as something to dance to, but now – it may be Alan's patient tuition, or the entirely new world he's stumbled into – it makes perfect sense. Only music can fairly summon Adele's face in the forest gloom, pupils enormous and kissed mouth so sad. In the heart of this simple duet is that swarm of butterflies, a yellow spiral rising and turning.

Alan comes back in, very pale but composed. He puts the linctus bottle on the table and picks up his beer.

'Sorry about that, old man. One last game?' He swirls the dominoes, clackety clack, then starts picking out his hand.

'This climate's not doing your lungs any favours.'

'Sure,' he agrees. 'But ever since I was a kid, I wanted to be in the Far East. Romance, adventure, you know.'

He leads off with the double six, Sandy follows. On evenings like this, the music and the game lets them talk or not talk.

'Any doctor would say you shouldn't be here,' he insists. 'You've got worse since I met you.'

Alan looks up from his little domino wall.

'I reckon on making the most of however long I have,' he says quietly. 'That's a reasonable choice, don't you think?'

For a moment their eyes meet. Then a sharp double rap and Li Tek sticks his head round the door.

'You have lady visitor,' he says. 'Mrs Doctor.'

A suspicion of a wink as he holds the door open wide for Adele. Alan stares at her. People do not call at this time, especially not women alone.

'Is something wrong with Ann?' he asks.

'No ... No,' she replies. 'She's fine.' Two red spots rise in her pale cheeks, she clutches her closed parasol with both hands. 'I was passing on my way back from ... a talk. Thought I'd drop by and say goodbye before we go off to the Highlands.'

Her voice tails off. She doesn't sound convinced. Alan looks at her, then at Sandy. At the two of them staring at each other.

Alan flicks over his dominoes then reaches for his hat.

'Reckon I'll hit the hay,' he says. 'Been a long day. Say, son, can you find me a rickshaw?'

Alan stops at the door with Li Tek. He glances round the room but it seems he can't look at either of them. He shakes his head and is gone.

38

'I like your friend Monica,' Roo says on the bus out to Stamford Hill. 'She's very clever, isn't she?'

'She's so sharp, she cuts herself,' I mutter.

'I think she wants to get back with you.'

She's looking ahead, watching for our stop. I wonder what was said between them while I was held up at the counter.

'People make mistakes,' she continues. 'Sometimes it's better to forgive.'

'I can't,' I say, and don't like the choke in my throat.

She shrugs, keeps peering out the mucky window. I can't read her at all.

'She came into my room during a storm,' I begin.

We're walking downhill on a broad tree-lined street with glimpses of a river at the bottom. A pale sun, first hint of real warmth in this new year. Here in the deep South the crocuses are done smearing yellow and purple over the grass, the daffs have tight curled beaks ready to open. The Golden Girl, my 'wee pal', is cruising along beside me and I feel nearly as young and fresh as she is.

'The way a relationship begins is its template,' I conclude. 'She was always something that happened to me.'

We slip through a gate and onto a towpath by a glittering river. The houses have given out, traffic sounds have faded. I can smell and hear the water ruckling along the banks.

'But what if you had a chance to *choose* to be with her? I mean, then it would be something that you had made happen.'

I look around, enchanted. It's so quiet down here, just a few morning strollers. The water is clear, slight chop on the surface, and on the far side a scrub of willows and birches stretches off into the distance. A woman potters on a houseboat, a rower sculls past, drops falling from his oars in little crushed suns.

'It's too late for that,' I say.

We cross over on the lock gate then set off down the towpath on the far side. It's a brilliant morning and the world is full to the brim.

'So how about the way we met?' she asks. 'What does that mean?'

'Well ...' I'm at a loss. 'We bumped into each other when I wasn't paying attention and you had broken down.'

We walk on in silence for a while. My pulse is a little raised and I'm terribly aware of my hands, how close they are to hers as we walk, how great that small distance is. She asked Mica along. This is not a date. She's a generation younger than me.

'So we're an accident.' Her voice is husky, I'm not sure if it's a statement or a question. She doesn't sound quite sure about it.

'A happy accident,' I say.

'Right.'

She stops, looking down at her trainers, frowning. A couple of paces on, I stop and come back to her. She looks up at me, I look at her. She's biting her plump lower lip, seems uncertain. I get a notion of what she's maybe about to do, and I think *I want to choose this*, and bend down just in time as she lifts her face to me.

'Alan knows?' Adele says into the silence.

'He does now.'

They are still standing apart. Sandy can't cross the distance that Alan's disgust has opened up.

'Do you have to go?' he says at last.

'It's pretty clear there's a three-line whip on the Cameron Highlands.' She shrugs, almost smiles. 'Four, if you count John.'

'Does he know?'

Adele closes her eyes for a moment. Standing by the table, her fingertips stray over the dominoes as if they were Braille.

'I haven't told him,' she says finally.

'Your health – is that just their excuse?'

Her fingers have settled over the double one.

'They had no right to tell you,' she replies. 'It's not that serious. I just have to be careful sometimes.' The tip of her index finger jumps from one little black pit to the other. Now for the first time, she looks right at him. 'It's probably as well I'm going,' she says quietly. 'Things have been . . . very strange at home.' She pauses, her mouth twitches. 'Pretty strange away from home, come to that!'

Sandy steps forward and awkwardly puts his arms round her waist. Her hips move in towards him but her head doesn't.

'Nothing like this has ever happened to me,' he says. 'I want more.'

Her gaze moves past his shoulder then meets his again. It's as though something has truly focused his eyes for the first time since he was a child. Certainly he feels as helpless as one.

'I know,' she says. 'But it'll be a chance to think things over.'

He doesn't like the sound of that. Thinking is the last thing he wants either of them to do. He clasps one hand round the back of her head and kisses her. For a moment, he feels her resist and then she doesn't and the two of them seem to be falling into each other without end.

At last she pulls back.

'I can't do this,' she says. 'Not when I'm going home to him. It's so unspeakably cheap.' Her voice is flat, matter of fact, and chills him more than any tears could.

'Then don't go home. Bide here!'

He stands shaking, appalled, thrilled. She stares at him.

'Don't be silly,' she says softly. 'You'd lose your job – gross moral turpitude. They'd have you out of here in a week.'

'They can't make me leave!'

She shakes her head.

'Sandy, Sandy, who do you think is in charge here?'

It's true. Of course it is. One isn't left alone with a revolver any more; instead a return to England for health or family reasons is suggested.

'Then we'll go together!'

She looks at him for the longest time. Her eyes begin to glisten.

'Yes,' she says. 'I suppose that's the choice. You'd have no job, no income, no savings, and I'd have no family.'

'I can get work! A friend of mine in Vienna, in the British hospital—'

She puts her fingers to his lips.

'John might give me a divorce because he loves me, but for the same reason, he might not. Is that what you want?'

He's about to reply when she pulls back.

'Don't answer that yet,' she says. 'Best not write to me directly – they'll ask about any personal letters. We'll send notes through Ann if possible.'

'I don't think she's very keen on me at the moment.'

'I told you she was possessive. For all that flapper front, she's the moral one. I'm the whited sepulchre who reads books and betrays my husband.'

There's a steady clicking sound. Only then does he realise he hasn't heard a note of the music since she came in. He lifts the needle, then looks at her. He must remember her like this, the yellow pleated dress, hair loose and damp. But that's all detail. He doesn't care what she wears or how her hair is. Only her eyes and mouth matter.

She opens her hand, puts the domino back on the table.

'Till later,' she says quietly. 'Let's wait and see.'

Before he can object, she is gone. He can hear her talking lightly with Li Tek outside. Their voices fade, the mongoose patters behind the walls and he stands by the hissing Tilly lamp, utterly lost.

We're following faint paths through an empty place, only there's nothing empty here. It's as though the houses have picked up their skirts and fled to the horizon. Along the rim of a pale blue sky rise a few office blocks, faint and unreal as a poor stage backcloth.

'Walthamstow Marshes,' she says.

The wind is brisk, stirs the tall dry grasses as she talks. It frisks the first green stubs on the scrub birch trees, stirs little willows as I lean towards her. We've come by overgrown ponds, pools, backwaters, even the pylons are well behind us now. I'm in London, I have kissed a young English woman I scarcely know, and yet it feels I have come home, in this most unexpected of places.

Roo is explaining her life. She seems to be at once organised and utterly lacking in ambition. After leaving school early, she worked in Boots, Woolworth's, Tesco, Dixons, working her way along the Newcastle High Street. Whenever she was offered promotion with more pay and more responsibility, she quit and moved on. Finally she found the Royal Mail and stayed there.

'So what do you do?' I ask. 'Pound the beat?'

She looks at me like I'm daft.

'I sort the letters that haven't got sorted. The ones that haven't got their blue dots, or got the wrong dots.'

'Is that interesting?'

'Of course not. But we have a good laugh, and you can do it stoned.'

As she walks she trails her hands out over the long ears of grass, a gesture so graceful and childlike I blink in amazement. She seems to be caressing the wind or this wasteland. Only it's not a wasteland, it's just being repossessed. A couple of mallards scutter down a lost canal. A heron leans forwards like a long grey pencil, wipes its neb on a branch, is still. The towers, docks, workshops, houses, roads and railways of one of the world's great cities are only a mile or two away, but here's peace and a silence that isn't silent. No people except us and that's plenty.

She's never been out of work, bought a small flat when she was twenty, she's never had a car. She doesn't go to restaurants or spend money on clothes or drink, so living in the North her low wages were enough to let her do what she wanted, the things that really matter to her.

Which was? Which are?

She looks surprised, as if it's obvious. 'Living, you know. Having time to potter, see mates, get stoned listening to music. *Clubbing.*'

She warms to her theme. I could as well be getting news from a distant planet. For ten years Roo has lived for dance music: hip-hop, acid house, techno sometimes, Italian disco, trance to chill.

'My cut-off point is music made by drum machines,' I confess. 'You have to take serious drugs to make that interesting.'

She flashes me a beaming smile.

'Aye!' she says.

Seems Roo has been taking Ecstasy most weekends for the last ten years. There's nothing like it when the music and the people come together, she insists. Beautiful, perfect, stonking mad. Better even than sex. Clubbing isn't about getting off with people, it's about that moment when the music goes inside you and you go inside it and everyone is in the same ... joy.

She stops, looks for my reaction. I feel a hundred years old.

'I can't think of anything worse than being stuck in a shed with hundreds of people flailing on mind-altering chemicals with some drum machine going a zillion beats a minute. If it was threatened as torture, I'd tell all.'

She laughs, caresses her fingers again through the tall grass.

'Didn't your generation invent drugs?'

'These days it's all I can do to stay in my right mind. Last thing I want to do is get out of it.'

'Is your mind such a good place to be?'

'I'm working on it.'

'And didn't you ever dance?'

'Sure,' I say. 'Not your kind of dancing.'

'Show me,' she says. 'Go on.'

And because I love the slightly goofy flash of her front teeth when she laughs, I show her.

In a small clearing, I go back to the beginning. Take her right hand in mine, set her hips alongside mine. She looks startled but interested. I take her left hand in mine behind my back and we're set.

'Back in the dawn of time,' I say, 'when I was but a lad, there was a very loud instrument called the accordion, and a man called Jimmy Shand. And this is the military two-step ... '

I holler 'Mairi's Wedding', and take her through it. Forward, back, heel, toe, heyeuch! Step we gaily on we go – heyeuch! She's gratifyingly gasping with laughter. My arm round her waist so warm. She gets the rhythm and the moves and then the bounce of it though she's still cracking up. Her fair head at my shoulder, golden bobbing ball.

And me, I feel inspired, lit up, at play. I feel light on the ground as I take her on a fast-forward history of the sixties and seventies. The Twist mutating into my Jagger impersonation, the sulky sullen pouting strut as

I camp through 'Satisfaction', then free-form floppy waving expressing inner cosmic events once the LSD kicked in.

She's on her knees with laughter now. The little grass joint we shared under a tree a while back seems to have caught up with her. And me, I feel weightless, a clown, liberated from the weight of my history by its absurdity and her laughter. She falls onto her back among the dry reeds as I demonstrate the loon-pant Mr Natural undulating walk. Her gold navel ring might as well be looped through my nose, it tugs me so.

'What happened then?' she finally manages.

'Oh, then came Disco and I stopped. Then a bit of leaping up and down when Punk happened.' I frog-leap maniacally then bend over gasping for breath. 'But I was already in my mid twenties and never liked amphetamines, so that didn't last long.'

'And that's it?'

I straighten up, still clutching my chest.

'Yeah, lots of interesting music to come, but no new moves for me.'

She nods sympathetically and for a moment I'm desolate. No new moves.

'I guess there has to be a cut-off point,' she says. 'I've kind of lost interest myself. The scene's lost its buzz – or maybe I'm just past it.' She shrugs. 'I'm starting to get into Folk and beer and, you know, world music. I haven't taken E since I came down to London, though I do kinda need this' – she feels in one of her more useful pockets and takes out the bag – 'to keep on the right side of my head. Want another?'

I sit down by her and pull flask and sandwiches from my pack.

'You go ahead, lass.'

One Saturday morning he stands uneasily outside the English Protestant church. The rainy season has passed, and the air is marginally less muggy. He watches 'the man of a hundred boxes' go by slowly up the road with his impossibly numerous apparatus dangling off his body. The man is a mobile haberdasher, pharmacist, ironmonger and sweetie-seller. Today he also has a pair of cockatiels, one tied to each shoulder. With his poles, strings and wires branching out in all directions, the man is a miracle of balance, a walking mobile.

Sandy watches him, envious. The young Chinaman turns the corner, still calling softly his melancholy, failing cry, and is gone.

He waits on, fidgeting. It's her way of tormenting him, making him wait for her here. Finally the big door opens and she comes out of the church.

'Here you are!' she cries. She runs down the steps, amused. He has to admit she looks good, tanned from afternoons out at the Lone Pine. She doesn't wear gloves, her arms are bare. More than ever, she has diverged from her sister.

Now she slips her arm through his.

'You look like a man waiting outside a bordello,' she murmurs. 'The church won't bite you, you know. You should give it a try.'

'No chance of that,' he replies. 'I can't sacrifice my intellect and believe nonsense just because it would be comforting.'

She laughs at that, starts to lead him towards the promenade.

'Your precious intellect! What sort of a guide has that been?'

'I don't think we need to feel we're under surveillance in order to behave well.'

She stops then, half inside the colonnade in the street of the shoemakers.

'And you have behaved well?' she enquires.

He will remember her like that, her fair head tilted to one side, the light running down one cheek, her clear eyes holding on him. And there's the smell in Achah Street, that sweet burnt stink of leather, it runs all the way back to his father's workshop. Perhaps that is why her words skewer him.

'I'm not her keeper,' Ann says quietly. She reaches into her pocket and quickly hands him Adele's latest folded letter, the one that would have come inside her own. 'And I don't like being your postman.'

He puts it away and they walk on in silence.

39

It turns out that Heaven is located near Hackney Marshes Filter Beds (disused). Or at least it did that windy bright March afternoon. Perhaps it moves on, like a travelling circus. That's why it's so hard to locate, because when we go back to where we last found it, it's somewhere else.

We sat on long dry reeds near the willows. I ate and drank, she ate and smoked and told her stories, lying beside me, not quite touching. I'd been alive long enough to know the radiance wasn't necessarily coming from her, but though it might be an illusion I was overwhelmingly glad to find I was still capable of it.

She told me she'd moved down to London last year to get away from someone. A man. A boyfriend. The boyfriend of ten years.

'Ten years!' I said. 'The only one?'

She looked at me, raised a dark gold eyebrow.

'I may have taken a lot of drugs,' she said, 'but I'm not promiscuous. It's not the same thing, see? There'd been a few before Paul but I don't screw around.'

'Sorry,' I said. 'I didn't mean—'

'My mum was the bohemian,' she said. She sort of smiled, a smile with little hooks down at the corners of her mouth that snagged in my chest. 'Though she was a wonderful person, I saw what that did. Not for me. That's why I have to be careful what I do.'

'I see,' I said. 'Gotcha.'

'Good,' she said, then rolled into me.

In Pitt Street the call to prayer rings out above the voices and the traffic, high and harsh and sweet.

'It's not all rules and threats of punishment,' Ann says suddenly. 'A lot of that I don't believe any more than you do. None of the religions of Penang are really about that, whatever you think.'

'So what are they about?' he asks, only half listening. Adele's unopened letter is burning in his pocket, though he doesn't expect it to be that different from the others – lively, amused, neutral.

She stops and watches the current of men drain into the mosque, some serious, some cheerfully nodding to each other. Then she looks at him, and her smile is a small wave breaking along her upper lip.

'Love,' she says.

It's been much on his mind, but it's not something to talk about.

'I think we can manage love without bringing God into it.'

'I don't mean just an affair of hormones,' she says impatiently.

He looks back at her, thinks he sees all kinds of things. He thinks of Adele, her restless eyes, the quirk of sadness and wit at the corner of her mouth.

'Nor did I,' he replies, and this time it is she who looks down.

'*All is vanity*,' he intones as he sips from his decapitated coconut.

'Nonsense,' she says briskly. 'Adele reads too many liverish books and you come from a depressed country, that's all. Delivering babies, bringing clean water to the towns as Alan does, teaching children to read, even going to the races, flirting and dancing and falling in love . . . That's not vanity, you silly man – that's life.'

Above their heads, the huge shade of the food stall trembles. Over the wall beside them, the sea has turned murky yellow, and one quarter of the sky over Gurney Drive is black. They hear a familiar thud-a-dud, turn to see Ellyot on his motorcycle. He raises one gauntlet in greeting, points towards the approaching storm, then accelerates on till he vanishes behind the courthouse.

That was the last time Sandy would see Freddie Ellyot, and he often thought on it. The eyes hidden behind goggles, the gloved hands, mouth open calling something, those splendid teeth . . .

Then the storm is on them. One canopy topples over, bringing down a couple more. People stand by their tables gripping the poles in the deluge amid laughter and shouting in the half-dark afternoon, warm crash of rain, her laughter and sodden hair as a bellyful of water poured onto her off the umbrella canopy, and he's braced himself to hold their pole up while worrying that the letter in his breast pocket is getting wet . . .

Those afternoon Sumatran storms! Half an hour later, the sky is clear again, the streets steaming, the umbrellas righted and the stall fires blown back into life. But Freddie Ellyot of the Public Works Department doesn't come back, and Adele's letter is a blue-stained rag.

We were walking again, drifting past reed beds that rattled in the wind, till at some point we came on a large-bore pipe across a canal. The sign on it said *Danger of Death by Failing*. I blinked, looked again, but there it was. Some wit or anxious soul had scratched a break in the upper part of the 'l'.

After we'd stopped laughing – so many fears seemed hilarious that afternoon – she'd turned to me. 'I won't mind getting older,' she said. 'I just don't want to ever be unable to—'

In her pause, I thought of all the disabilities of age. Unable to run, climb the hills, make love, taste food?

'—open my heart to the world!' she concluded, flung her arms out wide, and in that moment gave me something that she could never take back.

As we followed the river down to the city, she told me she'd finally fled to London to get away from her boyfriend's violent jealousy bordering on paranoia. It was complicated by some drug money, she said vaguely. She'd finally had him evicted and the flat let, got her job transferred. Now she couldn't go back. No one back home must know where she was.

We were holding hands and I was feeling absurdly innocent and happy. For we hadn't made love, nor had sex on the dry reed bed. When her hands tugged up my shirt, I'd thought that's what she had in mind. Instead we'd lain together for an unmeasured time with our bellies fused, warm skin on skin and her belly's beat on mine.

I can feel yet the cool hardness of her navel ring against the little scar left from my shunt operation. No amount of sex could have brought us closer, nor healed me so.

As the traffic sound began to carry to us on the breeze, she told me her new supervisor at the Royal Mail was always on at her to better herself. Saying she was bright, could make something of herself. She should study, get qualifications, take more responsibility and get paid more.

'And all through my twenties I've thought: that's rubbish. If I get paid more, I'll just spend more, and I'd be back where I started only with more things and more stress. *Make something of myself* – but I am something already, aren't I?'

I looked at her, so bright and earthed against A.V. Roe's brick arches where the first ever British manned flight was prepared. A cormorant flapped away behind her shoulder, and there was nothing adequate I could say.

He's on his way out the door, bathed and changed and mentally prepared for the contest, when Marsden hurries in.

'Sorry I can't come to watch, old man,' Marsden says. 'Bit of a flap on at work.'

The customary urbanity has gone. His breathing's rapid, he's nicked himself shaving.

'The Raman thing?'

'Four months' work! Maybe I've been too patient, or too greedy – God knows. I've sent Freddie—' He breaks off, stares at the gathering dark around the pinang trees. 'It may yet be all right.'

He holds out his hand. Sandy can feel a fine trembling pass through it.

'Good luck, Sandy. Oh, and remember to lock that door. Just . . . keep an eye out.'

The man is rambling. Sandy puts his hand awkwardly on his shoulder.

'Thanks,' he says. 'I must be off.'

They part at the rickshaw stand. Li Tek is hanging round there, talking to his cousin. Marsden nods to the waiting policeman, then they both stride off quickly and vanish round the corner. For this occasion, Sandy has decided to go by rickshaw, give himself time to settle.

'Good fortune, tuan!' Li Tek calls. 'Play good now.'

No doubt about it, the Penang Club is busier than usual tonight. The men he knows nod then look away. Those he doesn't just stare briefly then return to their drinks, but the glances keep coming his way. He orders a large gin and tonic without the gin, then goes through to the billiards room.

Alan's there, he appreciates that. They are still friends, though now there are some things they don't talk about. A couple of committee men wait by the scoreboard, two young MCS chaps break off their game on the far table. There's an odd sort of silence as he walks over to the cue rack where his opponent waits.

'Wondered when you'd get here,' Dr Trent says. He holds out his hand. 'Good luck, then.'

'Good luck,' Sandy echoes.

Trent's hand is dry and bony. How absurd to wish your opponent, the man you want to beat, good luck, Sandy thinks. The things we say! The things we do.

The matches he has played to get this far have been fairly casual. At least, his opponents seemed to take them lightly. In the quarters, that administrator chattered all the time; in the semi, Oerstrat was half-cut. Personally, Sandy can't see the point in competition unless you're trying your damnedest to win. It seems he'll never quite be a gentleman.

But tonight, the final, is different. For the first time there's a scorer. There are spectators, lounging round the walls, drifting in and out of the room as the match progresses. He has a feeling, or maybe it's just him, that their interest isn't entirely the billiards itself.

They toss for cue ball. Sandy calls right and chooses the spotted white. A grin and thumbs up from Alan as the two men chalk their cues then bend to the table.

We gradually re-entered the city, crossing under flyovers, over railway tracks. Then the buses, the traffic, the buildings, tremendously large and loud till we finally came on the Thames at Trinity Buoy Wharf, right across from the Dome. She released my arm and went and sat on an old bollard. She'd gone cold and withdrawn, huddled into herself.

I paced up and down the quay. The low sun was into mist now and there was a bitter wind off the river. I stared down into the grey water, low and a long way from home.

For ten minutes or an hour, however long we'd lain wrapped together on the dry reeds, I'd been utterly happy and reconnected. It hadn't lasted. We can't spend all our time lying down wrapped in each other.

My changes are done. No new moves. We all come to that point, and must accept it or become ridiculous. Could be that's what maturity is, knowing you've more or less arrived at yourself and the world will keep on changing but you won't much, and then living with that. No wonder my father had been heavy with dignity.

I looked back at her. She was hunched, arms round herself, looking tired and not golden at all. We had very little in common. We were at different stages of our lives and that would aye be the way.

I looked down into the Thames and was amazed to see seaweed drifting by. I'd forgotten it was tidal. Then I felt it – sweep of the river mingling with the sea, and the molecules and salts of that sea connecting all the way up the coast, one unbroken sea-road all the way up to Orkney. This same water swept by the Ness, buoyed up the *St Ola* rounding Hoy Head, broke on the shores at Warebeth in patterns we might succeed in making musical . . .

I looked over at Rowan and she didn't seem so far away. We both lived and breathed and were made of the same stuff.

I sat by her on the chill bollard. Put my arm round her. She said nothing. I kissed her cheek, then her lips as she turned towards me.

She pushed me back.

'What am I, Eddie? What do you want with me?'

I stared at her, had no idea what she was on about.

'I'm not educated, I've been nowhere except England and Ibiza. I'm not like your friends with degrees and everything, who can play music and do research, read books and fish and write stories! I can sort letters and roll joints, and that's about it. There's nothing about me that could interest you for very long.'

I'd told myself the same, but coming from her it sounded daft. I started to tell her but she cut me off, grabbing my arm.

'So you want to kiss me and bring me trouble. What am I to you – a sweetie in a jar?'

A sweetie in a jar. It makes me smile yet.

I protested my intentions were honourably dishonourable. That I really liked her, enjoyed her company, and, yes, fancied her like mad. Whatever else, I certainly wasn't playing with her.

She watched me doubtfully. Gradually her shoulders slackened and her head bowed.

'It's not all your fault,' she whispered to my chest. 'There's complications.'

'Such as?'

'For a start there's seven hundred miles between us.'

'I believe we live in the age of travel,' I said. 'Anyway, I don't expect to stay in Orkney once the tidal project's done.'

'And, well there's someone I've met recently. We've just been out a couple of times and I haven't committed yet but . . . ' She looked away at the Dome or something else of hollow purpose. Her next words were whispered as much to herself as anything. 'If only we'd done this when we first met.'

'I wish we had,' I said. 'Though I was probably too bound up with Mica.'

'And it's more complicated than that,' she said. She looked up at me. 'You see—'

'All I know,' I blurted, 'is right now I really want to kiss you. I understand you can't commit anything. You don't have to explain, you don't have to feel bound by it or anything, but please kiss me once more and save my life.'

And she did, and it felt like it did.

Then she shivered and we parted.

'I didn't plan on this happening,' she said fervently. 'I want you to believe that.'

She hesitated then shoved her cold hands in pockets and looked upriver at the lights in the dusk.

'Must be getting back – I'm on nights this week. People must get their lost letters.'

We parted outside the Underground. She hurriedly scribbled down her phone number on a packet of Rizla, tore off the flap and stuck it in my jacket pocket. She seemed about to say something, then kissed me on the mouth, quickly, softly, a butterfly kiss.

'Ta-ra,' she said.

Trent's the better player, he always was. He has a better feel for the recoil off the cushions, more experience, a smoother cue stroke. The match is best of three games, each first to 250 points, and Trent takes off like a train with a sequence of rapid pots and in-offs the red. He has scored eighty to Sandy's feeble twelve when he tries a near-impossible angle, misses the fine cut altogether and lets Sandy back onto the table.

Funny thing is, the man doesn't seem bothered. His shrug is casual, his eyes are dull. As Sandy tries to claw his way back in to the game, and Trent continues to have careless conclusions to fast brilliant breaks, he starts to realise Trent's indifference isn't feigned. The man's mind isn't on it.

It's almost insulting, and makes Sandy all the more determined. With a couple of flukey and entirely unintended pots, he makes up ground but just fails to win the first game.

A buzz of talk goes round the room. Sandy orders another non-gin tonic, notices Trent has double whisky and drinks it fast while chatting to his pharmacist friend. It's true, the man is genuinely indifferent to the match.

More fool him. Sandy runs the chalk around the cue tip, trying very hard to shut out thoughts of Adele. It's been two weeks since he got her unreadable letter, he's heard nothing since then. The short letters he'd received earlier were witty, disjointed and non-committal. Life in the Cameron Highlands is, it seems, cool and uneventful. Only at the end of one had she added rapidly, *I think of you all the time. I'm thinking so much.*

He blinks, puts her away. Trent reaches across him for the chalk, and for a moment the two men are close together. Sandy's looking at the white stretched skin of the temple wound.

'Had a letter from my wife,' Trent murmurs. 'She's coming home very soon.'

'Oh,' Sandy says. 'Good.'

'Yes,' Trent replies. 'We're all very pleased.'

For a moment, pale grey eyes stare into his, then Trent returns to the table for the second game. They both now play badly, Sandy still trying to get his heart rate under control and as for Trent, he just doesn't seem to care. The spectators start to murmur. Whatever they'd come for, it wasn't this.

Finally Sandy gets launched into a long break, a pretty series of cannons combined with in-offs the red. Suddenly it seems he just can't miss. Replace his cue ball, in-off, replace . . . Another couple of breaks like that, and he looks up to see he's passed two hundred and Trent's playing so badly he's still in single figures.

His concentration wavers, he overhits, his cue ball bounces away from the pocket and Sandy steps back from the table. Still, this game should be in the bag, then it's all down to the decider.

As he chalks his cue, Trent is beside him again, reaching for his drink.

'You may congratulate me,' he says casually.

'Game's not over yet,' Sandy replies.

John Trent smiles. At least, his iron-grey moustache twitches.

'Sorry I've been playing so badly. You see, I've been a bit distracted.' He drains his whisky then leans closer to Sandy. 'It seems I'm going to be a father at last.'

Trent goes back to the table and builds a very pretty break of nearly a hundred. Sandy seems unable to do anything other than watch the blue cue-tip flicker. The smells of chalk and hot baize and cigarette smoke occupy his brain completely.

Trent finishes to a smatter of applause, then comes back to him. Sandy is still frozen on the spot. If he stops leaning on his cue, he might fall over.

'Congratulations,' he manages.

John Trent smiles.

'Yes, it's a surprise,' he says. 'In fact, with my low sperm count, I'd say it was a miracle. Still, it will be good for her, and that's what matters, isn't it?' He puts his hand on Sandy's shoulder, squeezes. 'Your turn, Mackay.'

⁓

40

*T*his is the night male crossing the Border ...
Not often my wee inner voice has a sense of humour. Things must be getting better in there. I'm being carried lengthwise out of England, my body aligned north like a compass needle seeking its true home.

Hackney and Walthamstow Marshes drain into the Lee River which flows into the Thames which enters the North Sea, which connects to Scotland and on up to Orkney. Same sea, though the temperature and salinity of it alters a bit, but still molecules jostling with each other all the way. There are no gaps. Same land, same sky over it all – same night, same darkness, same light, though it arrives at different times.

I adjust the reading light over the narrow bed, prop up on one elbow, open the Penang file and try to read, but it's no good. I'm thinking, so what if she's English and I'm Scottish? It's only a matter of a few degrees of latitude and a shift of vowel sound and cultural history. And as for the eighteen years between us, well we're just at different points on the same journey, like London, Newcastle, Edinburgh, all joined by the same rails I'm rocking over on this midnight train.

We're born on the same planet, bound for the same end, and when she kissed me I felt myself redeemed.

I roll on my back, look up into the flickering dim yellow light as the midnight train rocks through middle England. I am high on a woman with a psychotic ex and a possible new fella, little formal education, an extended history of mind-altering drugs, to whom it's as incredible that I saw the Beatles on *Juke Box Jury* as that my father heard Yeats read his poetry in Dundee (one of his casual asides near the end of his life), or saw Buffalo Bill Cody with his Wild West Circus in Aberdeen, and his father in turn telling him how he just missed the train that went over in the Tay Bridge Disaster. Three generations and you go back into the mid nineteenth century ...

All right, she *is* a sweetie in a jar. The trick is not to get my hand stuck in the neck of it trying to extract her. Leave her be. Let that one magic afternoon be enough.

And then it comes, scattering all other thoughts of that day – Roo turning to me near that *Danger of Failing* sign. I'd made some silly bitter comment about people not knowing their heart. She'd stopped me, her hand on my arm, looked at me intently as she spoke.

'Eddie, once I'm committed I'm the most loyal person you will ever meet.'

Those words, and the look in her eyes – a promise? a warning? – fizz and crackle in me like the electricity lines which power this train as we lurch north through the night.

'Tough luck,' Alan says as they come down the steps of the Penang Club. 'I thought you had him till your cueing fell apart. Boy, did you play rotten!'

'Aye, I noticed,' Sandy mutters.

He's amazed he can speak at all. He's got through the handshakes, the drinks, the ribbing, on automatic. Worst was Trent's handshake at the end, those eyes fixed on him. Or perhaps he's imagining it. Now he needs to be alone with the night.

Alan looks around, signals a taxi.

'Say, what did old Trent say to you at the break?'

'He'd had some good news.'

'Yeah of course – Adele's coming back!' Then Alan stops grinning and looks embarrassed. 'You didn't know?'

Sandy doesn't reply. Alan's hand is on his arm as the taxi draws up. 'Share a cab back?' he suggests.

Sandy shakes his head. More than ever he wonders what was in her last letter, the one the rain washed out. He must, must talk to her.

'I'll walk home,' he says. 'Need a bit of air.'

It takes a long time getting home. The moon is shrouded, and once he turns away from the shore road to walk up Transfer Road, the night is dark and deserted. Penang doesn't stay up late except during festivals. A few night lanterns still burn, and the triple red eyes of incense sticks glow outside Chinese premises. The distant clack of wooden clogs, a drift of opium from the brothels on Chulia Street. This does not concern him, neither the whorehouses nor the drug. As a doctor, nothing is strange to him. Everything human is an object of study, not of judgement.

Near the top of Macalister Lane, he takes his usual shortcut up an unnamed back alley. It's very dark here, he has to step carefully round baskets of refuse. He's vaguely aware of a door squeaking behind him, and up ahead a pale movement at the top of the alley, but his thoughts remain on one thing only.

A click, then yellow light from a shuttered lantern held to his face. One word: *achee. Yes.* Then a blow from behind sends him staggering into the wall. He's protecting his head and kicking out. A searing whack to his kidneys. He's on his knees now in pool of yellow light, sees the stick coming, hears his arm crack. He's on his back, looking up at three men. Blows rain down, he keeps twisting and crawling to deflect them but it's no good. Lying on his side, he sees the blade. His good arm goes up, he feels the flesh slice open but no pain yet. Stupid, so stupid.

A cry, a shout. Torchlight in the alley. *Mata mata!* the man above him shouts. Sandy twists to glimpse Li Tek with two policemen, then a departing cudgel to his head brings on the blackest night.

I walked once again down Newhaven Road on my way to see Mrs Cunninghame. It was a dreich morning, rain spitting and the sky lowered over the city. There were changes happening all over it – Tollcross was scarcely recognisable, and there was a hell of a big hole off the Royal Mile that would be my country's Parliament building. I wondered how our Tidal Power Generation report would be received by the Executive Committee. It was nearly done now, and we all felt this was the future, that only a numpty could read it and fail to act. Trouble was, there were a lot of them about.

Coming up the drive, I glanced up at the tower window and once again saw a movement away from the glass. The companion opened up, offered a 'Good morning' which seemed to suggest a number of things, few of them uncritical, then told me to wait in the hall.

I sat on a heavy mahogany chair carved with dragons and demons, taking in again that smell of furniture polish, leather, fustiness and – perhaps I was imagining it on account of all the Far East bits and pieces – a lingering sweetness of incense. A tweed deerstalker cap perched on the top bough of the hatstand.

In the hall in that big not-quite-silent house, time hadn't stopped. Two grandfather clocks and one marble carriage clock kept chopping hours and minutes into different sized little bits. I pictured the mechanisms, the springs and weights, and the cogs like tiny gleaming axes, shredding the kindling for the conflagration . . .

I grimaced, brushed my palm over the right side of my head. It had become a habitual gesture, feeling the little bulge under my scalp, my very own hourglass, my portable memento mori. Rowan had touched it wonderingly after I'd told her.

Time hadn't so much stopped in that house as opened like a fan. I glanced up the staircase to see my father as a young man descending in a white cotton suit, holding his hat, talking with a little girl in a crinoline beside him. In through the side door comes Alan, smothering a cough as he puts down his golf bag by the hatstand. A doctor opens a panelled door with a stethoscope round his neck, calls 'Next!' The bulky man who was Mr Cunninghame puts on his mac and bustles out with a quick parting wave. And two young women with fair bobbed hair, one slimmer than the other, in frocks of different shades of green, are walking away down the passage exchanging confidences . . .

'Vanessa will see you now.'

I picked up my Penang file and followed the nameless companion up the stair, brushing my hand over the mythical beasts crouched on the newel post.

The coffee as usual was very dark and strong, so bitter I added two lumps of brown sugar with the silver sugar tongs. I noticed the tongs were fashioned as the body of a snake, the jaws with little fangs to grip the sugar.

'Karachi,' Mrs Cunninghame said briefly. 'Present from the Mission School.'

'Bit creepy, isn't it?'

'That may be your opinion, young man.'

She was sitting very erect in her high-backed chair set against the light coming in the great windows, so it was hard to see whether she was annoyed or amused.

'It is that,' I agreed.

I opened up my Penang file and spread the photocopies on the coffee table.

'My, you have been a busy lad,' she said in that clipped nasal drawl. 'Tell me, do you think your father honoured his own marriage vows, unlike the way he behaved in Penang?'

'Who knows what really happened there?' I'd had enough of this. 'And the woman presumably had a choice in the matter. So let's not be too quick to judge, eh?'

A long pause. The tall lacquer clock in the corner carried on splitting time into two-second splinters. Then her head inclined a fraction.

'Perhaps it was *because* of what happened in Penang that he was true in his marriage,' I added.

She seemed to consider this, weigh it inwardly. For some reason I pictured the deerstalker hat perched high on the hat-stand like a tweedy flightless bird.

'Yes,' she said at last. 'There are mistakes we learn from and those we repeat. The latter are the ones we haven't forgotten ...'

She drifted off to somewhere I couldn't follow. While I waited, I looked out the windows into the walled garden, the lawn and flowerbeds, the little green gazebo. It was bleak and chill out, no one was sitting reading there today.

'So,' she said briskly, returning to earth. 'What have you got here?'

I'd already decided to lead off with my third best card. So I told her how a friend who was helping me had gone back some months on the *Penang Gazette*, on impulse looked up her mother's birthday, and stumbled on the notice of the arrival of the *Amelia*, with the passenger list. I read it out: Mr P. Marsden; Dr A. Mackay; Miss Simpson ...

She took the photocopy from me, read through the list quickly, her pale fissured lips working.

'So,' she said. 'That would make sense. People often formed friendships and more on the voyage out. Cousin Ann must have come to take up her teaching post.'

'That's not all,' I said. 'I'll come back to that list. Are you all right?'

'It's this coffee,' she said. 'It's the only thing that keeps my heart beating, but sometimes it's over-enthusiastic. So odd to see those names again.' She fumbled with a silver cigarette case. It was old and dented, with initials in curly writing. She lit up, inhaled then sat back. 'Pray continue.'

I showed her the clipping about Ellyot's death, then his funeral. Her old tortoise throat constricted then relaxed.

'Poor Freddie,' she murmured. 'I'd quite forgotten. 'That motorbike of his – we girls thought it so exciting.'

'And then I really got lucky,' I said. 'Or rather, my friend did.'

I showed her *Alarming incident at Butterworth Quay*, the snatched photo of the boy hanging from the netting. She examined it through the magnifying glass I'd brought, ran it along the blurred faces at the rail. She stared and stared at them.

'Butterworth Quay,' she whispered. 'I remember . . . I can smell. I can hear . . .'

She was gone and for a moment I glimpsed it too – the milling crowd, the copra and rubber, the rickshaws and Asiatic swelter, the sweet-sour heady rot of life, and something more intangible, the atmosphere of a different age.

'Your father certainly knew how to announce his arrival,' she commented dryly.

'He did that.'

With a flourish, as though trumping my previous card, I put down *Dramatic operation in hurricane off Sumatra*. Then the accompanying picture of my father with the second mate and Dr Trent. For reasons of my own, I'd snipped off the names.

She put on reading glasses, scanned the article and photo carefully.

'Well done, Mr Mackay. It's not true, you know, what people say about old people living in the past. I open my eyes from my afternoon nap and am so surprised to discover I'm not dead . . .'

She trailed off.

'You've been extraordinarily lucky,' she said as she read the article again. 'Your *friend* must bring you good fortune.'

'I think she has,' I agreed.

She glanced at me with the amused, almost condescending smile of someone for whom these games are long past.

'So will you be seeing this fortunate friend again?' she enquired.

'I don't know,' I said. 'I hope so. But she's ... well there's complications.'

'Ah yes. There always are.'

By way of reply I put the Chulia Street dispensary photo next to the one of the two doctors by the man on the stretcher at the docks.

'It's the same man with my father both times,' I said. 'It's not Phillip Marsden as you suggested.'

She looked at them then glanced up at me.

'Quite possibly,' she said.

'But do you recognise this man? Do you remember him?'

She picked up the magnifying glass I offered, then examined the clearer photo. I noticed again a fine trembling in the waxy hand that held the magnifying glass.

'Perhaps,' she murmured at last. 'It's rather blurry.'

She put down the photocopies then let her other hand flop onto the arm of the winged chair. Her lower jaw dropped and I had to look away from the decay of her mouth. Then her eyes flicked open and her back straightened.

'Yes, I remember Trent.'

'Dr Trent?'

'He was an administrator of some sort.'

'He was Chief Medical Officer. And he was married to your oldest cousin?'

'Adele? Yes.'

'Who came off the same boat as her sister and my father. You said nothing about her.'

She gave me her most haughty look to date.

'I didn't have much doings with cousin Adele, let alone her shadowy husband. She was usually out, or had her nose in a book. He was almost never there. I'm not even sure that's him.'

I leaned closer to her. I heard the companion stir behind me.

'But he was a doctor, and in a way my father's boss – and you never thought to mention him when I first came here?'

'As I said, he was an administrator. The family just referred to him as Trent.' She raised her head and stared at me. 'What are you driving at, young man?'

'Do you think my father's affair could have been with Adele?'

She glared at me with incredulity and contempt in equal measures.

'Adele and your father?' She laughed, not pleasantly. 'Do you think there could have been an affair and family scandal without me knowing?'

This seemed to me to sit awkwardly with her earlier protests of a child's lack of interest in adult doings, but I let it go. Her anger was real enough.

'Do you think she'd have given him the time of day?' she continued. 'Anyway, if he was after anyone, it was Ann. Adele? Ridiculous!'

She screwed her cigarette out into the heavy brass ashtray. There was another long silence, so quiet I could hear my pulse in my ears.

'I'm sorry,' I said. 'I had to ask.'

She lifted her coffee cup to her mouth with both hands and drank carefully.

'Adele used to go around with Marsden,' she said at last. 'If there was anything going on, which I very much doubt, it would have been with him.'

'What happened to Adele and Trent?'

'What happened?' she cried. 'They died, like everybody else.'

'But they stayed together?'

'Of course,' she said impatiently. 'She went in the late forties, I think. She was tubercular, never very strong, and the Japanese occupation did for her. Trent had some injury from the Great War – I can picture it now, some kind of dent in his head. Still he outlived her, but not by a great amount.' She drummed her waxy fingers on the photo of Trent and my father on the docks. 'I was sent to school in England after that summer,' she said. 'When I moved back in '57, they were both gone. They're dust, you see, all of them.'

I started to gather the photocopies.

'Thanks for your time, Mrs Cunninghame.'

She dipped her head in acknowledgement, then smiled at me.

'Would you care to stay for luncheon? I do get so bored, and I may have a surprise for you afterwards.'

'It's an outrage!' Alan is saying. 'I've never heard of a Westerner being attacked here. Still, at least you hung on to your wallet.'

Sandy looks up at him. There'd been no attempt to get at his wallet.

'Aye,' he says. 'I'm the lucky fellow.'

He tries to sit up in the hospital bed, but needs Alan's help. Everything aches – ribs, back, head, legs, testicles. He's been thrashed like a bit of meat.

'It's a miracle they didn't kill you!' Alan says.

Sandy nods, though he's not at all sure it is. Lying here, he's had time to think about it. They could just have stabbed him at the first and been done with it. No hands had reached for his wallet. Even the knife had just cut his arm.

'I need to talk to Adele,' he says. Alan looks down. 'Or Ann,' he adds.

Alan looks up at him, his face is very grave as he slowly shakes his head.

'I'm afraid something else bad has happened,' he says.

Trent steps back from the bedside and looks down at him.

'You must have a thick head, Mackay,' he says. 'You say you've stopped passing blood?'

'Nearly.'

Trent nods. His grey eyes are neutral, professional, as they linger on Sandy.

'The registrar here is a chum of mine and perfectly competent. I just thought I'd look in.'

'To see for yourself.'

'It must be odd to be on the receiving end,' Trent says abruptly. 'To be the patient. I always found it so.'

'Aye, it's an education.'

'Perhaps a useful one.'

A long silence in the side ward. Shuttered sunlight lies in bars across the bed and Trent's on the far side of them. Sandy glimpses himself in a cell, shut behind those bars.

'I'm very sorry about Ellyot,' he says.

Trent nods, points at the ceiling.

'He's two floors up. Marsden's with him now, has been since he was brought in.'

'Prognosis?'

'Not good. He's still breathing, but . . .'

Marsden stares at him, then sits heavily on the bed. All bounce has gone, he's ashen, hollow-eyed. Unshaven, he looks much older. The hand that holds his cigarette shakes.

· 'We lost them,' he says. 'Raman's vanished into Siam with most of his network. And Freddie . . .'

He looks away, thumbs an eye.

'The paper says he'd had an accident on his bike.'

'If you call a steel wire strung across the road an accident. I sent him when it looked as though we were going to lose . . .'

'I'm sorry,' Sandy says. He clears his throat. Speech still hurts. More or less everything hurts. 'You couldn't have known.'

Marsden shakes his head, lets smoke hiss out from between his teeth.

'Vanity,' he mutters. 'My sister said it would be the death of me. I've been too clever by half.'

'You have a sister? A family?'

Marsden looks at him, arches an eyebrow and for a moment the old style comes back.

'I didn't spring into being on a half-shell!' he replies. 'I just prefer to keep my family out of my affairs – better for all of us.' He inhales, three quick little gasps. 'I'm not a safe person to be associated with.'

'You think I was attacked because of you?'

Phillip looks at him, smoke trickling past his moustache.

'Could be,' he says at last. 'Or it could be on account of that other thing.'

'Would Trent go that far?'

'I've given up being a soothsayer.'

Sandy grips Marsden's arm, so thin under the cotton jacket.

'I must see her!'

'She's . . . not going out much right now.' He gets to his feet. 'Must get back to Freddie, in case he regains consciousness.' Marsden is fidgeting now, eager to be away. 'I'll do what I can, old man.'

41

'In Upper Perak or Selangor, if you turned your back on that jungle for a week, you lost half your garden to it. I never thought I'd miss it, yet sometimes I wake in the night and the sound of rain . . .'

Mrs Cunninghame took a deep drink from her glass. She seemed revived now, a fresh fag in her steady hand as we sat between courses in the panelled dining room.

'You can't imagine rain like monsoon rain,' she continued. 'It explodes onto the ground like water bombs. And the smell afterwards, the freshness, and the birds all starting up again while drops still stream from the leaves. We'd close the chicks – blinds – during the afternoon lie-in, and the houseboy and the cook would play mah-jongg, and the clattering of the tiles went with the birds and the dripping . . .'

She closed her eyes and we both sat there. How many afternoons my father must have lain listening to just that. Through her stories and memories this last hour, I was getting a little bit of him back. What did the details of his affair matter?

'A terrible climate – too many mosquitoes and bugs for anyone's good,' she said briskly. 'Malaria and cholera got a lot of us sooner or later, especially in the more backward Unfederated States. Maybe that's why everyone drank so much – there was a theory it protected your liver. By the way,' she added abruptly, 'have you kissed your new friend?'

'Well . . . yes,' I said.

'Do you expect to again?'

'I'm still wondering about that,' I confessed.

She laughed. That seemed to be the right answer.

'Maybe things haven't changed so much,' she said. 'But you have this other friend in Orkney.'

'Not really. I mean, I did.'

She filled my glass and I swear she winked at me.

'I adore hearing about other people's affairs,' she said, 'having none of my own. Do tell.'

I talked about Mica for longer and far more frankly than I'd meant to –

the wine perhaps, and because I felt I owed Mrs C. something after my suspicions.

'Do you think she wants to get back with you?' she asked when I'd finished.

'Maybe,' I said. 'I think she wants us to be pals. Which we still are, in a way. It's just . . .'

I trailed off. I didn't know what it was just. Vanessa Cunninghame slid another cigarette from her case, lit it with the chunky dragon lighter, breathed dragon-smoke from her nose.

'Forgiveness,' she murmured. 'That can be hard to come by. You carry a wrong around with you for years and years, and then one day you look round and find you've put it down somewhere and didn't even notice.'

She took another deep draw on her cigarette and smiled at me.

'And who do you think would be better for you?' she enquired. 'Your difficult Orkney friend or your lucky one?'

I was still working on that when the companion came in to clear the table. She placed something flat wrapped in tissue paper on the white tablecloth, emptied the last of the wine into my glass, then left us. Mrs C. turned to me with a thin smile.

'Mr Mackay, time for your surprise.'

Ann arranges the fruit in the blue bowl by his bed.

'Sorry I couldn't think of anything more original.' She sits on the bed and studies him. 'You look terrible,' she says at last.

'I'll live. I had it coming.'

She picks out an apple, turns it slowly in her hand, drops it back in the bowl.

'Maybe,' she murmurs.

'Ann, I'm so sorry about Ellyot. I know you were fond of him.'

She looks down at her hands, the fingers twisting together on her lap. She stares as if they are nothing to do with her.

'I think he's going to die, Sandy.'

Staring straight ahead, she starts to weep.

At first all he can do is watch the water run from her eyes. Then he leans and puts his arms round her for the first time since the night in the gazebo. As she coories in, her head presses on one of his cracked ribs and something hurts like hell. Still he holds her, trying not to breathe more than absolutely necessary.

At last she stops. Eases away from him. She makes no attempt to wipe her face, he admires that. As with her joy, she gives herself over to sorrow in a way he never could, no matter how far he gets from his country.

'I must see Adele.'

She shakes her head.

'I don't think so.'

'But this baby—'

'Could be exactly what she needs.' She gazes steadily at him. Tears have washed her eyes very clear. 'I'm so happy for them.'

'But it's not the truth!'

Her hand rests lightly on his chest. He's aware of some deep ache as she stares into him.

'I love my sister,' she says. 'That's more important than truth.'

His mouth is open but nothing comes out.

'This is what she needs,' Ann insists. 'Marriage, stability, and now a family. If you care for her, let her have that.'

'Care? Christ Almighty, I love the woman!'

He's appalled. The word is out. It's only been whispered between him and Adele, a word so secret it can only be uttered in the dark. Ann's grip tightens on his pyjama jacket.

'I must talk to her,' he insists. 'To know what she wants. If you care for me at all, please tell her that. I'll not give up till I hear it from her.'

She shakes her head as she releases him.

'You just don't get it, do you?' she says quietly, and seems to be addressing her hands. 'I could have more than cared for you, more than Adele ever will.'

She stands up quickly, pauses at the door.

'I'll see what I can do,' she says. 'Once you get home, I'll send word.'

She is gone. The little ward is very silent. He looks at the mangoes, oranges, papayas, glowing in the bowl. *The fruits of our endeavour are not always sweet,* his father used to quote.

He picks out a bunch of grapes and slowly feeds them into his bruised mouth.

I was looking at a creased black and white photograph in a cardboard mount. Quite big, maybe ten by eight. The chemicals had reacted with light and turned it patchily to sepia. Still it was my Grail, or at least as near as I was likely to get to one.

'Taken at the Penang Races,' she said. 'Probably 1930 or '31. I found it among some old things in the loft.'

In front of a crowd of white blob faces, a small group of Europeans are on a low stand.

'Let me introduce you to the family,' she says.

Her finger descended on the older man with whiskers wearing a beehive hat.

'Uncle Donald. Awfully nice man. He must have died not too long after this was taken. Heart.'

The cheerful plump lady beside him was Aunt Isabella.

Then for the first time I looked on Phillip Marsden. Quite short, immaculate in white – those trouser creases! – he put me in mind of a conjuror or a jockey. Cigarette in his right hand, pale moustache, some kind of ironic grin as he fixes his eyes on the camera. I imagine his voice, urbane yet secretly mocking: *Our power in the Far East can depend on bayonets or prestige. On the whole, prestige is preferable.*

Here was Dr Trent looking worn and grim. Mrs C. pointed out the pale glimmer of his temple wound just below his hat.

In the centre, two young women, both fair-haired, stand with their arms linked. They both wear pleated skirts that are blown by the wind. The one on the left is exclaiming, pointing at something, laughing under a cloche hat circled with flowers. The other's hat has a couple of tall feathers, its broad brim shadows her eyes. At last, the Simpson sisters.

The cloche-hatted one was Ann, Mrs Cunninghame thought. I'd time to take in an easy full-lipped smile and a certain exuberant vitality – that pointing arm, the way she holds that parasol – which jumps across seventy years. Big eyes, wide-open and interested.

Then I studied Adele Trent née Simpson. The similarity was evident, but she was a little taller and thinner and even as she looked along her sister's pointing arm, there was something removed about her, as though commenting inwardly on what's happening. It could be irony or anger or concealed boredom in that tilted half-smile. *Jill isn't about to go back in the box.*

I took the magnifying glass and looked more closely. Unlike her sister, she's not carrying a parasol. Instead her left hand loosely grips a dark cane with a silver handle that looks like a beak. It gives her a certain impudence.

I remarked on it. Mrs Cunninghame took the glass and inspected the photo. She thought maybe it was Marsden's stick, which might explain the way Adele's holding it, like some kind of a trophy or joke.

'They were really quite close, you know,' she said.

I looked again at Marsden, who'd spoken at the young sportsman's funeral, who'd persuaded my father into the Penang Club, who had been close to Adele. Who might have known. Who is of course dead like all the rest.

Looking more closely at the photo, I noticed a little mischievous face peering out at waist height between the two sisters, and another by Ann's side.

'Cousin Emily,' Mrs C croaked, pointing at the first little girl. 'Ann and Adele's little sister. We were great chums.'

'She's—?'

Mrs C. just nodded. I pointed at the other little face, a dark-haired unsmiling child.

'That's you?'

'Not so appealing, am I?'

The unsmiling child is peering out from behind a man standing next to Ann. I left that for the time being as something struck me.

'Your parents aren't here.'

'They must have been in one of the other stands,' she sighed. 'Or maybe father was placing a bet. This would have been taken by one of those strolling photographers – it's not an arranged family portrait.'

Hat in one hand, not tall but stocky, white light splashing across brushed-back hair and onto his chunky face, the man next to Ann looks as though he's trying to suppress a grin as he follows her pointing arm.

'So who's this?' I asked casually.

She leaned in, glanced up at me, peered again.

'I'm not sure,' she replied. 'It may be Hayman.'

'Who was?'

'An American who was sweet on Ann.'

I opened my notebook, found the passenger list of the *Amelia* and read from it though I knew it by heart.

'Mr A. Hayman,' I read. 'That'll be Alan, my father's friend. You said you didn't know his second name.'

'I'd forgotten it,' she said. 'Seeing his face brought it back.' She drank some water and seemed to collect herself. 'We just called him *Ann's Yankee suitor*. I can't be sure,' she added, 'but it's possible the man next to him is your father.'

It was tall and slim enough to be him, standing at the edge of the group. What was he doing turning away from the camera like that, hand raised to his mouth? Just like him, that tail-dragging man.

'Do you think so?'

No matter how closely I squinted, there was just the side of the head, neck and ear, splashed in brilliant light. If only he could just turn back round, as he probably had in the next moment. Then again, it could be someone else altogether. I'd check a copy with my mum. Though it had been a decade before they met, she should surely still recognise the body shape.

Of the photos I ended up with from my quest, it is that image of a day at the races that haunts me still. The two sisters in the stand, shoulders touching, and the men grouped around them under the ferocious sun, the children peering between the grown-ups as the invisible wind blows the dresses out. Trent's pale wound glimmers in the shadow under his hat, Marsden and Mr Simpson confer, Ann points out something exciting to Adele while Alan Hayman plays along, and my father instinctively turns away.

A quick light rap then she slips into his bungalow, secures the door. As he tries to put his arms round Adele, she seems frail and frantic, difficult to grasp without damaging. His own body still aches all over.

She asks for a drink and sits down on the bed. It may be the poor yellow lamplight, but she looks older, different, insubstantial. None of her features are quite as he remembers. Still, she is Adele. The rest will come back in time.

She's not weepy but angry. At him. Why did he ignore her last letter?

He couldn't read it. It got soaked in a storm. He'd asked Ann to let her know.

She stares at him, her pupils huge in the poor light.

'Oh,' she says softly. 'Ann never told me. I thought . . . So I decided . . .'

She looks away, grips the bed cover. He sees her knuckles whiten as he sits beside her.

'It's mine, isn't it? Ours?'

Slowly, as if her neck were a stiff bar bending, her head comes round. 'No,' she says.

Part of his brain still runs through the little hints, Ann's words, Trent at the billiards final. Impossible to know whom to trust or believe.

There's a very small smile quivering at the side of her mouth. Nothing funny here. It may be embarrassment. Yes, that's it.

'I don't believe you.' She just looks back at him, waiting. 'Trent said that he, you know, couldn't.'

'And you believed him? Maybe he was trying to trick you into confessing. Or maybe it was just to put you off your game – John does like to win.' She chuckles softly, a bubble in her throat. 'Sounds like he succeeded.'

He stares at her. Is this some test? He puts his arms round her, she neither resists nor yields. Through the thin dress her body is hot and thin. He can feel her vertebrae, her scapula, her mortality.

'I'll know when you deliver,' he says. 'So will Trent. You can't fool us. I know when a baby is and isn't premature. I'll wait till then if I have to.'

As she looks back at him, her eyes seem to bloom, blue flower with black core.

'I was afraid you'd say that,' she said. She puts her hands on his shoulders. He winces when she presses his fractured collarbone as she stands up. 'Dance with me,' she says. 'Put some music on and hold me.'

His hands shake as they never have in even the most delicate of deliveries while he lowers the steel needle onto 'Moon River'. His life is in the balance as she sways into him and finally gives. Even as she raises her head and her lips open, he can glimpse what this would mean.

'I'm sorry,' she says. 'It's all too dreadful.'

He has never cried and kissed a crying woman before. It's like two open wounds bleeding into each other. They are lying on the bed, his head is on her breast. As she holds him there, for the first time he hears her heart, is awed to realise it's always beating whether he's there or no.

He tries to lift his head to tell her, but she clasps him tight.

The door opens.

She breathed the last of her cigarette through her nose, then stubbed it out.

'Do you think your generation invented a troubled world? Or created a virtuous one? That was how things were then. I see no reason to be censorious or sentimental about it.'

I stared at her. All I'd done was casually remark that it seemed likely a lot was going on behind the untroubled facade of photos like this one.

'Edward, the doings of grown-ups, the state of Europe, the price of rubber, the opium trade, the war in China – none of this meant anything to me. I was far more interested in my new butterfly collection and beating cousin Emily at croquet. That's how it is when you're ten, always will be.'

She paused, lit up another cigarette. I noticed they had no filters. She must have caught me looking.

'One of three positive aspects of old age,' she remarked, 'is it's much too late to give up smoking. Can I offer you one?'

'No thanks,' I said. 'I'm not old enough yet.'

She laughed, a sudden sharp bark. She was still giggling as she put the cigarette to her lips again.

'So what are the other two good things?'

She turned her aged, poised head my way, breathed out more smoke.

'You can do as you damn well please and people think you're charmingly eccentric.'

'And the last?'

For a moment I looked into her eyes.

'You realise nothing matters much. Not even dying.'

If I live long enough, I may find out for myself what I saw in her face then. She touched the napkin to her lips and tried to get up. I got behind her, helped move the heavy chair, awkwardly put my arm round her shoulder to steady her. Under her black cardigan, she was nothing at all. As I passed her the cigarette case, I finally realised she wasn't just old.

'Thank you, Edward,' she said. 'A word for you from one who'll soon be leaving.' A hint of a smile creased her time-battered lips. 'They say life is wasted on the young, but the truth is, life is wasted on the living. These people,' she gestured towards the photo on the table, 'would so envy just a minute of our time. Don't waste yours any more.'

She reached out and pressed the bell push. My time was up. I began gathering my papers into the Penang file.

As I bent to shake hands with her at the top of the stairs, the companion hovering impatiently at my side, Mrs Cunninghame gripped my hand tight. For a moment she looked into my eyes.

'Decide about these two women and what you want to do with your life and then do it. Give my regards to your mother.'

With that she released me, and I stumbled down the great staircase with the Penang file under my arm and a burning in my chest.

The last he sees of her: escorted out between the hospital superintendent – what is he doing here? – the night watchman and the constable from the street corner. Li Tek clings to his arm, a little anchor holding him back. As she goes out the door, she looks back at him – just for a moment – her mouth open, something stricken in her eyes.

Her mouth open, fair hair still in a tangle, eyes on him, then gone.

42

I leant on the playground wall of the old academy and looked down over the town, thinking on Mrs Cunninghame's parting words to me: *The truth is, life is wasted on the living.*

Cool March wind, thin sunshine through hazy cloud, shadows pursuing each other down Scapa Flow towards the Flotta flare stack, faint gleam from the oil storage tanks. The little twin-mast blue yole rocking at anchor. The *St Ola*, late again, was just turning past the edge of the Kame of Hoy, heading back to Scotland. A tractor and trailer inched across Graemsay from one farm to another. In the new school across the bay, kids on mid-morning break spilled out onto the playing fields.

This had been going on the ten days I'd been away – rhythms of clouds, tides, people, ferries. Whether in London or Edinburgh, driving or on trains, tubes and taxis, I'd always been aware Orkney was still there. No other place had affected me like this.

Ellen gripped the wall and swung herself up onto it. She parked her trim behind, looked down at Stromness.

'So, Eddie,' she said. 'Will you stay or will you go?'

A swarm of starlings rose up from behind the Post Office, went one way, ballooned, flexed then turned itself outside-in and vanished into Hillside Road. I don't know how they do that.

'Go, I think,' I said at last. 'I love this place but I can't hang around on the off-chance we'll get a funding extension.' With our tidal energy report nearly ready to print and submit to Scottish Enterprise, we had two weeks of contract left. 'So I might go to London.'

She looked at me sceptically. She'd got to know me pretty well.

'Haven't Melville-Stevenson approached you about working here?'

'I told them I'd be interested when they could actually commit to construction. I've had enough feasibility studies – I want to make something solid.'

'It's not just that, is it?'

Everywhere I went now gave me reminders – the Flying Dutchman, the Outertown Road where the For Sale sign was up outside her dad's house, Warebeth where we'd watched the Northern Lights and been briefly lifted out of ourselves, her high window above James Street, my own house where she'd lit up the kitchen, ravaged the bedroom . . .

'You shouldn't let what happened drive you away.'

'I haven't completely decided.'

'What's in London?'

'The sea-music project with Ray . . . And the Newspaper Library if I want to do more research.'

'Is that all?'

'Well . . .'

Fact was, I admitted, all lines to the Golden Girl had been cut. On my return here, I'd rung the number Roo had scrawled on the Rizla flap but it was unobtainable. I must have been reading it wrong, her writing was truly terrible. I tried various combinations of possible numbers, but none worked. Directory Inquiries would be useless without an address, and in any case she'd mentioned she was ex-directory on account of the ex-boyfriend.

She'd be wondering why I hadn't called. I'd tried phoning the Royal Mail but they wouldn't oblige. She'd draw all the wrong conclusions. She'd see this other bloke again, commit and that would be that. *You will never meet anyone as loyal as me.*

Sometimes I wondered if I'd truly lost my mind and invented her. I'd been around the romance block often enough to know that in some ways I had. But still, she wasn't all fantasy. Somewhere in London was a very real flesh and blood woman who had touched me uniquely. She was a portal into a richer, wider world, my own Penang.

I should have given her my number but she'd been in a hurry and I'd assumed hers would do. She wouldn't realise that in a place like Orkney a letter addressed to Eddie Mackay, Tidal Energy Project, Stromness, would find me.

Then again, perhaps it was a sign. The whole thing had been a brief delightful glimpse, a taste. A reminder that such things are possible, nothing more.

'Well, I think you should pursue it,' Ellen announced and slid down from the wall. 'Maybe you'll have another miraculous meeting in London.'

'It had crossed my mind,' I confessed. 'You wanting a shopping lift to Kirkwall this afternoon?'

'Duncan's been taking us through, while you've been away.' She hesitated, looked out at the Flow. 'When I heard him play with the Smoking Stone Band . . . '

'Lordy Lordy,' I said. 'Congratulations.'

And then the man himself came loping across the yard, big grin then they went off bumping shoulders down the high-walled lane to the town.

At the corner I saw them link arms, brief glimpse of her flushed face turned up to his.

'Sure is a small gene pool selection round here,' Ray said behind me. I turned round. He was grinning and bopping from foot to foot.

'It's just occurred to me,' I said. 'Duncan's not so dour. It's just he was unhappy.'

'Aye, love is a many-splendoured thing,' he said. 'I've secured that flat round the corner from Inga. Got a spare room that's big enough if you don't intend to swing a cat. '

'It's a start before we make our fortunes. Fancy a stale pie and flat pint on me at the Dutchman?'

'You know, Eddie,' he said as we trundled down the lane, 'this could be the end of a beautiful friendship.'

'I'm sorry,' Marsden says. 'Before, I could have pulled some strings, but now I'm a busted flush. They're moving me on too.'

He hands back the letter from the Chairman of the Board of Governors of the Edward VII Maternity Hospital. Li Tek had brought it in that morning, eyes lowered as though he shared the disgrace. *Unacceptable behaviour . . . Gross moral turpitude . . .* The phrases still cling and burn.

'They can't do this!'

'They certainly can, old chap. As my more unoriginal colleagues would say, they got you bang to rights. Hospital superintendent, watchman, constable . . . and a fairly compromising position, I understand? No point appealing this.'

'I can stay on,' Sandy says desperately. 'I've been saving. I can get locum work, even in Singapore or KL.'

Marsden puts his hand on his arm, gently. The sympathy is the worst of it.

'No, you can't,' he says. 'Once they revoke your resident status, you've no choice but to leave. I've been by the Commissioner's, and I know it's in the pipeline.'

'Then Adele and I will go together! Bugger the lot of them!'

Marsden fingers the condensation on his glass. The spark's completely gone, and Sandy realises the man's nearly elderly.

'Who do you think set this up?' he says quietly.

Of course it was set up. Had to be. He's had time to think about it. Could have been Ann. She knew. Or Alan, he could have opened the note. Or Li Tek, he could have been bought by Trent, to report any female visitor. Or Marsden himself – the man manipulates people as invisibly and adroitly as he does cards.

There is another possibility, of course there is.

'Are you saying you know?'

He could have sworn she'd locked the door when she came in. Perhaps she'd thought she had. But the music, the dancing, the kiss, her tears, the bed, it all seems now so orchestrated . . .

No, this is paranoia. This is what they want you to think.

'I'm saying she won't be coming with you.'

Marsden's face gives nothing away except a certain sympathy. Sandy knows there's no point in interrogating him.

350

'I've got to hear it from her,' he insists.

'They won't let you see her. Believe me.'

'You can get a message to her.'

Marsden drains his glass, puts it down carefully on the ring of its condensation mark, exactly, no overlap.

'You don't seem to understand, Sandy.' The grey eyes are fixed on him. 'I've no power left here. There's a bit of a witch hunt on for . . . my sort. This posting was my last chance, and all I managed to do was get Freddie killed. They'll have me counting coolies in Selangor. Worse, sent back to the Home Counties!'

He gets to his feet. Surely, Sandy thinks, he must have been tinting his hair fair before, because now it's mostly grey.

'I won't give up!'

Marsden leans on Sandy's shoulder as he passes. It's hard not to yelp.

'Good for you, old chap,' he says. 'Good for you. Let me know when you know when you're sailing.'

On his way to the door of the dim hotel bar, Marsden crosses with a man in the MCS. There's no mistaking it, the tutup jacket buttoned up to the neck. Sandy watches the messenger fix on him, sees the formal envelope.

Hands flat on the table, he sits and lets it come.

❧

I knew the writing of course, that vivid spiky scrawl like a seismograph in an earth tremor.

> *Because you make me laugh, sometimes when you mean to.*
> *Because you share my anxieties and know what I'm on about.*
> *Because you make solid things like bridges, buildings and tidal whatsits and I make airy nothings . . .*
> *Because we're pals and bed is good.*
> *I'm holed up in a friend's cottage in freezing Friston, trying to turn my nippy stories inside out. Much less about ME now, thank God. Come any time and we could do some re-writing ourselves. No excuses, but it was a difficult time, and surely we can learn from mistakes?*
> *Yours if anyone's – Mica*
> *p.s. Doctor pal sez check worldwide annual register thingy of all Brit medics with British Medical Association – addresses etc!*

I didn't burn it or reply. For the time being I stuffed it in the Penang folder, among the other pieces of the past that wouldn't quite lie down. However I did contact Peter and asked him to do me a wee favour next time he was in Edinburgh.

※

Here comes Ann now, out of the school gates behind a crowd of girls. He leaves the shade to intercept her as she crosses towards the Runnymede. She sees him coming and abruptly changes direction, lifts her long golden arm to wave for a rickshaw.

They owe him more than this. He signals the rickshaw away, pulls her arm down. She flushes, is about to protest. The headmistress with two assistants calls to ask if she's coming for lunch at the Runnymede. She shakes her head.

For a moment they stand looking at each other under the midday sun. Then she takes Sandy by the arm and leads him back to where he's been waiting – an old Hindu shrine backing onto the wall of the old cemetery, crumbling and its tiny door rusted solid.

Drifts of jacaranda tumble and smother over its roof, casting a few feet of shade onto the pavement. It's nothing very special, just a long-forgotten shrine dating back nearly to the founding of George Town, and it would disappear during the Japanese invasion a decade later. No one seems to remember who or what it's dedicated to, and for Sandy and Ann it's just the nearest place out of the sun, but to the end of his life he will remember it – the shade, the blinding light over the sea across the road, and Ann's eyes darkening as she lies to him.

※

43

My last morning walk to the harbour, pausing to read the latest paranoid conspiracy ravings in the window opposite the baker's. Last bacon roll from The Cafe, taken out on the pier in sun and fresh wind.

I looked along the waterfront, the few trawlers, the dive boats, Kipper's inshore boat just casting off. His brother was at the tiller and Kip was sorting creels as they went by. At the last moment he raised his hand, a wave of sorts. I raised my hand, an acknowledgement of sorts.

Then I ate my roll and watched reflected sunlight shake a bright grid over the sandstone pier opposite, looked down the line of little piers that run out towards the Hudson's Bay cannon and the Ness. This morning the Holms were connected to each other but not the shore. The blue yole still rocked in the wake from Kipper's boat, the Hoy ferry edged out from the pier, then it was time to climb Boys Lane for the last time.

I didn't say goodbye to that little grey and golden sandstone town. Not because I'm not sentimental – I am, hopelessly – but because it's not the kind of place you can say goodbye to, even if you never return.

Our joint feasibility study had emerged looking almost credible, then Anne-Marie whizzed it off to Scottish Enterprise to change the direction of our national energy policy. We'd had a small but authentically drunken celebration in our office that afternoon, continued in the Dutchman all evening. Now today we had to crawl back in to clear our desks so a Heriot Watt project – something to do with crustacean infestation – could move in.

Very end of term feeling, that clutch and plummet in the stomach as I took down my father's postcard photos – the Penang colonnades with the domino factory, one of Sumatra, him and Trent outside the dispensary standing awkwardly apart. Odd that he should keep that one . . . Then the toys I'd accumulated on my desk – razor shells from Waulkmill Bay, a perfect stone from Skaill, delicate skull and beak of a curlew, a wee dozing netsuke Buddha, the ambient Brian Eno CDs I'd brought in for long night sessions, calculator. Glancing through the drawerful of handwritten calculations, I could see now how shaky and uncertain my writing had been back in October.

Whatever and wherever next, a phase of my life was through. It had been some kind of convalescence, and I was grateful to all and everyone for that.

Even Mica? Her second note came later that morning, direct to the office

So you're not talking? Don't pretend you're not there – my spies are everywhere.

For my part: Because you're prepared to say you're scared, and that the world could be beautiful.

Because you should have been the writer and I the brisk engineer.

Because I admire competence and resolution, and you've hung in there.

It's a fight to the death between me and this damn book. One of us must submit. Best we can ask in life & work is joyous struggle rather than a pointless one?

I can't and won't grovel, but I am sorry. You never fuck up big time? Think about it. Pals, at the very least

Yrs – Monica

The 'pals' touched me, but I wanted much more than that. I wanted something glimpsed among the rustling reed beds of Hackney Marshes. Or perhaps the Golden Girl truly was a fantasy. Certainly she seemed to have disappeared off the map.

I tucked Mica's letter into the Penang folder along with the other, added that to the cardboard box. Then a last look at that view I'd spent so many hours gazing on – the rooftops, slates, chimneys of the tight-huddled houses coorying under the brae; the harbour and the Holms and Scapa Flow glimmering today smooth milky pearl like the inside of an oyster shell. I'd miss the graffiti too, miss the ghosts of gone schoolchildren and that wise warning *FUCK NO!*

Stevie hoisted one box, I took the other, then we closed the door for the last time. He peeled off our title TIDAL STREAMS RESEARCH PROJECT with Ray's handwritten scrawl below *Sorry no energy today.*

'Here,' he said, and dropped it in my box. 'You're the man for souvenirs.'

We carried the boxes down through the town and along the street to my place. We arranged to meet the next day for the first fishing trip of the new season, which would likely also be my last. I admitted it seemed perverse to be leaving after surviving the long dark, just as the light was flooding back, but WAMM would need me in London and there was nothing to keep me here.

Stevie abruptly held out his hand.

'You can aye come back, boy. We're not going anywhere.'

We shook hands, nearly hugged but of course didn't.

Indoors, I picked up the post, put aside the bumf and junk then opened with mild curiosity the brown A4 envelope, recognising my brother's writing.

Hope this might help lay some ghosts – cheers, bro! P

Stapled to his note were pages photocopied from the Medical Register compiled annually by the British Medical Association. Some entries long, listing publications and heavily abbreviated qualifications and career records, others quite brief. But Mica had been right, each carried details of current address and employment. It was the short cut I'd been looking for.

In 1929, Dad was in Manchester Hospital, must have been his second houseman year. The 1930 entry was terse and very different: *Mackay, Gordon Alexander, c/o Chartered Bank of India, Penang. M.D., Ch.B. St. And.* 1925. Chief Consultant Obstetrician, Penang Maternity Hospital.

I sat in the armchair by the window looking across the square to the slipway, making myself go slowly through each page. In 1931 his address had changed to c/o Chartered Bank of India, Bishopsgate, London. No employment listed. Had he been in Vienna? So that was him home in disgrace, but with enough saved to buy into a run-down practice in Perth the following year and carry on from there. The rest I knew, more or less – specialises in obs and gynae just before the war, meets Mum, gets married and leads hard-working blameless life, plays some golf, has two children, retires . . .

Now I had his departure from Penang down to the nearest year. If I ever had a couple of months with nothing else to do but read through the *Penang Gazette* I might eventually find a mention of his departure. But what would that achieve? Though I'd established his arrival date, the names of a small group of people he had associated with, and had a few photos that put faces to those names, it seemed that was the end of the line. I'd had a notion about Adele Trent but Mrs C. had been genuinely outraged at the suggestion.

On the next photocopied page, Peter had circled an entry on the other name I'd asked him on impulse to check out for me, just for completeness' sake.

Trent, John Broadie. He'd graduated ten years before my dad, from Edinburgh. *Chief Medical Officer, Penang and Province Wellesley.* He'd published a couple of papers on malarial complication and liver function, and the vaccination problem.

That was 1930. Peter had enclosed photocopies of the following years. No change, then in 1940 he was listed at an address in Singapore – looked like he'd been made Chief Medical Officer for all of the Federated States, just in time for the Japanese invasion. But he'd survived it, because in 1945 he was listed again in Singapore, different address.

There was only one more sheet. On top Peter had written *Didn't copy the others because no change till this one – of any use?*

It was for 1954. Immediately after Trent's name was *(retired)*. He'd come home.

I blinked and re-read that address.

I told myself I was hallucinating, another blip from a damaged brain. But like lightning arriving ahead of thunder, I saw it all in an instant, even before I reached for my file to check.

I'd thought I'd got this far on the Penang quest by application and a degree of luck. By the time I finally went to bed that night I knew I hadn't worked that hard, and no one gets that lucky.

'She doesn't want to see you,' Ann hisses. 'You must realise that!'

In desperation, he has been round three times to the Trents' house near Ayer Itam. Each time he has been turned away by a very large Chinese houseboy. Mrs Trent is resting, she is not to be disturbed.

'I don't believe you.'

'You should.' Ann seems to relent, her hand on his arm. 'Sandy, she's made her decision. The baby is John's. That's what she wants.'

He looks away, away from her and the busy road and the light, into the purple shadow.

'So – what? – She's got what she wanted from me?'

She looks him in the eye. 'Believe that if it helps. She regrets everything that's happened, except this baby. It will help her, I know it will. Put it down to experience.'

'Experience! Is that what you call it?'

'That is what people come to the Far East for, isn't it? Adventure and experience. Some never leave, some can't wait to. And others . . . have to.'

Someone calls from a passing rickshaw, a woman in white hat and gloves whose smile fixes as she recognises him. Ann smiles and waves, and they watch the rickshaw trundle away down Northam Road, the clock of the clogs of the rickshaw boy fading. He loathes the dismissive tilt of that hat.

'We're born to this,' she says abruptly. 'To the climate. To regular separations of husband and wife and children, to tiffins, afternoon lie-offs and our perishables all in tins. To being a small group among so many other races.'

Her hand tightens on his arm and he winces. He's beginning to suspect his radius is fractured.

'Sandy, you'll never know what's going on here, any more than you'll ever understand my sister. My advice to you is – go home and forget us.'

'I'm supposed to sail in four days,' he says, and suddenly feels close to tears. Maybe it's the heat, or the shock of being beat. Across the road, the Runnymede Hotel shimmers white, a great iced cake. He'll never again drink cold mangosteen with Adele under the fans among that high-ceilinged splendour.

'Don't miss us – we're not worth it.'

Her hand rests on his cheek a moment, fingers pass lightly over the bruising. She looks into his face intently, her lips move as though she's memorising something.

'I'll no go if she doesn't want me to.' He hears the begging in his voice, it makes him sweat more than the heat ever could.

'She wants you to go,' she says clearly. 'Goodbye, Sandy.'

Her hand drops away, she turns and passes from purple shade into white glare. She crosses the road as he stands and stares, runs up the steps of the Runnymede, her head bowed, then she is gone from him.

Maybe she didn't lie. It may be true. At one extreme possibility, he's been set up, used; at the other, Adele is more or less a prisoner in her home and weeps for him. And so many possibilities between those extremes.

As he stirs, a small shower of jacaranda falls onto the back of his hand and blends with the bruising there. This morning when he sluiced himself down from the Shanghai jar, his whole body seems to have bloomed yellow, green, blue, brown, purple, all the garish colours of the tropics.

He shakes the petals away, bends the brim of his hat down against the glare then sets off home to pack.

44

It was a warm May morning as I came up the drive in Trinity for the last time. The file under my arm was fatter now, for since finally leaving Orkney three weeks earlier I'd taken time to think things through and do some more research. I glanced up at the turret room, but there was no face there today. No matter.

The companion eyed me disapprovingly though I'd phoned the evening before.

'I've come to see Emily,' I said, and walked past her. On impulse I unhooked the deerstalker from the hatstand and wasn't so suprised at the name inside, then hurried on up the stairs while her mouth still hung open.

She rose to her feet as I walked in, all in black except for lace round her throat. The room was very bright with sunlight and her face more lined and wax-white than ever as we stared at each other.

'So, Mr Mackay, you got there in the end.'

She was almost Mica's height, upright and thin as a stair-rod. I had a very strong desire to throttle her.

'It *is* Emily, isn't it?'

She inclined her head graciously.

'I took the liberty of swapping lives with cousin Vanessa. She was my best friend, after all.'

I'd meant to play this calmly but it wasn't possible.

'What the hell did you do it for?'

I'd had weeks to ponder that. Malice, mischief, boredom? She didn't reply at first but moved closer to the mantelpiece as she opened her cigarette case.

'Do you think you'd have got this far without my help?' she croaked. 'Whenever you looked like giving up, I gave you another clue. I think you should thank me.'

Torn between walking out and a storm of questions, I focused on what was next to her on the mantelpiece. That silver tankard hadn't been there

on my earlier visits yet it looked awfully familiar. Even as I picked it up, I
think I knew.

Dr John Trent
Winner Class 'A' billiards
The Penang Club
1930

'Some you win . . .' she murmured behind me.

I took a step towards her. Her glance went to the companion who was
standing in the doorway, then she smiled.

'You could serve sherry, Susan. Though I have no doubt Mr Mackay
would like to throttle me – we have, after all, rather amused ourselves at
his expense – he has not his father's temper. I think you may safely leave
us alone, dear.'

The companion gave me a doubtful look but left the room, though she
left the door ajar.

'You knew what I'd find when you sent me to the Colonial Records
Office?'

'I felt you should know more about Phillip and poor Freddie,' she
conceded.

'And the passenger list from the *Amelia*, and that photo of my father
with Dr Trent on the quayside, all that stuff we found in the *Penang
Gazette* – I suppose that wasn't just chance?'

Emily Simpson snickered as she lit up.

'Chance would be a fine thing.'

I put down the billiards trophy and looked round, half-expecting the
elder Simpsons to come out from behind the sofa or Phillip Marsden to
stroll, smiling and debonair, from the cupboard, clapping quietly. It had
been stage-managed from the start, all those months of direction and
mis-direction. As I looked at Emily Cunninghame née Simpson and she
gazed calmly back, waiting, I knew we were getting very near the end.

I put my Penang file down on the table. We wouldn't be needing it any
more.

'Let me guess – Roo is the great-niece you once mentioned?'

'That was careless of me,' she admitted. 'Rowan is my sister's
granddaughter and the only family I have left.'

My mouth had turned drier than the Gobi. I swallowed twice while she
just stared at me with a slight smile fissuring her lips.

'Which sister?'

Ejected one more time from the door of the Simpsons' house, he comes at last to the Chinese temple and hesitates at those green and gold gates. Somewhere in there is a shaded courtyard, a statue and a fountain where an old man had swept leaves and he had felt at peace. Somewhere in there is calm.

He wants to sit there and feel some respite from this ... burning.

But Ng isn't here to show him how to find the little courtyard. This is not his culture, not his religion. It's not for him, never can be.

He hurries away, sweat squelching in his shoes.

Back under the arch of the colonnades on Acheen Street it is, fractionally, cooler. Off the street he is spared both the sun crashing on his shoulders and the stares he imagines coming his way. The word will have gone out, he knows that. This morning Daniel Ng had bowed briefly as he passed then hurried on without stopping towards the hospital. He knew then he was finished.

He opens up his Brownie and hurriedly takes a couple of pictures down the street – a rickshaw boy, a group of Chinese hawkers. He lowers his camera as a bunch of Malay schoolgirls come by, laughing gently.

It's true: he cannot stay. His contract is severed, his resident permit rescinded, his berth booked. More than that, he who has always said he doesn't care a damn what people think now realises he cannot bear being talked about when what they say is true. He knows he is now the man who was caught with the wife of the Senior Medical Officer, and that makes his personal and professional life here impossible.

God knows what it will make hers.

The reel of film is nearly finished. He's had the same one in the camera all the time he's been here. He's not a one for pictures – he knows where he's been, he knows what he's seen. Likely he'll never know what he failed to see.

Sumatra must be on this reel, including a couple he and Adele took of each other outside the hotel, under the traveller's palms. He can see those mountains yet, feel the cooler air, her laughter as he raises the camera ... He's only taking these for his mother, whose last letter ended, *It would be grand to see some photographs of such a foreign place.*

He puts away the camera, hails a vendor. A few cents buys him cool watermelon, pink as watery blood, but only leaving here will buy him any relief. He's given up. He's beat. Li Tek delivered the telegram along with the morning chai. *Temporary locum arranged Stop Vienna very cold Stop Will meet Stop Slainte Exclamation Bob*

Yet she might change her mind, if it was ever made up in the first place. Practicalities are important, and they have changed too. He now has six months' work in Vienna, nobody knows them there, they can start again, man, woman and child.

He must let her know he has work, an address. But the houseboy won't let him in, she can't or won't come to the door. They have no telephone. His letters have remained unanswered, and for all he knows, undelivered. They turn Li Tek away. She hasn't been seen at the Runnymede nor the E&O.

Ann, then? He can't trust her. Alan has come over all earnest and American, will not even discuss it. 'Can't help you there. Sorry.' How can he get a message to her?

One last shot. He steps out into the street to take a picture of the colonnades, raises the tiny viewfinder, operates the shutter, curses inwardly as a white-suit hurries by just as he clicks.

Then he blinks, looks again at what he has just photographed. On the pillar above the Good Fortune shrine: the familiar playing cards, the dominoes. He's looking at Mr Lu's Games Workshop and he can feel his carotid artery throb, for the game isn't over yet. In that moment he knows the message, he knows the means. It's just a matter of finding an innocent messenger, and thinking of those passing schoolgirls, he knows that too.

He parts the bamboo curtain and steps inside.

Fortunately for my criminal record, Susan came back in then bearing a silver tray of sherry glasses and a chilled bottle. I was persuaded to sit on the sofa and drink something so dry it disappeared without trace. My tormentor was going to answer in her own time.

'Everything fell apart in our family after that,' Emily said. 'My father died suddenly later that year, and I'm sure it was to do with the state Adele was in. Even before that the atmosphere was terrible, what with Ann and Adele scarcely speaking, and her and Trent so stiff and formal, and my mother trying to be glad to the world that there was a baby on the way. It seemed to me it all went wrong with your father's arrival.'

She cracked a salty wafer between her fingers.

'You saw him with Adele?' She nodded. 'And with Ann?'

She nodded again, tongued in some crumbs off her lips, more like a lizard than ever.

'On the voyage out, and later in the gazebo,' she said dryly. 'And other places. Kissing and canoodling. I'm afraid I was always an inquisitive child.'

'And you blame my father?'

She paused with another cracker halfway to her mouth, stared at me and for a moment I glimpsed the observant, overlooked, angry child.

'I had him down for Ann, who was my favourite,' she said at last. 'Though he seemed a bit intense and frightening, he was quite funny and gentle with me. He said I reminded him of a sister he once had. He did this trick with string ... '

I saw again a station platform, me and him waiting for a train. *Here, I've something to show you.* The complex knot that pulled out into nothing.

'Then I found out he'd kissed them both.'

'Or they'd both kissed him,' I interjected.

'As you wish. One afternoon I saw him and Adele talking in the Runnymede, and even at that age I knew what was happening. Then we were whisked off to the Cameron Highlands. She spent all her time mooning in her room, or walking up and down in the rose garden, and getting jumpy before the postboy came.'

Her eyes were fixed on another time. Even her voice had changed, as though the child were coming close to the surface.

'When we came back to Penang, I was told Adele was having a baby.' I leaned forward, she imperiously waved me to let her finish. 'In all the books I read that was a happy ending, but no one seemed to be happy about it. Adele scarcely spoke, she didn't leave their house. Trent, who I'd always put up with as a bit of a dry old stick, was being so horribly jovial I thought he was going mad. Ann was distant, cold and angry and not my friend any more. I think it was then I began to hate your father.' She paused, her mouth twisted in a smile of sorts. 'That's why it was so funny it was me he came to.'

The big clock's minute hand clunks to noon and out in the playground the ancient Chinese janitor lifts the brass bell. It clangs across the cry to prayer rising from the mosque, a sound that never fails to move Sandy. Something in the harsh, sweet, uncompromising clarity of that cry summons up his own country.

He waits in the shade of the bicycle sheds as the children stream out. He has met Ann before here, and knows it will another five minutes before she emerges with arms full of jotters. But here comes Emily, listening to her cousin Vanessa.

He grips the little wooden box and steps from the shade ...

'He said he was going away, which I knew, and that this box of dominoes was a farewell present to Adele. Would I give it to her in private when I had the opportunity? I knew from the way he asked that it was important. His big nose was gleaming with sweat – he never properly acclimatised. So I looked at him and said yes, I would.'

She gazed towards the big windows onto the garden and was silent a long time. I waited, seeing it myself: the serious child, the anxious man, the pregnant woman shut away, the scalding playground, the domino box changing hands. I was finally coming to the crux. I could nearly touch him.

'People underestimate children,' she said at last. 'Especially solemn little girls who look them in the eyes. I knew the present was some sort of message. When I got home I went up to my room, locked the door and drew down the chicks.'

In the shaded room the girl in the pink dress kneels on her bed and turns out the shiny set of dominoes. She looks for a slip of paper but there is none. So maybe there's secret writing in invisible ink on the box, or something scratched onto a domino.

As she searches, outside the wind is rattling a bamboo cup around the courtyard. There are muffled voices down the stair, her father and Ann arguing in low, urgent voices. Philomena the canary and Phyllis the cook are singing, and she can find no message. Perhaps she has got it wrong. She has been told often enough she is too clever for her own good.

Still she picks up each ivory tile in turn, squints at the surfaces looking for marks but there are none. The sweetness of cooking curry tiffin, durian and coconut drifts up the stair. Soon it will be lunch. These last few weeks she has come to dread family meals.

She frowns down at the domino in her right hand. It has a tiny dragon carved on the underside, but there's something else different about it. She picks up another in her left, weighs one against the other. She shakes the two:one domino, puzzled. Holds it to her ear, picks at the edges with her nails but nothing happens.

Then at last, thinking perhaps of her hated piano lessons and those ivory keys, she presses her fingertips on the little cups where the dots are, and feels the lid slide open.

'When I saw what was inside, I knew it would only cause more trouble. For a long time after, I felt rather pleased with myself, thinking I'd been rather clever, and responsible.' She lowered her glass and looked at me speculatively. 'If I had passed it on to Adele, you might well never have been. Odd thought, isn't it?'

I shivered, feeling my complete non-being pass through me. Odd wasn't the word for it.

'Things change,' she said briskly. 'After keeping it to myself for seventy years, maybe I wanted to explain to someone. When I saw your advertisement, I thought it would be interesting at least to find out what had happened to him, what sort of life he'd had. Maybe I wanted to confirm I'd done the right thing . . . ' She raised her glass at me then sipped. 'And perhaps to have some entertainment. One does get so bored, waiting to die.'

I stared back at her, shaking my head. If there was an apology in there somewhere, it was pretty well hidden.

'You mad, vindictive, old snake,' I said slowly. 'You had no right not to pass it on.'

As she looked back at me, her yellow-grey old tongue flicked across her lips, gathering in the last crumbs.

'He had no right to ask me to,' she replied.

'He would have been desperate. He was being forced away and they wouldn't let him contact her. He had to do something.'

Slowly she put her glass down. It rattled a little on the table, the veins on the back of her hand were like thick blue string. Her skin had that translucent sheen I remembered on Mica's dad towards the end.

'Susan!'

366

The companion must have been listening on the other side of the door because she was in straight away. My revelator waved a hand.

'The bureau,' she croaked. 'Left-hand drawer. Get it.'

As Susan did her bidding, Emily Simpson continued.

'I always held your father responsible for everything. Only recently have I begun to revise that opinion, with Rowan's help.' She glanced at me. 'It's possible he was as manipulated as you have been.'

I jumped up, went to the mantelpiece and glared back at her. I wanted to manipulate her scrawny neck. Susan straightened up at the bureau.

'Got it, Emily.'

'You once said you wanted something of your father,' she said. 'Well this is his. I think it's time you had it back.'

She nodded to Susan who crossed the room to put a yellowed ivory two:one domino into my not entirely steady hand.

It seems the Founder's Day ceremony has dwindled to the Assistant Commissioner standing by Sir Francis Light's tomb addressing a few words to a scattering of MCS people and wives, some chaps from Guthries and Bousteads, and a few redundant planters hoping for a free drink. Followed by a short prayer from the vicar about 'strength in difficult times'. It all strikes Sandy as rather perfunctory, like the singing in a church where people have ceased to believe.

Now the group are heading for the Penang Club. There'll be a special dinner, the inevitable vast curry, with drinks and a few words about standards and the spirit of adventure, but mostly drinks and talk of falling prices.

Sitting on an old tombstone under the frangipani trees, Marsden stirs by his side.

'Pretty clear we're not welcome.'

'I wouldn't want to go anyway.'

'Absolutely not, old chap. Are you packed?'

'Aye.'

It hasn't taken much. Some last-minute shopping at the markets for presents for his parents for their mantelpiece at home, to put alongside the carved seals from Nova Scotia, the wooden antelope from South Africa, the little bush piano from Australia. His tin-lined trunk is only half full with books, clothes, a few impulsive last-minute purchases from the stalls and colonnades on Light Street. The fibbing letter home is taking shape in his mind, something to do with 'broaden my medical experience on the Continent' and 'ready for a change'.

Marsden stands, adjusts his jacket over his shoulders. The sun's low and the heat's going out of the day.

'We're getting tired of being top dog, so let someone else do it – the Yanks, China, Japan.' Marsden's curt laugh fluffs up his moustache. 'It's all tosh anyway. Let's you and I take a stroll and read some very, very short stories on tombstones.'

As they wander through the graves in the long-disused Northam Road cemetery, over and over Sandy reads and does the small subtraction. Sailors, traders, administrators, the first women missionaries and teachers, all dying so young. Mostly of malaria, but also cholera, typhoid, dysentery, childbirth.

They've made some progress there, at any rate. Not everything gets worse. If he'd had a couple more years . . .

He looks away, walks on. As the shadows lengthen and they part grasses to decipher yet another cadet come out from England looking for adventure, another mother's son drawn by everything that whispers in the words *Far East*, then dying in his twenties, Sandy wraps himself in the melancholy of it and is obscurely comforted.

In the end they come back to Francis Light's tomb. Though it's been cleaned up for today's ceremony, it's easy to see the long neglect, the absence of any trodden path. *Died 21st October 1794.*

'Malaria got Light too in the end,' Marsden remarks. 'Still, he accomplished something, which is more than I have.'

What bounce is left in the man is like the twitching of a cockerel after the head comes off – reflex, nothing more. Sandy has some idea of what Marsden has lost in Freddie Ellyot. It's somehow fitting he spends his last dusk here with him.

Marsden sits on the tomb and produces – magician to the last – a hip flask and two little silver cups.

'But we're still alive, so let's sit and drink to the man.'

So Sandy Mackay spends his last evening in Penang sitting with Marsden drinking brandy and smoking to keep mosquitoes at bay, by Francis Light's grave under the frangipani trees and the falling dusk.

45

'I warn you, it's been seventy years since I opened that,' Emily Simpson said.

I turned the domino over and back again. Now it had come to it, I was almost reluctant.

'You haven't looked in since?'

She almost blushed.

'The contents seemed so ... personal,' she said. 'I'm not entirely without conscience. But I've no idea what condition they'll be in now.'

I nodded, preparing myself for disappointment as I fitted my fingertips to the little pits and pressed.

Mr Wu must have been a good craftsman, for the lid slid open at my second attempt. The little slip of paper on the floor of the compartment looked blank, then I noticed the faintest of marks as I tilted it to the light.

'Here,' she said, and handed me a magnifying glass. 'This might help.'

Very faint brown, his writing, a tiny version of the cursive script I knew.

73 *Rathausestrasse, Wien. Work. Love Allways.*

'I was surprised he couldn't spell 'always',' she remarked.

'It wasn't wrong,' I muttered. 'It's a family joke he used to crack – McKay equals son of both yes and forever. He called Peter *Sometimes* and I was *Maybe*. Not particularly funny.'

So that was his last message to Adele, the one she never got. Short and to the point, with a pun of sorts. For how long had he waited and wondered, watching the grim lines start to set around his mouth in his shaving mirror in the Viennese mornings?

'Try these, Mr Mackay,' the companion said and handed me a pair of tweezers.

At her direction, I lifted aside the slip of paper and found a folded scrap of some gauzy material, very fine. Emily coughed beside me.

'I'm afraid that's faded too,' she said. 'But when I first saw it, it was a tiny yellow butterfly.'

'What was that about?'

'God only knows.'

I lifted it aside with the tweezers, and looked into a yellowed but miraculously unfaded face of a man neither I nor my mother had ever known: my old man as a young man in Penang.

He stares straight out at the camera. Below his side parting, his forehead is splashed with light but his eyes are in shade. Behind him, out of focus, are some palm trees. Perhaps I imagine a hint of self-mockery in his wide smile, but for sure I never saw him so frank and unburdened, so complete.

I gripped the little photo by the tweezers, turned it over.

For ever and for aye.

I stared for a long while then slid the lid back in place, feeling some charge travel through me. Looked down again at the miniature tombstone in my palm. Thought of the note, the photo, the gauzy dust of the butterfly.

I knew he had prepared this domino, staked his future on it, a desperate, raw young man, then handed it over to a child and watched his future walk away. Contact at last. A slight easing even as I slipped it into my pocket.

One question remained, the big one. I was half-choked as I uttered it. 'Was Adele's child my father's?'

She steepled her fingers and looked at me for a long time. For once she didn't appear to be enjoying herself at my expense.

'I don't know,' she said at last. 'She never confided in me. Nor in Ann – they were never close after your father left. It was murmured in the family that Trent had some medical condition. It was certainly an issue that they had no children before, and they never had another after.'

I sipped the drink that left me drier than before, like curiosity itself. 'What became of it?'

'Him,' she said brusquely. 'My nephew Stephen died young, tubercular like his mother, a few years before Adele went in '45. Trent loved that boy and never recovered from his death. Probably your father never knew – to the best of my knowledge, there was no further contact between them.'

'My father married in 1946,' I said thoughtfully. 'Not long after Adele died.'

She nodded.

'I wondered about that when you first told me,' she said. 'It may be coincidence. I don't suppose we'll ever know.'

'So that leaves—?'

Emily Simpson chuckled at my urgency, sipped on her sherry again before replying.

'Ann and Alan Hayman married a couple of years after your father left. They had one child before Alan died – his lungs, you know. I'm afraid Mary was rather wild. Once she'd left boarding school, she went her own

371

way and never came back to Malaya. Rowan is her daughter by a most unsuitable man. Fortunately she has a lot more sense than her mother.'

I put my glass down carefully. I'd fallen for the granddaughter of a woman my father had once kissed and perhaps more. But not, thankfully, *his* granddaughter.

Still, it was a spooky idea, for Roo had affected me on an almost molecular level. I carried so much of my father's genetic code, just as she must have Adele and Ann's. I'd not forgotten our day on Walthamstow and Hackney Marshes, the sense of rightness as her belly beat on mine.

But all a set-up.

'The first time we met, when her car broke down outside my friends' house?'

She chuckled at that.

'Rowan's idea. She was visiting when you first called here.'

I thought of the face at the turret window that first time, the footsteps I'd heard going off down the hall, the reader in the gazebo.

'I thought it better to keep her out of sight, but when I told her about the purpose of your visit here she was intrigued to meet you. After all, it concerns her family too! And I wanted to form a better idea of who you were, so I could decide what to do with you. I must say your office was pretty free with your London address. The rest was easy.'

'And the day out we had – was that your idea too? Do you normally pimp for her?'

'No need to be coarse, Edward.' She screwed her cigarette into the Malayan dollar ashtray. 'No, I hadn't anticipated that, nor her feelings for you. I dare say she was touched by your attentions.'

She put her glass aside and looked at me without speaking for a while. When she reached for her battered cigarette case, I grabbed it first, turned it over and read the swirly engraved initials: *P.M.* 'He gave it to Ann when he had to leave Penang. Such a clever, amusing man,' she murmured, 'you'd have liked him.'

I pressed the little tag, the case opened and I offered her one. She drew it out with the smallest of grins, lit up then sat back in the winged chair.

'In any case, I decided perhaps your father wasn't the scoundrel I'd always believed. So it was time to give you the final clues.'

'The photo at the races?'

'You were taking so long to connect Trent and Adele.'

'But you said the very idea was outrageous!'

'I still think it so.'

'And the Medical Register?'

She inclined her head and there was a long silence.

Even in my more paranoid moments, I'd thought that was one

discovery I'd made unaided. When she glanced keenly up at me, I saw the spark of mischief or malice in her eyes.

'Of course, I do owe you an apology,' she said as she got shakily to her feet. 'I have enjoyed myself at your expense. So I have taken it upon myself to offer you something in return.'

She smiled almost coquettishly as she shuffled over to the big window. I could not but follow her and we stood together looking down onto the sunlit garden. Through the trellis of the gazebo, I was looking at a head of golden hair, longer now, grazing her shoulders as Roo leant forward over a magazine.

The scene had looked staged the first time I'd visited because it had been. The difference this time lay in the other woman who now sat across from Roo, leaning forward as she gestured and spoke, her head alert as a thrush probing a snail. *p.s. Doctor pal sez check worldwide annual register thingy of all Brit medics.* Of course, of course.

'A charming scene, is it not? They seem to have become quite good friends.'

She inhaled and exhaled happily till I remembered to breathe. Out in the garden, Roo gestured while Mica laughed and shook her head.

'It is time to make a choice,' Emily Simpson said briskly. 'The catch is, you can only have one of them.'

'They know about this?'

'Clearly.'

'You're quite mad, you know that? You can't offer me a choice between two people like they're sweeties in a jar, do I want the red one or the blue one!'

She exhaled and looked on me more kindly.

'Well put, young man. However, I didn't say you can have either of them. I said you had a choice. Choose wrongly and you end up with no one, for only one *might* have you. Choose rightly and I'll call down, then after a pleasant luncheon you will leave here with her. Whatever happens then is up to the two of you.'

I took a long look. Roo flicked over another page of her magazine, her head nodding in the sunlight as she turned eagerly to her companion with some enquiry.

You will never meet anyone more loyal than me.

I could see Mica's mouth move in reply, recognised that quick, sardonic twist, remembered the restless intelligence she employed to protect her heart.

Think about it – pals at the very least.

'Choose rightly, and I'd say you have a fighting chance of being happy,' Emily Simpson croaked at my side. 'I'm deeply fond of my great-niece – incidentally, she will inherit this house – who I think would prefer to have children rather than further an education she neither wants nor needs. You are not too old for that, are you?'

'You're completely mad,' I said.

She didn't seem in the least bothered as she stood beside me, took another sip from her glass followed by another drag on her fag with a slightly shaking hand, getting her pleasures while she could.

'On the other hand there's Monica. We've had some fine long chats recently, and I find she rather reminds me of myself at that age, so naturally I like and admire her. So – the young lovely easy one, or the difficult, challenging one? I do hope,' she added thoughtfully, 'you choose more wisely than your father did.'

I took a last look down into the sunlight garden, at the two women who had helped and fooled me, now laughing and talking together. I'd not easily forget.

I turned away, picked up my prize from the mantelpiece. At the door I turned to look back at Emily Cunninghame née Simpson, the last person alive who had known my father as a young man baffled in love.

'I think you owe me this much,' I said. 'Goodbye.'

I went down the stairs at a lick in case I changed my mind, nodded to Dr John Trent's old deerstalker on the hatstand. Apparently what survives of us isn't love but hats.

As I opened the front door, she may have called 'Well done' from the top of the stairs or maybe it was just my little inner voice muttering *Dae weel, dae richt.* In any case I left that time-suspended house to hurry away down the gravel drive with a hollow domino in my pocket and a Class A billiard winner's trophy from the Penang Club 1930 hanging from my hand.

The soft moist clinging dark wraps round them like an angora sweater that can't be pulled off. The lights come on in the Runnymede, but they won't be going there. Sandy swallows his third brandy then turns to Marsden.

'I played the hand you dealt me, didn't I?'

Marsden's face glows briefly as he draws on a cigarette.

'I can only deal what's in the pack,' he replies.

'We lost.'

'Freddie lost. We're still breathing. Here, might as well finish this.'

By the light of a passing taxi on Northam Road, Marsden fills up the two cups.

'I . . . cared for Freddie,' he says abruptly. 'Much more than he knew. Now he's dead because of me. Cheers.'

Nothing worth a damn Sandy could say to that.

'Slainte.'

Marsden has lost Freddie and his great game. And Sandy is leaving a child not yet born, that might or might not be his, and a love that had known four days in the Sumatran Highlands, one night in the Crag Hotel. Adele, absently tucking a lock of hair behind her right ear as she reads *Elmer Gantry* in bed. Her last look back as she was hurried out the door.

But still there's hope, just a flicker. Little Emily promised to deliver his innocent item, and Adele would surely know what to do with it. Then it's up to her.

'My only advice, old man,' Marsden begins then trails off. He is, Sandy realises, fairly drunk. 'If I may.'

'If you must.'

He feels a grip on his arm, then the fingers' heat coming through his jacket.

'I'm too old to put this behind me, but you're not. When you leave, don't dwell on it.'

Sandy lets the fire run down his gullet.

'How can I no dwell?'

The grip tightens.

'You put the war behind you?'

'For the most part.'

'I suggest you do the same with Penang. And if you ever dream about it

– about her, or Ann, or any of us – well, you're not responsible for your dreams, are you?'

A long silence. A firefly stitches its way across the tombstone. Yellow thread, darkness, yellow thread, darkness.

Sandy stands up, sways slightly. Reaches down to pull up Marsden.

'Retreat in good order.'

'Precisely.'

Arm in arm, two pale ghosts in their white suits, they stagger through the cemetery towards the sea and the road home.

The last visitors have finally left the broch site, but the custodian seems in no hurry to get home. Through the binoculars I watch him slowly carry in his noticeboard, emerge to potter over to his van, then potter back to the hut again.

I take a last look at the pink and yellow horizon in my rear-view mirror – the road, the track, the shore are all empty. No one's coming, I'll do this last act alone, which is fine by me.

About that moment of decision at Emily Simpson's: for once in my life I never second-guessed myself, never hesitated or regretted. The choice she offered was too insulting all round. Perhaps it was meant as her final test.

In any case, a few weeks later I got from her a long letter with all the scraps of memory she had left of him and the crowd he knew then. It may have been an apology of sorts, and certainly it must have cost her much effort, for her writing became shakier and more erratic as it went on. Her final P.P.S. was almost illegible. *You might be amused to hear your father's houseboy Li Tek went on to become Director of Harbours after Independence. Rather fitting, I thought!*

I sent her a short reply, which was returned, unopened, by Susan the companion. Emily Simpson had died in the afternoon in the winged armchair overlooking the garden. On the whole I was glad she never got to read my note. Susan also sent a small package. *She wanted you to have this.*

I feel in the glove compartment and take out the battered silver cigarette case, open it, draw out from under the crimson band Emily Simpson's last remaining cigarette, untipped. I wind down the window then light up my first in years, thinking on her.

It tastes rotten, but still.

I went to see my mother after leaving Trinity. This time she'd remembered I was coming and was ready for me.

'Don't tell me your father wasn't a passionate man,' she said, handing me a tiny envelope. 'I found this among some old cards in my desk.'

I opened it, took out a yellowed card with a single, roughly drawn flower on the front. *To my darling Mary who grows more lovely, more clever and more valued down the years. Let's get married again. 17th March 1957. "I will." Alexander.*

'So,' my mum said briskly, 'did you find out about this mystery lady?'

I blinked, carefully put the card back in its envelope.

'I think there was probably nothing in it,' I said.

She nodded as she put the card away in her drawer.

'I thought as much,' she said. 'Your father was very sensitive to slights and embarrassment, so I always took it with a pinch of salt.'

I draw deeply and this time the smoke gets past my tonsils. I tap the ash out the window, exhale, wait a little longer. It must be the nicotine that raises the heart rate, making the head spin slightly then settle like a compass needle, quivering as it points the way to go.

Our first full playback was just a fortnight ago, in Inga's black and silver octagonal bat cave. The walls, surfaces and much of the floor space were strewn with very expensive recording, playback, keyboard and programming equipment.

'This is very rough,' Ray warned us. 'Just trying out ideas, yeah?'

'Just run the bloody thing,' I said. 'See if it's anything like music this time.'

We'd had our first installation piece a few weeks back as a soundtrack at a conceptual art show. One reviewer had described it as *enticingly nihilistic*, another was excited by its *compelling authentic randomicity*. I had hoped we could do better than make people's ears bleed, though the grant had come in handy.

Curled up on her silver settee, Inga yawned and inspected her unfeasibly black fingernails.

'I been working like a bastard on this for months,' she said. 'I reckon it will never sound like what I call music.'

'That's hopeful.'

'Shut your cakehole, Ray, and run the fucker,' she commanded.

We were exhausted and on edge. Since walking out of Emily Simpson's house four months earlier, I'd given myself over completely to this project, faithful to it as any lover, and as open to disappointment if it failed. But it was right, I knew it, to be finally whole-hearted about something through all my waking hours. This was my true quest. What happened when I slept was my problem alone.

Ray selected a mini-disc from a rack of recent recordings.

'*Top of the tide in a light westerly, waning moon*,' he read, then slotted it in.

While it ran, we tweaked the settings, changed the scale, introduced a loop-tape delay, added reverb and a bass so deep it was subterranean. I finally slowed it right down and introduced some silence. A lot of silence.

Then we stopped and just listened. I see it still: Inga all black angles on the settee, Ray on his back on the floor, me at the window looking out on the London night thinking even if this is crap, it's been worth it. These are my friends and this is my work. Even if he'd have been baffled by what we produced, my father would have asked nothing more of me.

From the speakers came the sound of the shape of the sea, remodelled by human intervention. We'd guessed it would come out essentially as a duet of rising and falling broken arpeggios. And it did, though not like any we'd ever heard. Not like anything anyone had ever heard.

In the silence afterwards, Ray finally got up, pattered on the keyboard and the playback became a swarm of human polyphonic voices. Then musical rain on an over-sensitive roof. When he added our auto-chord programme and flicked to a Blues scale, Hendrix going up in flames crashed from the speakers. Another re-setting turned the Birsay waters and the sea off Warebeth into a bittersweet collusion of cello and clarinet.

So many possibilities. But however we tweaked it, through it all, like the word *Orkney* through a stick of rock, came the energy formed of sea, wind, bedrock, and the pull of the moon.

When we'd done, we could scarcely look at each other. Ray lay on the floor staring at the ceiling. I swear Inga flicked water from her eyes before she stirred and spoke.

'This is going to require lots of coke to get right.'

There's an amount of science-music starting to appear – music derived from DNA chromosome patterns, light defraction, that sort of thing. Most of it – we have to keep an ear on the competition – just goes to show Bach did it much better. Boring, however formally complex.

Music, as I pointed out to my co-directors, is just patterned sound like the heart is just a muscle for pumping blood. I mean we're *not* redundant here. Imagination is still required.

Our ambitions now went well beyond producing ambient sound. Music to chill by – a memory of dancing a musical history for Roo, the light flashing on her navel ring, her golden belly as she rolled on the dry reeds – well that could be only part of what we were after. There was a fairly large universe of renewable sound out there, and some corners of it might be habitable.

This could take years to explore, I thought as we talked late into that night. Personally, I wouldn't mind if it took the rest of my lifetime.

'A base line,' Inga insisted. 'I need a pitch and a tone I can cascade around. Think of it like the vanishing point in a painting.'

We looked at each other. What would it be? Middle C?

'Too square. A bottle opening?'

'I was thinking a death rattle would be cool.'

'You're one sick Goth, Inga. How about Billy MacKenzie's top note?'

Various low-minded suggestions later, Ray called us to order.

'You started this, Eddie – you pick.'

I had the beginnings of an idea. I decided to keep it mysterious so just said I'd bring the key-in sound when I got back from a quick trip. I needed the break. In truth, I think we were all starting to go a little mad.

As Ray and I wandered home in the early hours, in my mind I was already walking again the flagstones of a narrow silent street past cat-prowled alleys that led down to the sea whose heartbeat we had just attended to.

46

The custodian's van edges out of the car park, sidelights yellow in the dusk, potters up the hill and leaves the scene at last. I stub out the last of the cigarette, slip Phillip Marsden's case into my inside pocket, give the double one domino a last squeeze for luck then put it back in the glove compartment. The other one rests in my jacket pocket as it has all day.

What I've come to do is not such a big deal. It's not a deal at all, for you don't make deals with the dead. But you can, I think, dissolve them.

I get out, take the tools from the boot, pull on the big coat and set off alone across the Sands of Evie. Under my dad's coat the bolt-cutters thump on my hipbone, and the other pocket is stiff with hacksaw, file, chisel and head torch. The recording equipment fills my tweed jacket. I'm a one-man awkward squad.

Roo's note came some weeks after I'd walked out of Emily Simpson's. It contained various apologies and explanations but no excuses, which I appreciated. I can't remember her new boyfriend's name, but her ending lingers yet. *Passed my French!! We're going travelling. Keep the faith, have a stonking good time! Love – Rowan P.S. Walthamstow Marshes was for real.*

I sent her a disc of early WAMM music (House mix) with a note to say, *Don't think twice, it's all right*, and meant it. Even as I'd looked out the window at her in the gazebo, I'd realised you can't get youth back by kissing it. Renewal would have to come from elsewhere. But I believe still in the current that briefly flowed between us as we lay once with our breathing fused, the current that is what it's all about, for which I have no original words. For which I'm holding out.

Terns scutter and peep. A couple of swans come in low through the dusk, the *whap whap* of their beats resounding then fading over to Rousay. And me, I'm sharp, awake, all here, the way transgression brings us smack into the present.

I don't want to be unable to open my heart to the world. Dead right, kid. She gave me a pointer and a true thing. How are we to live in the face of the sure and certain knowledge we will lose parents, friends, lover, the whole shebang and caboodle?

Whole-heartedly. Of this one thing I am sure.

So I cross the empty car park, go through the gate and on towards the dark hull of the broch. Up the grass rampart, down the other side, round the back, stepping carefully by the tiny houses. I take a deep breath then walk up the causeway into the entrance. Duck low, and I'm in.

Dim inside. I can just hear the distant rush from Eynhallow's tidal bore, and a curlew's long sleepy cry as I pass by the red hearth and stand at last above the covered well.

This well is dangerous. Keep Out.

I lay out the tools and kneel. The bolt-cutters quickly snap through the grille. With gloved hands I peel it back. Now for the cast iron hatch. I try the cutters but there's no way.

Right then. Hacksaw.

The first stroke squeals. The backstroke is worse. Anyone within a hundred yards would hear this. I cut as fast as possible, leaning into it but trying to keep pressure steady. I'm sweating now and Dad's coat is hampering. I peel it off and carry on.

I made no effort to get in touch with Mica after Trinity, and I heard nothing from her. I wondered if that was indifference or tact. I wondered about a lot of things as the summer came and went in London, but it was still too soon to get in touch.

Finally through one bar of the hatch. Kneeling over the second, I feel that pricking up my back that says someone's watching. Look round, ready to run, but there's no one coming through that doorway. There's no one standing by the hearth, or keeping watch on the walls above me. Yet I feel them, I feel them so well. They might or might not be on my side.

I start on the second rung, feeling at all times my back exposed. All these bogles are in the mind. But the mind's real enough, isn't it?

Daft, man! The second bar is taking much too long and my wrist is cramping, and here I am looking at a padlock. I curse quietly, position the bolt-cutters and squeeze hard. Again. Then give it everything I have, and the blades clash together, the shock numbing my hands as the cutters spin to the ground.

Pull on the hatch but it's stuck solid. Out with the chisel and begin to lever. Twice it skites off. I've not brought a hammer, so I take a stone off the wall and use that. A sharp crack! and the hatch moves.

I tug hard and it lifts. I put the stone back while I still remember where. A last look round in the greying to check the only watchers are invisible ones, then I begin to feel my way down into the well at the heart of the broch.

One narrow wet step. Another. Another. With each step down the darkness became more complete. I think again on Tina, who never liked dark enclosures, lying deep in the earth. This is for her, among others.

I'm descending into the shadowlands again, voluntarily this time. My father's down here too.

You're good as gone.

But I'm not gone yet. My mortality is a reminder to pay attention, that's all. I obsess about it less these days, though it never goes away completely.

If I fall here and knock myself out—

If someone comes and closes the hatch—

I spread my arms, brace against the walls of the well and feel for the next step, going down.

Under Li Tek's supervision – the lad has insisted – Sandy's trunk is swung high in its net, swivelled then lowered onto the cargo deck. All his worldly goods rest there for a minute, then the purser has it taken below.

He's committed now. He's going to board this boat.

'Mind and work hard at the school.'

His father's words. Work hard, get on, get away.

'Oh yes, tuan. Absolutely first-class education.'

Li Tek is taking the mickey, Sandy knows that. Quite right too. But the money has been lodged with the school to take him on to his certificates. After that it's up to him.

He holds out his hand.

'Good luck.'

'Good luck to you, Doctor Sandy.' Then as his palm rests lightly against Sandy's, Li Tek sets his dark almond eyes on him. 'Thank you for mending me. I am sorry that ... '

For a moment they stare at each other. The boy looks away.

'Here comes your friend the American tuan,' then he slips into the crowd.

'Don't be an ass, Sandy, take it. You won it!'

Sandy glares at the box containing the billiards trophy Alan had picked up from the engraver that morning.

'Lost it, more like.'

'Hey, runner up is not so bad.'

Sandy grunts but takes the box and tucks it under his arm. The Butterworth Quay is heaving – passengers, cargo, crew, traders, stevedores, well-wishers, all swarming round the gangplank. That stench of copra, cloves, rubber, humanity. The few people he recognises avert their eyes. He feels like a criminal slinking away from the scene. He has heard nothing from Adele.

He holds out his hand to Alan.

'Cheerio, then.'

Alan grips his hand, then hesitates.

'You and Ann – there was nothing in it, was there?'

'Nothing at all. Marry the lass.'

'I sure will!'

'Good luck to you both.'

They drop hands. A last pat on the back, then Sandy is going up the gangway with the trophy box under his arm, thinking that was one of the more worthwhile lies he has told.

On deck at the rails, he looks back. Alan is bent over, coughing, handkerchief to his face. Finally he straightens up, looks and waves formally to Sandy, who in that moment senses he will never see or hear from him again.

Bellingham-Smythe pauses, about to descend the gangplank after seeing someone off.

'I tried to tell you, Mackay,' he says. 'Marsden's not right.'

Sandy looks at him, at the heaving quay, the rickshaws, taxis and bullock carts. She hasn't come, of course she hasn't.

'He's worth more than any of you.'

Bellingham-Smythe flushes even deeper red then turns to descend the gangplank. And there, over his shoulder, through the crowd comes a familiar car.

I'd not thought there could be so many steps. Perhaps I'm already dead and this is what I do for ever, stepping down and down into the dark.

I look up at a dim rectangle of less-black sky. It seems a long way off. One more step down, left foot then the right. I lean panting against the cold stone wall. I can go no further.

Behind the darkness I see my father by a steaming lily-pond. He reaches down to touch tepid water while staring urgently at a woman on the other side. Now I know who she is, and that is something. I know too that he once loved, and lost, and carried on, as I will do though differently, and that is something more.

I too reach down, and when my right hand touches icy water I nearly faint.

I brace myself against the ancient wall, take out the two:one domino. I have of course made a copy of the tiny photo and it, like the Happy Buddha, will follow me wherever I choose to live next. But the original is inside, together with his ghostly note of his Vienna address and the scrap of yellow butterfly.

I squeeze it, hesitating. So hard to let go.

Out with the mini-disc recorder. As I feel for the mike switch, the darkness deepens. I look up, and a head-shaped blob wavers against what light remains.

'Yoo hoo!'

I damn near fall. Steady myself, steady my voice.

'You took your time.'

A torch clicks on, lighting Mica's face demonic.

'You didn't think I was going to miss the ending, did you?' she says.

'Hold your wheesht for ten seconds, woman.'

I set the recorder running, hold the domino out over the blackness at my feet. Only one take at this. Life, eh?

And release.

Marsden's blue Austin putters slowly through the crowd, halts by the food stalls. He gets out, is joined by a tall, slender, fair-haired woman in a blue dress, cream hat. Ann. Both beautiful, one a gazelle. Even at this distance, he can easily distinguish them.

Sitting near the window in the dimness of the back seat, a pale blur looking his way. She has opened the domino, she has got the message.

Adele will get out, then force and push her way up the gangplank at the last minute, carrying only a small suitcase, leaving all else behind. She will step onto the deck, stare into his eyes then enter his arms, and they will leave for Vienna and whatever life will bring.

The oval blur of her face remains unmoving as the ropes slacken. Alan gives a thumbs up; Ann waves slowly; at her side Marsden raises his Panama with a hint of a self-mocking bow. On the very edge of the quay, Li Tek in his best shorts and shirt, black hair neatly brushed back, is waving wildly. Standing by his Daimler at the side of the crowd Daniel Ng inclines his head, touches his palm to his heart then extends it towards Sandy in the soft farewell of the East. But Adele, she just sits, and dwindles along with the car, the quay, George Town, the shores and green dark slopes of Penang.

Alexander Mackay tucks the box holding his runner-up trophy under his arm, turns his back on the island sinking back into the haze, and goes below.

✖

47

We divide up the break-in kit, then pick our way out of the site by hazed light of the moon. As we exit the gate Mica brandishes the bolt-cutters exultantly once above her head, then we set off back along the track towards my car.

The key-in sound for renewable music, the splash of the falling domino, is secure in the mini-disc in my father's coat pocket. The ivory tile now lies for ever at the bottom of the well, returned to the dead to whom it belongs. Though the darkness must be complete down there, one way or another people will be hearing from it for a long time.

When a parent dies, sooner or later you may search for the details or meaning of their life, to make some kind of peace. And in that search you may come to glimpse not your father or mother but yourself now they are gone. That's their last gift to you, the one they give through being dead. Make a kirk or a mill of it.

A tern peeps alarm into the dark and the night wind brings peat smoke across from Rousay as we stumble on with the sea on our right, a scatter of yellow house-lights high on the brae to our left, and the rest of our lives still up ahead.

What happens next, there is no telling.

I link my arm to hers, pals at the very least as we bump along, feeling our way back to the world, its action, and all the people dying to live there.

It's owre late for fear:
Owre early for disclaim;
When ye come hameless here
And ken ye are at hame.

Scotland, William Soutar